Whispers of Humanity

Adam McKim

For my wife, who waited patiently
as I was lost in my own world
working on this novel

Part One

Whispers of Silence

Prologue

Saul hadn't seen the sun in days. He couldn't remember the last time he felt its warmth. The cold had settled deep in his bones, and no matter how many layers he wrapped around himself, the chill persisted, gnawing at his resolve like a patient predator.

He staggered down the empty road, eyes scanning the horizon with the intensity of a starving wolf. The landscape was barren—burned-out cars lined the roadside like skeletal remains, their empty frames rusted and crumbling in the elements. The buildings he passed were hollow shells, gutted by fire and years of scavengers taking everything of value.

Saul knew these ruins held no food. He had picked them clean before but wandered through them anyway, driven more by habit than hope. He had learned that to stop moving was to invite death, to let hunger take root and consume what little strength he had left. It had been days since he last ate—two cans of stale, metallic peaches, but enough to keep him going for a little while. His hunger was now different, an all-encompassing, agonizing emptiness that twisted his insides and clouded his mind. He stumbled on weakened legs, leaning against the blackened walls of an old grocery store to steady himself. The windows were shattered, and the aisles had been stripped bare long ago. A sign that once read Fresh Produce now hung askew, its letters faded and peeling.

"Fresh," Saul muttered, a bitter laugh escaping his chapped lips. The word sounded absurd in his mouth, like something from a dream.

He reached the edge of town, where the ruins met the endless expanse of dead fields. The wind blew across the open plain, carrying the faint scent of decay. Saul ignored it, focused instead on the dark speck in the distance—a house, isolated and barely visible against the horizon.

He set off toward it, each step a battle against his failing strength. The house grew more prominent as he approached, and he felt a flicker of something akin to hope. Maybe something would be left inside, overlooked, or hidden in a place where no one else had thought to look.

The door was ajar when he arrived, swaying in the breeze. Saul pushed it open with the barrel of his rifle, wary of what might be inside. The hinges creaked, a sound too loud in the silence, and he stepped into the entryway.

The interior was dark, lit only by the pale, diffused light filtering through the broken windows. Dust motes drifted in the air, and the floor was littered with debris—old newspapers, shattered glass, and remnants of furniture that had long since rotted away. He moved cautiously, stepping over the mess, and went deeper into the house.

Room by room, he searched. Kitchen—empty. Pantry—bare. Bedrooms—stripped of blankets and anything else useful. By the time he reached the last room, he was shaking with exhaustion, his breaths shallow and uneven. The hunger was gnawing at his insides like a ravenous beast. Then he smelled it—faint but unmistakable—the scent of death.

He turned, scanning the shadows, until he saw the body slumped in the corner. A man, thin and emaciated, his eyes half-open and glassy. There were no signs of a struggle; the man had simply wasted away, like so many others. Saul felt a pang of pity, quickly swallowed by the ever-present hunger.

He should have left. He knew what happened to those who lingered near the dead—they became easy prey for others…or worse…lost themselves. But something held him there, his feet rooted to the floor. The hunger gnawed at him relentlessly, whispering in his ear and blurring the line between desperation and morality.

No one will know, the voice seemed to say. *It's already too late for him.*

Saul's stomach twisted painfully, and he sank to his knees. His hands trembled as he reached for his knife, the blade catching a faint glimmer of light. For a moment, he hesitated. He thought of his mother's stories—stories of honor, sacrifice, and holding onto one's humanity even in the face of despair. She had always believed that doing the right thing mattered, even when no one was watching.

But his mother was dead. The world she had believed in was dead. And Saul was still alive. He closed his eyes and brought the knife down. For the first time since the world had succumbed to the disease, he crossed the line.

This was survival…

Chapter 1

Saul had long since lost track of time—whether it had been a week or a month since his last decent meal was beyond him. Hunger played tricks on the mind, stretching time like a taut rope, fraying at the edges, and slowly unraveling the spirit.

Ten years had passed since the first whispers of the disease. It had begun quietly, almost unnoticed, with reports of dying plants and animals trickling in from distant regions. At first, people thought it was a localized issue, something the scientists and governments would resolve. But as the months dragged on, trees stopped bearing fruit, the fields turned barren, animals rotted away, and the grim reality set in. This wasn't a crisis that could be fixed. This was extinction, and for some cruel, twisted reason, humans were spared.

The road he walked was barely recognizable anymore—its asphalt cracked, buckling under the weight of years without maintenance. Saul had ventured far from his hometown of Millerton, hoping against hope that he might stumble upon some overlooked cache of supplies. But out here, there was nothing—just memories and bones.

He stopped beneath the withered skeleton of what had once been a tree. Now, it stood as a monument to what had been lost. He leaned against the brittle bark, feeling it flake away beneath his fingers.

The air was colder than it should have been, more frigid than he remembered autumn being. However, seasons became more chaotic without plants and trees to regulate the climate. Summers baked the land, scorching everything in sight, followed by winters that froze everything in their path. Saul tightened his coat around his body. The fabric frayed at the seams, slowly giving way to the same decay that had claimed everything else.

This can't go on much longer, he thought, *not like this*.

Saul reached into his coat pocket and pulled out the last piece of jerky he had saved. It was tough and dry, more a memory of meat than actual nourishment, but it was all he had. He took a small bite, chewing slowly, but it was gone too quickly, leaving only the bitter tang of salt on his tongue—and the same hollow ache in his gut.

He closed his eyes and leaned his head back against the tree. As they often did, his thoughts drifted to the times when hunger had driven him to cross lines he never thought he'd cross.

He could still see the faces. Strangers, mostly—people he had found in the ruins, already dead. He had only one rule: take what he needed to survive the day. He knew that there would be no turning back if he gave in to the monster desperately trying to come out of him. He would become like them—the hunters—the ones who prey on others for survival. But Saul did everything he could to hang onto whatever humanity he had left.

He opened his eyes. For a brief moment, he considered staying there, letting the cold take him, letting hunger win. But then, in the distance, he saw the smoke—a thin column rising into the air, barely visible against the darkening sky. Someone had lit a fire, and that meant there were survivors nearby. Saul felt a surge of conflicting emotions—fear, hope, and caution.

He knew what fire could mean in a world like this. It could mean warmth, safety, and food. But it could just as easily mean danger, traps, and violence. He watched the smoke drift upward, trying to decide what to do. Every instinct told him to stay away, to avoid others at all costs. He had seen too many encounters end in blood, too many strangers turn to threats when desperation set in. But the whispers in his ear stirred up again.

Maybe they have food, it said. *Maybe you can trade. Or beg. Or steal.*

He took a deep breath. He could continue on his way and risk starving, or he could approach, risking everything. In the end, it wasn't really a choice. The hunger made sure of that.

Saul rose to his feet, wincing as pain shot through his legs. He pulled his coat tighter and started walking toward the smoke. As he drew closer, he began to make out the details—flickering light, shadows of figures moving around a fire. He crouched low, gripping his rifle, keeping to the edges of the camp's light. He didn't know if they would welcome him or kill him on sight. But he had no options left.

He saw three figures, two men and a woman, huddled close to the flames. They looked worn, their clothes patched, their faces gaunt and hollow. One of the men stirred a pot over the fire. The other two spoke quietly, their voices too low for Saul to hear.

For a moment, he considered retreating into the darkness. But his body refused to listen as if the fire and the scent of food had a magnetic pull on him.

Just one meal, the voice whispered again. *One meal, and you can keep going.*

Saul swallowed, forcing down his fear. He took a step forward, emerging from the shadows. "Hello?"

The three figures turned toward him, eyes narrowing in suspicion. Saul kept his rifle slung over his shoulder, his hands open, trying to appear non-threatening. His heart raced as he stepped closer.

The woman drew a small revolver and pointed it at Saul. "Who are you?" she asked.

"A traveler," Saul answered, his voice steady. "I saw your smoke."

One of the men stepped forward, his expression hard. "We don't have anything for you," he said bluntly. "So just move along."

Saul hesitated, then spoke quietly, almost pleading. "Please...just a little something, and I'll be gone. I'm no threat to you. I'm just trying to survive, same as you."

The group exchanged uncertain glances, weighing their options in the silence. Finally, the woman lowered her gun. "Come closer," she said.

Cautiously, Saul stepped into the firelight. The warmth hit him, but it was the smell of the stew that nearly overwhelmed him. He watched as the man scooped a small portion into a metal bowl and handed it to him. It was no more than a few bite's worth, but he wouldn't complain.

"This is all you get," the man said flatly.

Saul nodded, accepting the bowl. He sat near the fire, the heat almost unbearable after so long in the cold. The scent of the stew was intoxicating. He took a spoonful and brought it to his mouth. As soon as the taste hit his tongue, he knew. But he didn't care. He just needed to make it another day until he could find something else.

They ate in silence, the quiet crackle of the fire the only sound between them. Saul glanced around at the group. They seemed like good people, a rare find these days. But he knew better than to trust in that too much. He had seen it before—good people didn't last long, especially when they stayed together. Groups were fragile. Starvation made sure of that. Desperation had a way of warping even the best intentions and always ended the same way.

They would turn on each other. They always did.

Saul scraped the last of his meal from the bowl and stood up. There was no need for goodbyes or acknowledgment of the understanding they all shared. It was time to go. He gave them a nod, turned, and continued into the night.

Chapter 2

The snow had begun falling later that week, blanketing the landscape in a deceptive purity. The world looked almost beautiful under its thin layer of white, the jagged edges of ruin softened by the delicate frost. But beauty had no place here. Not anymore.

Saul moved cautiously through the snow, each step deliberate and slow. The cold bit through his worn boots, numbing his toes and making each footfall a quiet struggle. He needed to find his next camp before nightfall, or he would freeze to death.

The wind whispered through the crumbling buildings, stirring the loose snow into spirals that danced in the corners of his vision. Saul scanned the landscape, his breath fogging in the frigid air, his senses on edge. Snow made it harder to hear footsteps—harder to tell if he was truly alone.

He kept his rifle slung over one shoulder, one hand resting lightly on the strap. He didn't want to look ready to fight, but he needed to be prepared. It was a delicate balance that often meant the difference between life and death.

Saul approached a narrow alley between two buildings, the snow drifting in knee-deep piles where the wind had blown it. He moved carefully, placing each foot down with practiced precision, listening for anything that seemed out of place. The alley was a dead end, blocked by a collapsed wall and a pile of frozen debris. He turned to leave but stopped when he heard something—a muffled voice.

Saul crouched down, pressing his back against the wall. He strained to listen, his heartbeat quickening. The voices were coming from the other side of the alley. He couldn't make out the words but could hear the tone—angry, tense. He peered around the corner, careful to stay in the shadows.

A group of men emerged from a nearby building, moving quickly through the snow. There were five of them, dressed in ragged coats and heavy boots, their faces obscured by scarves and hoods. They carried rifles and knives, their weapons gleaming in the pale morning light. Saul's eyes narrowed as he watched them— they moved with purpose, their steps heavy.

The group stopped at the mouth of the alley. The leader raised a hand to signal silence, then motioned to one of his men, who moved forward cautiously, his rifle ready. Saul tightened his grip on his rifle but stayed hidden, waiting. He watched as the man approached a pile of snow-covered crates, crouching to peer behind them. A gunshot rang out, sharp and deafening in the stillness.

The man fell backward into the snow, a spray of blood marking the point of impact. Saul's heart jumped in his chest, but he didn't move. The rest of the group reacted instantly, raising their rifles and spreading out, searching for the source of the shot. There was shouting, frantic and disorganized, and more gunfire—short, controlled bursts that cut through the air like thunder.

Saul pressed himself against the wall, keeping low. He watched as the group engaged with their unseen attackers, gunshots echoing through the narrow streets. The snow quickly turned red, staining the pristine white with splashes of blood.

Bodies fell in the chaos, the sound of gunfire mixing with the shouts and cries of the wounded. Saul could see the desperation in their movements, the way they fought with a fury born of starvation and fear.

The leader's group began to falter, their numbers dwindling as the ambush took its toll. The attackers—another group of survivors, moved in quickly, pressing the advantage. They fought ruthlessly, their knives flashing in the dim light, their boots crunching through the snow as they advanced.

The attackers weren't just killing their enemies—they were butchering them. As the last of the leader's men fell, the victors moved in, their knives already slick with blood. They worked quickly, stripping the bodies of clothing and supplies. One of them pulled out a long, serrated knife, and Saul closed his eyes.

He knew what was next and didn't want to watch. He had seen it too many times before. But the sounds of the harvest were still there—the wet, tearing noises. When he opened his eyes again, the attackers were finishing their work. They gathered their spoils— packs, clothing, weapons—and began to move away, leaving the bodies where they lay. The smell of death hung heavy in the air.

Saul waited until he was sure they were gone before he moved. He slipped out of the alley, avoiding the bodies, his steps quick and silent. He kept his eyes on the ground, not wanting to see the faces of the dead, not wanting to remember them. But the image of what he had witnessed was burned into his mind.

Saul walked on, leaving the town and the blood behind him. The snow continued to fall, covering his tracks and erasing the evidence of what had happened. It was almost as if the world itself wanted to forget, to bury the past beneath a layer of cold and silence.

He couldn't shake the feeling that he was running out of time —time to hold onto the last remnants of his soul, time to find something worth living for. In this new world, survival came at a price—and he wasn't sure how much more he could afford to pay.

Chapter 3

The flames flickered as Saul sat by the small fire he had built. He only risked a fire on nights like this, when the moon was concealed behind thick clouds, letting the darkness swallow the smoke and hide it from prying eyes.

As he slowly ate from the rusted can of green beans he had scavenged from a car just outside of town, Saul tried to cling to the silence around him. But no matter how hard he focused, the memories crept in. He couldn't escape them—not in this silence or emptiness.

He couldn't escape *them.*

Saul's mind drifted back to the early days of the outbreak when the world was still coming to terms with what was happening. He had been in his hometown then, a small place in the Midwest with rows of old brick houses and wide, tree-lined streets. Saul remembered standing in his backyard, watching as the leaves on the trees withered and fell long before autumn should have come. He had noticed that the birds were gone, and the squirrels and rabbits had disappeared from the neighborhood. He had felt a growing sense of unease, a gnawing feeling that something was terribly wrong. But even then, he had held onto hope that it was just a passing blight, that things would get better if they just waited it out.

His wife, Laura, had been more pragmatic. She had always been the realist, the one who saw things for what they were and didn't waste time on wishful thinking. She had been the one to insist they stock up on supplies, start growing what they could in their backyard, and prepare for the possibility that the world might be changing in ways they couldn't control. Saul had humored her at first, thinking it was just another one of her overcautious tendencies. But Laura had been right. And by the time he realized it, it was too late.

The memories came in flashes now, fragments of moments that felt distant and painfully close. He remembered the last time they had all sat together at the kitchen table, trying to make a plan as the news reports turned from confusion to panic. He remembered how Laura held his hand, her grip tight and steady, even as the fear showed in her eyes. He remembered their daughter, Emily, asking questions they couldn't answer—questions about why the animals were dying, why the plants were sick, why everyone was so afraid.

They had tried to keep things normal for Emily's sake, to shield her from the worst of it. But normal had become fragile, cracking under the weight of a world that was falling apart.

When the food shortages began, they had turned to their neighbors, hoping to find strength in numbers. Saul had always believed in community, in the idea that people could come together in times of crisis and help each other through. He had been raised with that belief, taught by his parents and reinforced by the small-town values that had shaped his life.

The first signs of trouble came when the grocery stores were stripped bare, and the lines outside the few remaining supply depots stretched for blocks. People grew restless, angry, and violent. Rumors spread like wildfire—stories of government conspiracies, secret stockpiles, and neighbors hoarding supplies. Trust broke down, and the sense of community that Saul had tried so hard to foster crumbled into suspicion and fear.

The night the riots reached their neighborhood was the night everything changed. Saul had stood on his front porch, shotgun in hand, watching as the streets filled with angry, desperate people. He had heard the shouts, the breaking glass, the distant sound of gunfire. Laura had begged him to come inside, lock the doors, and wait it out, but he had felt helpless standing there, knowing that the world was tearing apart.

When the fire started, Saul had known there was no going back. They packed what little they had and fled, joining the exodus of people trying to escape the chaos. They hoped to find refuge in the countryside, away from the violence, away from the madness. But the disease didn't care about boundaries. It spread through the soil, through the water, and through the very air they breathed. The crops failed, livestock died, and wild animals disappeared into the silence.

Saul and his family had held on for as long as they could. They had rationed their supplies, tried to grow what little they could in the barren soil—and hunted for whatever scraps of life still lingered in the forests. But it wasn't enough. It was never enough.

The day Laura died was the day he lost the last of his hope. She had fallen ill, weakened by hunger and exhaustion, her body unable to fight off the infections that came with malnutrition. He had tried to take care of her, tried to keep her warm and fed, despite his own failing health, but there was nothing he could do. He had watched as the light faded from her eyes, feeling helpless and broken in a way he had never known.

Emily had cried for days, her small hands clutching at his shirt, begging him to bring her mother back. Saul had held her, whispered empty promises, and tried to be strong for her sake. But he could feel the cracks forming inside him, the weight of his failures pressing down on him like a stone.

They had buried Laura in the woods behind the house, marking her grave with a simple wooden cross. Emily had wanted to leave flowers, but there were no flowers left—only the dry, brittle stems of plants that had long since withered and died.

In the following weeks, Saul had tried to hold onto what little remained of their life. He had tried to protect Emily, to keep her safe from the horrors of the world outside. But the disease didn't just kill plants and animals—it killed hope, too. It left people empty and hollow, stripped of everything that made them human. In the end, it took Emily, too.

Saul's last memory of her was the sound of her shallow and uneven breathing as she lay in his arms. He had rocked her gently, whispering the lullabies Laura used to sing, trying to soothe her and pretend everything would be okay. But he knew the truth even then. He knew that there was nothing he could do to save her.

When Emily's breathing finally stopped, he felt something inside him break. He had sat there for hours, cradling her small, lifeless body, unable to let go. When he finally did, it was as if he was leaving a part of himself behind—a part he could never reclaim.

He had buried Emily next to Laura, marking her grave with another wooden cross, and then walked away—leaving his home and everything he had ever known behind.

He had wandered ever since, searching for something he couldn't name. Maybe it was redemption, or maybe it was just the hope of finding a place where he could finally stop running. But every step he took, every town he passed through, and every encounter with other survivors only reminded him of what he had lost.

The memories were always there, lurking in the corners of his mind, waiting for moments of silence to resurface. They were the ghosts that haunted him, the remnants of a life that felt like a distant dream.

Saul put out the fire and pulled a thick, tattered blanket from his bag, settling in for the night. There were countless abandoned houses he could have chosen for shelter, but the dead forest offered something those ruins couldn't—solitude. Houses were unpredictable, and there was no telling when a scavenger might stumble in or whether they'd be a fleeting ally or a ruthless hunter. Saul closed his eyes, waiting for the memories to leave him in peace. Only then did he finally drift into sleep.

Chapter 4

Saul moved cautiously through the crumbling remains of another long-abandoned town. He had been searching the outskirts, avoiding the more prominent locations like grocery stores and gas stations, which had long since been stripped bare. Instead, he focused on the forgotten places—the basements of old houses, storage sheds hidden behind fences, anywhere others might have overlooked in their desperation.

The day was cold and grey, the sky heavy with the threat of more snow. His breath hung in the air as he crept, keeping to the shadows, his eyes scanning the ruins for any signs of movement.

He entered a small house, the front door hanging loosely on its hinges. The interior was dark, the windows broken and boarded up. He let his eyes adjust before moving deeper inside, his hand resting on the grip of his rifle. In the kitchen, he found a single can of beans, the label faded and torn. It wasn't much, but it was better than nothing.

He slipped the can into his pack and moved on, his footsteps barely making a sound on the dust-covered floor. He approached the living room, where an old couch lay overturned, its cushions ripped open and the stuffing spilling out. He was about to turn away when he heard a faint rustling sound—a movement that didn't belong in the stillness.

He froze, listening, his heart pounding. The rustling grew louder, coming from the hallway behind him. Saul tightened his grip on the rifle, turning slowly to face the source of the noise. He couldn't see anything in the shadows, but he felt the hairs on the back of his neck stand on end.

Then he heard it—a quiet shuffle, the sound of feet moving cautiously across the floor. Saul backed away, his eyes searching the darkness for any movement. He knew he couldn't afford to let his guard down, not now, not when he was so close to exhaustion, and the cold was seeping into his bones.

"Who's there?" he called out, his voice steady despite the fear tightening in his chest.

There was no response, only the continued rustling. He stepped back, raising his rifle, his finger hovering over the trigger. He didn't want to shoot, didn't want to draw attention to himself, but he knew he couldn't take any chances.

Suddenly, a figure lunged at him from the shadows, moving with a speed that caught him off guard. Saul stumbled backward, raising his rifle to block the attacker's swing. A sharp pain shot through his arm as something heavy struck him—a pipe—or maybe a crowbar—and he gritted his teeth, trying to keep his footing. The attacker pushed forward, shoving Saul against the wall, their face obscured by a hood and scarf.

Saul struggled to push the attacker away, but his strength was failing. He was too weak and tired and knew he couldn't keep this up for long. He braced himself for another blow, preparing to fight back with whatever energy he had left. But he had nothing left.

His legs gave out, and he slumped to the floor as the attacker came down on top of him. Saul felt the warm hands of the attacker wrap around his neck and begin to squeeze.

This is it, he thought. *This is how it ends.*

Saul closed his eyes and prepared for his final breath. Just as he was about to let it all go, a sharp crack echoed through the empty house.

The attacker staggered—his grip on Saul's neck loosening. Saul watched in confusion as the figure slumped to the floor, blood pooling beneath him. He looked up, trying to make sense of what had just happened, and saw a woman standing in the doorway, a revolver in her hand. She was tall, with dark hair pulled back into a tight braid. She wore a patched coat and a heavy scarf. Her eyes scanned the room for other threats. Satisfied that there were no more attackers, she lowered the gun and turned to Saul.

"You alright?" she asked.

Saul didn't respond at first, still trying to catch his breath, his arm throbbing with pain. He felt the weight of his exhaustion pressing down on him, the adrenaline slowly fading. He glanced at the attacker's body, then back at the woman.

"Yeah," he said finally, his voice hoarse. "I think so."

The woman holstered her gun and approached him cautiously, her eyes still wary. "You're lucky I came along when I did," she said. "This guy would've been preparing you for lunch a few minutes from now."

Saul nodded, still unsure of what to say. He didn't trust her— he didn't trust anyone—but he knew he owed her his life, at least for now. He watched as she knelt to inspect the attacker's body. She took a knife from the man's belt and pocketed it, then checked his pack for any supplies.

"What were you doing here?" she asked without looking up.

"Scavenging," Saul replied. "Looking for food."

The woman nodded, seemingly satisfied with his answer. She stood and wiped the blood from her hands on a rag she pulled from her coat. "Same here. This place looked empty, but I guess it wasn't as abandoned as I thought."

Saul remained silent, still trying to decide whether he could trust her. Trust was a dangerous thing—a mistake that could cost you everything. But the woman didn't seem hostile, and she had saved his life. That counted for something, even if it wasn't enough to put his guard down.

"I'm Hannah," she said, extending a hand.

Saul hesitated for a moment before taking it. "Saul," he replied.

Hannah studied him for a moment as if she was trying to read him. "You look like you could use some rest," she said. "And some food."

Saul nodded, his exhaustion catching up with him. He didn't have the energy to argue, and the thought of food was enough to weaken his resolve.

Hannah reached into her pack and pulled out a small bag of dried jerky. She tossed it to Saul, who caught it clumsily, his hands shaking from the cold and fatigue. He stared at the bag for a moment, unsure if it was a trick, before tearing it open and eating quickly.

"Slow down," Hannah said, her voice softer now. "You'll make yourself sick."

Saul forced himself to stop, taking deep breaths to steady himself. He hadn't realized how hungry he was until he started eating, and the sudden rush of real food made his head spin. He glanced at Hannah, still wary, but her expression was unreadable.

"Why did you help me?" he asked finally.

Hannah shrugged. "Didn't seem right to let you die," she said simply. "And besides, I could use the company for a little while. Safer to travel in pairs, at least for now."

Saul didn't respond. He wasn't sure what to make of her answer, and he couldn't shake the feeling that there was more to it than she was letting on. But he didn't have the strength to question her motives. He just needed to rest, to gather his strength for whatever came next.

Hannah gestured toward a corner of the room where she had set up a small bedroll and a few supplies. "I was already set up here for the night. You can stay if you want," she said. "It's not much, but it's better than freezing to death out there."

Saul considered her offer, weighing the risks and the potential benefits. But he was too tired to keep moving, too weak to face another night on his own. And if she had wanted to kill him, she could have done it already.

"Alright," he said.

Hannah nodded and turned away, giving him space to settle in. He set his pack down and sank to the floor, his body aching with every movement. He kept his rifle close, his fingers resting lightly on the trigger, just in case.

He felt a strange mixture of relief and unease as he lay there. He had spent so long on his own, relying on no one but himself, and now he was faced with the possibility of something he hadn't dared hope for in a long time—companionship.

For now, though, he would rest. Tomorrow would bring new challenges, choices, and maybe a chance to find something worth holding onto. But that was a question for another day. Tonight, he would close his eyes and let the world fade away.

Chapter 5

The morning came cold and quiet. When Saul awoke, he didn't know where he was, his mind still lingering in the haze of restless sleep. Then the events of the previous day came rushing back—Hannah, the fight, the small room where they had taken shelter.

He stirred quietly, sitting up and rubbing the sleep from his eyes. Hannah was already awake, crouched by the remnants of the campfire she had built the night before. She was sharpening a knife with slow, methodical strokes. Saul watched her for a moment, trying to gauge what kind of person she was. She seemed calm, but there was a tension in her posture—a readiness that spoke of someone living on edge for far too long.

She glanced up, catching him watching her, and slightly nodded. "Morning," she said, her voice low and rough.

"Morning," Saul replied, his voice equally hoarse. He cleared his throat, feeling the ache in his chest from the cold night.

They didn't speak for a while after that. The silence between them was thick with unspoken questions, but neither seemed ready to break it. Saul didn't trust Hannah—didn't know if he could—but he could sense she felt the same way about him.

Hannah finished sharpening her knife and slipped it into a sheath at her belt. Saul could tell she was used to surviving alone, just as he was. It was in the way she moved, kept her eyes on her surroundings, and held herself as if expecting danger at any moment.

"Ready to move?" she asked, breaking the silence.

"Yeah," Saul replied, pushing himself to his feet. He gathered his things quickly, not wanting to linger in one place for too long. Hannah had been right about one thing—it was safer to keep moving.

They set out together, moving through the town. Saul noticed that Hannah kept a hand near her sidearm, her eyes scanning the ruins for any sign of movement. She didn't speak much, and Saul didn't push for conversation. He was used to traveling alone; silence felt more comfortable than forced words.

Still, something was unsettling about having another person nearby—someone whose thoughts and motives he couldn't read. He found himself watching her out of the corner of his eye, studying how she walked, how she checked their surroundings, and how her fingers drummed lightly on the handle of her revolver when they passed a particularly dark alley.

He found himself respecting her caution, recognizing in her the same instincts that had kept him alive for so long. But there was more to it than just survival skills. There was a way she carried herself. It was the look of someone who had seen too much, lost too much, and couldn't afford to let their guard down. He had seen that look in the mirror often enough to recognize it in someone else.

They stopped briefly to rest near a collapsed office building. Saul leaned against a concrete pillar, his eyes scanning the horizon for movement. Hannah crouched nearby, drinking from a canteen, and watched him with the same wary expression he had seen in so many others.

"Where were you before all this?" Hannah asked suddenly.

Saul hesitated, unsure how much to share. He wasn't used to talking about his past—he wasn't used to talking to anyone. But something about the question felt genuine, as if she was trying to understand him and decide if he was worth trusting.

"Small town," he said finally. "Midwest. Had a family. A house."

Hannah nodded as if she understood without needing further explanation. She didn't press for more, and Saul was grateful for that. He didn't know if he could put the rest into words, even if he wanted to.

"You?" Saul asked.

Hannah took a long drink from her canteen before answering. "I used to live in a city," she said. "I worked at a hospital… watched it all go to hell when the food ran out. I stayed as long as possible, trying to help people…but you can't help everyone."

There was a bitterness in her voice and a weight to her words that made Saul wonder what she had seen and lost. He didn't ask, though. He knew better than to pry into wounds that were still healing. He wondered if she was running from her past, just as he was.

The sun was beginning to set by the time they were a few miles out of town. The light was fading, casting long shadows across the road ahead. Saul glanced at Hannah, who was scanning the horizon.

"Think we should stop for the night?" Saul asked.

Hannah nodded. "There's an old farmhouse up ahead," she said. "Should be secure enough if we clear it out first."

They approached the farmhouse cautiously, moving in silence. The building was in better shape than most; its walls were still intact, and its windows were only partially broken. Hannah signaled for him to cover the front while she checked the side entrance. He watched as she moved quietly, her footsteps barely making a sound on the snow-dusted ground.

The interior was cold and dark, but there were no signs of recent activity. They barred the doors and set up a small camp in the living room, using what little furniture remained to create a makeshift barricade. Saul took the first watch, sitting near the window with his rifle ready, while Hannah set up her bedroll in a corner.

They ate a small meal in silence, each lost in their own thoughts. Saul kept glancing at Hannah. There was something about her that felt familiar, something that made him think she wasn't like the others he had met—those who had lost all sense of right and wrong, who had given in to the darkness that came with desperation. Hannah seemed different, and Saul couldn't shake the feeling that maybe she understood what it meant to hold onto your humanity, even in a world that seemed determined to strip it away.

As the night wore on, he relaxed slightly, letting his guard down just a little. It wasn't trust, not yet, but it was something close. He didn't know if she felt the same, but she didn't seem as wary as when they first met. They were still strangers, still circling each other cautiously, but there was a sense of understanding growing between them—a recognition that maybe, just maybe, they were both trying to survive without losing who they were.

Chapter 6

Saul and Hannah continued scavenging as the days passed, but their efforts yielded almost nothing. The cold deepened with each passing day, forcing them to take shelter in a factory. Despite its crumbling walls, the building provided some refuge from the biting wind—if only for a short while.

Saul found an old oil drum in a corner and, with some effort, managed to start a small fire. The flames cast flickering shadows on the walls, creating fleeting illusions of movement that kept both of them on edge. But at least the warmth was real. The two of them sat close to the fire, the silence between them almost comfortable now.

Hannah was tinkering with something she had pulled from her pack—a small, battered radio receiver. It looked ancient, its casing chipped and worn, and it was missing one of the dials. Saul hadn't given it much thought when she'd first pulled it out, assuming it was just another broken relic she'd picked up along the way. But she seemed intent on fixing it as she adjusted wires and tightened screws.

He watched her quietly, curious but unwilling to break the silence. He had come to appreciate the quiet moments they shared, moments when words weren't necessary. But as he listened to the wind outside and watched the firelight dance on the walls, he couldn't help but wonder why she was so determined to get the radio working.

"Think that thing will actually pick up anything?" he asked finally.

Hannah didn't look up. "Maybe," she replied. "Found it in an old communications station a while back. It's mostly junk, but the receiver still works. Thought it was worth a shot."

Saul wasn't sure what she expected to hear. The radio stations had gone silent a long time ago, along with everything else. In the early days of the outbreak, there had been a flood of messages—desperate calls for help, garbled transmissions from military outposts, chaotic reports of mass die-offs.

But as the disease spread and the world unraveled, the voices on the airwaves grew fewer and farther between until there was nothing left but static. He had stopped listening a long time ago.

But Hannah seemed to hold onto the hope that someone might still be broadcasting somewhere. Maybe it was just a way to pass the time, a distraction from the endless monotony of survival. Or maybe it was something more—a thin thread of hope she wasn't ready to let go of. Saul didn't press her. He knew better than to question the things that kept people going.

They sat in silence for a while longer, with only the sounds of the crackling fire and the faint hum of the radio as Hannah adjusted the frequency. Saul leaned back against the wall, closing his eyes and trying to let the warmth of the fire soothe his tired muscles. An hour passed, and Saul was on the verge of drifting off when he heard it—a faint, crackling noise coming from the radio.

He opened his eyes and glanced at Hannah, still fast asleep beside him, her breathing steady. The crackling grew louder, and a low hum filled the air. Saul's pulse quickened as he leaned forward. Then, through the static, a voice emerged.

Faint, barely more than a whisper, distorted by interference but undeniably human. Saul's breath caught as he strained to hear, his heart pounding. He reached for the dial with trembling fingers, adjusting it carefully. The crackling shifted, and the voice became clearer.

"...repeat, this is... safe haven... coordinates... 39.2...-120.1..."

Saul's eyes widened. His mind raced as the fragmented transmission continued. The voice repeated the coordinates, cutting through the static just long enough for him to catch them. He fumbled for a piece of paper and a pencil from his pack. His hands shook as he quickly scribbled the numbers down.

"...safe haven... repeat... 39.2... -120.1..."

As the voice faded, Saul leaned over and gently shook Hannah awake. "Hannah," he whispered, urgency thick in his voice. "Wake up. I've got something."

Her eyes fluttered open, confused for a moment before locking onto his intense expression. The signal cut out abruptly, leaving only silence. The voice was gone, swallowed by the void of static and dead air.

Hannah sat up, rubbing her eyes, "What is it?" she asked.

"I heard a message," Saul replied. "It wasn't much, just fragments, but I caught the coordinates. Someone out there said there's a safe place."

Hannah's eyes widened slightly, surprise flickering across her face. "Coordinates?" she asked. "Where?"

Saul held out the paper, showing her the hastily scribbled numbers. "Safe haven," he murmured. "I think it's something."

Hannah frowned, her doubt obvious. "Or it's nothing. Could just be a trap, Saul."

Saul shook his head. "No, this was different. It wasn't just static or garbled nonsense. I heard coordinates. A place. A safe haven."

Hannah sighed, her shoulders slumping. "And what if it's not? What if we go chasing after this, and there's nothing there? We could waste days, maybe weeks, going in the wrong direction. What then?"

Saul met her gaze, the flicker of hope in his eyes unwavering. "We've both been surviving for years, Hannah. Just…surviving. But what if we have a chance at something more? We can't keep wandering forever, living day to day like this. If there's even the slightest chance of finding a safe place, don't we have to try?"

Hannah looked away, her lips pressed into a thin line. "I just don't want us chasing ghosts," she muttered. "I don't want us to get our hopes up only to find nothing but more ruins."

"I'd rather chase a ghost than stay stuck like this," Saul replied. "We've been in worse situations before. And I think…I think this could be different."

Hannah crossed her arms. "You really believe that, don't you?"

"I do," Saul said without hesitation. "Something about this feels right. We've come this far—we can't just ignore it."

Hannah sighed again, rubbing her eyes. "And if it's another dead end…?"

"Then we'll deal with it," Saul replied softly. "But at least we'll know we tried."

"Alright," she said quietly. "We'll head in that direction. But if we see any signs of trouble, we turn back. No risks."

Saul nodded. "Agreed."

Chapter 7

Saul and Hannah rested and gathered their strength, preparing for the journey to the safe haven. The factory had served as their refuge, but staying too long would be risky. They had kept the barrel fire burning in a small room, its warmth pushing back the cold. Fuel wasn't an issue—there were plenty of old filing cabinets in the offices, their contents long forgotten but now useful. The warmth and quiet had given them a rare moment of peace, a brief escape from the harsh world outside. But they both knew it was temporary. This fragile calm couldn't last.

On their final morning, after the cold snap had finally eased, Saul tended to the fire's dying embers while Hannah quietly packed the last of their supplies.

Hannah glanced at Saul, her voice quiet. "You still think it's worth it?"

Saul nodded without hesitation. "I do."

Hannah sighed, slinging her pack over her shoulder. "We'll see."

They left the factory behind, returning to the cold, desolate landscape. The wind bit their skin as they began their journey toward the coordinates.

After hours of walking, they came across what looked like a makeshift settlement. A low, rotting wooden fence marked its boundaries, and the gate hung loosely on its hinges. The wind stirred it just enough to make it creak softly. They exchanged cautious looks before moving forward, and Saul gripped his rifle a little tighter as they stepped through the gate.

The settlement was small, no more than two dozen buildings arranged around a central square. The structures were simple, made from weathered wood and rusted metal. It reminded Saul of old frontier towns where people once believed they could build a life, even in the harshest conditions. The square's centerpiece was a stone well. There was no sign of recent activity—no footprints, smoke, or voices. The place felt like a memory swallowed by time.

"Looks abandoned," Hannah murmured.

"Has been for a while," Saul replied, scanning the buildings. "They tried to build something here. Something better."

"You think hunters found them?" Hannah asked.

"Maybe," Saul replied. He remembered the events he had witnessed in the alley a few months back. The hunters who ambushed a group, taking everything they had, including their lives.

"Places like this never last, "Hannah said. "People try to build something safe, but the world takes everything from them in the end."

"We should keep moving," Saul said. "We still have a ways to go to the next town."

Hannah nodded, "Good idea," she said. "This place just has a sadness that doesn't seem to go away."

They left the settlement behind, the gate creaking shut as they stepped back onto the road. A few hours later, the sun began its slow descent toward the horizon. Darkness crept in faster than expected, and the distance ahead seemed daunting.

"We're not going to make it," Hannah said, glancing at the map. "It's going to get too dark and cold soon."

Saul scanned the road ahead, his eyes catching on a van stuck in the ditch a little farther down. "Let's check it out."

They slowly approached the van, the cold stinging their faces as the wind picked up and whipped across the empty road. The van was old, its once-white paint now chipped and streaked with rust. The windows were cracked and clouded from years of exposure to the elements.

Saul leaned closer and peered inside, confirming the van was empty. He pulled the door hard, the metal groaning as it finally gave way, rust having nearly sealed it shut. Inside, the van was a wreck—torn upholstery with stuffing spilling out, shards of broken glass scattered across the floor, and the faint, musty odor of mildew hanging in the air. Despite the mess, the interior was dry.

"It's not much," Saul said, stepping back to glance at Hannah, "but it'll keep the wind off us."

Hannah nodded, tightening her coat around her shoulders. "It'll have to do."

Saul pushed aside some debris, making room for them to settle in. "We'll leave at first light," he said. "I don't like being out in the open like this."

"I agree," Hannah replied. "But it's all we got right now."

They shared a small can of beans, passing it back and forth in silence. The portions were tiny, just enough to keep their stomachs from collapsing in on themselves but not nearly enough to satisfy the gnawing hunger that seemed to grow with each passing day. The cold air only worsened as their bodies burned through the little energy they had left to stay warm. Each bite was a cruel reminder of how little food remained. Hannah scraped the bottom of the can with her spoon, scooping out the last remnants before handing it back to Saul.

"This isn't going to cut it," she said quietly, her voice edged with frustration. "We need to find more. We're getting too low."

Saul nodded as he set the empty can aside. "I know," he muttered. "The next town's our best shot. Maybe we'll find something—anything worth scavenging."

Hannah looked down at her hands, rubbing them together to fight the chill. "It has to be more than just scraps this time. We're not going to make it much longer like this."

Saul didn't answer right away. He knew she was right. They were already stretching their rations as far as they could, but the hunger caught up faster than they could keep up. His mind raced, wondering what they might find in the next town—if anything was even left.

"We'll make it," he said finally, though even he wasn't sure if he believed it. "We have to."

As they turned in for the night, the confined space felt almost suffocating, but the warmth of their bodies filling the small space felt comforting compared to the outside. Saul shifted, trying to find a comfortable spot, but the tight quarters made it difficult. His arm brushed against Hannah's side, and he immediately pulled it back.

"Sorry," he mumbled quietly. He wasn't used to being this close to anyone—not since the world had changed.

"No worries," she replied softly. She adjusted her position, making space the best she could. "At least it's warmer like this," she added, her voice a little more relaxed.

"Yeah, there's that," Saul agreed.

They settled back into silence. Saul closed his eyes, listening to the wind and the quiet breathing beside him. As they drifted to sleep, the subtle awareness of each other's presence remained—an unspoken understanding that this was just survival.

Chapter 8

Saul awoke to the dim light of dawn filtering through the dirty windows of the van. It wasn't the chill that stirred him from sleep. It was the unexpected warmth against his side. Hannah. She was pressed up against him, her body close, her breath soft and steady in her sleep. They had both shifted during the night, seeking whatever comfort they could find in the narrow confines.

For a moment, Saul lay still, his mind sluggish from the fatigue. He hadn't been this close to another person in a long time —not like this. Before he had a chance to move, Hannah stirred beside him. Her breathing hitched, and her eyes fluttered open. It took her a second to realize where she was and how close they had gotten. Her body tensed, and she immediately pulled away, her face flushed with embarrassment.

"Sorry," she mumbled, quickly brushing a hand through her tangled hair.

Saul gave her a slight nod, his voice low and calm. "It's fine."

They climbed out of the van without another word, stepping into the crisp morning air. The morning chill wasn't as biting as it had been in recent weeks, hinting that maybe winter was beginning to lose its grip. Saul stretched his stiff limbs, his muscles protesting slightly after a night spent in the cramped van.

Hannah did the same beside him, rolling her shoulders and rubbing the back of her neck. She looked up at the pale sky, exhaling slowly as if shaking off the last remnants of sleep. The promise of warmer days lingered in the air, faint but present, though they both knew better than to trust that relief would come too soon.

They worked in silence, gathering their supplies from the van. Saul slung his pack over his shoulder when he noticed Hannah had stopped. She was standing by the edge of the road, staring at something. Frowning, she bent down and picked it up—a small object.

"What is it?" Saul asked, moving closer.

Hannah held it up, her brow furrowed in confusion. "A flashlight."

Saul's eyes narrowed as he studied it. "That wasn't there yesterday, was it?"

"No," she said, shaking her head. "We would've noticed it when we found the van."

Saul stepped closer, taking the flashlight from her hand. It was battered but intact—the rubber grip worn from use. He clicked the button, but nothing happened.

"Dead batteries," he muttered, turning it over in his hand. He handed it back to Hannah, a sense of unease settling over him.

"Maybe someone passed by during the night," Hannah suggested. "The batteries probably died, and they just tossed it."

Saul's eyes scanned the empty road around them. The idea of someone passing so close while they slept unsettled him. "Could be," he said. "Either way, we should get off the road. If someone did pass through, we don't want to be here when they come back."

They left the road behind and cut through the forest. In the pale morning light, the trees stood like skeletal sentinels. Their brittle branches creaked in the wind, and the ground beneath their feet was soft with decay. The forest's silence pressed in on them, broken only by the occasional crunch of their boots on the dead earth.

As they moved deeper into the forest, Saul couldn't shake the feeling that someone had been nearby during the night. The flashlight had been left too conveniently, too close to their shelter. Whether it had been discarded by someone passing by or deliberately left behind, it didn't matter. They couldn't afford to take any more chances out in the open. Suddenly, Hannah drew her gun, her posture tense as she stood frozen.

Saul tightened his grip on his rifle. "What is it?" he asked. "Listen," Hannah replied.

Saul turned his head, looking for any signs of movement. Then he heard it—faint at first but unmistakable.

"Help…Help…please…someone…"

The voice was weak, hoarse, and full of desperation. Saul exchanged a glance with Hannah. Her eyes were cold and unreadable.

"Could be a setup," Saul said.

The voice continued, weaker this time. There was something in the tone, something that struck a chord in Saul. He had been in that place before—the edge of survival, where every breath felt like it could be your last. It wasn't an easy place to be, and it wasn't an easy thing to ignore.

"Let's check it out," Saul said, keeping his voice low. "Carefully."

Hannah didn't argue, but her grip on her gun tightened. They moved through the trees, their steps silent, their senses heightened. The voice grew louder as they approached. Saul motioned for Hannah to stop as they crept closer, staying low to the ground as they peered through the branches. There, slumped against the base of a large tree, was a man. He looked to be in his thirties, though it was hard to tell with the grime and exhaustion etched into his face. His clothes were torn and dirty—his face was pale, covered in sweat, and his chest heaved with labored breaths.

"Please," the man rasped, barely able to lift his head. "I fell...I think my leg's broken. I've been here for hours...please...help me."

Saul's gaze swept over the scene, searching for any sign of danger, but there was nothing. Just the man, clearly in pain, looking like he'd been left for dead.

Hannah moved closer; her eyes studied him. "Who are you?"

The man swallowed hard, his breath shaky. "Carl...my name's Carl. I was with a group, but we got separated. I fell, and...they didn't come back for me. Please...I need help."

Saul knelt a few feet away from Carl, his hand resting on his gun. "You've been out here all day?" Saul asked.

Carl nodded, wincing as he shifted slightly. "I don't know how long it's been. I was running, and I fell...landed wrong. Please...I just need help. If I stay here any longer, I won't make it."

Saul glanced up at Hannah. She hadn't put her gun away, her expression still guarded, but something flickered in her eyes. A shared understanding. They had both been where Carl was now— alone, hurt, and clinging to hope.

"We'll help you," Saul said finally. "But we can't stay here. You'll need to move with us."

Carl's face tightened with pain, but he nodded. "I'll try."

They set to work quickly. Hannah fashioned a splint for Carl's leg from branches and strips of cloth while Saul monitored their surroundings, alert for any sign of movement. They couldn't afford to be caught off guard.

Once Carl could stand, they led him farther into the woods, where they found a small clearing. It was a risky move, stopping to help a stranger, but leaving him there to die felt wrong. At least to Saul, it did.

Carl sat down and leaned back against a tree, his leg stretched out in front of him. "Thank you," he murmured, his voice hoarse. "I didn't think anyone would stop. Not anymore."

Hannah sat nearby, her gun resting close within reach, her silence heavy with unspoken thoughts. Saul didn't need words to sense her unease—it mirrored the doubts that had already begun to gnaw at him. He glanced at her briefly, their eyes meeting in mutual understanding before he turned back to Carl.

"We're not staying long," Saul said. "Once you've rested a bit, you'll have to figure out your next move."

Carl's face shifted. "You're not leaving, are you?"

Saul's gaze hardened. "We can't stay. We've got to keep moving."

Carl's eyes widened, his head shaking in disbelief. "No, no… you can't just leave me out here. Please, you can't."

Hannah stood up. "We don't have much time left today, and we don't have much trust left either." Her voice was calm but carried a clear warning.

Carl's shoulders slumped, his eyes dropping to the ground. "Just stay the night," he muttered. "Help me get to town in the morning, and you can leave me there. I won't slow you down, I swear. We can leave before dawn."

Saul studied him for a moment, feeling the weight of the decision pressing down on him. He glanced over at Hannah, then motioned for her to step aside. They walked a few paces away from Carl before Saul spoke.

"What do you think?" Saul asked.

Hannah didn't hesitate. "I think something doesn't feel right. He's desperate, but something is off about him."

Saul exhaled slowly. "Maybe you're right. But when I saw him, all I could think about was when you found me. I was done for, and if you hadn't stepped in…"

"That was different." Hannah interrupted. "I saw something in you that night, something worth saving. I don't see that in him."

Saul nodded. "Then we move on," he said quietly. "Trust is hard to come by, but I trust you."

Hannah blinked as if caught off guard by his honesty, then nodded. "Let's get back over there and pack up."

They turned and headed back toward Carl. Saul couldn't shake the feeling that Hannah had been right all along. She was still on guard, her instincts sharp, while his had softened for reasons he couldn't explain. For a brief moment, he felt grateful that she was with him—grounded where he wasn't.

As they broke through the tree line and stepped into the clearing, they stopped cold. Carl was crouched low beside their packs, rifling through their supplies. His hands moved fast, stuffing food and gear into a makeshift bag. The leg he had claimed was broken moved effortlessly, without hesitation.

Saul's breath caught. He slowly pulled his rifle from his shoulder, leveling it at Carl. Hannah followed suit, her revolver steady in her grip.

"Don't move," Saul called out.

Carl froze, his back still to them. The tension was thick. Neither of them moved for a moment. Carl finally turned. His eyes were wide, filled with fear as he stood there, clutching the bag of stolen supplies.

"I...I didn't have a choice," Carl stammered, his voice trembling. "I needed the supplies. I didn't think you'd help me if I asked."

Saul took a slow step forward, his rifle aimed squarely at Carl's chest. "You lied to us. Played us."

Carl's eyes darted between Saul and Hannah. "I didn't mean any harm," Carl pleaded, his voice frantic. "I just..."

Saul pulled the trigger. The gunshot echoed through the forest. Carl's body jerked as the bullet hit him square in the chest. For a moment, he stood there, his face twisted with pain and shock, before collapsing to the ground. He gasped once, twice, and then he was still.

Hannah looked at Saul, her face still with the same cold expression. "He would've killed us if he had the chance," she said quietly.

Saul nodded in agreement. "Yeah, I know."

Hannah crouched beside Carl's lifeless body, her expression unreadable, calm, almost detached. Saul couldn't see her face clearly, but he knew exactly what was coming.

"No," he said firmly.

Hannah rose to her feet and turned to face him. "We need to harvest him."

Saul shook his head, turning away from her. "No," he repeated, his voice quieter. "We're not doing that."

Hannah grabbed his arm, forcing him to turn back and meet her gaze. "Saul, look at me," she said.

He hesitated, then raised his eyes to hers.

"Believe me," she continued, "I don't want this any more than you do. I'd give anything to just pack up and leave right now. But look at us—we haven't had anything sustainable in weeks. We're surviving on scraps to nothing. We won't last much longer if we don't do this."

Saul knew she was right, but it turned his stomach. He could barely bring himself to consider it. "I…I can't," he said, his voice cracking.

Hannah's eyes softened. "Listen, Saul. If we hadn't come back when we did, Carl would've taken everything, and we would have been the ones left with nothing. This—" she gestured to Carl's body "—this was his mistake. And because of that mistake, we have a chance to survive."

Saul lowered his gaze. He didn't want to accept it, but he knew she was right. The truth was inescapable. After a long pause, he finally nodded. "You're right. It has to be done."

Saul walked over to Carl and stood over him for a long moment. He felt sick as he drew his knife. He hated it. He hated himself for what he knew had to happen next.

Chapter 9

The following weeks brought more sunshine, a welcome change from the harsh cold they had endured. Though the nights remained cool, the days were warmer, making travel easier. Saul and Hannah continued their journey through the woods, keeping just far enough inside the tree line to catch glimpses of the open fields but not so close as to risk being seen from the outside.

Since they had relied on their grim "harvest" for sustenance, they hadn't needed to scavenge as often. Each trip into town brought the threat of danger, and after weighing the risks, they decided to bypass several towns along their route. Avoiding trouble had become as essential as finding food.

The day stretched, the sun casting long shadows across the dead landscape. As the air began to cool again, signaling the approach of night, they ventured deeper into the forest, seeking a safe spot to set up camp before darkness settled in.

They ate silently, as they always did, but the silence was eerie this time. Saul stared at his meal, the food on his plate seeming more like a challenge than nourishment. His hand hovered over it, hesitating before lifting another small piece to his mouth. He couldn't bring himself to look at Hannah, and he knew she was doing the same—keeping her gaze fixed on the ground as though acknowledging the other's presence would make it all too real.

The fire crackled in the quiet of the night, its orange glow casting flickering shadows across their small camp. Beyond the light of the flames, the forest was pitch black, its silence almost oppressive. There was no wind—just the stillness of the cool air.

Saul sat hunched near the fire, staring into the flames as if they held some kind of answer to the questions swirling in his mind. He felt the familiar weight pressing down on him, the weight that came every night when he let his guard down, even for a moment. It was the weight of guilt, regret, and memories that wouldn't let him sleep.

He hadn't told Hannah how bad it had gotten, how much the nightmares plagued him. He rubbed his hand over his face, trying to scrub the memories away, but they clung to him, refusing to leave. He felt Hannah's presence nearby, sitting across from him by the fire. She had finished her meal and was sharpening her knife, the blade scraping against the stone in a steady rhythm. She hadn't said much all day. She rarely did anymore.

Saul hesitated one last time as he took his final bite, setting his plate off to the side. His eyes went back across the flames. "Hannah," he said quietly.

She looked up from her knife, her eyes meeting his. She didn't say anything; she just waited for him to speak. She was just as worn down as he was, carrying the same weight and guilt.

"I've been having these nightmares," Saul admitted. "Every night. I see them. The people I've killed. They're always there."

Hannah's gaze didn't waver, but he saw the flicker of recognition in her eyes. She knew what he was talking about. She always knew.

"Yeah," she said softly, setting her knife aside. "I see them too."

Saul sighed, the confession pulling at something deep inside him. He had kept it all bottled up for so long, thinking he had to carry it alone. But now that he was saying the words, they felt like a flood he couldn't stop. "It's like they're always with me. No matter what I do, I can't get rid of them. Carl…raiders, people who lost their way in desperation and turned on me. So many people over the years. I see their faces every time I close my eyes. And then there's my family…"

His voice trailed off, the words catching in his throat. He had never talked about his wife and daughter with Hannah. It was too painful, the wound too deep. But tonight, the weight of it all was too much to bear.

"They're gone, and I couldn't save them," Saul continued, his voice trembling with the emotion he had tried to suppress. "I couldn't save anyone."

Hannah didn't say anything at first. She just watched him. But after a long moment, she spoke, her voice softer than usual. "I know what you're feeling," she said. "I feel it, too. Every time I think about the people I've lost, the people I've killed…it's like they're still here, haunting me. My family…I wasn't there when they died. I was out scavenging. I came back, and they were gone."

Saul glanced at her, surprised by her admission. Hannah rarely talked about her past, about the people she had lost. She kept it locked away, hidden behind the tough exterior she had built over the years. But tonight, something was different. Maybe it was the exhaustion or the weight of the guilt they both carried, but for the first time in a long time, she was letting her guard down.

"I keep thinking," Hannah continued, "that if I'd just been faster, if I'd been there when they needed me…maybe things would've been different. Maybe they'd still be alive."

Saul nodded, feeling the familiar ache in his chest. "I think about that too. About what I could've done differently. About all the things I didn't do."

Saul felt their shared guilt lingering heavily, yet there was something more—an unspoken tension that had been quietly growing between them for a long time. They had been through so much together—long treks through various terrain, scavenging town to town, sharing meals and shelters. And yet, despite everything they had shared, there was always a wall between them—a wall built by the horrors of this world, the violence and loss that had shaped them.

But tonight, in the quiet of the night, with the fire burning low and the memories of the dead swirling around them, that wall seemed to crack.

"I'm scared," Saul admitted. "I'm scared that we're losing ourselves. That every time we have to kill, every time we cross that line and take from others, we're losing a little more of who we used to be."

Hannah's gaze softened, and for a moment, Saul glimpsed a rare vulnerability in her eyes, something she rarely allowed anyone to see. She stood, then made her way around the fire, settling down beside him.

"I'm scared, too," she said quietly. "But we're still here, Saul. We're still fighting. And as long as we're still fighting, we haven't lost everything."

Saul nodded. "But how much more can we take? How much more before we're not even human anymore?"

Hannah looked away. Her gaze drifted to the fire as if she was searching for her own answers in the flames. "We're not monsters, Saul. As long as we care and feel guilty about what we've done, we're still human."

The fire crackled again, louder this time, as a log shifted and sent a spray of sparks into the night sky. Saul watched them rise and disappear into the darkness. Hannah shifted beside him, her leg brushing against his. The touch was brief, almost accidental, but it sent a jolt through him, a spark of something he hadn't felt in what seemed like forever. Saul turned his head to look at her, and their eyes met in the dim firelight. Something in her gaze mirrored the storm inside him—something vulnerable, something hungry.

Without thinking, Saul reached out, his hand brushing lightly against her cheek. Hannah didn't pull away. Instead, she leaned into his touch, her eyes closing for a moment as if savoring the warmth of his hand. He wasn't sure who moved first, but the space between them suddenly vanished. Hannah's lips met his, soft but urgent, and all the tension, unspoken emotions, and fear of losing themselves poured out in that moment.

Their kiss deepened, the fire crackling softly beside them, and everything else—every nightmare, every ghost, every weight they carried—faded into the background. For the first time in what felt like forever, they weren't thinking about survival or the next fight. They weren't thinking about the people they had lost or the things they had done. They were just Saul and Hannah—two people trying to feel human again.

When it was over, they lay together in the quiet aftermath, their bodies still pressed close, their breathing slowing as the fire burned low. The night had grown colder, but the warmth of each other's presence was enough to keep the chill at bay. For a long time, neither spoke, the silence between them now comfortable, no longer weighed down by the things they couldn't say.

Hannah rested her head on Saul's chest, her fingers tracing slow, lazy patterns on his skin.

"We're still human," she said softly.

"Yeah," he whispered. "We are."

Chapter 10

T he fire had long since burned to embers, leaving the camp shrouded in an early morning chill. Saul stirred from his restless sleep, his body stiff and sore from the hard ground, but his mind sharper than it had been in days. Hannah lay curled beneath her coat beside him, her breathing steady and slow. Saul watched her for a moment, the events of the previous night hanging between them. The warmth of her body and the closeness they had shared had been real. But now, that moment felt distant, as if it had happened in another world.

Saul sat up slowly, his muscles protesting the movement. The aches and bruises of their journey were now a constant companion, but his mind was alert, focused on what lay ahead. He glanced around the small clearing where they had made camp, taking in the quiet of the morning. There was a stillness to the world, a kind of fragile calm that only existed in the brief hours before the day truly began. It was peaceful, in a way, but Saul knew better than to trust it. The world was no longer a place of peace.

They didn't speak as they packed up camp. There was no need to. The silence between them was a mutual agreement to let the night's events remain in the past. Survival didn't leave much room for reflection, and they both knew that the day ahead would demand all their focus.

Hannah moved efficiently as she gathered her belongings and prepared for the road ahead. Saul did the same, his thoughts already turning to the journey that awaited them. They still had a long way to go, and the rumors of the sanctuary were still just that: rumors. But it was something to hold onto and guide them through the endless days of walking, fighting, and surviving.

As they finished packing, Hannah turned to Saul, adjusting her pack on her shoulders. "I'll be back in a minute," she said quietly. She gestured toward the edge of the forest. "Nature calls."

Saul nodded, his eyes following her as she disappeared into the trees, leaving him alone in the clearing. The quiet settled over him, and for a moment, Saul allowed himself to breathe deeply, the cool air filling his lungs. Despite the tension that always seemed to accompany their journey, these brief moments of solitude allowed him to center himself. But as the silence stretched, his instincts began to stir, that familiar prickling at the back of his neck.

He turned back toward the forest, his eyes scanning the treeline for any sign of movement. It was an old habit. Every sound, every shift in the wind, set his senses on edge. But it wasn't the wind that caught his attention. A figure stood at the edge of the clearing.

Saul's hand instinctively moved toward his gun. The man seemed to have appeared out of nowhere, his body blending into the shadows of the trees. He was older, his face lined and weathered, his clothes tattered and worn. He leaned against a gnarled tree, his hands in the pockets of a long, threadbare coat, watching Saul with an unreadable expression.

For a moment, neither of them spoke. Saul's body tensed, his fingers brushing the grip of his gun. The man didn't move or make any sign of threat, but there was something unsettling about the way he stood there—calm, relaxed, as though the chaos of the world had no hold on him.

"You alone?" Saul asked.

The man nodded slowly, his lips curling into a faint smile. "Alone," he said, his voice was raspy. "I've been alone for a long time."

Saul narrowed his eyes, glancing around the clearing. He didn't hear anyone else or see any movement beyond the man. But that didn't mean the stranger wasn't part of something larger.

"What are you doing out here?" Saul asked, keeping his hand close to his gun but not drawing it yet.

The man tilted his head slightly as if considering the question. "Walking," he said simply. "Same as you, I imagine."

Saul's grip tightened. "Where are you headed?" he asked, his voice firmer now.

The man's smile widened just a fraction, but it never reached his eyes. "Nowhere," he said with a shrug. "Everywhere. It doesn't much matter these days, does it?"

Saul felt a surge of frustration rising in his chest. He didn't like riddles, didn't like the ambiguity of the man's answers. There was no room for vagueness in a world where every decision could mean the difference between life and death. His jaw tightened as he took a step closer.

"You've been out here a long time, haven't you?" the man continued. "I can tell. You've got that look. Tired. Hungry. Searching for something…something that might not even exist."

Saul's pulse quickened, but he kept his face neutral. "What's that supposed to mean?"

The man chuckled softly. "You're looking for the sanctuary, aren't you? The place everyone talks about. The place where the world hasn't fallen apart."

Saul's chest tightened at the mention of the sanctuary. *How did this man know?* he thought. *Who was he?*

"Do you know where it is?" Saul asked.

The man's smile faded slightly, and he shook his head. "No

one does. It's a story, a dream people tell themselves to keep moving. To keep hoping. But hope can be dangerous in a world like this. It can blind you to the truth."

Saul's frustration grew. "What truth?"

The man's eyes softened. "The truth that sometimes…there is no sanctuary. No safe haven—no place where the world hasn't gone mad. Sometimes, all that's left is survival. And chasing after false hopes will only get you killed."

Saul stared at the man, the words settling uncomfortably in his chest. It was what he had feared all along and wondered in his darkest moments. But hearing it spoken aloud from the mouth of a stranger felt like a punch to the gut.

The man shook his head. "I'm not telling you to give up. But be careful what you're chasing. Sometimes, the things we want most aren't worth the price we pay."

Before Saul could respond, he heard the soft crunch of footsteps behind him. He turned to see Hannah emerging from the trees. She had a look of confusion as she approached.

"Who were you talking to?" she asked, her voice cutting through the tension.

Saul turned back toward the tree where the old man had been standing—only to find it empty. The man was gone, vanished into the shadows as quietly as he had appeared.

"No one," Saul muttered, his voice tight as he scanned the treeline again. "We need to go."

Hannah gave him a questioning look but didn't press the issue. She had learned to trust Saul's instincts, and if he said they needed to move, she wouldn't argue. Saul hoisted his pack onto his shoulders, his mind still racing with the old man's cryptic words, the doubts he had tried to push aside now bubbling back to the surface.

The two of them set off down the path, but Saul's mind was anything but calm. He glanced over his shoulder, half-expecting to see the man watching them from the shadows. But there was nothing there, only the endless stretch of forest.

"Let's keep moving," Saul said quietly. "We're not turning back now."

Chapter 11

The ground shifted beneath their feet, each step scattering dust into the dry air. The landscape grew broader and flatter around them as though the world itself had been stretched thin. The first signs of sand lay scattered across the earth, pooling in small patches that seemed to gather like warnings.

"This place…" Hannah murmured, her voice trailing off as she eyed the ground. Her boot sank slightly into a patch of sand, the grit clinging to the worn leather. "It's like it's swallowing us whole."

Saul gave a tight nod, his eyes fixed on the faint horizon. "Just keep going," he said. "We'll get through it."

But as they walked, the sand grew thicker, spreading until it became a relentless sea of soft, shifting dunes. The sun climbed higher, casting harsh light over the wasteland, bleaching the world around them to shades of white and gold. Saul squinted against the glare, feeling the sun's relentless heat digging into his skin, sweat rolling down his brow and stinging his eyes.

"Strange," Hannah whispered. "A whole world stripped clean. Makes you wonder if maybe this is the end of everything."

Saul shook his head, his gaze fixed ahead. "Not yet," he replied. "Not while we're still walking."

She gave a slight nod, her lips pressing into a tight line, and they trudged on in silence. They hadn't spoken much since they'd left the last stretch of trees behind. Out here, conversation seemed to vanish, swallowed by the vast emptiness around them. Each step forward felt like a promise—to keep moving, to stay alive.

A gust of wind kicked up, and dust swirled around them, coating Saul's throat and catching in his lungs. He pulled the thin scarf from around his neck, draping it over his mouth and nose to keep out the grit. But the wind grew stronger, clawing at his face and hands as if the desert was trying to drive them back.

"Here." Saul reached out, offering his scarf to Hannah. Her face was already red from the heat; her eyes narrowed against the brightness.

"Thanks," she said. "Didn't realize the sun could be this unforgiving."

"Better get used to it," Saul replied. "This place doesn't know how to show mercy."

"How long do you think we can keep this up?" she asked suddenly.

"As long as we have to," Saul replied, though his voice was as tired as he felt. "Stopping isn't an option."

Her gaze softened as she looked at him. "No, I guess it's not."

The silence returned, thick and heavy as the heat pressing down on them. Hours slipped by until Hannah's voice broke the quiet once more.

"Water," she said, her tone strained.

Saul halted, reaching for the water bottle hooked to his belt. He lifted it, giving it a gentle shake. The sloshing sound was faint —almost nonexistent.

"Not much left," he warned, unscrewing the cap and taking a

small, careful sip. He passed the bottle to Hannah, watching as she took a sip that was just as careful and restrained.

She swallowed, closing her eyes briefly as if savoring the faint relief. "We'll find more soon," she said.

"Yeah," Saul agreed, though his voice was uncertain, and neither wanted to acknowledge it. His vision wavered, the horizon blurred and shifted, and he stumbled slightly. Hannah reached out, her hand steadying him, her touch lingering for a moment longer than necessary.

"Are you alright?" she asked.

"Fine," he muttered. "Just…need a minute."

As they continued, something caught Saul's eye on the horizon—a shape, indistinct at first, then sharpening into the outline of a body, half-buried in the sand. They slowed as they approached, the silence growing heavy as they saw it. It was a person—what was left of one, anyway—reduced to a husk, with clothing torn and bones bleached under the sun.

Hannah stared at it. "Another one," she said quietly.

"Another one who didn't make it," Saul replied.

Hannah crouched beside the body, eyeing the torn backpack slung over its shoulder. She hesitated, her hand hovering above it before glancing up at Saul. "Do you think…?"

"Go ahead," he said. "Might be something we can use."

She opened the pack carefully, sorting through its contents. A dull knife, a tattered map, a cracked water bottle—nothing of value, nothing that would help them now. She stood, wiping her hands on her pants.

"Nothing," she murmured.

The hours bled together as they walked. The sun crawled toward the edge of the sky, its heat finally beginning to wane as shadows stretched across the sand. As dusk settled, Saul could see something in the distance—a jagged outcrop of rocks standing like bones against the darkening sky.

"There," he said, his voice rough with exhaustion. "We can

rest there for the night."

Hannah nodded, her face drawn and weary. They quickened their pace, pushing through the last stretch until they reached the shelter of the rocks. They sank against the cool stone, the relief immediate, though it did little to ease the ache in their bones.

Saul leaned back, closing his eyes as he tried to catch his breath. They were both exhausted, their bodies pushed to the breaking point, but they didn't have the luxury of stopping—not really. They had to keep going, even if they were walking into nothing.

For a long while, they sat in silence, the cool air a balm against the heat that had burned them all day. The stars began to appear, scattering across the darkened sky, and Saul could feel sleep pulling at him.

"Do you think…" Hannah's voice cut the silence. "Do you think this place we're looking for is real?"

Saul opened his eyes, staring up at the stars. "I don't know," he admitted. "But I need to believe it is. Otherwise…what are we doing here?"

She nodded. "Then I guess we keep going. One more day. One more night."

Chapter 12

The sound of the river was like a lifeline. After days of relentless walking, the rushing water cut through the silence and brought hope to Saul and Hannah. The desert had been brutal, leaving them with cracked lips and sunburned skin.

Saul dropped his pack with a heavy thud, his legs trembling from exhaustion. He knelt by the river, cupping the icy water in his hands and letting it pour over his face. The sensation was immediate, a shock that brought him back from the weary fog of survival. Beside him, Hannah knelt to fill her bottle, her eyes scanning the treeline with that quiet vigilance that never left her. Even here, she didn't let her guard down, her hand resting near the hilt of her knife, every muscle primed.

"We should rest for a bit," she murmured, glancing over at him. "Just long enough to refill our bottles and eat something. Then we need to move."

Saul nodded, lowering himself onto a fallen tree by the riverbank. Leaning back against the rough bark, he felt his muscles finally begin to relax. The river's steady roar was calming, a rare sound in a world that had lost its gentleness. It was almost enough to make him believe they could stay here. But that illusion shattered in an instant.

A faint rustling from the treeline across the river snapped Saul's attention back. His fingers instinctively found his rifle, gripping it as his gaze narrowed.

"Hannah," he said quietly.

Hannah's head shot up, her hand tightening around her revolver as she scanned the treeline, her body tense and ready.

"I hear it," she whispered, her voice barely audible.

The rustling grew louder, unmistakable now. A group of figures emerged from the trees, moving with predatory intent. There were at least seven, maybe more—ragged and armed, with eyes that shone with hunger and desperation.

"Raiders," Saul muttered, gripping his rifle tighter.

In an instant, the raiders charged, splashing into the river with reckless abandon. Saul raised his rifle, aiming at the man leading the pack. He took a steadying breath and fired, the shot ringing across the water. The man stumbled, clutching his shoulder, but didn't stop. His face twisted with pain and fury as he pushed forward, weapon raised.

"Move!" Hannah shouted, diving toward a boulder for cover. Saul fired again, the bullet hitting another raider in the thigh.

The man staggered but kept coming, driven by sheer desperation. The lead raider reached the bank, raising his rifle and firing, the bullet zipping past Saul's head. Saul dropped to one knee, returning fire and hitting the raider square in the chest, sending him sprawling into the water.

Hannah fired her revolver at another raider who was closing in fast, the bullet hitting him in the chest. But as she turned, another raider lunged from her blind side, grabbing her arm and twisting it with enough force to send the revolver spinning from her grasp. It clattered onto the rocks before tumbling into the river, sinking out of sight.

"Damn it!" she hissed, grabbing her knife as she spun to face her attacker. She moved like a shadow, her knife glinting as she intercepted another raider climbing up the bank. He raised a machete, his mouth twisted in a snarl as he lunged at her. She sidestepped smoothly, her blade flashing as she struck, cutting deep into his side. He gasped, his eyes wide with shock as he fell back, clutching his wound. Hannah didn't hesitate. She stepped forward and finished him.

Another gunshot cracked through the air, and Saul felt a sharp, burning pain as a bullet grazed his arm. He bit back a curse, gritting his teeth as he spun around, spotting the shooter—a woman with wild eyes, her finger poised on the trigger of her gun. He aimed and fired, hitting her shoulder. She cried out, dropping her weapon, but before he could catch his breath, another raider was upon him, swinging a metal pipe.

Saul barely managed to dodge the pipe whooshing past his head. He swung his rifle up, blocking the next strike, the impact jarring his arms as he fought to push the raider back. With a quick movement, he drove the butt of his rifle into the man's stomach, doubling him over. Saul followed with a strike to the side, sending the raider stumbling back, but he didn't fall.

"Saul…behind you!" Hannah shouted, her voice cutting through the chaos.

Saul glanced over his shoulder, spotting two more raiders closing in, their weapons raised. He fired, taking one down, but the other lunged at him before he could reload. They crashed to the ground, the raider's hands closing around his throat. Saul struggled, his vision blurring as his mind flashed back to when he met Hannah.

"Hannah!" he choked, feeling his strength fade.

But Hannah was already there. She drove her knife into the raider's side, forcing him off Saul with a strangled cry. She yanked him off, her eyes fierce as she helped Saul to his feet.

"They're not letting up," she said, her voice grim. "We need to get out of here, or they'll wear us down."

Saul nodded, his breathing ragged. Another gunshot rang out, and they ducked, pressing themselves against the nearest rock for cover as bullets peppered the ground around them.

"We're pinned," he muttered, glancing at her. "We need a plan."

Hannah assessed their surroundings. "I'll create a distraction. You circle around and take out the ones in the trees. We can get to the higher ground if we break their line."

Saul hesitated, but he knew she was right. "Be careful," he said.

She gave him a quick nod. "Go."

Without waiting, she sprang from their cover, darting toward the treeline. Shots followed her, the raiders' attention shifting as they tried to track her movements. Saul moved swiftly, circling around, his rifle at the ready. He aimed at the raiders concealed in the trees, firing at the closest one and hitting him square in the chest. The man fell, and Saul didn't waste a moment, moving on to the next.

Hannah dodged and weaved through the trees, her movements fluid as she avoided the gunfire. She reached one of the raiders hiding in the brush, her knife flashing as she struck. Another raider lunged at her, and she twisted, using his momentum against him as she drove her knife into his neck. He collapsed, his body hitting the ground with a dull thud.

Saul pressed forward, firing at another raider, who ducked behind a tree. He crouched, waiting for the man to show himself, his finger poised on the trigger. The raider leaned out to fire, and Saul didn't hesitate, pulling the trigger and watching as the man slumped against the tree, his rifle slipping from his hands.

"Hannah, on your left!" he shouted, spotting another raider closing in on her with a gun raised.

She spun around, her knife raised just as the raider fired. She dropped to the ground, the bullet missing her by inches. In one swift movement, she rolled forward, coming up behind him, and slashed at his legs. He let out a howl, dropping to his knees, and she finished him with a brutal thrust.

Saul exhaled, his chest heaving as he watched the final raider collapse to the ground. The world seemed to stop for a moment, and he felt the quiet settle over them like the earth had paused to draw breath. The only sound was the rushing of the river, its steady roar a stark contrast to the chaos that had just unfolded.

He looked at Hannah, who was leaning heavily against a tree. Her face was smeared with sweat and grime, and her hand was still clenched around the hilt of her knife. She caught his gaze and managed a slight nod. Her eyes were dark with exhaustion but sharp with that familiar determination.

"We're clear," she panted, pushing herself upright though her legs wobbled under her. "At least…for now."

Saul took a step toward her, reaching out to steady her. His own body ached, his arm throbbing where the bullet had grazed him. But they were alive. They had made it through.

"Let's…move a little upstream," he said, his voice rough. "Just in case any more decide to show up. We can't stay here."

Hannah nodded, wiping her blade on the edge of her shirt before sliding it back into its sheath. Together, they stumbled upstream, moving through the trees until they found another spot where the river curved and offered some shelter from the open bank. Once they were in a safe spot, Saul sank onto a fallen log, pressing his hand against the wound on his arm.

"You alright?" he asked, glancing at Hannah as she crouched beside him.

"Better off than you, but…" She shifted, pulling back the torn fabric of her pants. A thin, jagged cut stretched across her leg, shallow but bleeding steadily. "I think one of their knives got me."

Saul's expression tightened. "Here," he said, handing her a scrap of cloth from his pack. "Press down on that to stop the bleeding."

She nodded, pressing the cloth to her leg, wincing slightly. "Looks like we both could use some patching up."

"Let's start with yours," Saul said, pulling out another strip of fabric. He tore it into a smaller piece, dabbing it against the wound on her leg to clean away the dirt. Hannah winced but held still, letting him wrap the cloth tightly around the cut. Once he tied off the makeshift bandage, he turned to his arm.

"Here," she said, taking another cloth and moving closer. "Let me help you wrap it." She worked with quick, careful hands, tearing another strip of fabric and wrapping it firmly around his arm. He sucked in a breath as the pressure flared the pain, but he didn't pull away. Instead, he focused on the feel of her hands, the calm it brought him even amid the pain and exhaustion.

When she finished tying off his bandage, Hannah sat back on her heels, wiping a smear of blood from her forehead. "They really came at us hard," she said, glancing back at the river.

"Yeah," Saul replied. "Didn't hold back at all."

"We need to keep moving," she said. "They might have friends nearby."

Saul adjusted the bandage on his arm, wincing as a wave of pain shot through him. He glanced at Hannah, feeling a strange calm settle over him. He couldn't remember the last time he'd felt anything close to safety, yet here, beside her—scars, wounds, exhaustion, and all—it felt like enough.

"Let's go," he said softly, extending his hand to her. She took it without hesitation, her grip steady, and together they rose, turning their backs on the bloodstained river and the chaos they had just survived.

Chapter 13

The town was silent, the only sound the faint whistling of wind through hollowed buildings. Saul's boots crunched on the cracked asphalt as he and Hannah moved cautiously down what had once been the main street, eyes scanning the shadows for anything useful.

The sun was dipping lower, and their supplies were dwindling fast. As they passed the remains of an old grocery store, Saul noticed an open doorway leading into a narrow storage room at the back. Most of the building had collapsed, but the small room was sheltered, the walls still holding up under the weight of fallen beams and rubble.

"Hold on," he said, catching Hannah's arm. "There might be something in here."

"You think so?" Hannah asked.

Saul looked at the doorway again. "I don't know, but it's worth a shot."

They ducked through the doorway, carefully stepping over

broken glass and debris as they entered the dim space. Rusted shelving lined the walls, and a few scattered boxes that had long since collapsed. Saul scanned the shelves, his eyes adjusting to the shadows.

"Nothing," he said, his voice sounding defeated.

Hannah placed a hand on his shoulder. "We'll find something…somewhere," she reassured him.

"Yeah," he said. "Let's get out of here."

As Saul turned to leave the storage room, his shoulder bumped into a shelf. The rusted legs buckled, causing the shelf to crash to the floor.

"Damn it," Saul said. "I hope that wasn't too loud."

Hannah pointed to the floor. "Well, look at that," she said.

Saul's eyes followed to where she was pointing. There, lying on the floor where the shelf had stood, was just one solitary can.

Saul chuckled. "It must have rolled under the shelf a long time ago and sat there ever since."

He reached down and brushed away the grime coating its surface. "No label, but it's intact," he said.

"All this time, and it's still here," Hannah said. "I'd say that's a rare stroke of luck."

Saul stashed the can carefully in his pack, and they made their way back out to the street—a small victory in the growing shadows as they continued through the abandoned town.

He pulled the worn, tattered map out of his pocket and examined it. They had been using the same map for weeks. The lines were faded, and the edges were frayed.

"We need a new map," Saul muttered, looking at the crumpled paper.

Hannah looked at the map and nodded. "Better find one while we're here," she said.

They passed several darkened storefronts before spotting a brick building at the end of the street. A rusted satellite dish clung to the roof, and above the door was a weathered sign: "COUNTY

NEWS HERALD."

Hannah glanced at Saul, who shrugged. "Journalists kept maps on hand," he said.

"Worth a shot," she said, and they made their way up the cracked steps and through the heavy double doors.

Inside, the air was stale and thick with dust, and the dim hallway lingered with the scent of old paper and mildew. The silence felt heavy, and every sound they made seemed to echo, the emptiness amplifying each small step and movement.

"Maps would probably be in a back office," Saul murmured, glancing down the hallway. The shadows grew more profound in the corners, and he gestured to the largest door labeled "Newsroom."

Hannah nodded. "Let's start there."

They pushed open the newsroom door, stepping into a large, dimly lit space. Rows of desks were scattered with papers and notes, drawers left open, and chairs upturned as if people had left in a rush. Old monitors sat dark and caked with dust, while the walls were plastered with headlines, photographs, and hastily scribbled notes—a snapshot of a world that had unraveled as the reporters had tried to capture it.

"Let's split up," Hannah suggested. "I'll check the desks near the back."

Saul nodded, setting his pack down as he searched through the first desk. Most of the papers were unreadable—water-stained, worn, or faded from years of neglect. He flipped through folders and stacks of old newspapers. Eventually, he spotted an atlas book on a shelf in the corner of the room. He pulled it down, brushing off the dust, frowning at the tears and fading lines. But it was still better than what they'd been using.

"Better than nothing," he muttered, tucking it carefully into his pack.

As he turned to rejoin Hannah, a manila folder on a nearby desk caught his eye. Its label was thick, black ink: **"BIOGEN**

ACCIDENT—DRAFT."

He hesitated, a strange feeling settling in his stomach as he reached for it.

"What's that?" Hannah asked, noticing the shift in his expression as she came over.

"Not sure," he replied, flipping open the folder carefully. Inside were typewritten pages, photographs, and clipped notes. He scanned the first page, his pulse quickening as he read the headline: ***EXCLUSIVE: BIOGEN'S ECO-STUDY PROJECT GONE WRONG?***

"Biogen's Eco-Study Project, conducted at multiple rural test sites, was meant to enhance sustainability through genetic modification of local ecosystems," he read aloud, his voice thick with disbelief. "Confidential sources reveal that containment protocols were weak, and unforeseen mutations began spreading beyond control...."

Hannah's face grew grim as she leaned in, reading the words over his shoulder. "This...wasn't just nature taking its course, was it?"

"No," Saul said, flipping through the pages, feeling a chill as he took in the details. He continued reading. "They were conducting genetic experiments on plants, soil microbes, and even native vegetation, hoping to accelerate growth. But the modifications spread outside the testing grounds immediately. The mutations began causing unexpected die-offs, and Biogen classified it as 'low risk' for nearby towns."

He held up a photo clipped to the page. It showed a wide shot of a field of crops, their leaves blackened and curling and the surrounding trees stripped bare. A scribbled note at the bottom read, *"Animal fatalities confirmed. Mutation spread uncontained."*

Hannah let out a slow breath, looking around the dark newsroom with an uneasy expression. "If the outbreak started here, we're closer to the origin than I thought. It's almost like we're standing on ground zero."

Saul's throat tightened as he processed her words. They weren't just in another abandoned town—they were in a place that had been at the center of it all, where people had gone about their lives unaware of the catastrophe brewing beneath their feet. He turned the pages, skimming over internal memos and frantic notes, some in barely legible handwriting.

"Listen to this," he read. "Despite early signs of widespread mutation, Biogen pushed forward with testing, convinced it was an isolated issue. Internal findings were kept confidential to avoid public backlash, even as reports of ecosystem failures began surfacing."

He flipped to a memo marked *"Confidential,"* the ink smudged from hurried handling: "Containment measures failed at multiple sites. Mutations spreading beyond projections. Recommend full confidentiality on all project findings."

Hannah's eyes flashed with anger as she took in the details. "So they knew what they were doing and didn't stop. They just kept it quiet."

Saul continued skimming the documents, the words becoming more disturbing with every page. "Staff instructed to maintain public silence on project activities. All findings marked confidential…first reports of animal fatalities linked to plant mutations." He paused, lifting a photo of a deer carcass lying in a desolate field, its body twisted and covered in wilted brown leaves. "They were just…left to die," he muttered, the realization dawning painfully.

Hannah's fists clenched as she looked over the papers, her jaw set. "All for an experiment they thought would help. These people here didn't even know what was happening right in front of them."

"This article was never published," Saul said. "The news never left this office."

He carefully folded a few of the most damning pages, slipping them into his pack. "It's late," he said, looking back at the darkened street. "Might be better to stay here tonight. No one will come looking for food in a place like this."

Hannah dropped her pack onto the floor, rolling her shoulders. "And honestly, a roof over our heads doesn't sound bad after the day we had."

Saul opened his pack and pulled out the can they'd found in the storage room. "Let's see what we've got here."

Taking his knife, he carefully punctured and pried open the lid. He peered inside and raised his eyebrows.

"Well, look at that," he said, holding the can out for Hannah to see.

She leaned in, a smile spreading across her face. "Ravioli," she said. "I can't remember the last time I had that."

They set to work building a small fire, the flames casting a warm glow as they heated the food—the smell drifting between them. After enjoying their meal, they unrolled their mats near a row of desks, settling in as the night deepened around them. Saul lay awake for a long while, his gaze fixed on the cracked ceiling above, the weight of their discovery heavy on his mind. Beside him, Hannah was curled up and had already drifted off. After a moment, he let his eyes close, surrendering to sleep.

Chapter 14

Saul and Hannah moved cautiously down the road. Their muscles ached from the last few days of travel, and hunger had once again settled into an ever-present gnawing that no amount of rationing seemed to ease. Each step was heavier than the last as they scavenged what they could find. The light was already dim, and the air grew cooler as evening approached. Saul pulled his jacket tighter around him, grateful for any warmth he could find.

Then, just as the gray light began to wane, Saul froze, his eyes narrowing as he caught a faint column of smoke rising in the distance. He gestured to Hannah, who stopped beside him, her gaze following his.

"Smoke," she said, her voice tense.

"Let's just keep clear," Saul said. "Give it a wide berth."

They veered off the road, slipping quietly between the decaying shells of old buildings, doing their best to stay out of sight. But the rubble slowed their progress, forcing them to navigate carefully through piles of fallen concrete and exposed beams. Every step seemed to pull them closer to the source of the smoke, and the maze of buildings funneled them back toward the camp.

As they edged around the corner of a crumbling wall, Saul nearly stumbled into an open clearing, the scent of smoke and food hanging thick in the air. They both froze. Just ahead, a small campfire crackled, and a handful of people sat around it, some tending to what looked like a pot hanging over the fire. Several makeshift tents were pitched around the clearing, and Saul counted at least half a dozen people, each weathered and worn.

A tall, broad-shouldered man with long dark hair noticed them first. His expression flickered with mild surprise before a guarded smile spread across his face. He raised a hand in greeting, his voice friendly as he called out, "Hello there! I didn't expect to see anyone else out here."

Hannah's grip tightened on her knife—her posture tense. Saul's stomach knotted, but he forced a calm expression, giving a brief nod. They hadn't sought out this encounter, but they were caught now.

The man took a step closer. "No need to worry—we're just passing through, same as you, I'd guess," he said, keeping his tone casual. "Name's David. We're good people here, just trying to survive, like everyone else. You're welcome to join us by the fire if you need some warmth."

Saul glanced at Hannah, who kept her expression unreadable, her gaze flicking warily between the other camp members. They didn't seem overtly hostile; in fact, they seemed almost normal, a group of weary survivors taking refuge for the night. But every instinct Saul had told him to stay alert. He offered a cautious nod.

"Didn't mean to intrude," Saul replied. "We were just moving through."

"No intrusion at all," David said, gesturing to the fire. "We don't see many people around here. Safety in numbers, right? We've been on the road a while ourselves, moving from one old town to the next, scavenging what we can. Always ready to lend a hand to good folks who need it."

The offer sounded well-practiced, almost rehearsed, and Saul felt a prickle of unease, but he kept his tone neutral. "Just passing through, like I said."

David's smile faltered. "No need to rush. It's safe here, and it's not often you find that these days." He paused, glancing at the others. "You can even stay the night if you'd like. No one's going to bother you here. We're all just survivors. Doing what we have to." They continued watching, their eyes flicking between him and Hannah.

"Look," Saul said, his tone guarded, signaling to Hannah. "We're going to move along now. But thanks for the offer."

David's smile disappeared entirely, replaced by an expression far more predatory. "I think you might be underestimating your options," he said. "We're survivors, same as you. Food's hard to come by these days, and out here, we make the most of whatever… or whoever we find."

Just as Saul had suspected, this wasn't an offer of kindness; it was an invitation into a trap. "Run!" Saul shouted, grabbing Hannah's arm as they broke into a sprint through the crumbling buildings. Behind them, David's group shouted and gave chase, their footsteps pounding the ground as they surged forward.

Saul and Hannah darted between the buildings until they reached the edge of town and into the trees. Saul's lungs burned with every breath, but he didn't dare slow down, adrenaline fueling each step as they plunged deeper into the forest.

Finally, when the sounds of pursuit had vanished, they collapsed against a large tree, gasping for breath. Saul looked over at Hannah, her face pale and eyes wide, with the same mix of fear and anger he felt.

"You alright?" he asked.

Hannah nodded, though her hand was still clenched around her knife, her knuckles white. "Yeah…but that was too close."

He leaned his head back, his heart racing as he tried to steady his breathing. They'd almost fallen into another trap, nearly becoming victims of this brutal world once more.

"I don't think there's anyone left in this world to trust anymore," Saul said, his voice cold. "No one but us."

Hannah didn't argue. She only nodded.

Hannah's face tightened as they stood, and she instinctively reached for her leg. Saul's eyes dropped, noticing the cut on her leg was bleeding again.

"You're leg," he said, alarm tightening his voice. He hadn't even noticed her limp while they'd been running, and by her expression, she likely hadn't either—not until now.

"It's nothing," she replied, brushing it off. "I think I hit my leg on a rebar while we were running through town. It just opened up the cut again."

Saul shook his head, catching her arm as she shifted her weight and winced again. "That's not nothing," he said, his tone firmer than intended. "That looks infected. Your leg isn't healing right, and you just cut it open even more."

Hannah exhaled sharply, the exhaustion catching up with her. Saul knelt down, gently pushing up the fabric around the wound to get a better look. The cut wasn't gushing, but it was more than a surface scrape, deep enough to be a problem if they didn't clean and dress it soon.

"We need to stop the bleeding," he said.

Hannah gave him a faint smile, though her expression was strained. "It's not exactly like we have a first aid kit lying around, Saul."

He pressed a piece of fabric from his pack over the wound to slow the bleeding, tying it firmly. "We'll have to make do," he replied, standing up and offering her a steadying hand.

He pulled the Atlas out of his pack and opened it up, studying the map. "The next town is only a few miles across this patch of woods."

"A few miles?" Hannah asked.

"Only a few," Saul replied. "Let's go."

They pushed through the forest in silence, focused on the uneven terrain as night began to creep in. Hannah's breaths grew shorter, and each step became more of a struggle as the pain in her leg intensified. She tried to keep her weight off the injured leg, but the effort only slowed her down.

"Hannah, let me take your pack," he offered, but she shook her head, jaw set with determination.

"I can handle it," she muttered. But as they navigated the twisting roots and jagged rocks, her control slipped, and she stumbled occasionally, the pain breaking through her calm façade.

Saul stayed close, catching her when her leg buckled or she faltered against a rough patch of ground. "We're close now," he reassured her each time, though he knew he wasn't sure how much farther they had to go. As they crested a small hill, the remains of the town appeared on the horizon, silhouetted against the dim moonlight. Saul's eyes narrowed as he scanned the area, his gaze settling on a large building a short distance ahead. Faded lettering across its front read: "*ST. ANNE'S HOSPITAL.*"

"There," he said, gesturing to the outline. "We have to find something in there."

Hannah's eyes flickered with cautious relief. "Think they left anything useful inside?"

"If we're lucky," he replied. "At the very least, there should be some supplies we can scavenge."

Chapter 15

The interior was worse than Saul had expected—everything was in various stages of decay. Walls were covered in black mold, the floors scattered with debris, and the once-sterile corridors damp and filthy. Broken glass crunched under their boots as they moved deeper inside, their footsteps echoing in the thick silence.

He guided Hannah through the long, dark hallway, her steps slowing with every shuffle forward. She leaned heavily on his arm, her face pale, and he could feel her body trembling from the pain and exhaustion.

They reached a small room off the main corridor—a doctor's office, by the looks of it, with a broken desk tipped onto its side and scattered medical charts littering the floor. Though the air felt stale, the ceiling here was primarily intact, offering protection from the elements. Saul led her to the driest corner, helping her settle onto a pile of old blankets that had been pushed against the wall.

Hannah let out a shaky breath, her face twisting in pain as she adjusted her weight. Her leg wound had soaked through the fabric of her pants, and though she tried to hide it, Saul could see the tightness in her expression with each movement.

"I'll look for supplies," he said, trying to keep his voice steady. "There's got to be something left in this place—bandages, medicine, anything."

Hannah nodded weakly, leaning her head back against the wall, her eyes already half-closed as fatigue pulled her under. "Be careful," she said softly.

Saul swallowed the knot of fear rising in his throat. He wasn't a doctor. He didn't know much about treating wounds beyond the basics. But he couldn't let her suffer alone. He had to find something—anything that could help her.

With a last glance at her slumped form, he left the room and headed down the dark hallway, his eyes scanning each doorway, his heart pounding. The hospital felt like a mausoleum, an abandoned monument to a time when wounds could be treated with ease and illness wasn't a death sentence.

The rooms he passed offered little but a haunting reminder of what had been lost. He moved through empty exam rooms, peering into dark corners where rusted medical equipment lay scattered like discarded bones. There were overturned gurneys, wheelchairs missing wheels, and piles of brittle paperwork strewn about as if tossed aside in a rush. Each empty room only deepened his frustration and his fear. He could almost hear the ghosts of doctors and nurses hurrying through these halls; their voices faded, replaced by the quiet decay of the world they'd left behind.

After what felt like an eternity, Saul spotted a slightly open door near the end of the corridor. Heart racing, he pushed it open, revealing a storage closet. Dust covered every shelf, and the air was thick with the scent of mold and stale antiseptic, but his eyes landed on a few precious items left behind.

He grabbed an old package of bandages, their edges yellowed with age but still sealed. Next to them, he found a half-full bottle of rubbing alcohol and, miraculously, a small tin of antibiotic ointment. His hands shook as he scooped up the supplies, grabbing a roll of gauze as well. It wasn't much, but it was more than he'd dared to hope for.

With his arms full, he returned to the room where Hannah waited, her breathing shallow and strained. She looked up as he entered, her eyes barely focusing on him, but a faint hint of relief softened her expression.

"I found some supplies," he said, dropping to his knees beside her and setting the items carefully on the ground. He opened the bottle of alcohol. "This is going to hurt," he warned, his voice gentle.

Hannah gave him a slight nod, her jaw clenched. "Just do it," she whispered.

Saul soaked a cotton ball with alcohol, glancing at her one last time before pressing it to her wound. She tensed, a hiss of pain escaping her lips, and her fists clenched tightly as he worked. The gash was deep and ragged, the edges inflamed, and though he tried to be careful, every touch made her wince.

He worked quickly, cleaning the wound as best he could before applying a thin layer of antibiotic ointment. Finally, he wrapped the wound with gauze and bandages, securing it as tightly as he could. When he finished, he sat back, his heart racing, his hands slick with sweat.

"It's not much," he said quietly, draping a worn blanket over her shivering form, "but it'll help."

Hannah's breathing steadied a little, and she offered him a faint smile. "Thank you, Saul," she said, her eyes drifting shut again.

He settled beside her, watching her face as she slipped away into sleep. Her cheeks were flushed, a sure sign of the fever that was beginning to set in, and her body trembled beneath the thin blanket. He could only hope that the small bit of ointment would keep the infection at bay.

The hours crept by, and the silence was interrupted only by the soft patter of rain on the windows. Saul felt a gnawing guilt that he couldn't shake. He should have been more careful. He should have kept her safe. They'd survived so much together and had fought through starvation, hostile survivors, and the brutal, relentless cold of winter. Yet here, in this abandoned hospital, a simple injury might be the thing that took her from him.

"I'm sorry," he whispered, though he knew she couldn't hear him. "I should've protected you better."

He leaned his head back, and memories of their journey flashed through his mind—the quiet conversations by dwindling campfires, the way she had always been the one to keep moving when he wanted to give up. She had been his anchor in this shattered world, the only person he trusted.

Outside, the rain began to fall harder, the sound like a dull heartbeat against the windows. The air grew colder, seeping through the cracks in the walls, but Saul barely noticed, his attention focused on the faint, labored breaths that rose and fell beside him. She drifted in and out of consciousness, her face tight with pain, her lips moving in whispers he couldn't understand.

As night fell, he reached for her hand, holding it tightly, feeling the faint tremor that ran through her. Her skin was cold, and he could feel the fever radiating from her, a warmth that was anything but comforting. The darkness seemed to close in around them.

"I can't lose you," he whispered. "Not like this."

Hannah's eyes opened briefly. She squeezed his hand, her voice so faint he had to lean closer to hear.

"You won't," she whispered, her lips curving into a weak smile. "We've...been through worse."

The minutes stretched into hours, each one marked by the faint sound of her breaths, the feverish murmurs that spilled from her lips. He held her hand through it all, his eyes never leaving her face, as if sheer will alone could keep her here.

Sometime in the early hours of the morning, she stirred again, her fever-bright eyes meeting his. For a moment, clarity returned, and she gave him a look that was as steady as it had been when they'd faced countless threats together.

"You need to sleep," she whispered.

"I'm not leaving you," he replied, the exhaustion thick in his voice.

Hannah's smile was faint, her hand tightening around his. "I know…but if you don't rest, you'll…be no good to either of us."

Saul hesitated; the thought of closing his eyes and leaving her vulnerable was gnawing at him. But she was right; the exhaustion was dragging at him, blurring the edges of his vision, making it harder to stay alert.

He finally nodded, leaning against the wall beside her, his hand still holding hers. "I'll rest," he said, "but I'm not letting go."

Hannah's fingers curled around his, her touch a quiet reassurance that anchored him as he closed his eyes. The rain continued to patter softly against the windows, a lullaby in the silence of the empty hospital. For the first time since he had led her into this building, Saul allowed himself to drift, his mind easing into a light, fitful rest, still tethered to the sound of her breathing beside him. As the hours passed, the storm outside softened, the rain turning to a gentle drizzle. Saul and Hannah lay side by side, their hands entwined. They held onto the only light left to them— each other.

Chapter 16

Saul stirred from his restless sleep. He groaned softly as he sat up, rubbing the stiffness from his neck, and glanced over at Hannah. She was still asleep, her chest rising and falling in shallow, uneven breaths. The fever had finally broken during the night, but it had left her weak, her body battered from fighting the infection. Saul had spent most of the night watching over her, afraid that the fever might return or that the wound on her leg would worsen. But for now, she slept, her face pale and drawn but peaceful.

Saul stood, wincing as his muscles protested the movement. His boots scraped against the cold tile floor. It was a small room—once a doctor's office, perhaps—the air inside was stale, but at least it was dry.

He crossed the room to the broken window, brushing aside the tattered remnants of a curtain as he peered outside. The rain had stopped, but the sky was still dull, the clouds hanging low and heavy over the horizon.

He leaned against the windowsill and sighed, his breath fogging the glass for a moment before dissipating. They couldn't stay here much longer. The hospital had offered them shelter from the storm, but it was far from safe. The building was crumbling, and they had no food. What little medical supplies he had found were nearly gone.

But Hannah wasn't ready to move. The wound on her leg, though no longer bleeding, was still raw, the infection lingering just beneath the surface. She needed more time to heal—more rest. If they moved too soon, it could cost her life.

Saul's hand gripped the windowsill tightly, his knuckles white. He was torn between the need to protect her and the growing desperation that gnawed at him with every passing day. The world outside was unforgiving, and every decision felt like a gamble between two equally dangerous outcomes.

As he turned from the window, something caught his eye. At first, he thought it was nothing—just a flicker of movement in the distance, a trick of the light caused by the mist rolling over the hills. He blinked, his tired eyes struggling to focus. Through the haze, the landscape was nothing more than a blur of shadows and shapes, the outlines of the trees barely visible. But there it was again—just for a moment—a faint shimmer of color.

Green.

Saul squinted, his heart suddenly quickening as he leaned closer to the window. It seemed impossible, but there, on the distant slope of a hill, just barely visible through the fog, was a small patch of green. It was faint, like a streak of paint on a canvas, but unmistakable. Green. A color he hadn't seen in…he couldn't remember how long. It felt like forever since he had seen anything but the dull, dead hues of the world they had been left with.

The more he looked, the more the green seemed to waver, fading in and out of the mist like a mirage. But almost as quickly as it came, the green was snuffed out by a cold, creeping dread. It couldn't be real. It had to be a trick of the light, an illusion conjured by his mind in its desperate search for something—anything—that might offer a reprieve from the relentless bleakness of the world around them.

Saul forced himself to look away from the window. He couldn't allow himself to get caught up in it. Not when Hannah's life hung in the balance, not when the world had shown them repeatedly that it had nothing left to give.

He turned away from the window, his mind pushing the image aside, and walked back to where Hannah lay. She was still sleeping, her brow furrowed slightly in discomfort, her face pale and slick with sweat. Saul knelt beside her, and her eyes fluttered open, blinking slowly as she came back to consciousness. She looked disoriented for a moment, her gaze sweeping across the room before settling on Saul.

"Saul?" Her voice was weak.

"I'm here," Saul said softly, reaching out to touch her arm, offering what little comfort he could. "How are you feeling?"

Hannah grimaced, trying to shift under the blanket but wincing as pain shot through her leg. "Better, I think," she said, though her voice lacked conviction. "Did you find any more supplies? Any food while I was out?"

Saul hesitated for a moment, his mind flashing back to the distant hill, the flicker of green that had appeared through the mist. He could still see it in his mind's eye and feel its pull, but he forced himself to push it aside.

"No," he said quietly, shaking his head. "There's nothing left in this place. I checked again this morning."

Hannah's face fell slightly, and she let out a soft sigh, her hand brushing against her leg. "We can't stay here much longer," she said.

"I know," Saul said gently. "But we can't leave yet. You're still healing, and if we move too soon, it could make things worse. We need to give you more time."

Hannah opened her mouth to protest, but Saul cut her off

before she could argue. "The hospital's safe for now," he said. "At least we can lock the door to this room. We've got at least another day here, maybe two. You need to rest."

She hesitated, her eyes meeting his in silent argument. Saul could see the frustration in her expression, the way her jaw clenched as she struggled with the feeling of helplessness that had settled over her. Hannah was never one to sit still or let herself feel vulnerable, and he knew it was killing her to stay here, to depend on him when she was used to standing on her own. But eventually, she relented.

"Alright," she said quietly. "I'll rest. But we need to leave soon. We can't risk staying in one place too long."

"I know," Saul said with a smile. "We'll leave soon. I promise."

Hannah nodded, though her eyes were still clouded with worry. "What about food?" she asked after a moment. "We're almost out, Saul. We can't wait much longer."

"I'll go out and find something," Saul replied, standing up and pulling his pack onto his shoulders. "There has to be something nearby—I'll look for a few hours, and then I'll come back."

Hannah looked at him, her eyes full of concern. "Be careful," she said softly.

"I will," Saul promised. He gave her one last reassuring look before turning toward the door.

As he stepped into the hallway, the cold, damp air hit him like a wave, and the hospital felt even darker and hollower than before. The walls seemed to close in on him, and shadows stretched long across the floor as he approached the exit. But as he reached the door, he couldn't shake the image of the distant hill, the patch of green that had flickered into view through the mist. It was still there, lingering in the back of his mind like a whisper.

A promise of something more. Something better. He pushed the thought aside as he stepped out into the dying world once again, leaving the safety of the hospital—and Hannah—behind.

Chapter 17

They pushed through the forest, shadows deepening as night settled around them. Saul could see the strain etched into Hannah's face, the tightness in her jaw with each stride. They had left the hospital that morning after a week of much-needed rest—a chance for Hannah's leg to heal from the infection that had nearly taken her out of the fight. Her limp was barely noticeable now, and Saul felt relieved.

During their time in that small room, Saul had scavenged a few cans from nearby houses—beans, a small tin of corn, even a lone can of sardines. They'd stretched the food as far as they could, savoring each bite, but now the last of their rations were gone, and the familiar, gnawing ache of hunger had returned, sharper than ever. Saul stumbled slightly, catching himself against a tree, and Hannah shot him a concerned look.

"You alright?" she asked, though her voice was as drained as his.

He nodded, managing a weak smile. "Just a little dizzy.

Running on fumes, I guess."

"Feels like we've been running on fumes for years," she said as she reached down to adjust the strap on her bag. "I just thought we'd find something by now."

"There's always another town ahead," Saul replied.

But those towns were rarely a relief these days. As they kept moving, a new sound broke through the stillness—a snap of a branch. They froze, exchanging a look as Saul's hand reached for his knife. Hannah stiffened, her gaze sweeping the trees around them, her muscles tensed. They had both heard it, the unmistakable sound of footsteps nearby.

Before they could react, hands grabbed them from behind, yanking them backward with sudden force. Saul struggled, his adrenaline spiking, but the men who held him had firm grips, and he felt the cold press of a gun against his head.

"Stop struggling," a rough voice ordered. "We don't want to hurt you, but if you fight, we won't hesitate."

Saul felt his heart pound, and his mind raced as he quickly absorbed the situation. He glanced sideways, catching sight of Hannah, who was similarly restrained. Her face was a mask of tension as she tried to keep calm. She met his eyes, giving a subtle nod of understanding.

Bound and silent, they were forced to march through the forest, their captors guiding them with firm hands and little conversation. Saul could feel the adrenaline beginning to fade, replaced by the gnawing dread that came with the unknown. He studied the men flanking them, noting the wary glances they exchanged. These weren't wild, unhinged raiders—they were more organized, more deliberate. And that, in some ways, made them more dangerous.

After what felt like hours, they emerged into a wide clearing. Saul's eyes widened as he took in the sight before him: a large camp surrounded by walls of tin and wood—a testament to the camp's determination to keep intruders out. Saul exchanged a look with Hannah, and they both took in the setup.

They were led through a metal gate, which clanged shut behind them with a sound that resonated through the quiet camp. Inside, the camp was larger than they had expected, with tents and makeshift shelters arranged in a rough circle around a central fire pit. About a dozen people moved between the shelters, their faces marked with the same caution and wariness that Saul felt in his own chest.

A tall, broad-shouldered man with a graying beard stepped forward, critically studying Saul and Hannah. His clothes were worn but clean, and his stance radiated command.

"You're not raiders," the man said, his voice deep. "Raiders don't travel in twos. So…what are you?"

Saul met the man's gaze, choosing his words carefully. "We're just trying to survive. That's all."

The man raised an eyebrow, glancing between the two of them. "And we're supposed to take your word for that?"

A tall, dark-haired woman standing nearby stepped forward, her eyes sharp and her posture rigid. She had an air of authority that was hard to ignore, and Saul felt her gaze sweep over him with a calculated intensity.

"My name's Evelyn," she said. "And this is Peter." She gestured toward the bearded man. "We don't take chances with strangers. You might not be raiders, but that doesn't mean you're trustworthy."

Hannah's voice was steady, though her exhaustion was evident. "We're not here to cause trouble. We're just passing through."

Evelyn's eyes narrowed as she considered their words, and after a moment, she gave a slight nod to one of the guards, who stepped forward and cut the ropes binding their wrists. Saul rubbed at the soreness, his gaze never leaving Evelyn and Peter, trying to gauge their intentions.

Peter gestured toward the fire, his expression softening

slightly. "Come, sit. You look like you could use a meal, and we've got enough to share tonight."

The offer made Saul's stomach twist with hunger, but he hesitated, glancing at Hannah. She gave him a slight nod. They couldn't afford to turn down food, not in their current state, but at the same time, Saul couldn't shake the feeling of what kind of 'food' they were in for.

They settled around the fire, and Peter ladled out steaming bowls of stew, the rich scent of meat and broth filling the air. Saul took a tentative bite, savoring the warmth that spread through him as he tasted the familiar flavor of real meat—something he hadn't had in as long as he could remember.

"What kind of meat is this?" he asked, glancing at Peter.

"Freeze-dried beef," Evelyn answered, her gaze fixed on him. "We stockpiled it when things started falling apart. We ration it carefully to make it last."

Saul raised an eyebrow, surprised by the admission. "You were prepared for all this?"

Evelyn's expression grew somber, her gaze distant. "Some of us saw the signs early on. We knew things weren't going to stay the same, so we did what we could to make sure we'd survive."

Hannah looked around the camp, taking in the walls, the organization, the sense of order. "How have you managed to keep it this whole time?"

Peter gave a nod toward the camp's perimeter. "We don't keep everything here. Our main stockpile is hidden underground, far from here. We bring back only what we need each day."

Saul exchanged a glance with Hannah, the realization settling in that these people had prepared for survival in a way he and Hannah had never been able to. In a world where desperation ruled, a stockpile like this could be a dangerous possession.

"So, what happens when it runs out?" Saul asked quietly, meeting Evelyn's gaze.

Evelyn's expression hardened slightly. "That won't happen for a while. But…if it happens, then we adapt. We'll figure something out like we always have."

They ate the rest of their meal in silence, the warmth of the fire contrasting with the cool evening air. As the flames crackled, Saul couldn't shake the feeling of unease that had settled over him. With its walls and careful planning, this camp might seem secure, but it felt fragile—a sense of control that could easily slip away if desperation pushed its inhabitants too far.

"Say," Peter said as he looked at Saul and then at Hannah, "Just out of curiosity, have you ever…you know…"

Saul hesitated for a moment before he slightly nodded. "Yeah…we have," he said. "But we have never killed for it."

His mind flashed back to Carl, but he quickly dismissed it. That was a different situation that was unavoidable.

Peter nodded, and the camp fell quiet again. As the night deepened, the other camp members drifted into their tents, though a few stayed up, casting wary glances at Saul and Hannah. Saul could feel the tension in their stares, the silent suspicion that came with the presence of outsiders. They had been given food, but they still were not trusted.

Once they were alone by the fire, Evelyn looked over at them, her gaze sharp. "If you plan to stay here, know this—we protect what's ours. We don't tolerate betrayal, and we won't hesitate to defend what we've built."

Saul nodded slowly. "We understand. We're just looking to rest and keep moving."

Peter gave a faint smile, though his eyes held a hint of caution. "Good. You're welcome to rest here tonight."

They settled in near the edge of the camp, close enough to feel the warmth of the fire but far enough to keep a distance from the others. As they lay down, Saul felt the familiar weight of uncertainty pressing on him, the knowledge that security was an illusion even in a place like this.

Once the camp had fallen into a quiet lull, Saul leaned close to

Hannah, his voice a low whisper. "We're leaving at dawn."

Hannah nodded, her gaze drifting over the camp's walls. "I agree. This place might look safe, but it feels…unstable."

Saul looked back at Evelyn and Peter, who were deep in conversation by the fire. "They've built something solid here," he said quietly. "They seem decent, but there's a tension about them. After all these years, whatever stockpile they've got won't last forever. And when that food's gone…so is the camp."

They turned in for the night and as the first light of dawn began to lighten the sky, they began to gathered their things.

"Leaving so soon?"

They both turned, surprised to find Peter standing by the fire, watching them with a knowing look. He didn't seem angry, just… understanding.

"Yeah," Saul said, his voice quiet. "We appreciate the food and shelter, but we're…not the type to stay in one place too long."

Peter nodded. "I understand. But remember—this world can be a lonely place. Don't be afraid to find people you can trust."

Saul didn't respond, but Peter's words lingered heavily in his mind.

"Stay right there," Peter said. He turned and stepped into his tent. A moment later, he returned with Saul and Hannah's weapons. "Here you go," Peter said as he held them out.

Saul reached out and took his rifle and knife while Hannah retrieved her knife. "Thanks," Saul said.

"Hope you didn't mind us holding onto them," Peter said with a smile.

Saul nodded. "We understand."

They walked to the gate, and Peter unlatched it. He stood back to let them pass. Saul and Hannah glanced over the quiet camp, the embers of last night's fire barely glowing, the makeshift shelters still and silent. With a final nod to Peter, they turned and slipped into the forest, the pale morning light guiding them back onto their path.

Chapter 18

The sun climbed higher into the sky as Saul and Hannah pushed forward along the narrow path. They had been walking for hours since leaving Evelyn's camp, their minds occupied by the tense feeling that lingered between them.

Hannah finally spoke. "You think we're far enough from Evelyn's camp yet?"

Saul shrugged, "Maybe. But I've had a feeling for a while now…"

Hannah stopped walking and turned to face him. "What kind of feeling?"

Saul met her gaze. "I think we're being followed."

Hannah's hand moved to the knife at her side. Her eyes darkened, and her voice dropped. "How long?"

"Since this morning," Saul replied, scanning the trees behind them as he spoke. "Could be someone from Evelyn's camp. Could be someone else."

Hannah's gaze narrowed. "Do you think it's Evelyn?"

Saul hesitated before answering. "Maybe. I don't know. But whoever it is, we can't let them keep tracking us."

Hannah nodded in agreement. "We set a trap; figure out who's behind us."

"Exactly," Saul said. "We need to get the upper hand before they make a move."

They moved off the trail and into the forest, making a wide circle around the area they had just walked through. Time seemed to stretch out as they waited, tension building between them. Saul's grip tightened on his rifle as they listened for any movement. He caught Hannah's eye, and she gave him a slight nod—she was ready.

After several long, tense minutes, they heard it—the faint sound of footsteps approaching, slow and deliberate. Saul's muscles tensed as a figure emerged from the trees, moving cautiously along the path.

Saul recognized her immediately. Beth, the quiet woman from Evelyn's camp. She moved with the kind of nervousness from someone who wasn't used to this kind of thing. Her eyes darted around the forest, unaware that Saul and Hannah were watching her.

Hannah's eyes flicked to Saul's, confusion and suspicion mingling in her gaze. Saul motioned for them to step out of hiding.

"Beth," Hannah called out, her voice sharp, cutting through the quiet.

Beth froze, her body rigid as she turned to face them. Her hand instinctively reached for the knife at her waist. Her hand dropped when she saw Saul and Hannah standing there, though she still looked startled.

Saul stepped forward, keeping his posture non-threatening but firm. "What are you doing out here, Beth? Why are you following us?"

Beth's face flushed with embarrassment and fear. She opened her mouth to speak but hesitated, her eyes darting between Saul and Hannah.

Hannah took a step closer, her gaze hard. "We won't hurt you, but you better start talking. Now."

Beth looked down at the ground, wringing her hands together nervously. "I wasn't…I didn't mean any harm," she stammered, her voice shaky. "I just…I was following orders."

"Orders?" Saul repeated, his jaw tightening. "From who? Evelyn?"

Beth nodded, her voice trembling as she spoke. "She didn't want you to leave. She thinks…she thinks you two are important. That you could help with her plans."

"Plans for what?" Hannah demanded.

Beth swallowed hard, avoiding their eyes. "She's trying to build something. A new society. She thinks you two could be useful to her…that you could help her vision. When you left, she sent me to follow you. To try and bring you back."

"Why follow us alone?" Hannah asked, her voice cutting through Saul's thoughts. "If she wanted us back so badly, why didn't she send more people?"

Beth looked down. "Because I volunteered."

Hannah raised an eyebrow. "You volunteered?"

Beth nodded again, her face pale. "I thought…I thought maybe I could talk to you. Convince you to come back, but not by force. I didn't want to…I didn't want to do it like that."

Saul studied her carefully, noting how her hands shook as she spoke. She seemed genuine, but he knew better than to trust appearances. Still, something about her didn't scream threat. Desperation, maybe. But not malice.

"So what now?" Saul asked, his tone softer but still wary. "You've found us. What do you want?"

Beth hesitated for a long moment before looking up at them, her eyes filled with fear and uncertainty. "I…I don't want to go back. I want to leave."

Hannah crossed her arms. "Leave? You're part of Evelyn's

group. Why would you want to leave now?"

Beth's voice wavered as she spoke. "I don't want to be part of her plan anymore. At first, I thought what she was trying to do made sense. Rebuild and create a place where people could be safe. But…it's not like that. She doesn't care about people, not really. She cares about control. And when the food runs out…it's going to get bad."

Beth's words hung in the air, and Saul and Hannah exchanged glances.

Beth continued. "I don't want to be part of that. But I can't survive on my own. I'm not like you two. I thought maybe you'd let me come with you."

Saul felt a pang of sympathy for her, but he quickly pushed it aside. He couldn't afford to let emotions cloud his judgment.

Hannah's eyes softened for a moment, but her tone remained firm. "We can't, Beth."

Beth's face crumpled, and she looked at Hannah with pleading eyes. "Please. I don't want to go back to Evelyn. I can help you. I'll do whatever you need me to do. I won't slow you down."

"No," Saul said, shaking his head. "We can't take the risk."

Beth's lip trembled, and her voice broke as she spoke. "Why? I…I'm not like them. I swear."

Hannah took a deep breath, her voice softer now but still resolute. "It's not about you, Beth. It's about survival. We've been on our own for a long time, and letting someone else in…it's dangerous. We can't afford to take that chance."

Beth's eyes filled with tears, and she wiped at her face with trembling hands. "I understand," she whispered, her voice thick with emotion.

Saul felt a heavy weight settle in his chest. He knew it was the right decision, but that didn't make it any easier. Beth was clearly terrified of what would happen when the food ran out, and she wasn't wrong to be afraid. But that didn't change the fact that bringing her with them would be too risky.

"You're safer with Evelyn for now," Saul said. "As long as there's food, you'll be okay. But before it runs out…you must be ready to leave."

Beth nodded slowly, her shoulders slumping in defeat. "I'll try," she whispered.

Hannah took a step closer, her gaze softening. "Listen, don't follow us again, Beth. Go back to camp and tell them you couldn't find us."

Beth sniffled, nodding once more. "Ok, I promise."

"Good," Saul said.

Without another word, Beth turned and walked away, disappearing into the trees. The forest quickly swallowed her figure.

As Beth's footsteps faded, Hannah let out a long breath, her shoulders relaxing slightly. "Do you think she'll be okay?"

"I don't know," Saul admitted, his voice quiet. "But we made the right decision. We couldn't risk it. If she comes with us, they'll come looking for us all. Besides, she's not made for this world. She can't survive out here."

Hannah nodded slowly, her gaze still fixed on the direction Beth had gone.

"Come on," Saul said finally. "We need to keep moving."

They continued on the trail, but as they walked, Saul couldn't fight the feeling that he made the wrong choice. Beth was a good person, and he knew that. But he felt that he had just sent her back to a death sentence.

Chapter 19

The sky hung low with heavy clouds that seemed to mirror the exhaustion gripping Saul and Hannah as they trudged through the barren landscape. They had been moving across this jagged, unforgiving terrain for days, the wind whipping harshly across the rocky ridges. Saul's feet felt like blocks of stone, heavy and uncooperative, as though every ounce of energy had been drained from his body. The hunger had long passed from sharp pain into a dull ache, an emptiness that now felt like part of him. His legs trembled with every step, his chest tight, and his breath coming in shallow, uneven gasps. The world around him blurred slightly, the edges of his vision dimming as fatigue clawed at him, threatening to pull him under.

Hannah moved with purpose ahead of him, though Saul could see the strain in her movements. She was strong, but even she was beginning to falter under the weight of their endless journey. Still, she pressed on, scanning the landscape with sharp eyes, ever vigilant for any sign of danger or shelter.

"Saul," she called back, her voice carried by the wind. "You doing okay?"

Saul swallowed hard, forcing the words past his dry throat. "Yeah," he muttered, though even he could hear how unconvincing it sounded. His voice was weak, barely more than a rasp, and he knew Hannah had heard it too. He could feel her concern, even if she didn't say anything.

They continued in silence for a few more minutes, the sound of their footsteps on the loose gravel the only thing breaking the oppressive silence. The path narrowed into a thin ledge, clinging to the side of a steep drop-off that stretched down into a rocky ravine below. The wind picked up as they moved along the ledge, whipping at their clothes and tugging at them as if it wanted to throw them off balance.

Hannah moved carefully, her steps deliberate as she navigated the dangerous terrain. Saul followed behind her, but his steps were slower, more uncertain. His legs felt like they might give out at any moment, his body rebelling against him as he fought to keep up. His vision wavered, and his breath became more labored with each step. And then it happened.

Saul's foot slipped on a patch of loose gravel, and in an instant, the ground beneath him seemed to disappear. His arms flailed out, grasping at the air, but there was nothing to hold onto. His body tipped sideways, and before he could even register what was happening, he was tumbling down the side of the ridge.

The world spun around him as he fell, the jagged rocks tearing at his clothes and skin as he hit the ground again and again. The impact knocked the wind from his lungs, sending shockwaves of pain radiating through his entire body. He tried to grab onto something, anything, but his hands found only sharp edges, his fingers slipping uselessly against the rocks.

Finally, with a heavy thud, Saul landed at the bottom of the ravine. The pain was overwhelming, and for a moment, he couldn't breathe. His vision blurred, the world tilting around him as he lay still, gasping for air. The taste of blood filled his mouth, metallic and bitter, and his entire body felt like it had been shattered.

"Saul!" Hannah's voice echoed from above, distant and filled with panic.

He tried to respond, to call out and let her know he was alive, but his voice wouldn't come. Every breath felt like a struggle, the tightness in his chest making it nearly impossible to speak. His limbs felt heavy and unresponsive, and the pain that wracked his body left him feeling paralyzed.

It didn't take long before he heard the sound of Hannah scrambling down the steep slope, her boots kicking up dust and small rocks as she rushed to get to him. Within moments, she was at his side, her face pale with fear as she knelt beside him.

"Saul, can you hear me?" she asked, her voice tight with worry as her hands moved over him, checking for injuries.

Saul winced as her fingers brushed against his ribs, the pain shooting through him like fire. "I'm…I'm alive," he managed to say, though his voice was little more than a whisper. The effort it took to speak felt like it drained what little strength he had left.

Hannah's expression was grim as she continued to assess his injuries. "You're hurt bad," she muttered. "I need to get you out of here."

She glanced around, her eyes scanning the landscape for any sign of shelter. She spotted a small cave a short distance away, nestled into the hillside. It wasn't much, but it would protect them from the wind. It would have to do.

She helped Saul to his feet with great effort, draping his arm over her shoulder as she bore most of his weight. Every step was unbearable for him—the pain making it hard to even think, but Hannah didn't slow down. She gritted her teeth and kept moving, her determination unwavering as she guided him toward the cave.

By the time they reached the cave entrance, Saul was barely conscious. His body slumped against the cool stone wall as Hannah lowered him to the ground, her breath coming in short, ragged bursts. His face was pale, his skin clammy with sweat, and his breathing was shallow.

"You're going to be okay," Hannah said softly, though the uncertainty in her voice was evident. She quickly began rummaging through their packs, pulling out the last of the medical supplies they had salvaged from the hospital. There wasn't much left—just a few bandages, some antiseptic wipes, and a handful of painkillers—but it would have to be enough.

Her hands moved quickly and methodically as she cleaned the deep gashes on Saul's arms and legs, bandaging the worst of his injuries. He was still conscious, but barely. Now and then, a low groan of pain escaped him, but mostly he remained silent.

Once she had done all she could with their supplies, Hannah sat back on her heels, her body trembling with exhaustion. She looked down at Saul, her heart pounding with fear. He was alive, but he was in bad shape, and she didn't know how long they could survive like this.

She reached into her bag, hoping to find something to eat, but as her fingers sifted through the contents, she felt something unexpected—a small, half-eaten ration pack. Her brow furrowed in confusion. She hadn't put that there. Quickly, she checked the rest of her bag and found more of the rations she thought they had already eaten.

Realization hit her like a wave. Saul had been slipping his rations into her bag. The weight of it settled heavily on her chest as she stared at the ration packs in her hand. He had been starving himself, giving her his food, making sure she stayed strong while he wasted away. And now, because of it, he was lying there, barely able to move, his body weakened and fragile.

"Damn it, Saul," she whispered, her voice breaking as she looked over at him. "Why didn't you tell me?"

The anger and frustration bubbled up inside her, a mix of emotions she didn't know how to process. She wanted to yell at him for being so selfless, for risking his life just to keep her going.

But more than that, she felt an overwhelming sense of guilt. She hadn't noticed. She had been so focused on surviving, so caught up in the day-to-day struggle, that she hadn't realized he was giving up what little he had for her.

Hannah clenched the ration pack tightly in her hand, her mind racing. She knew why he had done it. Saul had always been the protector, always putting her needs before his own. But this…this was too much. He had nearly killed himself for her, and now they were both paying the price. She knelt beside him again, gently brushing a strand of hair away from his forehead. His skin was cold, but he was still here—still fighting.

"You don't have to do this alone," she whispered, her voice thick with emotion. "We're in this together."

They had to rest—to wait for Saul's strength to return before they could go any further. The cave would shelter them for the night, but tomorrow was uncertain. She couldn't carry him the whole way. They needed to find more food and supplies—something to keep them going. But right now, the only thing that mattered was that they were still alive.

After ensuring Saul was as comfortable as possible, Hannah lay beside him, her body trembling with exhaustion. She felt the cold stone beneath her, the chill of the night air creeping into the cave. But the sound of Saul's slow and steady breathing was a small comfort.

Without thinking, she shifted closer to him, gently resting her head on his chest. His faint but steady heartbeat was reassuring beneath her ear, anchoring her to the present and reminding her that despite everything, he was still with her. Hannah's eyes grew heavy, and as the wind howled outside, she let herself drift off to sleep. His breath's steady rise and fall lulled her into a fitful yet much-needed rest.

Chapter 20

The pale, early morning light crept slowly into the cave. Outside, the wind had stilled, leaving only the soft whisper of a new day. But inside, the silence was heavy. For Hannah, it felt like the calm before the storm. She sat against the cold stone wall, her knees pulled to her chest, her arms wrapped around her legs as she stared at Saul. He was still asleep, his face pale and his body motionless except for the slight rise and fall of his chest. His breathing was shallow, each breath labored and uneven, but it was a sound that reassured her.

Hannah hadn't slept much. The events of the previous day played over and over in her mind. The moment Saul had slipped on the narrow ridge, the sickening sound of his body hitting the rocks as he tumbled down the slope, the panic that had surged through her as she rushed to his side, desperate to make sure he was still breathing. She had been so scared, so utterly terrified that she had lost him.

He was in bad shape, but he was still alive. That was the only thing that had kept her from falling apart. But even now, as she sat beside him, watching him sleep, she couldn't shake the feeling that they were on borrowed time. Her eyes drifted to the ration packs beside her, and her chest tightened with emotion.

Hannah sighed, resting her head against the cold stone wall. She had always cared about Saul. From the moment they met, she felt a connection to him, a bond that had only grown stronger as they faced the horrors of the world together. But this was different. It went beyond friendship, beyond survival. Somewhere along the way, her feelings for him had deepened into something more.

She looked down at him again, her heart aching with the weight of her emotions. If Saul had risked everything to keep her alive, then maybe—just maybe—he felt the same. Maybe he had been protecting her not just because they needed each other to survive but because he cared for her in the same way she cared for him.

But now wasn't the time to think about that. Not when everything was still so uncertain, when the world outside their small cave was as dangerous as ever. They were still fighting to survive, and there was no room for anything else.

She reached for the ration packs again, her fingers tracing the edges of the small, half-eaten packs. They had to be rationed carefully now—more carefully than ever. Saul was weak and needed every bit of strength he could get. She wasn't going to let him sacrifice himself for her again.

Saul finally began to stir. His face twisted in a grimace of pain as he shifted. Hannah immediately sat up, leaning closer to him as his eyes opened. Saul blinked against the light, squinting slightly as he tried to focus. His face was drawn with exhaustion, but he was awake.

"Hey," Hannah said softly, her voice filled with relief. "How are you feeling?"

Saul groaned, lifting a hand to his side where the worst of his injuries were. "Like I've been hit by a truck," he muttered. "But

I'm more hungry than hurt."

Hannah smiled faintly though her worry hadn't lessened. "That's a good sign," she said, reaching for one of the ration packs beside her. She tore it open and handed it to him. "Here. Eat. You need your strength."

Saul took the pack slowly, his hands trembling slightly as he tore off small bites of the dried food. His jaw worked mechanically as he chewed, but his appetite was minimal. Still, he forced the food down, knowing he needed it to recover.

As he ate, Hannah watched him, her mind racing with everything she needed to say. She couldn't keep it in any longer. The weight of what she had discovered the night before was too heavy to bear alone.

"Saul," she began in a steady voice. "I know what you've been doing."

Saul paused mid-bite, looking up at her with a confused expression. "What do you mean?"

Hannah took a deep breath, her fingers twisting the edge of her sleeve as she tried to gather her thoughts. "The rations," she said. "I found them in my bag. You've been giving me your food, haven't you?"

Saul's expression shifted, a flicker of guilt crossing his face as he lowered his gaze. He nodded slowly, his voice barely audible as he spoke. "Yeah. You needed it more than I did."

Hannah's heart clenched at his words. "You didn't need to do that," she said softly. "I can take care of myself, Saul. We're supposed to be in this together."

"I know," Saul said, his voice still quiet. "But you're stronger than me, Hannah. You've always been stronger. I couldn't let you get weak. If something happened to you…"

His voice trailed off, and Hannah's throat tightened as she looked at him. She could see the vulnerability in his eyes, the fear that had been hiding behind his usual strength.

"I don't need you to protect me like that," she said. "We're supposed to look out for each other, Saul."

Saul sighed, leaning his head back against the cave wall as he stared up at the ceiling. "I know," he said again. "But I've been questioning everything lately. I don't know if we're making the right decisions. We have been running for so long. It feels like we're just…existing. Maybe it would've been better to stop a long time ago."

Hannah's heart twisted at his words. She had never heard him talk like this before, this uncertainty, this doubt. Saul had always been the one to push them forward, keep them moving, and keep them fighting. But now, he was questioning everything. And she understood why. The constant running, the hunger, the exhaustion —it all wore on them, day after day. But she couldn't let him give up. Not now. Not after everything they had been through together.

"Saul," she said. "We can't stop. We have made it this far. We have survived when we shouldn't have. We have fought, and we have kept each other alive. We are not giving up now."

Saul looked at her. "But what if we're just chasing something that doesn't exist? What if there's nothing out there, no sanctuary, no better life? What if this is all there is?"

Hannah shook her head. "I don't believe that. And I don't think you do either. You were the one who heard the radio. You were the one who started us on this path to a safe haven. There's got to be something more out there, and we'll find it. We'll keep going until we do."

Saul's gaze softened as he looked at her, the uncertainty in his eyes slowly giving way to something else—something that looked a lot like hope, or at least the faintest glimmer of it. But before he could say anything, Hannah reached out and grabbed his hand, squeezing it tightly.

"I'm not letting you give up," she said softly, her voice steady. "If we don't find a better place, then we die together. But we're not stopping. Not now."

For a moment, Saul was silent, his eyes locked on their

intertwined hands. His breathing was shallow, his chest rising and falling slowly as he processed her words. She could see the conflict in his expression, the battle between his doubt and the part of him that still wanted to fight.

And then, without warning, Hannah leaned forward. It was sudden, a rush of emotion that she hadn't fully processed until it happened. Her lips pressed softly against his, tentative at first but filled with the intensity of everything she had been holding back. The world outside the cave seemed to disappear, the cold wind and the endless struggle fading into the background as she let herself feel something other than fear and survival. Saul didn't react for a moment, his body frozen in surprise. But then he kissed her back, his hand tightening around hers.

When they finally pulled apart, Hannah's heart was racing, her mind spinning with what had just happened. She had kissed him. And he had kissed her back. The reality hit her like a wave, but it wasn't overwhelming—it felt right.

Saul's mind flashed back to the first night they had come together, that desperate, raw moment when they shared themselves with each other—not out of love but to feel human again in a world stripped of its humanity. Back then, it had been something that had just happened, a way to reclaim a flicker of warmth in the cold shadow of survival.

But this was different. This kiss was a bridge, carrying the unspoken emotions they had held onto for so long. In that single, quiet moment, their true feelings were finally laid bare, a silent confession that spoke more deeply than words ever could.

Saul stared at her in shock. "Hannah," he whispered. "I didn't know…"

Hannah smiled faintly, her hand still wrapped around his. "I didn't either. Not until now."

Saul's gaze softened, the doubt and exhaustion in his eyes fading, replaced by a warmth that made her heart ache. They had both been holding back for so long, too afraid to let themselves feel anything beyond the immediate need to survive. But now, in the quiet of the cave, it felt like they were allowed to be something more than just survivors.

"I couldn't lose you," Saul said quietly, his voice filled with raw honesty. "I think I've felt this way for a while, but...I didn't want to make things harder."

Hannah nodded. "We're going to keep fighting," she said softly. "And we'll find something worth living for. Together."

Saul smiled and nodded in agreement. "Together."

Chapter 21

The path stretched before them, narrow and uneven, as they resumed their journey after a few days of rest. Saul's body still ached from the fall, but thanks to Hannah's careful tending, he felt strong enough to move on.

As they walked, Hannah broke the silence with a gentle smile. "You know, you're lucky nothing was broken. That fall could've been so much worse."

Saul nodded, glancing at her with gratitude. "I know. When I hit the ground...I thought that was it. Guess I have you to thank for making sure it wasn't."

"Don't mention it." She smiled, her eyes softening. "Those few days, taking care of you...it was hard, sure, but it was also nice. Just being there with you."

"Thank you, Hannah," Saul replied. "I know I haven't exactly been the easiest person to look after."

She shrugged. "We've been looking out for each other this whole time, haven't we? That's how we're still here."

"Thinking back..." Saul said. "It's strange, isn't it? How different everything feels now. Like back then, we were just trying to get by, day by day."

Hannah nodded. "Yeah. I think somewhere along the way...it changed. Like it's not just about surviving anymore."

They exchanged a quiet look, one that said more than words could. Their journey was no longer about just making it through; it had become about sharing something real, something lasting.

After a few moments, Hannah glanced back at him with a warm smile. "Come on. Let's keep moving."

Saul returned her smile, nodding. "Right beside you." Then they saw him. A man in the distance, walking toward them. He moved slowly, unlike someone rushing or running from something. Saul's hand tightened around his rifle.

"Saul," Hannah whispered.

"I see him," he replied.

The man got closer, raising a hand in a casual wave as he came into full view. He didn't look like a threat at first glance—tall, with a rough beard and worn clothes. A rifle hung loosely over his shoulder, but his posture wasn't aggressive.

"Hey there," the man called out, stopping a few paces away from them. His voice was calm and friendly but cautious.

Saul exchanged a glance with Hannah before stepping forward. "Who are you?"

"Name's Luke," he said, his eyes steady on them both. "I'm out scouting. There's a settlement not far from here."

"A settlement?" Hannah asked, her voice skeptical. "Where? We haven't seen anything like that."

Luke smiled, though it was clear he wasn't surprised by her reaction. "It's well hidden. Massive, fortified, and safe. We've got room for more. We've managed to survive pretty well. You two look like you've been on the road a long time."

Saul kept his eyes on Luke, measuring the man. "We're not interested," Saul said flatly. "We've got our own direction."

Luke's smile faltered slightly, but he didn't back down. "I get it. People are wary. You don't know me; you don't know the settlement. But at least come with me and meet Marcus—he's the leader. Hear him out. If it's not for you, you can leave. No strings attached."

Saul clenched his jaw, glancing at Hannah. She looked just as wary as he felt, but there was also a flicker of something else in her eyes—weariness. They were tired, hungry, and out of options.

"Why do I feel like if we don't at least meet Marcus, we're going to have a problem?" Saul asked.

Luke's expression softened, and he raised his hands. "No problem. I'm not here to force anyone. But trust me when I say it might be worth your while."

Hannah gave Saul a look. They both knew refusing outright could lead to more trouble than it was worth. Even though they didn't trust this man or what he was offering, they also knew they couldn't keep walking forever. They needed to resupply, at the very least.

"All right," Saul said after a moment. "We'll talk to Marcus. But that's it."

Luke grinned, his posture relaxing. "That's all I ask. Follow me."

The trek to the settlement wasn't far, but Saul kept his guard up as they walked, watching for any signs of danger. Hannah did the same; her hand was never far from her weapon. As they approached, the massive walls of the settlement came into view. The structure was even more impressive than Luke had let on. The walls were reinforced with metal, towering high above the ground. Barbed wire lined the top, and guard towers stood at intervals along the perimeter, manned by armed sentries.

"This is it," Luke said proudly as they neared the gate. "Pretty impressive, huh?"

Saul didn't answer. His eyes were fixed on the settlement, trying to read the place. The gate opened with a heavy groan, and

Luke motioned for them to follow him inside. Once through, they found themselves walking down wide streets lined with buildings that were mostly intact, some even reinforced to look nearly new. The people seemed busy collecting scavenged materials, repairing structures, and organizing supplies.

As they walked, Saul's unease grew. The place was thriving, but in a way that felt unnatural. There was a sense of forced order, as if everything was designed to run a certain way, and no one dared step out of line.

Luke led them to a large, sturdy building at the center of the settlement. It looked like it had been some kind of government office before the world fell apart. Reinforced windows and doors made it clear that this was the hub of the settlement's leadership.

"Marcus will meet you inside," Luke said, motioning toward the door. "He'll explain everything."

Saul and Hannah exchanged glances, their unease deepening. But they followed Luke inside, stepping into a well-organized room with maps pinned to the walls and papers stacked neatly on a large desk. The room smelled clean, like it had been scrubbed recently, and that alone felt out of place in a world where filth and decay had become the norm.

A tall man with dark hair streaked with gray stood behind the desk, his clothes spotless. He looked too calm and composed for a man living in this world. His eyes were sharp, assessing Saul and Hannah as they walked in.

"Welcome," the man said, smiling in a way that made Saul's skin crawl. "I'm Marcus. I run this settlement."

Saul kept his tone neutral. "Luke said you have a system here. A way of keeping things...safe."

Marcus's smile widened slightly. "Yes, we do. We've created something special here that most people out there have forgotten—order and discipline. Everyone in this settlement has a role, a purpose. We send out scouts regularly to pick clean the ruins of the world, bringing back whatever we can find. Food, supplies, anything of use. We don't waste time waiting for things to grow that never will. We scavenge far and wide."

Hannah raised an eyebrow. "And the people you bring back...what happens to them?"

"They join us if they're willing," Marcus replied smoothly. "The more people we have, the more scouts we can send out. The stronger we become."

Saul felt a knot tighten in his gut. The system Marcus described sounded efficient, but there was something too cold about the way he spoke—too detached, as though the people in the settlement were little more than cogs in a machine.

"We're not looking to stay," Saul said, his voice firm. "We're heading in our own direction."

Marcus's eyes gleamed with curiosity. "And what direction is that, if I may ask? It wouldn't happen to be chasing some kind of dream, right?"

Saul stiffened. He hadn't mentioned the safe haven to anyone. "You've heard of it?" Saul asked carefully.

Marcus chuckled, leaning back in his chair. "You're not the first people to come through here chasing a dream. I've heard it all. An island where animals flourish—a city of greenhouses with all the fruits and vegetables you can eat. Hell, I've even heard of an underground city so deep that people down there don't even know what's going on up here. But there is one thing that all these dreamers have in common—they never make it, realizing it was never there to begin with."

"We have coordinates to a safe haven," Saul said, pulling the crumpled paper from his pocket. "I heard it myself over the radio."

Marcus smiled and shook his head. "Haven't heard that one yet."

Hannah frowned. "So, you don't think it's real?"

"I don't," Marcus said simply. "I think it's a story people tell themselves to keep going. But if you want to find out for yourselves, I won't stop you. But I'm sure you know that the world outside is merciless. And if you decide that the search isn't worth it, this settlement will be here. You're welcome to return if you choose. Some of the residents here used to be those dreamers. The rest of them…well, they just didn't make it."

Saul didn't like the way Marcus was speaking, the way he seemed so sure that they would fail. But the man had planted a seed of doubt that was hard to shake.

"We'll take our chances," Saul said, standing up.

Marcus nodded, his expression calm. "So be it," he replied. He stood up and walked over to a cabinet tucked against the wall. When he opened it, Saul and Hannah saw shelves stocked with canned goods. Marcus picked up a few cans, then turned and held them out.

"Before you go, take these for the road," he said. "Consider it a gesture of goodwill. I wish you both good luck."

Saul hesitated, glancing over at Hannah. Then he reached out and took the cans from Marcus. "Thanks," he said.

Saul's mind was racing as they walked out of the building and back toward the gate. He didn't trust Marcus, and the settlement felt too controlled, too unnatural. But as they neared the exit, something caught his eye. A familiar face slipping through the crowd.

"Beth," he muttered under his breath.

Hannah turned, following his gaze. "Is that...?"

"Yeah," Saul replied. "It's her."

Saul's heart skipped a beat as Beth saw them. The look she had on her face was unmistakable—fear.

"We need to keep moving," Saul said quietly. "We can't stay here."

Hannah nodded. They walked away, leaving the heart of darkness behind. But the image of Beth's face lingered in Saul's mind.

Chapter 22

The night air was heavy with silence, and the crackling fire between Saul and Hannah barely gave off any heat. It had been a long day, and they were both exhausted. Saul sat staring into the flames, his mind racing with thoughts of Beth. The way she had looked at him, the fear in her eyes—something was wrong in that settlement, and Saul couldn't shake the feeling that they had walked away from a problem far from over.

Hannah sat beside him. She could see the tension etched in his face. She had known Saul long enough to understand when something was eating away at him, and she could tell that Beth's appearance at Marcus's settlement had stirred something in him. He hadn't spoken much since they left, his thoughts clearly elsewhere.

"You've been quiet," Hannah finally said. "What's on your mind?"

Saul looked up, blinking as if coming out of a daze. He met her gaze across the fire, but it was clear his thoughts were still tangled in the past few hours. "Beth," he said after a long pause. "Seeing her at that settlement…it doesn't make any sense. Why is she there?"

Hannah studied him, trying to piece together his train of thought. "I'm guessing she left Evelyn's camp like she said she would," she replied. "Maybe she thought Marcus's settlement was a better option."

Saul shook his head, frustration evident in his voice. "Maybe. But there was something off about her, Hannah. The way she looked at me…like she was scared."

Hannah sighed, leaning forward to toss another stick into the fire. Sparks flew up into the air, quickly fading into the night sky. "Maybe she is scared. You said yourself that Marcus's place felt off. But Saul, we've been through enough. Do we really need to get involved in whatever's going on there?"

"I don't know," Saul admitted, running a hand through his hair. "But I can't just walk away from this. Not when we know something isn't right. Beth is a good person, and we turned her away before. She doesn't deserve to be turned away again."

Hannah watched him carefully, her arms crossed over her chest. She didn't like where this conversation was heading.

"You want to go back," Hannah said.

Saul met her gaze. "I do. I have to."

Hannah shook her head, a frustrated sigh escaping her lips. "You can't go back there alone, Saul. If something happens—if Marcus or his people figure out what you're doing—you'll be trapped."

"I'll be careful," Saul replied, though he knew it wasn't enough to ease her worries. "I just need to talk to Beth. Find out what's really going on. Then we'll decide what to do."

"I'm coming with you," Hannah said firmly.

But Saul was ready for this. He had already made up his mind before the conversation had even started. "No, you're not," he said.

Hannah's eyes widened in disbelief. "What? You can't

seriously expect me to stay behind while you walk into a situation that could get you killed!"

"I'm serious, Hannah," Saul said, his tone unwavering. "It's too dangerous. If something happens to both of us, we're done for. But if you stay behind, at least one of us will be safe."

"I'm not a damsel, Saul," Hannah snapped, her frustration bubbling to the surface. "I've survived just as much as you have. We've made it this far by sticking together. Why would you want to change that now?"

"Because I need you to be safe," Saul replied, his voice softening. "This isn't about you not being capable. I know you can handle yourself. But if something goes wrong, I need to know that you're here, waiting for me. If we're both in there and it's a trap, we're both screwed."

Hannah's jaw clenched, her fists tightening at her sides. She hated that he was making sense, hated that she understood his logic. But it didn't make the idea of him going back alone any easier to swallow.

"Promise me you'll come back," she said, her voice breaking slightly despite her attempt to stay strong.

"I promise," Saul said.

The hours ticked by slowly, each minute stretching into an eternity as the fire dimmed. Saul could feel the tension between them, but he also felt a strange sense of calm. He had made up his mind. He would go back to the settlement in the morning, talk to Beth, and figure out what was really happening there.

Eventually, Hannah stood. She paused for a moment, looking down at Saul before lying down. "Just...be careful," she whispered.

"I will," he replied softly.

* * *

The following day, Saul set off before dawn, leaving Hannah behind at their camp. The air was crisp, and the faint light of the rising sun bathed the landscape in a pale glow. His mind was focused, and his body moved instinctively as he retraced the steps to Marcus's settlement. The road felt longer this time with every step he took.

When he finally reached the settlement, the guards at the gate recognized him immediately. The tall one with the rifle—Luke, Saul remembered—greeted him with a nod.

"Back already?" Luke asked, his tone casual. "Thought you two were heading in another direction."

Saul forced a smile, trying to keep his tone light. "I wanted to take a closer look. Get a feel for the place. Hannah's still on the fence about it."

Luke raised an eyebrow, but he didn't seem suspicious. "Marcus'll be glad to hear that. Go on in."

The gate creaked open, and Saul stepped inside, the familiar sense of unease settling over him once again. The settlement was as orderly as ever—too orderly. The people moved about their daily tasks with almost a robotic precision, their faces blank, their movements mechanical. It was unsettling, and now that Saul knew what he was looking for, it was impossible to ignore.

He made his way to the central building where Marcus had first met them, but before he could enter, the man himself appeared, stepping out into the open with a smile that didn't reach his eyes.

"Saul," Marcus said, his tone warm. "Back so soon? I wasn't expecting to see you again so quickly. Changed your mind about joining us?"

"Not yet," Saul replied, keeping his voice neutral. "But I wanted to get a better look around. See how things work here before I talk to Hannah again."

Marcus's smile widened, though there was something predatory in his gaze. "Of course. Take your time. We're always open to new people—especially those who can see the value in what we've built."

Saul nodded, forcing himself to stay calm despite the growing unease in his chest. He could feel Marcus watching him as he walked away, and he had the distinct sense that the leader wasn't one to take no for an answer lightly. He needed to find Beth fast.

He wandered through the settlement, keeping his eyes open for any sign of her. The streets were eerily quiet, the people moving about their business without much conversation or interaction. It was as if they were all afraid to speak, afraid to draw attention to themselves.

Eventually, he spotted her—Beth, sitting alone near a statue, her eyes distant as she stared off into the horizon. She didn't notice him at first as she was lost in her own thoughts, but when Saul called her name, she looked up, her eyes widening in surprise.

"Saul?" she asked. "What are you doing here?"

"I need to talk to you," Saul said, crouching beside her. "Why are you here, Beth? What's going on in this place?"

Beth's face paled, and she glanced around nervously as if making sure no one was listening. "You shouldn't have come back," she whispered, her voice trembling. "It's not safe here."

"I figured that much," Saul replied, keeping his voice low. "Tell me what's happening. Why did you leave Evelyn's camp?"

Beth swallowed hard, her eyes darting around as if she were expecting Marcus or one of his people to appear at any moment. "A scout came by Evelyn's camp," she began. "He talked about this place, about how they had food, safety, order. Evelyn was furious and told the scout to leave. But...I was tired of Evelyn's way of doing things. I thought maybe this place would be different, so I went with the scout."

"And is it?" Saul asked.

Beth shook her head, her expression growing darker. "It's worse. Much worse. I didn't realize it at first, but...things here aren't what they seem. Marcus...he's not who he pretends to be."

Saul's heart sank, but he forced himself to stay calm. "What do you mean?"

Beth glanced around again before leaning in closer, her voice trembling with fear. "Marcus runs this place through fear, Saul. People disappear. Anyone who questions him, anyone who doesn't follow the rules, they just...vanish. And the scouts? The ones who go out to scavenge? If they don't bring back enough, if Marcus isn't satisfied with what they find...he kills them."

Saul's blood ran cold. "He kills them?"

Beth nodded, her eyes wide with terror. "He takes them outside the walls, executes them, and then...he harvests their bodies. He uses them to keep the settlement fed. That's why the food supply here hasn't run out. He's using people, Saul. His own people."

Saul felt a wave of nausea wash over him. He suspected something was wrong with this place, but this...this was worse than he could have imagined.

"How do you know this?" Saul asked, his voice tight with anger.

Beth hesitated for a moment before answering. "One of the missing scouts...he was the other person who left Evelyn's camp with me. When he disappeared, I got suspicious. I started sneaking around, listening in on Marcus's conversations. I overheard him talking about it—about the executions. He said it was a necessary evil to keep the settlement running."

Saul's hands clenched into fists, his rage barely contained. "We need to get you out of here," he said.

Beth shook her head, her eyes filling with tears. "I can't just leave. If Marcus catches me, he'll kill me."

"I'll come back for you," Saul promised, his voice firm. "But right now, I need to get out of here. I need to get back to Hannah."

Beth nodded, though fear still gripped her. "Just...be careful, Saul. He's watching everyone."

"Don't worry about me," he replied. "You just come back to this statue tonight and wait for us."

"Ok," Beth said. "I will."

Saul stood, his heart pounding as he approached the gate. He had to get out of there and get back to Hannah and tell her what he had learned. But as he approached the exit, he saw Marcus standing there, watching him with that same cold smile.

"Saul," Marcus said smoothly. "I trust you've had time to look around. What do you think of our little community?"

Saul forced a smile, keeping his voice calm despite the terror racing through his veins. "It's impressive. I think I'm in favor of joining, but I need to talk to Hannah about it first. She's still hesitant."

Marcus's eyes gleamed with something dangerous, but his smile never faltered. "Of course. Take your time. The gate will be open for you whenever you're ready to come back."

Saul nodded briefly, trying to keep his expression neutral as he stepped past Marcus and out of the settlement. The moment he was outside, he quickened his pace, his heart racing as he put as much distance between himself and that place as possible.

When he finally reached the camp, Hannah was waiting for him, her face etched with worry.

"What did you find out?" she asked.

Saul sat down beside her. "Beth's in danger," he said. "They all are. Marcus...he's killing his own people, Hannah. He's using their bodies to keep the settlement fed."

Hannah's eyes widened in shock. "What?"

"It's worse than we thought," Saul replied, his voice heavy with disgust. "That place...it's built on lies and fear. We need to get Beth out of there and get as far away from it as possible."

Hannah hesitated for a moment. "I don't like this one bit," she said. "But I know Beth is good. She's just trying to find her way." She continued to hesitate before looking at Saul. "We'll leave tonight."

Chapter 23

The night cloaked them as they crept through the landscape, the cool air sharpening their senses as they neared the walls of Marcus's settlement. Saul gripped his knife. He had left his rifle back at their camp. They needed to do this as quietly as possible. Beside him, Hannah readied her knife as they moved along the settlement wall. They crouched behind a row of abandoned vehicles near the gate.

"Stick to the plan," Saul whispered. "Wait for the guard switch, then we move."

Hannah nodded, her eyes steady despite the tension in her stance. Minutes passed, dragging on like hours, until finally, Saul saw movement above—the guards switching places, their backs turned as they completed their routine patrol.

"Now," he whispered.

They moved quickly, slipping through the shadows. Saul took the lead, signaling for Hannah to follow close behind. With quick movement, Saul dispatched the first guard with his knife, the man crumpling to the ground without a sound. Hannah followed suit, using her knife to take down the second guard. They dragged the bodies into the shadows, wiping their blades clean before continuing to the gate. They quietly slipped inside.

Once within the walls, an eerie stillness greeted them. The structures stood silent as if the entire place was holding its breath. Saul glanced at Hannah, who nodded, her grip tight on her knife.

"I'll go for Marcus," Saul said. "You find Beth near the statue."

Hannah hesitated for a brief second, worry flashing in her eyes. "Be careful."

"You too," Saul replied, though his mind was already focused on what lay ahead.

Saul navigated through the dim alleys, his heart pounding with a steady, unrelenting rhythm. When he finally reached Marcus's quarters, he took a deep breath, bracing himself for the confrontation as he pushed open the door.

Marcus stood waiting inside. But Saul's gaze quickly shifted to a familiar figure beside him—Beth. She looked pale, her face streaked with tears. The regret in her eyes was unmistakable, and her hands trembled as she met Saul's shocked gaze.

"Saul…" Beth's voice was barely a whisper. "I'm so sorry."

Marcus let out a low chuckle, an unsettling smirk crossing his face. "Ah, yes. Quite a reunion," he said coolly, stepping forward. "You really should be more careful, Saul. I saw you speaking to Beth before, plotting your little rebellion. It was only a matter of time before I got the full story from her."

Beth shook her head, her voice choked. "I didn't want to tell him, Saul. I swear…but he said he'd kill me if I didn't. I had to. I had no choice."

Marcus's smirk widened, his gaze flicking back to Saul. "You think you're a hero, Saul? You think you can come in here, disrupt everything, and leave? You're just another fool in a long line of fools, each one convinced they're making a difference."

Saul glared at him, his voice sharp. "It's over, Marcus."

Marcus raised an eyebrow. "Over? Hardly. You think killing me will fix anything? These people survive because of me. I keep them in line. Without me, they'd tear each other apart."

Saul took a step forward, his voice thick with anger. "You're not helping them. You're enslaving them."

Beth's voice broke in, her tone raw with desperation. "Saul, I didn't mean for any of this to happen. I just…I thought maybe if I talked, he'd let you go."

Marcus chuckled, his expression darkening. "Oh, Beth. Do you really think I'd let either of you walk away that easily?"

"Beth, it's okay," Saul said, sparing her a reassuring glance. "But this ends tonight."

Before he could say anything more, Marcus lunged at him, drawing a knife from his belt. Saul barely dodged the blade as it sliced through the air. The room was filled with grunts as they fought, knives flashing in the dim light.

Beth gasped, stepping back. Her eyes were wide with fear as the two men struggled. "Saul, watch out!" she cried, her voice trembling.

Marcus's strikes were wild and desperate, his movements fueled by rage. But Saul kept his focus, and each motion was calculated. Their knives clashed, and Marcus sneered, his breath coming in ragged gasps.

"You think you're some kind of savior?" Marcus taunted—his face inches from Saul's. "You're nothing, Saul. Just another dreamer in a dead world."

Saul gritted his teeth, pushing back with all his strength. "I'm not here to save you. I'm here to end you."

With a swift motion, Saul twisted his knife free, knocking Marcus off balance. As Marcus stumbled, Saul seized the moment, driving his knife deep into Marcus's chest.

Marcus gasped, his eyes wide with shock. "You think this changes anything?" he rasped, blood staining his lips. "The fear…

will never leave them."

"Not if I can help it," Saul replied, pulling the knife free. Marcus crumpled to the floor, his body going still as the last breath left him.

Silence filled the room. Beth stared at Saul, her face pale, her hands still trembling.

"I'm so sorry, Saul," she whispered.

Saul walked over to her, placing a reassuring hand on her shoulder. "It's okay, Beth. You did what you had to do to survive. But we need to leave now."

At that moment, Hannah appeared at the doorway, her eyes taking in the scene. She looked from Marcus's body to Beth, then to Saul. "Are you both okay?" she asked.

Saul nodded, his expression resolute. "It's over."

As they left the building, people were spilling into the streets, confusion and fear spreading through the crowd. Saul, Hannah, and Beth kept to the shadows, blending in as they approached the gate. As they neared the exit, Saul turned to face the crowd one last time.

"Marcus is dead!" he called out, his voice carrying over the noise. "You're free."

Some people stared at him in disbelief, while others looked terrified. A man stepped forward. "What are we supposed to do now?" he asked.

Saul scanned the crowd again. "Leave…stay here and continue scouting…whatever you need to do to survive," he said. "But Marcus does not control you anymore."

After a moment, a quiet voice broke the silence. "Thank you."

Saul and Hannah slipped through the gate, and Beth followed close behind. When they were far enough away, Hannah looked at Saul. "They won't make it," she said quietly.

"Maybe they will, maybe not," he said. "But they are free."

Chapter 24

eth sat closest to the fire, staring into the flames as though searching for something she couldn't quite find. Her knees were pulled up to her chest, her arms wrapped around them tightly. She hadn't said much since they fled Marcus's camp, and the weight of her survival seemed to rest heavily on her shoulders. She had survived, yes, but at what cost?

Saul sat a little farther back, his knife in hand, cleaning the blood from the blade. His movements were deliberate, his focus distant. Every time his mind wandered back to the moment Marcus had fallen, there was a brief flicker of doubt, of guilt. He told himself it had been necessary. They couldn't have left Marcus alive, not after what they had learned, not after what Beth had told them. And yet, that knowledge didn't make the burden any easier to bear.

Hannah sat beside Saul, staring into the night beyond the campfire's reach. She could sense the heaviness over Saul that lingered after killing Marcus, after ending someone's life, even someone as cruel and dangerous as him. It had to be done, but still, the consequences were settling in.

Eventually, it was Beth who broke the silence. "Why did you come back for me?"

Her question wasn't accusatory but instead filled with quiet disbelief. She kept her gaze fixed on the fire, her eyes shimmering in the flickering light.

"You didn't have to," she continued. "You could have just left…I wouldn't have blamed you."

Saul paused his cleaning, his hand hovering over the blade. He exhaled slowly, glancing at Hannah before turning to Beth. The truth of it had been gnawing at him since they'd made the decision to return for her, but hearing Beth ask that question brought it all to the surface.

"When we left you back at Evelyn's camp, I thought it was the right call," Saul began. "But afterward…I couldn't shake the guilt. I couldn't stop thinking that maybe we made a mistake. That we'd left you in a place you didn't belong."

He ran a hand over his face, letting out a breath. "When I saw you again in Marcus's camp, I saw the fear in your eyes…I couldn't leave you behind a second time. I couldn't live with that."

Beth wiped a tear from her cheek, though she tried to hide the motion. She looked up at Saul. "I thought I was going to die there. I was sure of it."

"We weren't going to let that happen," Hannah said. There was a quiet intensity beneath her words. "We weren't just saving you, Beth. We were trying to save a part of ourselves, too. If we left you there, we would've lost something more than just you."

"Thank you," Beth whispered. "For coming back. For… everything."

"You don't owe us anything," Saul replied softly. "We're in this together now. We look out for each other."

Beth nodded again, though her face grew troubled. She bit her lip. "But…what if the world doesn't get better? What if this is it?

What if we're just…surviving until there's nothing left?"

Saul didn't have an answer, though he wished he did. The truth was that the world might never heal, and they might be fighting for something that would never come. The only certainty they had was each other.

"I don't know," Saul said finally. "But we can't stop now. We've come this far because we haven't given up. If we stop believing in something better, we've already lost."

Hannah reached out and put a hand on Beth's shoulder. "We keep moving forward. Together. Whatever happens, we face it side by side."

Beth looked between them, her eyes softening as their words sank in. "Together," she echoed.

As the night deepened, the weariness of the day began to catch up with them. Beth finally allowed herself to relax, curled up closer to the fire, and soon drifted asleep. The fire's embers glowed softly in the forest's darkness as Saul and Hannah remained awake. Saul couldn't shake the heavy feeling in his chest. They had saved Beth, but the world beyond Marcus's settlement was still just as dangerous, just as unforgiving.

Hannah shifted beside him, sensing his turmoil. She watched him in the flickering light of the fire, her gaze lingering on his face. She had seen that look before—the quiet, brooding one that meant he was carrying too much. She wanted to ease his burden, even if only a little.

"Saul," she whispered. "Come with me."

She reached out and gently took his hand, her fingers warm against his cold skin. Saul glanced at her, confused for a moment, but he followed without question as she led him away from the fire and into the quiet, dark woods. When they had walked far enough that the glow of the fire was just a faint glimmer in the distance, Hannah stopped and turned to face him. The moonlight filtered through the trees, casting a soft glow on her face.

"I need to tell you something," she whispered. She hesitated as though the words were too heavy to say, but her voice was filled with emotion when she finally spoke. "Saul…I love you."

Saul's breath caught in his throat. He hadn't expected her to say it or prepared for the flood of emotions that surged through him in response.

"Hannah," he said. He stepped closer, reaching out to cup her face in his hands. "I love you too."

Relief flickered across her face, and before either of them could say another word, their lips met. The world around them seemed to fall away, leaving only the two of them wrapped in the warmth of each other's presence.

At that moment, all the fear, uncertainty, and violence were gone. It was just them together, finding something worth holding onto despite everything that had been lost. And once again, they surrendered to the temptations and felt human again.

Chapter 25

The days stretched endlessly, each one more grueling than the last. The sun beat down relentlessly, its harsh light bouncing off the rocky landscape as Saul, Hannah, and Beth trudged onward. What little they had left was rationed to the barest minimum, each sip of water and bite of food a reminder of their dwindling resources.

Beth had grown quieter over the past few days, her usual anxious murmurs replaced by a hollow, distant silence. Her face was gaunt, her skin pale and drawn, eyes wide with a constant, flickering fear. Saul and Hannah had noticed the change but hadn't spoken of it. They knew the weight of the journey was bearing down on her in ways neither could fully comprehend.

As they walked, Saul kept his eyes ahead, scanning the horizon. The narrow pass they had been heading toward was now in view, a jagged canyon splitting the landscape. The wind howled through the rocks, and the cliffs on either side loomed like dark sentinels, offering no sign of shelter, only more treacherous terrain.

Saul felt a pit in his stomach as they approached—it would be difficult to cross, but there was no other option.

"We're getting close to the pass," he said. "It's not going to be easy. We'll need to climb."

"We'll make it through," Hannah replied. "We've done worse."

Saul glanced back at Beth and could see the fear in her eyes, the way her hands trembled as she fidgeted with her water bottle, holding it like it was the only thing grounding her to reality.

"Beth," he called softly, slowing his pace until he walked beside her. "We're almost at the pass. We'll have to climb, but we'll get through it. Just stay close, okay?"

Beth looked up at him, her lips parted as if she wanted to say something, but no words came. Her eyes darted from Saul to the looming cliffs ahead, and a flicker of panic crossed her face.

"I don't know if I can," she whispered. "It's too much. I can't...I can't breathe..."

"You can do this," Hannah said, coming up on Beth's other side. "Just stay close to us. We'll help you if you need it."

Beth shook her head, her breath quickening as her eyes darted around the canyon. "It's not just the climb...what's the point of all this? Why are we even still going? There's nothing out there. We're just chasing a dream that isn't real."

Saul's heart clenched at the desperation in her voice. His mind recalled what Marcus had said about people and their dreams. He knew Marcus planted that doubt in Beth's head.

"We don't know that," Saul replied, trying to keep his voice calm. "We don't know what's out there, but we have to keep moving. We've come too far to stop now."

Beth stared at him, her eyes filling with tears. "I don't know if I can keep going. I'm so tired. I'm so scared."

Saul reached out, placing a hand on Beth's shoulder. "It's not for nothing. We're still here. We're still alive. That's what matters."

Beth nodded, though her face remained pale, her body

trembling. Saul could tell she wasn't convinced, but there was no more time for words. They had to keep moving.

The three of them reached the base of the pass. The narrow canyon stretched before them, flanked by cliffs that looked almost impassable.

"It's steep," Saul said, "but we can make it if we're careful."

He moved first, finding a handhold in the rock and pulling himself up, testing the stability of the surface. Although the rock was loose in places, it held. He climbed a few feet higher, looking back down at Hannah and Beth.

"Just take it slow," he instructed. "One step at a time."

Hannah followed, her movements sure and steady. Beth hesitated at the base, staring up at the climb with wide eyes. Her hands shook as she reached for the first handhold, her breath coming in shallow, panicked gasps.

"I can't…I can't do it," she stammered, her voice pitching.

"You can," Saul urged. "Just focus on your hands and feet. Don't think about the rest."

Hannah glanced down from her position on the rock. "We're right here, Beth. You're not alone. Just take it slow."

Beth swallowed hard. Her movements were shaky as she started to climb. Saul and Hannah watched her closely, ready to help if needed. For a few minutes, it seemed like Beth might make it. She climbed slowly, inching her way up the rock face. But then, halfway up the pass, her foot slipped on a loose rock, and she froze.

"I can't…I can't do this!" Beth cried, her voice trembling with panic. "I'm going to fall!"

"You're not going to fall," Saul said, trying to keep his voice calm. "Just hold on."

But Beth's breathing grew more frantic, her grip on the rock weakening. She was paralyzed by fear, her body shaking uncontrollably.

"Beth, listen to me!" Hannah shouted, her voice cutting

through the wind. "You're almost there! Just keep going!"

But Beth didn't move. Her eyes were wide with terror, and her hands slipped further.

"Beth!" Saul called, panic rising in his chest. "Hold on! Just hold on!"

But it was too late. Beth's fingers lost their grip on the rock, and with a terrified scream, she fell. The sound of her body hitting the rocks below echoed through the canyon, and Saul's heart dropped into his stomach.

"Beth!" Hannah shouted, scrambling back down the cliffside as quickly as she could.

Saul followed, his mind reeling. When they reached the bottom, Beth's body lay still on the rocks, her limbs twisted at unnatural angles. Her wide, unseeing eyes stared up at the sky, and Saul knew in an instant that she was dead.

Hannah knelt beside Beth, her hands trembling as she reached out to touch her. She let out a choked sob, her voice breaking as she whispered Beth's name. Saul knelt beside her, his grief catching in his throat. They had tried. They had done everything they could. But it wasn't enough.

For a long moment, the world seemed to stop. The wind howled around them, and the sun beat down mercilessly. Saul reached for Hannah, pulling her close. She buried her face in his chest, her body shaking with quiet sobs. They held each other for a long time, mourning Beth, mourning the world they had lost. But even in their grief, they knew they couldn't stay. The world wouldn't wait for them to mourn. They had to keep moving.

"We have to go," Saul whispered, his voice thick with emotion. "We can't stay here."

Hannah nodded against his chest, wiping the tears from her eyes as she pulled herself together. They stood together, taking one last look at Beth's lifeless form before turning away. There was no time for a proper burial, no time for words. The world had taken her, just as it had taken so many others.

Chapter 26

The days following Beth's death felt like a blur. The world around Saul and Hannah had always been quiet, but now, after losing her, the silence seemed to carry more weight. It was heavier, more suffocating, as if the earth itself was mourning alongside them. The stillness of the plains stretched out in all directions, and each step they took only seemed to deepen the sense of isolation that enveloped them.

Saul and Hannah moved forward in silence, and the hunger gnawing at their stomachs became harder to ignore. Their rations had been dwindling, and they were now down to their last can of peas and sips of water. Saul could feel the weakness creeping into his limbs. He glanced at Hannah, who walked with the same determination as his but with exhaustion evident in her eyes.

"We need to find food soon," Hannah said quietly.

Saul nodded, though his expression was grim. "I know."

He reached into his pack, pulled out the canned peas, and offered it to Hannah. "Here," he said. "Take the rest."

Hannah shook her head. "No, we'll split it."

But Saul insisted, pressing the can into her hands. "You need it more than I do."

"Saul," Hannah said, "we'll split it."

Saul nodded. There was no arguing it. They divided the small portion between them, chewing slowly, savoring every bite despite how little there was. It was flavorless, but it was all they had.

Saul scanned the horizon as they continued walking, hoping to see anything that might offer them shelter or food. The plains stretched uninterrupted until something caught his eye in the distance. It was barely visible at first—a small, dark shape against the gray sky—but as they drew closer, Saul realized it was a structure.

"Hannah," Saul said, nodding toward the distant shape. "Look."

Hannah followed his gaze, squinting against the fading light. "A cabin?"

Saul's heart quickened. It could be dangerous—there could be other survivors inside. Then again, this world didn't have many survivors left.

"We should check it out," Saul said.

"We need to be careful," Hannah replied.

They made their way toward the cabin, the wind picking up as the sun began to dip below the horizon. The building looked old and weathered, its wooden walls gray and worn from years of exposure. The windows were dark, and the door hung slightly ajar, swaying gently in the breeze. It looked abandoned, but Saul knew better than to assume it was empty.

Saul motioned for Hannah to stay close as he approached the door, slowly pushing it open. The hinges creaked, the sound unnervingly loud in the silence. He stepped inside, his knife drawn, scanning the room for any signs of movement. But the cabin was empty. Dust coated everything, and the air was thick with the musty smell of abandonment. It didn't look like anyone had been here in a long time.

Hannah followed him inside, her eyes scanning the room cautiously. "Looks empty."

"We should check for food," Saul said, moving toward the small kitchen area.

They searched the cabin thoroughly, opening cupboards and drawers and checking under the bed and behind the furniture. But there was nothing—no food or supplies—just dust and empty shelves. Saul felt a wave of frustration rise in his chest. After everything, they had hoped this cabin might be a lifeline, but it was just another dead end.

"There's nothing here," Hannah said.

Saul sighed, running a hand through his hair as he paced the floor. He couldn't shake the feeling that they were running out of time, that their options were growing slimmer with each passing day. As he walked, his boot caught on something—a soft creak beneath his foot. He froze, looking down at the floorboards. Something didn't feel right.

"Hannah," Saul said, his voice sharp. "Come here."

Hannah quickly crossed the room, kneeling beside him as he inspected the floor. One of the boards under the rug felt loose. He moved the rug away, revealing a hidden trapdoor underneath.

Saul lifted the trapdoor, revealing a narrow set of stairs leading into the darkness.

"A cellar," Hannah said.

Saul's heart raced with anticipation as he grabbed his flashlight from his pack and descended the stairs. The beam of light cut through the darkness, and what it revealed made his breath catch in his throat.

Shelves. Rows and rows of shelves, all lined with neatly stacked cans of food: canned vegetables, fruits, soups—more food than they had seen in years.

"Hannah," Saul called up, his voice filled with disbelief. "You need to see this."

Hannah hurried down the stairs, and when she saw the stockpile of food, her eyes widened in shock. "Oh my God," she whispered. "We found it."

They stood there for a moment. It felt like a miracle, like the universe had finally given them a reprieve. After so long of barely scraping by and rationing every bite, they found enough food to last them for weeks.

That night, they ate their first real meal in what felt like an eternity. They heated cans of soup and vegetables—the smell of warm food filling the room and lifting their spirits. They ate until they were full, the hunger that had gnawed at them finally easing.

After dinner, they went to the small, worn bed in the corner of the cabin. The mattress was thin, and the blankets were old and frayed, but it was a bed. After sleeping on the cold, hard ground for so long, it felt like a luxury.

Hannah rested her head on Saul's chest, her fingers tracing soft patterns on his arm. Saul held her close, giving her a soft kiss on her forehead.

"We're getting close to the coordinates," he said. "It's not much farther. What we found here will keep us going the rest of the way."

Hannah smiled, still tracing his arms. "We're so close," she replied.

As their breathing slowed, they drifted off, the steady rhythm of their hearts syncing as they surrendered to sleep—feeling as close to peace as they'd been in a long, long time.

Chapter 27

T he sun had dipped low, casting the sky in shades of burnt orange and fading indigo as Saul and Hannah approached the final stretch of their journey. The landscape had changed in the last few days, shifting from the open plains to a more rugged terrain with slopes and scattered outcroppings. Ahead of them rose a steep hill, its crest barely visible against the evening sky. They exchanged a look, an unspoken thrill passing between them. This was it—the safe haven was not much farther.

"Just over that hill," Saul said, his voice tinged with anticipation.

Hannah's eyes sparkled with the last light of day as she took in the hill, her breath coming a little quicker. "Feels like it's taken forever to get here," she said.

"Too long," Saul agreed, a faint smile tugging at his lips. He pulled out the map, though he hardly needed to check it. They'd been following the coordinates for so long that they were practically etched into his memory. But seeing the markings, the numbers that had guided them through every mile, made the moment more real.

Saul glanced back up at the hill, squaring his shoulders as he felt a new burst of energy. The exhaustion from the day's journey seemed to lift, replaced by the pulse of excitement. "Ready?"

Hannah nodded, determination sharpening her gaze. "Ready."

The incline was steeper than it looked, the ground loose underfoot and scattered with jagged stones. But they climbed steadily, the air thick with anticipation. With each step, their hearts beat faster, their breaths coming in short, excited bursts as they imagined what might be waiting for them just beyond the ridge.

"Do you think it's there?" Hannah asked.

"It has to be," Saul replied.

They climbed higher, each step bringing them closer to the crest. The air was cooler up here, a light breeze brushing against them, and Saul felt his pulse quicken with every inch they gained. He was acutely aware of Hannah beside him. Together, they'd endured so much, and now—finally—this journey felt like it was reaching its peak.

"Almost there," he said, glancing over his shoulder. Hannah flashed him a quick, encouraging smile, her eyes bright with anticipation.

They slowed as they neared the top, the sky stretching like an endless canvas painted in twilight hues. Saul felt his chest tighten, and a surge of excitement filled him as he prepared to take those final few steps.

They reached the crest of the hill side by side, their eyes widening as they gazed out over the horizon.

Saul's eyes scanned ahead before looking down at the map again. The coordinates were correct. They were exactly where the map had led them. But there was nothing. No sanctuary. No safe haven. Just a barren, desolate plain that stretched out endlessly before them. The same cracked earth, the same lifeless sky.

Saul's hands trembled as he looked at the map again, checking the coordinates one more time as if hoping that he had made some kind of mistake. But there was no mistake. This was the place. This was where they were supposed to find their salvation. But there was nothing.

"This can't be right," Saul muttered, his voice shaking with disbelief. "This…this has to be it."

Hannah stood beside him, her face pale as she took in the sight before them. She didn't speak or move as the crushing realization settled over them.

"This can't be it," Saul said again, louder this time. He looked at the map, then back at the empty plains. "It can't be."

But no matter how many times he looked, the truth was staring him in the face. There was nothing here. The safe haven they had been chasing was nothing but a mirage, a false hope that had led them into the middle of nowhere.

Saul felt something inside him break. The hope he had clung to for so long—the belief that they would find something at the end of this journey—was gone, shattered into pieces by the brutal reality of what lay before them.

"It's not here," Saul whispered, his voice thick with emotion. "It's not here…"

Before Hannah could say anything, Saul started running down the hill towards the plains. Though weak and trembling from exhaustion, his legs carried him forward as he sprinted. He couldn't accept it. He couldn't believe that this was all there was. There had to be something. There had to be.

"Saul, stop!" Hannah shouted, but her voice was distant, drowned out by his racing thoughts.

He ran, his feet pounding against the cracked earth, his breath coming in ragged gasps. He scanned the horizon, his eyes wild with desperation, searching for any sign that they had missed something. But there was nothing—just endless, lifeless land.

"It has to be here!" Saul shouted. "It *has* to be!"

He kept running, pushing himself harder, faster, as if he could outrun the truth. But no matter how far he went, the landscape remained the same. Empty. Barren. Dead.

"Saul, please!" Hannah's voice was closer now, but Saul barely heard her. He was consumed by the need to find something —anything.

His legs gave out beneath him, and he collapsed to his knees in the dirt. His body shook with sobs, his hands clutching the dry earth as the weight of everything came crashing down on him. The hopelessness, disappointment, and crushing realization that they had been chasing a dream that had never existed was too much to bear.

Hannah caught up to him, her chest heaving as she knelt beside him. She wrapped her arms around him, pulling him close as his body shook with grief. For a long moment, they stayed like that, the two of them huddled together in the middle of the empty plains, the only sound the quiet, broken sobs that escaped Saul's lips.

"Marcus was right," Saul said finally, his voice was hoarse. "It was nothing but a dream. Nothing but false hopes."

Hannah's heart ached as she listened to him, her eyes filled with tears. "But what about the radio?" she asked. "You heard the radio."

Saul shook his head as he realized the grim truth of it all. "But you didn't," he said, wiping his tears.

Hannah looked confused. "What are you talking about?"

"Hallucinations," he muttered. "Every desperate survivor had them. We were all on the brink of starvation, and we made them up. We created our own false hopes of survival."

"I don't believe that," Hannah said softly, though even she could feel the doubt creeping into her mind.

Saul's mind flashed back to the old man he spoke to in the woods. Hannah never saw him. She never heard the radio, and she never saw the old man. They were never real. They were all in his head. Another image slowly appeared in his memories.

"The hospital," he said, his voice distant.

Hannah frowned, confused. "What about the hospital?"

"At the hospital," Saul continued, his eyes filled with sadness. "I looked out the window and thought I saw green…a field of green grass. I could have sworn it was real. But now I know it was just another illusion. It was nothing."

"We still can't give up," Hannah said, her voice firm. "Even if there is no safe haven, even if it was all just a dream…we can't give up on each other."

Saul looked at her, his eyes filled with pain and confusion.

"I love you, Saul," she said. "And I won't give up on you." She wiped a tear from Saul's face. "Don't give up on me. Don't give up on yourself."

For a long moment, Saul was silent. Then, slowly, he nodded, the tension in his body easing as he took a deep breath. Hannah helped him to his feet, and together, they stood at the edge of the barren plain, the empty land stretching out before them. They began to walk again, their pace slower and more deliberate. The sun was setting in the distance, casting a soft, orange glow over the empty landscape. They didn't know where they were going, but they knew they had to keep moving.

As they walked, they spotted something in the distance—a small, weathered shack half-hidden by the shadows of the treeline. It was a simple structure, barely more than a wooden shell, but it was shelter—and right now, that was all they needed.

"Looks like a hunting shack," Saul said as they entered.

The shack was small, with a single room inside. The only furnishings were a bed, a small table, and a chair. Saul and Hannah set their packs down, exhaustion settling into their bones as they took in their new surroundings.

"We can stay here for a while," Saul said quietly, his voice still hoarse. "We have enough food from the cabin to last a little while."

They lay together on the small bed, wrapped in each other's arms, their bodies warm, keeping the world's cold at bay. Hannah nestled closer, her head resting on Saul's chest, feeling the steady rhythm of his heartbeat beneath her ear. For a while, neither of them spoke. They simply lay there, absorbing the moment's peace, letting it wash away the echoes of all they'd endured. Saul traced gentle circles along her back, his touch soothing, as if his hand alone could reassure her that she was safe.

After a long stretch of silence, Saul's voice broke through. "All this time…all the miles we walked, all the places we searched…thinking we'd find something to save us."

Hannah's fingers brushed over his, intertwining with his hand. She lifted her gaze, meeting his eyes in the dim light. "Maybe we did find it," she whispered, her voice trembling with a truth that had only begun to reveal itself.

Saul's hand tightened around hers. "If I hadn't found you, Hannah…" His voice cracked, and he had to pause, swallowing back the emotion. "I don't think I would've made it."

Hannah blinked back tears, pressing herself closer to him. "Neither would I," she replied.

"It was never about finding a place, was it?" he whispered. "We thought it was out there, waiting for us somewhere, but the haven we needed was within us all along." He brushed a strand of hair from her face, his thumb lingering gently on her cheek. "We found a safe haven within each other."

Tears slipped down her cheeks as she kissed his hand, her lips soft against his skin. "We don't need anything else," she said. "We have everything right here."

As they lay there, drifting on the edge of sleep, Hannah whispered, "We'll be okay…"

Chapter 28

They spent the next week in the shack, each day mirroring the last in a quiet, steady rhythm that brought Saul and Hannah a fragile sense of peace. Mornings greeted them with the same gray sky and still air, and as days blended into nights, they found themselves growing accustomed to the routine they had built together in this temporary refuge. Though the world outside remained barren, they had created something that felt like home within these walls.

With each passing day, the sting of disappointment over the failed sanctuary faded, replaced by the gentle comfort of familiarity. They had found what they needed in each other, and while the shack wasn't the dream they'd clung to for so long, it was enough. They had shelter, warmth, and a space where the outside world felt a little farther away, its dangers kept at bay for a while.

Saul, however, hadn't entirely let go of the map. Despite knowing in his heart that the destination he had longed for didn't exist, he would sometimes pull it out, tracing the faded lines with a sense of lingering purpose. The map was more than just coordinates now; it had become a record of their journey, a reminder of the miles they had traveled together. And though the safe haven they had sought wasn't waiting at the end of that path, it felt impossible to let go of the small hope it still represented.

Hannah had settled into a comforting routine. She would wake with the sunrise, sometimes before Saul, and gather kindling from the brittle remains of nearby trees, organizing the small supplies they had left. There was little to occupy her time, but she kept their small space tidy, creating an order to the day that felt grounding.

Each night, they would sit by the fire, talking quietly or just enjoying the silence, sharing memories of a world that seemed further away with each passing day. They'd learned to find peace in the simple routines and in each other's presence. In the glow of the flames, they would sometimes fall into conversations about dreams, distant futures, or the fragments of lives they'd once had, and those moments—brief but cherished—became the heart of their new reality.

On the seventh morning of the week, Saul woke just as dawn began to creep over the horizon. He lay still for a moment, watching Hannah as she slept beside him, her face peaceful in the soft morning light. Careful not to wake her, he slipped out of bed, pulled on his boots, and went outside. The land lay quiet under the first light of dawn, the sky shifting from gray to soft pink as the sun rose. Saul took a deep breath, savoring the calm settling over the landscape.

As he gazed out over the lifeless land, something caught his eye. A flicker of movement in the distance. It was faint, barely noticeable against the static landscape, but unmistakable. Saul blinked, rubbing his eyes as if to clear away the last remnants of sleep, then squinted into the distance. His heart quickened. It couldn't be—but he couldn't look away.

Without thinking, Saul turned and rushed back inside the

shack, his eyes darting around the room until they landed on a pair of binoculars hanging on the wall. They had been there since the day they arrived, dusty and worn, a relic of whoever had lived in the shack before. Saul grabbed them and hurried back outside, raising them to his eyes and focusing on the distant movement.

His hands trembled slightly as he lowered the binoculars for a moment, his mind struggling to process what he had just seen. He raised the binoculars again, adjusting the focus, and his heart skipped a beat as the image became clear.

He turned and hurried back into the shack. "Hannah! Wake up! You need to see this!"

Hannah stirred, blinking as she sat up, her face creased with confusion. "What is it?" she mumbled, brushing sleep from her eyes.

"Outside," he said, practically pulling her out of bed. "You won't believe it."

She grabbed her coat and stumbled out after him, still half-asleep as she tried to make sense of his urgency. "Saul, what's going on?" she asked, shivering slightly in the morning air.

Saul handed her the binoculars, pointing toward the distant treeline. "Look over there," he said. "Near the edge of the field."

Hannah raised the binoculars, squinting as she focused on the horizon. She saw only the same empty landscape, the familiar stretch of dead land and skeletal trees.

She lowered the binoculars. "I don't see anything, Saul."

Saul grabbed the binoculars and looked again—then handed it back to Hannah. "Over there," he pointed. "Look again."

Hannah raised the binoculars to her eyes. As she adjusted the lens, her breath caught. A flicker of movement appeared in the distance. A deer.

It stood at the edge of the field, its sleek body silhouetted against the dead trees, its head lowered as it grazed. For a moment, she thought it must be a trick of the light, a mirage born from days of empty landscapes. But the deer was real, its graceful form moving slowly through the field, tentative and alive.

"Oh my God," she whispered, lowering the binoculars, her hands trembling. "Saul…it's a deer. It's actually real."

Saul took the binoculars from her, his pulse racing as he looked through them again. The deer was still there, moving with a quiet elegance, its head lifting now and then to check its surroundings.

They stood side by side, watching the deer in stunned silence. It grazed for a while, moving slowly, its presence a testament to the resilience of life itself. For that brief, perfect moment, the world felt different—gentler, as though it hadn't fully surrendered to the ruin that surrounded them.

They watched as the deer lifted its head, its ears twitching, before disappearing into the shadows of the trees. The silence that followed felt profound, a reminder that the world, however broken, still held small miracles within it.

Saul lowered the binoculars, glancing at Hannah with a smile he couldn't hold back. Her eyes shone with a newfound hope, her face softening in a way he hadn't seen in a long time.

"It's amazing," she whispered, looking at him. "I never thought I'd see something like that again."

"Neither did I," Saul replied, his voice tinged with wonder. "But maybe things aren't as empty as they seem."

Hand in hand, they walked back to the shack, a quiet joy settling over them. That morning, they had learned that hope didn't have to be grand or sweeping. Sometimes, it was as small and simple as a single deer, a creature brave enough to emerge into a world scarred by desolation. And maybe, just maybe, they could find a way to live within that tiny, persistent spark of life.

Epilogue

A year had passed since they saw the first signs of life. They had moved on from the old shack, leaving behind the plains and finding a cabin hidden deep in the woods. Remote and well-concealed, it had become their home, their sanctuary. It was a far cry from the life they had once known, but it was theirs.

The air was cool and still, with only the faintest hint of a breeze rustling the tops of the trees surrounding their cabin. The sun hung low in the sky, casting a soft, golden light over the small clearing where Hannah knelt in the dirt. Her fingers sifted through the soil, careful and deliberate as she tended to the struggling plants. Most were barely clinging to life, their leaves withered and frail, but a few—just a few—showed signs of hope. Small, delicate shoots pushed through the earth, stubbornly refusing to die despite the odds stacked against them.

Life was beginning to return slowly but surely. What had once seemed like a complete extinction of all plant and animal life hadn't been as final as she and Saul had feared. The disease that had wiped out so much of the world hadn't taken everything. Some creatures had survived. Nature, in its resilience, was quietly reclaiming what had been lost. Hannah paused in her work, wiping her brow and looking out across the small garden she had painstakingly cultivated over the last several months. It wasn't much, but the fact that it was there at all was a miracle in itself.

She leaned back on her heels, taking a deep breath of the crisp air. It smelled like the forest—damp, earthy, alive. It was hard to believe how much had changed in just one year. In the quiet of the afternoon, Hannah's thoughts drifted to Saul, as they often did when he was out hunting. It had become their routine over the past year—he would leave in the early mornings, venturing deeper into the forest to search for whatever small game he could find, while she stayed behind to tend to the plants and keep the cabin in order. The hunts had been sparse at first—a squirrel here, a rabbit there—but it was enough to keep them alive.

She remembered the early days of their life here, how every creature Saul brought home had been carefully rationed, each bite measured and stretched to last as long as possible. They had learned to live with less, to make do with what they had, and in the process, they had found a strange peace in the simplicity of it all. Life was hard but also simple now—survive, nurture, endure.

A soft sound in the distance pulled her from her thoughts. It was faint at first, a low, rhythmic noise almost swallowed by the stillness of the forest. But as it grew more distinct, Hannah stood, wiping her hands on her pants and turning toward the sound.

Her breath caught when she saw him. Saul was emerging from the treeline, his broad shoulders hunched slightly under the weight of the deer he dragged behind him. It was larger than any of the animals he had brought home in the past year, its sleek body catching the last rays of the setting sun. Blood stained the deer's fur where Saul had made the kill, and its lifeless form trailed through the dirt as he pulled it toward the cabin. Hannah's heart swelled with relief—a deer. After months of surviving on small game and scraps, Saul had managed to bring down a deer.

Saul glanced up as he approached, his face breaking into a tired smile when he saw her. His dark hair was damp with sweat, his clothes stained, but there was a quiet pride in his eyes—a look that said he had done what needed to be done and that he would do it again tomorrow and the day after that, for as long as it took.

Hannah crossed the clearing in a few quick strides. She barely hesitated as she reached him, throwing her arms around him. She leaned up and kissed him as his arms tightened around her, pulling her closer. When they finally broke apart, Saul looked down at her, a smile tugging at the corner of his mouth.

"We're eating good tonight," he said.

Hannah pulled back slightly, her eyes meeting his, and in that shared look, there was an understanding—a recognition of how far they had come and how much further they still had to go. But for now, they had this, and they had each other. And as the world continued to reclaim its life, the whispers of silence faded into the past and stirred up whispers of hope.

Part Two

Whispers of Hope

Prologue

The fire flickered low in the hearth, casting uneven shadows over the rough-hewn walls of the cabin Saul and Hannah had called home for the last three years. Outside, the world lay in unbroken silence—a silence so deep it seemed to press in on them, a constant reminder of the empty land beyond their walls. They had each grown accustomed to that quiet expanse of nothingness, but tonight, it felt heavier, as if some invisible force were watching, listening.

Saul added another piece of wood to the fire and settled back, stretching his legs toward the warmth. He glanced at Hannah, her face partially hidden by the hood of her worn jacket. She sat across from him, legs drawn up, arms wrapped around her knees, gazing into the flames as if trying to extract meaning from their silent dance.

The fire crackled, briefly illuminating her face, and Saul could see the shadows beneath her eyes—faint lines that spoke of countless sleepless nights and the weight of too many thoughts.

"It's been too quiet lately," she murmured, almost as if speaking to herself.

Saul nodded slowly. He felt it, too, that shift in the air, the way the silence outside seemed almost watchful. "Sometimes, it's hard to tell if that's a blessing or a curse."

Hannah's gaze drifted as if her thoughts had taken her far from the cramped walls of their cabin. "I think…" she hesitated, pulling her arms tighter around herself, "I think we're hiding here. We keep telling ourselves this is survival, but it's starting to feel like something else."

"Like we're stuck?" Saul asked.

She nodded, her eyes flicking up to meet his. "When we first found this place, I thought we'd be safe. And we have been, in a way. But…" she trailed off, glancing at the dark windows where faint frost had gathered along the edges. The winter was close to ending, yet the cold had not entirely let go of the land.

"It's not just about safety anymore, is it?" Saul said. "It's about finding…something more. Someone."

They had skirted around the topic for months, each too cautious to bring it to the forefront. But now, the unspoken words hung heavy between them, an unacknowledged burden.

"I keep thinking about other people," she said softly. "We can't be the only ones left, can we?"

"No," Saul replied. "We're not the only ones." He let the silence linger, trying to picture the lives of the people they might find out there, imagining what kind of world awaited them beyond the safety of their cabin.

Hannah's face tightened, her hands curling around her arms as if bracing herself. "And if we find them, what then? How do we know they won't still be desperate? That they won't be willing to do whatever it takes to survive?"

"Trust is a gamble," Saul admitted, "but staying here alone feels like giving up. Like we're just waiting for the world to swallow us whole."

"Maybe that's exactly what we're doing," she whispered. "Just waiting, hoping that somehow things will change without us having to step out into that nothingness."

They sat in silence, each lost in the enormity of the decision ahead. The fire crackled softly, the only sound within the cabin, while the darkness outside pressed against the walls.

Eventually, Saul spoke. "When I close my eyes, I see the road stretching out, empty, silent, but filled with possibilities. I wonder how far we'd get before we found something." He looked at her, searching her face for a sign of reassurance. "What if it's worth the risk?"

Hannah didn't answer right away. She let her gaze drift to the fire again, her fingers tracing a faint pattern over her worn sleeves. "What if we're wrong? What if we find something worse?"

"We've faced worse before," Saul replied. He thought back to their early days of survival, the lengths they'd gone to for food, the moments of desperation that had tested their humanity. "We've made it this far, haven't we?"

She nodded, a faint smile curving at her lips, though it didn't reach her eyes. "I used to dream about a place—a community where people hadn't lost themselves to fear and hunger. I think I clung to that idea even when everything seemed hopeless. But it's been three years, Saul. Three years of silence, of empty roads and abandoned places. What if that dream is just fantasy?"

"Or what if it's just waiting for us to find it?" he countered, leaning forward. "Think about it, Hannah. We've stayed alive this long, but for what? Just to survive a little longer, hidden away? Or do we dare to believe there might be more out there?"

She exhaled a shaky breath, her fingers tightening around her knees. "I don't want to be naive. I don't want to lead us into something we can't escape."

"Maybe it's not naivety," Saul said, "maybe it's hope."

Hannah's shoulders dropped, her gaze softening as she looked at him. "Hope feels like a dangerous thing."

"Yeah," he agreed. "But so does staying here, pretending we're fine in a world that's already left us behind."

Hannah reached over, placing her hand on top of his. Her fingers were cold, a reminder of the winter outside, the world that lay in slumber beneath frost and shadow. "If we're going to do this, we need to be sure. We need to be ready for what's out there."

"We will be," Saul said, squeezing her hand. "When spring comes, we'll have supplies packed, weapons, everything we need."

Hannah nodded, but he could see the uncertainty in her eyes. Yet, beneath that, there was a spark—a glimmer of resolve that had been buried under fear and isolation for too long. She held his gaze, and in that moment, he knew she felt it too—the faint, stubborn pull of something more.

"When spring comes," she echoed, "we'll go. We'll leave this place and see what's out there. Maybe we'll find that dream…or maybe just a new kind of silence."

Saul nodded and squeezed her hand gently. "Whatever's out there, we'll face it together."

Hannah's fingers tightened around his. She glanced toward the window, her face softened by a faint smile. For the first time in a long while, Saul thought he saw a spark of light in her eyes that matched his own. Spring would come soon enough, and with it, a new chapter in their lives—a journey that held the promise of hope and the threat of everything they feared.

Chapter 29

The morning broke over the horizon, bringing the tender warmth of early spring. The cabin looked almost peaceful in the first light as if it had been spared the world's devastation. The walls, now speckled with creeping green moss, stood sturdy, a final fortress in the endless wilderness. They'd repaired, reinforced, and made it their own, filling the small, cold space with their stories and memories. It was the only home they had known since the world fell silent.

Saul stood by the cabin door, a small, rough sack slung over his shoulder, and looked around the clearing. The thaw was just beginning, and patches of stubborn snow lingered along the edges of the trees, resisting the season's warmth. A few early shoots pushed their way up from the earth, defying the winter that had held the land in its grip. This small and fragile new growth was a subtle promise that perhaps the world, battered and empty as it was, might recover.

"We're really doing this," he murmured to himself.

Hannah was gathering the last of their supplies inside. She looked at the walls, noting the makeshift shelves they'd built, the corner where they had piled their meager belongings, and the fire pit that had kept them warm through endless winter nights. Her gaze was warm but tinged with the sadness of farewell.

"Everything's ready," she said softly.

Saul turned to her, his eyes briefly catching on her face. He noticed the small changes in her expression, the way her lips pressed together, the distant look in her eyes. He knew the cabin had been more than just a shelter for her. In many ways, it had been her sanctuary, a place where she had allowed herself to believe in safety, even for brief moments.

"We'll miss it," he said.

Hannah nodded, her gaze sweeping over the cabin's interior. "Do you remember when we first came here? We thought it was too small, too cold. But after a few weeks, it felt like…" She trailed off, not quite willing to finish the thought.

"A home," Saul said gently, offering a faint smile. He looked around, letting his mind drift back to those early days. The cabin had barely provided enough space for them to sleep, but in time, it had become a safe haven, a shield against the desolation outside.

He picked up a small tin cup from the counter, turning it over. "I never thought a place like this would mean so much," he admitted. "It's strange, isn't it? How quickly we can grow attached."

Hannah reached out, resting a hand on his arm. "I know. But we have to go. We've outgrown it. If we stay…we're just hiding."

They turned their attention to their supplies, organizing them into packs. Their modest collection included dried foods, a few tools, two knives, and what remained of their medical supplies. Every item had a purpose, and each one carried the weight of necessity.

"Let's go over the plan one more time," Saul said, sitting beside the door as he pulled out their map, a worn piece of parchment marked with small, faded notations.

Hannah joined him, her fingers tracing the map's edges. "We'll follow the river south for a few days. Then, we'll head west toward the city ruins. From there, we look for signs of other people."

"You're worried about the others," he said gently.

Hannah looked down, her fingers fidgeting with the strap of her pack. "Aren't you? We don't know what we'll find out there, Saul. For all we know, it could be monsters."

"Maybe," he conceded, "but maybe there's something better, too. We've stayed here for safety, but that safety becomes a cage at some point."

She nodded, her expression thoughtful. "It's just when I think about the people we might meet, I keep picturing what the world has done to them. People can lose themselves out there."

"They can," he agreed, resting a hand on her shoulder. "But we've managed to hold on, haven't we?"

Hannah exhaled, her shoulders softening slightly as she looked at him. "It's strange…you always know what to say."

He shrugged, a small, rueful smile on his face. "I'm as scared as you are, believe me. But I've made peace with it. The world isn't what it was, but we're still here, and maybe that counts for something."

They shared a quiet moment, letting the words sink in. Saul's gaze drifted toward the small window, where faint sunlight filtered through, casting warm patches over the floor. The light had a quality he hadn't seen in months—soft and promising, the kind of light that heralded new beginnings.

"Are you ready?" he asked, breaking the silence.

"I'm ready," she replied.

They stepped outside, the world beyond seeming larger, more expansive than it had before. Each sound, from the rustling of leaves to the distant trickle of melting snow, felt like an invitation, a reminder that life, in its own way, was beginning again.

They walked a few paces from the cabin and turned to look back one last time. The small building stood quietly among the trees, yet it held a world of memories. Hannah squeezed Saul's hand, her fingers tightening briefly around his.

"Goodbye," she whispered, though the words felt strange on her lips.

"Goodbye," Saul echoed.

They stood in silence, letting the moment linger before they turned, stepping toward the unknown. The path ahead was rough, winding through forests still cloaked in patches of frost and mud. As the cabin faded behind them, Saul felt a strange feeling of loss. The life they had built was behind them, but a new one lay ahead.

"Do you think we'll ever see this place again?" Hannah asked.

Saul glanced back, though the cabin was now just a faint outline among the trees. "Maybe," he replied, though he knew they both understood it was unlikely. They couldn't look back, not if they wanted to survive what lay ahead.

With one last look back, they turned toward the road ahead. The silence of the cabin, the safety of its walls—all of it was gone now, replaced by a future filled with hope.

Chapter 30

Saul and Hannah ambled down the cracked, uneven road, eyes scanning their surroundings with practiced ease. They had been traveling for days, their feet aching, shoulders sore from the weight of their packs, yet they pressed on, driven by the need for survival and a spark of hope that they might find something beyond the desolation.

They could get by just fine now, living off what they hunted in the woods and fields, but exploring the deserted towns had become a ritual—a reminder of how things once were, a quiet nod to a world left behind.

By late morning, they'd reached the outskirts of a small town, its buildings partially hidden under thick layers of overgrown vines and weeds. Asphalt cracked underfoot, fragments of a forgotten life scattered around: rusted car frames, crumbling street signs, and broken storefront windows. It was like walking through a memory, fragments of normalcy frozen in time.

"Wonder if anything's still standing in there," Hannah mused, nodding toward a small grocery store at the corner.

"Maybe," Saul replied. "Good to check. Never know what might surprise us."

They moved through the street with cautious ease out of habit more than worry. Their lives didn't depend on these scavenges anymore, but the pull of the past was too strong to ignore. Inside the grocery store, dust covered empty shelves and cans scattered across the floor, long since emptied by desperate hands. Still, Saul and Hannah searched, their curiosity tempered with a quiet reverence for the remnants of a world that once was.

Hannah's hand brushed against something cool beneath a shelf—a lone can of beans. She held it up with a grin. "Guess luck's on our side."

Saul chuckled, giving her a nod. "Always a little luck left, I suppose."

These small moments, these little pieces of the past, reminded them that they were still here, still holding on to something that felt real, even if the world around them had changed beyond recognition.

As they moved toward the back of the store, a faint sound caught Saul's ear. He froze, raising his hand to signal Hannah to stop. She stilled immediately, her body tense as she listened. The sound was faint but unmistakable—footsteps approaching from the other side of the store. Saul's heart pounded as he held his breath, straining to make out any further noise.

Saul motioned for Hannah to follow him, and they crept toward an aisle near the back, ducking low to stay out of sight. The footsteps grew closer, and a voice murmured something too low to make out. Saul felt a shiver of unease settle over him. There were at least two people, possibly more. As the footsteps neared, he caught a glimpse of movement. A figure stepped into view, wearing a heavy jacket with the hood pulled up, obscuring their face. They were tall, their shoulders hunched with weariness, but their movements were cautious, as if they, too, were aware of potential threats. Another figure followed closely behind, a smaller woman with her hand resting on a makeshift spear.

Saul's hand tightened on his knife as he weighed their options. They could try to stay hidden and wait for the strangers to leave, or they could reveal themselves and hope for a peaceful encounter—a gamble, given how desperate and hostile people had become.

Before he could decide, Hannah shifted beside him. She stood slowly, her hands raised slightly, and Saul followed suit, hoping the gesture of peace would be enough to stave off any hostility.

"Hello," Hannah called, her voice calm yet firm. The strangers froze, their eyes narrowing as they turned to face her. For a tense moment, nobody moved, the air thick with the possibility of violence.

The tall man lowered his hood, revealing a gaunt face marked by lines of exhaustion and suspicion. He held up a hand, signaling the woman beside him to stay back, though she kept her spear raised, watching Saul and Hannah with a wary gaze.

"We don't want any trouble," Saul said, his voice steady. "We're just passing through, looking for supplies."

The man's gaze flicked over them, assessing, calculating. "Same as us," he replied, his voice rough and low. "Didn't think there'd be anyone else left in these parts."

Hannah took a cautious step forward. "We're just travelers. Looking for food, maybe some news. We don't mean any harm."

The woman with the spear relaxed slightly, lowering her weapon, though her eyes remained vigilant. The man nodded, seeming to accept their words, and motioned for them to sit. Saul and Hannah slowly lowered themselves to the ground, keeping a safe distance between themselves and the strangers.

"I'm Saul, and this is Hannah," he introduced. "We've been on our own for a while."

The man grunted, his eyes flicking to the dusty floor. "Name's Nate, and this here's Clara," he said, nodding toward the woman beside him. "We're from up north…or what's left of it."

Clara let out a dry, humorless laugh. "Ain't much of anything left anywhere, is there?"

Hannah nodded slowly, her gaze shifting to Clara. "It's been like that for a long time. We haven't seen many people out here, either."

Saul noticed the haunted look in Nate's eyes, a look he'd seen in the mirror enough times to recognize—the look of someone who had seen too much, endured too much.

"Where are you headed?" Nate finally asked, breaking the silence.

Saul exchanged a glance with Hannah, uncertain how much to reveal. "South, maybe further," he said carefully.

Nate's expression darkened, and he shook his head. "If you're looking for a community, be careful. Some of them have rules you won't like. Desperation changes people."

"We'll keep that in mind," Saul replied, glancing at Hannah, who seemed just as unnerved.

Clara shifted, her gaze fixed on the door as if watching for threats. "You two seem decent enough," she said. "But we've run into people who aren't so kind. They'll take what you have and leave you with nothing."

Hannah's fingers twitched, brushing against her knife. "We know," she said quietly. "It's why we keep moving."

Nate's face softened slightly as he looked at them. "There are rumors," he said. "About settlements, places where people have banded together. Not all of them are good, but some are trying."

Saul's heart quickened, a spark of hope flickering to life within him. "You think it's true?" he asked.

Nate shrugged. "Could be. Or it could just be a story people tell themselves to keep going. Hard to say what's real anymore."

Despite the doubt in Nate's words, Saul felt a renewed sense of purpose. Maybe their journey wasn't as hopeless as it had seemed. "We'll take our chances," he said.

Nate gave a nod. "Good luck, then. Just remember…not

everyone out here has held onto their humanity. Some people will do whatever it takes to survive."

Nate and Clara rose to their feet. They exchanged brief nods with Saul and Hannah. Then, without another word, they slipped out of the store, disappearing into the shadows of the town.

Hannah exhaled, her shoulders relaxing slightly as the tension faded. She looked at Saul. "Do you think we'll see them again?"

Saul shrugged, though he doubted it. "Maybe. But at least now we know there are others out here. We're not alone."

As they stepped back onto the empty street, Saul glanced at Hannah, a faint smile tugging at his lips. "Ready to see what's out there?"

She nodded. "Let's keep moving."

Chapter 31

Saul and Hannah moved silently through the underbrush, the forest floor damp and littered with fallen leaves that muffled their footsteps. It had been a week since they'd left the cabin, and although the silence of their former refuge haunted them, the days had begun to blur together, becoming a new kind of routine. There was a strange comfort in the familiarity of survival, even as the ever-present threat of the unknown loomed around every bend.

They had just passed a clearing, edging closer to the remains of what might have once been a small farm, when Saul heard it—a faint rustle, like the shifting of leaves, but purposeful. He raised his hand, signaling Hannah to stop. She froze instantly, her gaze sharpening as she scanned the surrounding trees, her fingers brushing the handle of her knife.

"Did you hear that?" he whispered.

Hannah nodded. "I did."

They waited, breath held, every muscle tense. After a few

moments, the sound came again—this time a deliberate footstep, too cautious to be random, too quiet to be anything but someone intentionally moving through the brush. Saul's heart pounded as he gestured for Hannah to take a position behind a nearby tree.

Suddenly, a figure stepped into view, emerging from a cluster of thick bushes a few yards away. He was young, barely in his twenties, with disheveled dark hair and sharp, wary eyes that darted around as he moved. His clothes were worn, patched with scraps of fabric, and he clutched a small knife in his hand, holding it defensively.

Saul raised a hand in a gesture of peace. "Easy there," he said, keeping his voice calm. "We're just passing through."

The young man stiffened, his eyes narrowing as he scanned them. He didn't lower his knife, but he didn't make any sudden moves. His gaze flicked between Saul and Hannah, measuring, assessing, as if weighing his chances.

"Who are you?" he asked, his voice steady but laced with a hint of fear. "You part of a group?"

"It's just the two of us," Saul replied. "We're not looking for trouble, I promise."

The young man hesitated, his grip loosening slightly. "Everyone says that until they decide they need what you have."

Hannah stepped forward, her hands open in a show of goodwill. "We get it. We've had our share of run-ins. But we're not like that. We just want to survive, like everyone else."

After a long moment, the young man exhaled. "I'm Finn," he said, lowering his knife.

Saul gave a nod, relieved to see a glimmer of trust forming. "I'm Saul, and this is Hannah. We've been traveling for a while now. Haven't run into many friendly people."

"Yeah," Finn replied with a tinge of bitterness. "Friendly people don't last long out here."

Saul noticed the hardness in Finn's gaze. "We've learned a few things. Mostly how to stay alive without losing ourselves."

For a moment, Finn's guarded expression softened, a flicker of something almost like hope crossing his face before he looked away. "You said it's just the two of you?"

Saul nodded. "It's been that way for a while now. We had a place, but it's time to move on. We're looking for people who haven't lost themselves to all this."

Finn hesitated, his gaze dropping as he fidgeted with his knife. "I was a little kid when all this started," he said quietly. "Five… maybe. I don't really remember much back then. I've been on my own for a while now. Since I was eighteen…I think. I lost track. I don't really know. I've been scavenging ever since, trying to survive."

"You were just a kid," Saul said, glancing at Finn. "What about your parents?"

Finn's expression hardened, and he shook his head, looking away. "I don't…I don't talk about that," he muttered. "I just try to keep going, live off plants and whatever I can trap these days. Before that…it was horrible. I did…" his voice trailed off, and then he looked at Saul. "I did…things to survive."

Saul nodded, understanding the boundaries Finn had built around his past. "I get it. Believe me, we all have that same past." He glanced at Hannah, who gave him a slight nod before returning his gaze to Finn. "If you don't have anywhere else to go, you're welcome to join us. For as long as you want."

Finn looked at him, surprised. "Why would you trust me?"

"Because we could all use a little more trust these days," Hannah replied gently. "It's hard enough out here without going it alone."

Finn's expression softened, and after a moment, he nodded, slipping his knife back into the makeshift sheath on his belt. "Alright," he whispered. "I'll join you. Just don't kill me."

Saul couldn't help but chuckle. "Don't worry, kid. But if it matters, all the same to you too."

Finn smiled. "Sounds good to me."

They continued along the trail, explaining their plans to Finn as they moved through the forest. Finn listened, but his eyes darted around. Saul noticed how he stayed slightly behind them. Their newfound camaraderie was tested sooner than they expected. Less than an hour later, Saul caught sight of movement out of the corner of his eye. He stopped, motioning for the others to halt, his eyes scanning the trees.

"What is it?" Finn whispered.

Saul didn't reply, his gaze fixed on a group of figures moving through the forest ahead. Rough-looking men with ragged clothes and weapons slung across their backs. Raiders. They hadn't seen them yet, but they were heading their way.

"We need to move now," he whispered, turning to the others. "Those men are raiders."

Finn's face went pale, his hand going to his knife, but Hannah grabbed his arm, pulling him back. "Stay quiet and follow us," she murmured.

They moved swiftly, ducking behind a cluster of bushes and slipping down a narrow incline. The raiders' voices grew louder, their laughter harsh and unsettling as it echoed through the trees. Saul's heart pounded as they crouched low, every muscle tense, waiting for the men to pass.

But fate had other plans. Just as the raiders reached the spot where they'd been moments before, one of them paused, sniffing the air. "Wait," he muttered suspiciously. "I smell smoke."

Saul's stomach clenched. They'd lit a small fire earlier to warm up, and though they'd doused it, the faint scent must have lingered. The raider gestured to his companions, and they began to spread out.

Hannah shot Saul a look, her eyes wide with alarm. Just as they started to back away, Finn stumbled, his foot slipping on loose soil. He tumbled forward with a muffled grunt. The raiders' heads snapped toward them.

"Go!" Saul hissed, grabbing Finn and pulling him up. They

took off through the trees, the raiders' shouts echoing behind. Branches whipped against their faces, and roots threatened to trip them, but they didn't stop, survival instincts taking over as they barreled through the underbrush.

They managed to put some distance between themselves and the raiders, ducking behind a large fallen tree to catch their breath. Finn slumped against the trunk, face pale, clutching his side where blood seeped through his shirt.

Hannah knelt beside him, worry on her face as she tore a strip of fabric from her sleeve to press against the wound. "It's not too deep, but we need to stop the bleeding."

Finn winced but nodded. "Thanks…I'm sorry. I didn't mean to mess things up."

"You didn't mess anything up," Saul said firmly. "We were all in danger, and you kept moving. That's what matters."

Finn looked down, a faint blush coloring his cheeks as he murmured, "I…I've never really been part of a group. I'm just on my own out here. I don't know how to do this. I'm used to just hiding all the time."

Hannah placed a reassuring hand on his shoulder. "We're all learning. Just stay close, keep your eyes open, and we'll be alright."

After tending to Finn's wound, they continued, sticking to the forest to avoid detection. The encounter had shaken them, but as they walked, Saul noticed a new look in Finn's eyes, a cautious hope he hadn't seen before. They were three now, bound by danger and trust, and for the first time, Saul felt a flicker of hope that, despite the darkness, they were not as alone as they once believed.

Chapter 32

The river moved slowly, winding its way through a narrow valley nestled between hills thick with wild underbrush. Saul and Hannah had made camp along its banks, their small fire flickering gently in the growing darkness. Across the river, the trees stretched high, their branches reaching over the water like fingers trying to bridge the gap. It was a peaceful spot, an unlikely oasis in the chaos of a world that had crumbled beyond recognition.

They'd chosen this place to rest after days of trekking through dense forests and skirting abandoned towns, keeping mostly to themselves and avoiding the dangers of open roads. Tonight, they could almost pretend they were safe. The sound of water rippling over rocks and the crackle of the fire brought a rare sense of calm, a brief escape from the reality that had become their lives.

Finn sat across from them, busy sharpening a knife he'd found along the way, his face illuminated by the fire's soft glow. He was still new to their routines, and though he watched them closely, picking up on their habits, there was an eagerness in his manner that spoke of youth and inexperience. Saul had noticed the way Finn's gaze would linger on him and Hannah, studying their every move. It was clear he was trying to learn, adapting to their rhythm with a determination that was both endearing and a little heartbreaking.

Hannah's voice broke the silence. "You ever wonder…if there's a place out there untouched by all this?"

Saul looked up, his gaze meeting hers across the fire. "Untouched?" he repeated. "You mean a place where the disease didn't spread?"

Hannah nodded, her gaze distant as she stared into the flames. "Maybe not the disease, but…I don't know. Somewhere remote, isolated enough that it escaped the worst of what happened here. I keep thinking about it—a place where people don't exist. An island, maybe?"

Saul considered her words, turning them over in his mind. The idea seemed both far-fetched and tantalizing, a spark of hope buried beneath layers of doubt. "An island…" he murmured. "I suppose it's possible. Hard to reach, though. And hard to know if we'd find anything better than what we have here."

Hannah gave a small shrug, though her eyes held a flicker of excitement. "It's just a thought. But think about it—an island, away from raiders, away from the desperation of the mainland. Somewhere we could rebuild. Even if it's just us."

Finn, who had been listening intently, looked up, his face lighting up with interest. "An island sounds incredible. You really think there could be a place like that?"

Hannah smiled, glancing at Saul before answering. "I don't know, Finn. But I think it's worth considering. We're already moving. If there's even a chance, maybe it's worth aiming for."

Saul leaned back, the idea taking shape in his mind. An island would mean isolation, a chance to start fresh, far from the violence and desperation that seemed to plague every step of their journey so far. But it would also be a gamble, a journey toward the unknown with no guarantee of success.

"How would we get there?" he asked. "Even if we found the coast, we'd need a way across the water. A boat…supplies. It's not like there are ports with ferry schedules anymore."

Hannah chuckled softly. "No, but…if we made it to the coast, there might still be boats. Maybe ones we could fix up."

"Assuming there's no one else with the same idea," Saul added, though he couldn't keep a small smile from forming on his face. "Still, you're right. It's an idea."

Finn was watching them both closely, his eyes alight with curiosity. "I know it's risky, but…it sounds like a place where we could actually be safe. Away from all this…madness." His voice trailed off, and he looked down, a hint of sadness crossing his face. "I've lost so many people. The idea of a place where we don't have to keep running…"

Hannah reached across, her hand resting briefly on Finn's shoulder. "You're with us now, Finn. And if we can make this happen, we'll do it together."

They sat in silence for a while, each of them lost in thought, the fire crackling softly between them. Saul stared into the flames, the image of an island flickering in his mind. He imagined rocky shores, thick forests, and the vastness of the sea stretching out as a barrier between them and the rest of the broken world. It was an enticing thought—a chance to escape, to leave the mainland's dangers behind.

"Suppose we did make it," Saul said. "We'd need supplies, shelter, a way to fish or hunt, depending on what's out there. It would be rough…but we've survived rough before."

Hannah nodded. "We've adapted so far. If we find a few more people, people we trust, we could make it work. It's not just about surviving anymore, Saul. It's about living."

Her words hung in the air, and Saul felt a small spark of something stir within him—a sense of purpose that had been dulled by the endless cycle of survival. The idea of a goal, something beyond the next day or the next meal, breathed new life into him.

Finn shifted. "I could help. I don't know much, but…I know how to fish. My dad taught me back when things were…normal. If we made it to the coast, I could help with that."

Saul gave him a nod of encouragement. "That's good, Finn. Every skill counts."

A breeze rustled the trees, and the firelight flickered, casting shadows that danced across their faces. The night felt alive, filled with the tentative promise of something new, something beyond the isolation they had come to accept as their reality. Saul glanced at the river, watching the water flow under the moonlight. If they could make it to the coast, if they could find a boat, there was a chance—however small—that they might reach an island and carve out a life there.

"The coast won't be easy," he said. "There will be raiders, scavengers, people trying to claim whatever's left. But if we're careful…we could make it."

Hannah looked at him. "Then that's our plan. We keep heading west until we reach the water. And along the way, if we find people…we invite them to come with us, as long as we trust them."

"Alright," he said finally, meeting Hannah's gaze. "We'll look for others. But we'll be careful. We can't afford to take unnecessary risks."

Finn looked between them, a grin spreading across his face as he absorbed the magnitude of what they were planning. "An island," he murmured, almost to himself. "Somewhere we can be safe. Somewhere we can…belong."

They spent the next hour discussing plans, going over the supplies they would need and the potential threats they might encounter. Hannah's voice was filled with a quiet intensity as she outlined the steps they would take. Saul listened, nodding, his mind racing with possibilities.

When the fire burned low, they finally settled in to rest, each of them cocooned in their own thoughts. The idea of the island had taken hold, filling the empty spaces within them with hope and purpose. As they lay beside the river, listening to the water's gentle murmur, they felt the weight of the journey ahead but also the strength to face it.

When the first light of day touched the horizon, Saul rose, stretching as he looked out over the river. Hannah stirred beside him, her eyes opening slowly as she sat up, blinking against the soft morning glow. Finn lay curled on his side, his breathing steady, his face peaceful in sleep.

"Ready?" Hannah asked quietly, her gaze steady as she met his.

Saul nodded, his resolve firm. "Let's go find our island."

Chapter 33

The journey had been relentless—days of navigating unfamiliar trails, the constant vigilance against danger, and the ever-present weight of uncertainty pressing down on them. Saul, Hannah, and Finn settled down for the night. They had chosen a secluded spot beneath a tall oak, its branches stretching wide above them, leaves rustling softly in the gentle breeze. After hours of trekking through dense underbrush, they welcomed the chance to rest.

As the evening wore on, Finn drifted to the edge of the clearing, his head resting on his pack as he gazed up at the night sky, his eyes reflecting the faint starlight. Saul and Hannah sat closer to the fire, their shoulders almost touching, the heat from the flames mingling with the warmth that radiated between them.

He glanced at her, his gaze lingering on the soft curve of her face illuminated by the firelight. Her expression was peaceful, her eyes fixed on the flames, and for a brief moment, she looked like someone untouched by the hardships they'd endured. He felt a surge of gratitude, an unexpected wave of affection that made him reach out, his hand gently finding hers.

Hannah turned to him, and they shared a quiet smile, a silent acknowledgment of the connection that had grown between them —a bond forged in the fires of survival, strengthened by every moment of trust and every unspoken promise to protect one another.

After a while, Hannah spoke. "I used to have nights like this," she said, her gaze distant. "Back when…back before everything. My family had a cabin by a lake, and we'd sit by the fire just like this. My parents, my brother, and I…we'd talk for hours, or sometimes we'd just sit in silence, watching the stars."

Saul listened, his heart aching as he pictured the life she described, a life filled with warmth and love that now felt like a distant dream. "They sound like good memories," he said softly, his thumb brushing gently over the back of her hand.

"They are," she replied. "But sometimes, they feel more like ghosts. It's like…holding on to something you know you can never have again. You try to keep it close, but every day, it slips a little further away."

He nodded, understanding all too well the feeling she described. "I know what you mean. I used to have a life like that, too. My wife and I…we had a small house in a little town not far from the city. We had a daughter…" His voice trailed off, the words hanging in the air as he struggled with the memories that surfaced, each one laced with both love and loss.

Hannah's hand tightened around his, her expression softening as she looked at him. "Tell me about her," she said, her voice gentle.

Saul hesitated, the pain of remembering mingling with the urge to share, to let someone else carry the weight of his grief, if only for a moment. "My wife's name was Laura. She was kind, patient…she could make me laugh even on the worst days." He paused, a faint smile tugging at his lips. "She loved to bake, even though she was terrible at it. Our kitchen was always filled with smoke, but she'd just laugh and try again. Said she'd get it right someday."

Hannah chuckled softly, the sound mingling with the crackle of the fire. "She sounds wonderful. I would've liked to meet her."

He nodded, his gaze fixed on the flames. "She would've liked you too," he said quietly. "You remind me of her, sometimes. The way you look out for others, the way you keep going, no matter what."

A soft smile spread across Hannah's face, her cheeks flushing slightly as she looked down. "Thank you," she said. "That means a lot." She squeezed his hand again. "So what about your daughter?"

"Emily..." Saul began. "She was such a sweet little girl. She was always full of questions. Every morning, she'd ask, 'What are we going to learn today?' Like the world was this endless adventure."

Hannah laughed softly. "Sounds like she kept you on your toes."

"Oh, she did," Saul replied.

They sat in silence for a while longer, the warmth of their shared memories enveloping them, creating a fragile bubble of peace amidst the darkness that surrounded them. For so long, he had kept his heart guarded, protecting himself from the pain of loss by keeping others at a distance. But with Hannah, that barrier had slowly eroded, replaced by a trust and closeness that felt exhilarating.

Hannah's gaze softened as she looked at him, her eyes reflecting the same emotions he felt. She leaned closer, her head resting gently on his shoulder, their fingers still intertwined. Saul let himself relax, his head tilting to rest against hers. They stayed like that, wrapped in each other's warmth, the fire crackling softly beside them.

"Do you think we'll find it?" he asked softly.

Hannah lifted her head, her eyes meeting his. "I do," she

replied. "We'll find our island. And if we don't…we'll still find a place to rebuild."

"We will," he said. "No matter what it takes."

As the night wore on, they finally drifted off to sleep, huddled close for warmth and comfort, Finn resting nearby, their small circle a beacon of hope in the vast emptiness.

Chapter 34

The sky had darkened in a matter of minutes as heavy clouds gathered overhead. The wind picked up, whistling through the trees and carrying with it the scent of rain. Saul, Hannah, and Finn were only halfway through their day's hike when the first drops began to fall, heavy and cold, pelting down through the branches and quickly soaking their clothes.

"We need to find shelter," Saul called over the rising wind, glancing back at Hannah and Finn as they trudged behind him.

Hannah shielded her eyes from the rain, scanning the surroundings. "I think I saw something back there, near the trail," she said. "Looked like an old building."

"Let's go," Saul replied.

They quickened their pace, pushing through the underbrush and stumbling over roots as the rain intensified. The sound of thunder rumbled in the distance, growing louder with each step, and within moments, they were drenched, their clothes clinging to their skin. But just as Hannah had said, an old stone structure loomed up ahead, partially obscured by vines and foliage—a small, crumbling church, its weathered walls standing defiantly against the elements.

"Thank God," Finn muttered.

They hurried to the entrance, pushing open the heavy wooden door with a groan that echoed through the empty interior. Inside, the air was thick with the smell of dust and damp wood, and the remnants of once-vibrant stained glass windows glowed faintly in the dim light, casting muted colors over the cracked stone floor.

The church was small, no more than a single room with rows of wooden pews, most of them broken or overturned. An altar stood at the front, draped in a moth-eaten cloth, and a few wilted flowers lay scattered around its base, long since dried and forgotten. Despite the decay, the space held a strange kind of peace, a quiet refuge from the storm raging outside.

"Let's make ourselves comfortable," Saul said. He set his pack down on one of the pews and began wringing the water from his shirt. "Looks like we'll be here a while."

Hannah nodded, shivering slightly as she wrapped her arms around herself. "At least we're out of the rain," she said as she settled onto a dry spot beside Saul. She glanced around, taking in the quiet beauty of the place, its worn stone walls, and fading colors somehow comforting.

Finn was already exploring, his eyes wide with curiosity as he moved around the room, brushing his fingers over the cracked pews and the faded remnants of painted saints on the walls. "You think anyone comes here anymore?" he asked.

"Doubtful," Saul replied, glancing up at the cobwebbed rafters. "Places like these…people probably left a long time ago. Or maybe they just stopped believing."

They fell silent, each of them listening to the steady rhythm of the rain pounding against the roof. The storm showed no sign of letting up, the wind howling through the cracks in the walls and sending shivers through the room.

It was Finn who noticed them first. In the shadows near the altar, a faint rustling sound broke the silence, and he turned, his eyes narrowing as he peered into the dim corner. "Hey," he whispered. "Someone's there."

Saul's hand went to his knife, and he rose slowly, his gaze fixed on the movement in the shadows. But before he could take a step forward, a voice called out.

"Easy there, friends," it said, followed by the sound of slow, shuffling footsteps. "We're not looking for trouble. Just here out of the rain."

A figure emerged from the shadows, an older man with graying hair and deep lines etched into his face, his clothes tattered and patched. He was followed closely by a woman, equally worn and weathered, her eyes sharp but kind as she took in the group with a cautious gaze. They moved slowly, leaning on each other for support.

"Name's Jace," the man said. "And this here is Marla."

Saul relaxed slightly, giving the newcomers a nod. "I'm Saul. This is Hannah, and that's Finn," he replied. "We're just waiting out the storm, same as you."

Jace nodded, his gaze drifting over them. "Didn't think anyone else would be out here. Not many people left these days who travel by choice."

Finn offered a smile, though his eyes remained guarded. "We're looking for something…better," he said.

Marla's eyes softened as she looked at him, a hint of sadness in her expression. "Aren't we all," she replied as she sat on one of the pews. "Been searching a long time now. It seems like every place we find is worse than the last."

They settled into conversation, the storm raging outside as they shared stories of their travels. Jace spoke of his days before the world had changed, tales of a small farm he had once owned, a quiet life with crops and animals to tend, a life he had lost when the disease swept through, taking everything he'd built with it. His voice was heavy with regret, and his words tinged with a bitterness that spoke of countless years of hardship and loss.

"We tried to rebuild," he said. "After the disease, after… everything. Thought maybe if we held on, if we just kept going, we could find some kind of peace. But the world out there—it's different now. People have changed."

Marla reached over, her hand resting gently on his. "It's hard to keep going sometimes," she admitted. "But we keep hoping… that somewhere, somehow, there's something left worth finding."

Hannah glanced at Saul, a silent question in her eyes, and he nodded, taking a deep breath before he spoke. "We've been thinking the same thing," he said, his gaze shifting to Marla. "That maybe there's a place…far from here, isolated enough to be untouched. An island, somewhere out on the coast."

Marla's eyes lit up, a spark of interest flaring to life as she listened. "An island?" she repeated, her voice filled with wonder. "A place away from the mainland…a fresh start."

Saul nodded. "That's what we're hoping for. Somewhere we can rebuild away from the violence and the despair. Somewhere we can make a life again."

Jace let out a scoff. "An island, huh?" he muttered, shaking his head. "Sounds like a dream. And in a world like this, dreams don't mean much."

"Maybe not," Hannah replied gently. "But it's something. And sometimes…a dream is all you need to keep going."

Marla's face softened as she looked at Hannah. "You're right," she said. "Hope is fragile, but it's worth holding on to."

The storm outside had begun to subside, the thunder fading into the distance, leaving only the gentle patter of rain against the roof. Saul looked at Jace and Marla. "You're welcome to join us," he said. "If you're willing to take the risk. We don't know what we'll find, but if there's a chance, it might be worth it."

Jace's face hardened as he considered Saul's words. After a long moment, he sighed and nodded. "Alright," he muttered.

"We'll go with you. If there's even a chance…I suppose it's better than waiting around to die."

Marla's face broke into a hopeful smile, and she reached out, taking his hand in hers. "Thank you," she whispered. "It's worth a try. For both of us."

The group settled in for the night, sharing what little food they had and huddling together for warmth as the last remnants of the storm passed. The old church was quiet, its worn walls and faded colors a reminder of the lives they had left behind, the world that had once been.

Chapter 35

The day had barely begun, but already, the climb was exhausting. They were moving through uneven, rocky terrain, and each step felt harder than the last. Saul led the group, his face set with determination, though he couldn't ignore the fatigue etched into each of their expressions.

"I'm starting to think this mountain doesn't end," Finn muttered.

Hannah shot him a sympathetic look, her own face pale with fatigue. "I know it feels endless, but there's bound to be a clearing ahead. Somewhere safer to rest, somewhere with water. We just have to keep going."

Behind her, Marla let out a tired laugh, wiping a hand across her brow. "I'm getting too old for this. I never imagined I'd be trekking up mountains and scrambling over rocks in my final years."

Jace, who had been walking beside her, chuckled softly. "It's not exactly the retirement we'd planned, is it?"

Marla reached out, patting his shoulder with a gentle smile. "No, it's not. But I'd rather be here with you, struggling together, than anywhere else."

Jace's face softened as he looked at her. "Same here, Marla. I don't think I would've made it this far without you."

Their quiet exchange brought a faint smile to Saul's face, though it was tinged with sadness. He glanced at Hannah, who met his gaze with a look that said she understood—they all did. In a world where so much had been lost, small comforts and shared moments had become precious.

The path narrowed as they continued, the ground growing steeper and more precarious with each step. Loose rocks slid underfoot, and they clung to the rocky walls for balance, their movements cautious. A wrong step could mean a fall, and Saul's stomach churned at the thought.

"Careful here," he called back. "One step at a time. Stay close to the wall."

Hannah went first, leading Finn across the narrow pass. Saul waited, watching as Jace and Marla followed. Marla moved carefully, her hand gripping the rough stone as she navigated each unsteady step. Jace kept close, his hand ready to catch her if she stumbled.

But then it happened—so suddenly that none of them could react in time. Marla's foot slipped on a patch of loose gravel, her hand reaching out, but there was nothing to grab. Her balance faltered, her eyes widening with panic as she tumbled sideways, her body twisting toward the edge.

"Marla!" Jace's scream tore through the air as he lunged forward, but he was a second too late. She fell, her fingers brushing his for a brief, heartbreaking moment before she slipped over the edge, her body plummeting down the rocky slope.

Time seemed to freeze, the world narrowing to the sound of Jace's anguished cry echoing through the mountains. Saul and Hannah stood frozen, their faces pale with shock, as they watched

Marla's figure disappear down the jagged cliffside. The only sound that remained was the faint rustling of stones falling after her until even that faded into silence.

"No," Jace whispered. He dropped to his knees, his hand still reaching out to the empty space where she had been. "Marla…no. Please, no…"

Finn stood motionless, his face ashen, his mouth opening as though he wanted to say something, but no words came. Hannah took a shaky step forward, her hand covering her mouth as tears filled her eyes. "Oh God…Marla…"

Saul finally found his voice, though it came out as a strained whisper. "Jace…" He moved toward him, placing a hand on his shoulder. "I'm so sorry."

Jace's shoulders shook, his head bowed, his hand clenched into a fist against the rocky ground. "This wasn't…she shouldn't… I should've saved her. I promised her…I promised her I'd protect her."

Hannah knelt beside him, her face streaked with tears as she reached out, her hand resting on his. "Jace…it wasn't your fault. You couldn't have known. You did everything you could."

But Jace shook his head, his face contorted with sorrow. "No. I failed her. She trusted me, and now she's…she's dead." He looked up, his eyes filled with anger as he turned to Saul and Hannah. "What's the point of this shit? We keep losing people. We keep getting hurt. What are we even doing this for?"

Saul took a deep breath. "We're doing this because it's the only way forward, Jace. Marla believed in this. She believed in all of us, in finding something better. We can't give up now—not after everything we've been through."

Jace let out a hollow, bitter laugh, his gaze fixed on the cliff's edge. "Something better," he repeated. "You think this shit is better? She's dead, Saul. What could possibly be better than being with her?"

Hannah reached out, squeezing his hand. "Jace, Marla

wouldn't want you to stop now. She'd want you to keep going, to find that peace she believed in. She'd want you to live."

Jace's face twisted with grief, and he buried his head in his hands, his shoulders shaking with silent sobs. Finn took a step closer, his own face streaked with tears as he looked at Jace. "Jace…I know it hurts. I…I lost my family, too. I know it feels like there's nothing left, but…but you have us. We're here with you. We won't leave you."

Jace lifted his head, his gaze settling on Finn's tearful face, and for a moment, something softened in his expression. He looked around at the others, at the faces of those who had shared his pain, who had fought alongside him and Marla. And though his heart ached, though he wanted nothing more than to give in to the overwhelming grief, he felt a small, fragile thread of connection holding him to them.

After a long, agonizing silence, Jace finally spoke. "Then… let's bury her. We owe her that much."

Saul nodded. "I agree," he said as he helped Jace up. "Let's go get her."

They found a small, sheltered spot beneath an ancient tree, its roots twisting into the rocky soil. The group worked in silence, digging into the earth with whatever they had on hand. When the grave was ready, they stood around it. Jace knelt by the grave, his hand resting on the soil, his face etched with sorrow as he whispered a few words.

"You deserved better, Marla. You deserved so much more than this world gave you. But I'll keep going for you. I'll carry you with me."

Hannah placed a small stone at the head of the grave, her fingers lingering on it. "Thank you, Marla. For everything. We'll never forget you."

Finn stepped forward, his face pale. "Goodbye, Marla. I…I wish I'd known you longer. Thank you for being with us."

Saul was the last to speak. "Marla was more than just a fellow traveler. She was a friend, a light in the darkness. She reminded us why we keep going and why we still hope. And for that…we owe her everything."

They stood in silence, the weight of Marla's absence pressing down on them, the realization settling in that she was truly gone. Jace remained by the grave long after the others had stepped back, his hand still resting on the soil, his head bowed, his face a mixture of anger, sorrow, and guilt.

As dusk settled over the mountains, they finally made camp nearby. Jace sat apart from the group, his gaze fixed on the grave. Saul glanced at Hannah, who gave him a faint nod, her expression filled with concern as she watched Jace.

"We'll get through this," Saul whispered.

Hannah nodded. "She believed in us."

One by one, they settled in, but sleep was elusive. Even as the night deepened and the mountain's silence pressed in, each of them lay awake, carrying Marla's memory into the quiet. It wasn't only rest they sought now but the strength to honor her by pressing onward.

Chapter 36

Saul and Hannah moved quietly, side by side, letting the calm settle over them like a balm. The night's grief for Marla still weighed heavily on their hearts, yet they took comfort in each other's presence. At one point, as they paused by a brook to fill their canteens, Saul took Hannah's hand, his thumb brushing softly over her knuckles. The touch was warm and familiar, grounding her in a way that words couldn't.

"You holding up okay?" he asked, his eyes meeting hers. Hannah offered a tired smile. "I think so," she replied. "Losing Marla…it just reminds me how fragile all of this is. How one moment we're together, and the next…we're not."

Saul nodded, his grip tightening on her hand. "I know. It's like every loss leaves this…hollow space. And sometimes, it feels like there's too much hollow space inside me. But being here with you, it's like a reminder that I don't have to carry it alone."

Hannah squeezed his hand. "We'll keep each other going," she said. "One day at a time."

The morning wore on, the fog slowly lifting as they continued down the winding path. They stopped for a break by midday, settling on the mossy ground under a towering tree. As Saul and Finn went off to refill their water, Jace took a seat beside Hannah.

"Marla and I…" he began, his voice hesitant. "We were married, you know…for over thirty years. She was my best friend, my partner. Losing her was like losing a part of myself."

Hannah looked at him, her heart aching for the sorrow etched into his face. "You loved her deeply," she said softly.

Jace nodded. "She was my light in the dark. I was never a man who said a lot of pretty words, but she understood me and knew me better than I knew myself sometimes. We used to talk about retirement, about taking trips together, maybe settling down somewhere quiet. She wanted to grow a garden."

Hannah's eyes softened. "I wish I'd known her better. She had such a kindness about her."

"She did," Jace said. "And she brought that kindness with her, even when everything else was falling apart. Sometimes, I think maybe she was too good for this world."

Hannah gave his arm a gentle squeeze. "I think she'd want you to keep going, Jace. To find that garden you talked about. To keep her memory alive, to keep that kindness she showed you in your heart."

He nodded, swallowing hard as he looked away. "Thank you, Hannah. I didn't think I'd ever find people like this again. People who cared."

A short distance away, Finn stood by the stream with Saul, his hands fidgeting as he glanced over at Jace and Hannah.

"I miss having people like that," Finn said. "I miss family."

Saul turned to him. "It's hard, isn't it? Feeling like you're drifting, like there's no one left to hold on to. I felt that way for a long time."

Finn looked at him. "Do you think it's possible to find that again? To have something like family?"

Saul considered his words, his gaze drifting over to Hannah. "I do," he replied. "It may not look the same as it did before, but we find ways to care for each other, to hold each other up. That's what family is, isn't it?"

Finn looked down, his hands tightening around his canteen as he nodded. "Yeah. Yeah, I guess it is."

When they were done filling their canteens, they set out again. They moved through the last of the forest. The air felt lighter here, the dense canopy giving way to patches of open sky as they emerged from the trees, stepping onto the edge of an open plain.

The sight of the vast expanse before them was beautiful. Fields of tall grass stretched out as far as the eye could see, swaying gently in the breeze, their golden tips catching the late afternoon sunlight. But with that openness came a sense of exposure, a vulnerability they hadn't felt in the shelter of the forest.

"Feels like we're on display," Finn muttered.

Saul nodded. "We'll have to be careful. There's no cover here. If anyone's out there…"

Hannah placed a hand on Finn's shoulder. "We'll keep a low profile and move quickly," she said. "We're not far from the coast now. If we can make it there, we'll find somewhere safe to rest."

Jace, who had been silent since they'd left the forest, looked out over the plains. "She wanted me to keep going," he said. "Marla would want me to see this through. To find a place where we can finally stop running."

Saul gave him a nod. "And we will, Jace."

They walked in silence, but there was a new strength in their steps. They were no longer just survivors drifting aimlessly through a broken world—they were something more, something stronger.

Chapter 37

Saul and Hannah moved cautiously as Jace and Finn followed closely behind, their eyes scanning the horizon. After so many days in the dense forest, the openness felt exposed, as if the world could see them as clearly as they could see it.

They'd been walking for hours, hoping to cover as much ground as possible while the weather held. As they crested a small hill, Hannah spotted movement in the distance—a few figures, barely visible, making their way toward a low grove of trees. She stopped, holding up a hand, and the others gathered around her, following her gaze.

"Looks like we're not the only ones out here," she said.

Saul squinted, his eyes narrowing as he focused on the small group. "Could be raiders," he said."

Jace let out a weary sigh, rubbing a hand over his face. "Survivors, raiders—it all feels like the same thing these days," he muttered.

They exchanged uncertain glances. After everything they'd

been through, it was tempting to avoid any potential encounter, to keep moving and leave these strangers to their own journey. But Hannah's gaze held steady.

"We should at least see who they are," she said. "Maybe we can trade. Or maybe they might tell us what we can expect ahead."

Saul nodded. "Alright. But we stay cautious. No sudden movements, and if anything feels off, we leave."

They made their way toward the grove, moving slowly and keeping their weapons within reach. As they approached, the figures came into clearer view—three of them, two men and a woman, their clothing patched and worn, their faces thin and lined with exhaustion. The woman noticed them first, straightening and holding up a hand in greeting, though her eyes were sharp.

"Stay there," she called out. "We don't want trouble, and I'm guessing neither do you."

Saul stopped a short distance away, holding his hands out to show he meant no harm. "We're just passing through," he said calmly. "Thought we'd see if you needed anything—or if you'd be open to a trade."

The woman eyed them carefully, her gaze lingering on each of them in turn. "Trade, huh?" She glanced at the two men beside her, who nodded slightly, and then looked back at Saul. "Alright, but keep your distance."

She took a few steps forward, her eyes never leaving them. Up close, they could see the lines etched into her face. Her dark hair was pulled back in a tight knot, and there was a small scar that cut across her cheekbone, giving her an air of fierce resilience.

"My name's Tara," she said. "These are my friends, Ben and Ollie. We don't have much, but we've managed to scrape together enough to get by."

Hannah stepped forward, offering a smile. "I'm Hannah, and this is Saul, Jace, and Finn. We're trying to reach the coast... looking for something safer. Maybe even a place where we can start over."

Tara let out a short, humorless laugh. "Start over? Good luck with that." She folded her arms across her chest. "We've seen what's left of this world. 'Starting over' is just a fancy way of saying 'delaying the inevitable.'"

Her words hung heavy in the air, and Finn shifted uncomfortably, glancing over at Saul, who remained calm.

"Maybe," Saul replied evenly. "But we'd rather take our chances out there than give up."

Tara's gaze softened for a brief moment. "We all have our ways of surviving," she said. "But the bigger your group, the harder it gets—more mouths to feed—more attention you attract. People see a large group, and they start thinking you have something worth taking."

Jace nodded slowly. "You've run into trouble, I take it?"

Tara's expression darkened. "More than I'd care to remember. People get desperate out here. It doesn't matter if they're good or bad—the need to survive can turn anyone into a threat."

Saul cleared his throat. "We understand the risk. But we believe there's strength in numbers. You don't have to come with us, but if you have anything you'd be willing to trade, we'd be grateful."

Tara nodded, her face relaxing slightly as she reached into her pack, pulling out a small cloth bundle. "We've got some dried herbs and a bit of salt," she said. "And Ollie managed to catch a couple of rabbits yesterday. We could spare one."

Saul reached into his own pack, pulling out a small tin of ointment they'd scavenged a few days before. "We have some medicinal salve," he offered. "It's good for cuts and scrapes."

Tara's eyes lit up with interest, and she took the tin, examining it with a nod of approval. "This will do," she said, handing over the rabbit and herbs in exchange. "Thank you."

As they packed up, Tara's eyes lingered on their group. "I know you're hoping to find others out here," she said. "Just be careful. The more people you bring in, the harder it'll be to stay safe. In my experience, most groups that grow too big…they don't last."

Hannah nodded. "We appreciate the advice. But we're willing to take that risk."

"I used to believe that too," Tara admitted. "But now…I don't know. Maybe I just lost the will to believe in something better."

After a tense silence, Tara nodded. "Well, good luck," she said. "Hope you find what you're looking for."

With that, she turned, leading Ben and Ollie back toward the grove. Saul, Hannah, Jace, and Finn stood silently, watching them go.

"She's not wrong," Jace said quietly. "More people does mean more risk. She has a point."

Saul sighed. "She does," he agreed. "But I still believe that finding others like us…people who still have hope, who can help us rebuild…it's a chance worth taking."

"We're stronger together," Finn said softly. "I've been alone before. It's no way to live. I don't ever want to go back to that."

Hannah nodded. "Tara's had a hard journey," she said. "She's lost faith in people, and I understand why. But that doesn't have to be our story."

Jace took a deep breath. "Maybe you're right," he said. "Marla would've said the same thing."

"Then we keep going," Saul said. "We trust each other, and we stay smart. But we don't close ourselves off from the world—not yet."

Though the road ahead was uncertain, they held onto their hope, their belief that somewhere, beyond the dangers and doubts, a place of peace and possibility awaited them.

Chapter 38

The air was crisp and clear as the group crested a gentle slope, their footsteps slowing as they took in the scene below. Spread out before them, glittering in the early afternoon sun, was a vast lake, its surface a rippling expanse of silver and blue that stretched out toward the horizon. The sight took their breath away—a rare, unexpected beauty in a world that had been stripped of so much.

Saul came to a stop, his eyes widening as he absorbed the lake's immensity. "It's…huge," he said.

Hannah stepped up beside him, her gaze fixed on the water. "It almost looks like the ocean," she said softly. "Like we're already there."

Finn let out a low whistle, his face breaking into a grin. "I've never seen anything like it. It just keeps going."

Jace moved forward, his expression shifting as he stared out at the lake. "Reminds me of the sea," he said. "Used to take Marla to the coast every year. She loved it. Said there was nothing like it."

"She'd be proud of you, Jace," Hannah said. "For still being here, still moving forward."

He nodded, his gaze never leaving the water. "I like to think so," he replied. "And I think seeing this makes me feel closer to her. Like maybe she's part of that horizon now."

They stood there for a few moments, watching the gentle waves lap against the distant shore. After weeks of trekking through forests and across fields, this felt like an oasis. They made their way down to the lake's edge, and Saul noticed an old wooden dock jutting out into the water. Tied to the end of the dock was a small rowboat—worn but seemingly intact.

"Would you look at that," Jace said, a small grin breaking across his face. "Seems like someone left us a gift."

Hannah raised an eyebrow. "Do you think it's still seaworthy? It's been here for years."

Jace shrugged. "Only one way to find out, isn't there?"

Finn let out a chuckle. "You think we could take it out? Just a little trip around the lake?"

Saul glanced at the boat, then at the group. Despite the exhaustion and the hardships they'd faced, he saw something new in them—anticipation, a kind of childlike eagerness. He looked back at Jace, who was already rolling up his sleeves, inspecting the boat with a critical but hopeful eye. "What are you thinking, Jace?"

"I'm thinking if we're serious about finding an island," Jace said, "it wouldn't hurt to learn how to row. This lake might be as good a training ground as any."

"So…you think we should try it?" Hannah asked.

Jace nodded. "It's a small boat, and we'd be close to shore. But if we're serious about this, we'll need every bit of practice we can get. I won't lie—it's been years since I took a boat out. But Marla and I used to sail, and I'd like to think I remember a thing or two."

"Alright," Saul said. "Let's give it a go."

Jace took the lead, his hands moving with ease and familiarity.

He adjusted the oars, explaining the basics to the others, his voice steady as he instructed them on the rhythm and timing needed to row smoothly.

"It's all about balance," he said, his gaze focused as he demonstrated the stroke. "You have to move in sync. Otherwise, you'll end up turning in circles."

Hannah and Finn exchanged amused glances, but they listened carefully, taking in every word. They'd never seen Jace so animated, so alive with purpose, and it was clear that the prospect of rowing—even just across a lake—had stirred something in him, a piece of himself he thought he'd lost.

They climbed into the boat. Jace and Saul took the oars, with Hannah and Finn sitting across from them, bracing themselves as the boat rocked gently on the water.

"Alright," Jace said. "Let's see what you've got."

They began slowly, Jace setting the pace with Saul following his lead, his movements a bit clumsy at first but gradually smoothing out. The boat glided across the lake, the oars cutting cleanly through the water, the soft splash of each stroke filling the quiet air.

Hannah and Finn watched in awe, their faces filled with wonder as they looked out over the vast expanse of water. The shoreline grew smaller behind them, the distant edge of the lake drawing closer with each stroke, and for a moment, they could almost believe they were on the open sea, bound for distant shores.

"This feels amazing," Finn said. "It's like we're flying."

Jace chuckled, his face filled with pride as he glanced over at him. "That's the magic of the water," he said. "It has a way of setting you free, of making you feel like anything's possible."

Saul nodded. "I can see why Marla loved it," he said. "Out here, everything feels open. Like the world is still wide and full of possibility."

"This is what we're working toward," Hannah said quietly. "A place where we can feel this free. Where we don't have to look over our shoulders all the time."

Saul looked at her with a smile and nodded. "Yeah. And if we can make it this far, then maybe that place is out there."

They continued rowing, their movements growing more synchronized as they found their rhythm, the boat gliding smoothly across the lake. The sun dipped lower, casting a warm, golden light over the water, and for a brief, perfect moment, they felt a peace they hadn't known in a long time.

As they reached the far shore, they clambered out of the boat, their muscles aching, but their spirits lifted. They pulled the boat up onto the sand and set up camp under a stand of trees overlooking the lake. They gathered around the fire, their faces flushed with the thrill of the day. Jace sat with a contented expression, a smile tugging at the corners of his mouth as he looked out at the lake, the memories of Marla's laughter and the smell of the ocean filling his thoughts.

"You know," he said after a while. "I never thought I'd get back on the water again. It was Marla's thing, really. But today felt right. Like maybe this is part of the journey she wanted me to take."

Hannah leaned toward him. "I think she'd be proud of you, Jace," she said. "For not giving up, for finding your way back to something you loved—even if it was hard."

Jace nodded. "You're right."

Finn looked around the group. "So, are we really thinking about sailing? Like, actually going out on the ocean, looking for an island?"

Saul grinned. "I think so, Finn. Today showed us that it's possible. If we can cross this lake, maybe the ocean isn't so impossible after all." He paused for a moment. "Of course, we'll probably get something bigger than a rowboat."

They all laughed, and the thought lingered, filling them with a renewed sense of purpose. As they settled in for the night and drifted off to sleep, the gentle lapping of the lake against the shore was like a lullaby, a promise of new horizons, a reminder that their journey was far from over.

Chapter 39

The valley stretched out before them, desolate and unyielding, a harsh landscape of rocky terrain and dry, cracked earth. The sky was a slate gray, heavy with clouds that seemed to press down on them, trapping the air and making each breath feel thick and oppressive. A cold wind swept through the valley, cutting through their clothes and chilling them to the bone.

It had been days since they'd seen any sign of wildlife or any hint of water, and the weight of exhaustion was taking its toll. The last of their supplies had been rationed so tightly that each meal was little more than a few bites, enough to take the edge off their hunger but never enough to satisfy. Every step felt like a struggle, their feet dragging over the uneven ground as they trudged forward.

Jace's face was drawn and pale, his eyes shadowed with fatigue as he pressed a hand to his side. "Feels like this valley's never going to end," he muttered.

Saul slowed his pace, glancing back at Jace. He, too, looked worn down, his shoulders hunched under the weight of his pack.

"We'll make it through," he said. "Just a bit further, and we'll find higher ground. Maybe even some shelter."

Hannah walked beside him, her gaze scanning the landscape with a wary eye. "The ground's too open here," she said. "We're exposed. If anyone's watching…well, they'll see us long before we see them."

Finn, trailing behind with his hands shoved into his pockets, looked up at the sky, his face tight with frustration. "And what if we don't find anything? What if we're just walking until we can't anymore?"

Saul glanced back at him. "We don't have a choice, Finn. We keep moving, one step at a time. We don't know what's up ahead, but staying here isn't an option."

Finn's expression darkened, but he didn't argue. The truth hung between them painfully clear—every day was a gamble, and there were no guarantees. Their survival depended on their ability to keep going, to push through the hunger and exhaustion, to hold onto the faint hope that somewhere beyond the barren landscape lay something better.

Hours passed, each step feeling heavier than the last. By the time they stopped to rest, the sky was growing darker, the first hint of evening settling over the valley. They found a rocky outcropping that offered some shelter from the wind, and they huddled together. Jace pulled out a small cloth bag, carefully unwrapping the last of their food. He divided the portions evenly, passing each piece to the others.

"It's not much," he said. "But it'll get us through the night."

Hannah took her portion, her hands trembling slightly. "We'll have to find more soon," she said. "This won't last us another day."

Finn looked down at his portion, his jaw clenched as he swallowed hard. "This isn't enough."

Saul looked at him. "I know it's hard, Finn, but we have to ration what we have. Pushing ourselves too far…it's too dangerous."

But Finn's face twisted with frustration, his fingers tightening around his meager portion of food. "Maybe for you," he muttered under his breath. "I'm not just gonna sit here and starve."

Saul's gaze hardened, but before he could respond, Finn stood up, shoving his portion into his pocket. "I'm going to look around," he said abruptly. "There has to be something out here. I can't just sit here and do nothing."

Hannah rose quickly, reaching out to grab his arm. "Finn, wait. We're all hungry, but wandering off on your own—"

"I can take care of myself," Finn interrupted. "I know what I'm doing."

Jace let out a heavy sigh. "Finn, listen to them. Going out alone in this kind of territory…it's a risk none of us can afford."

But Finn shook his head. "I'll be careful," he insisted. "I'll stay close. I just can't sit here starving. I'll be back soon."

He turned and strode off before anyone could stop him, his figure quickly disappearing into the shadows of the rocky landscape. Saul clenched his fists, but he knew chasing after him would only add to the risk.

"He'll be alright," Hannah said. "He's young and reckless, but he's not completely without sense."

"Hope you're right," Saul replied. "But we'll give him a bit of time. If he doesn't come back soon, I'm going after him."

The minutes dragged by, each one stretching into the next. They sat in silence, their gazes drifting toward the shadows, listening for any sound, any sign that Finn was returning. But as the sky darkened, worry began to creep into their hearts.

Suddenly, a faint rustling reached their ears, followed by the sound of hurried footsteps. Saul shot to his feet, his heart pounding as he saw Finn racing toward them, his face pale, his breaths coming in quick, shallow gasps.

"Run!" Finn's voice was laced with fear as he stumbled toward them, his hands shaking as he gestured frantically.

"Raiders…they set traps. I…I almost got caught!"

Saul grabbed his pack. "Move. Now!"

They scrambled to gather their belongings, adrenaline surging as they followed Finn back up the path. The shadows seemed to close in around them, every step echoing in the silent valley as they moved quickly, their breaths labored, the fear of being hunted driving them forward.

They found shelter in a shallow cave tucked into the rocky hillside, their movements quiet as they huddled together, their bodies pressed against the cold stone, hidden from view. Saul's hand gripped Finn's shoulder.

"What were you thinking?" he whispered. "Going off alone… you could've gotten yourself killed!"

Finn's eyes were wide with lingering fear as he looked down. "I didn't know," he stammered. "I thought I could find something, just…anything."

"We know you're trying to help, Finn," Hannah said, "but this…it's too dangerous to act alone. We have to be careful. Reckless moves could cost us everything."

Finn nodded. "I'm sorry. I didn't mean to. I just couldn't stand the thought of all of us starving. I wanted to do something."

Jace let out a sigh. "We're all doing the best we can, Finn. But we're in this together. We watch each other's backs; we move as a group. No one does anything alone, understand?"

Finn nodded. "Understood."

Saul's face softened. "Alright. We'll figure this out. Together."

"We need to find a safer route," Hannah said. "Sticking to the open valleys like this…it's too risky. If we move through the hills, keep to the hidden paths, we'll be harder to track."

Saul nodded. "It'll be slower, but it might be worth it. We can't afford any more close calls."

Jace leaned back, his gaze drifting to the darkening sky. "Marla always used to say, 'Better late and safe than quick and dead.' Looks like she was right."

The night pressed in around them, the cold air filled with the scent of earth and stone, and they huddled closer. In the quiet,

Finn's voice broke the silence. "I won't make that mistake again. I'll stick with you all. I get it now."

"Good," Saul replied. "We'll get through this. But we do it as a team."

Chapter 40

The village lay nestled in a shallow valley, a scattering of old buildings that seemed half-swallowed by vines and tall grass. Yet, even from a distance, there were unmistakable signs of life. A thin ribbon of smoke rose from one of the roofs, and Saul's sharp eyes caught the faint movement of figures between the structures. They slowed as they approached, taking in the sight with curiosity.

"Looks like a real community," Saul said. "Didn't think we'd see this again."

Hannah gazed toward the village with a soft look in her eyes. "It feels normal," she said. "Maybe even peaceful."

As they reached the outskirts, a man with a sturdy frame and graying hair stepped out of one of the houses, eyeing them cautiously. He held an old hunting rifle, though he didn't raise it; instead, he studied them carefully, his eyes lingering on them.

"You're strangers here," he called out. "We don't get many visitors."

Saul raised his hands, palms up. "We're just passing through," he replied. "No trouble, I promise. Just been a long road and… well, this place looked like you've found a way to make it work."

The man studied them for a moment longer, then lowered his rifle and gave a brief nod. "We have," he said simply. "Or at least we try. Come in—if you're honest folk, you'll find welcome enough here. Name's Lars."

They introduced themselves, each taking in the village as Lars led them past a cluster of old houses with makeshift roofs patched with tarps and salvaged wood. Small vegetable gardens, orderly and tended with care, filled every available patch of ground, and the air smelled of herbs and earth, mingling with the faint scent of woodsmoke.

Lars stopped at a large communal fire where a group of villagers gathered, a mix of faces, old and young alike, some with lined faces marked by years of hardship, others with the bright, curious eyes of children. An older woman with a braid of silver hair and a steady gaze approached them.

"Welcome," she said. "I'm Mara. We don't see travelers too often these days, but we're always glad to help where we can."

Hannah's face softened, and she offered Mara a small, grateful smile. "Thank you. It's been a long time since we've seen a place like this."

Mara gestured to the fire. "Sit with us for a while. We'll get you something warm to eat."

The invitation felt like a balm after so many weeks on the road, and they gratefully joined the villagers around the fire. A woman ladled bowls of hearty vegetable stew, thick with potatoes, carrots, and bits of wild greens, passing them around with a quiet smile. They ate slowly, savoring each bite, the warmth seeping into their bones, easing the tightness in their shoulders.

Finn looked up from his bowl, glancing around at the village. "You all live here together? Like a real community?"

Lars chuckled softly. "Took us a while, but yes. We found

each other over time. Some of us just stumbled through. Others heard rumors and made the journey here. We make do with what we have and help each other where we can."

Jace leaned forward. "I don't think I've seen a setup like this since…well, since before everything went to hell."

Mara nodded. "It's not easy, believe me. But we made a choice. Life out there is hard. Together, we stand a better chance. We share what we have and teach each other what we know. It may be small, but it's something."

Saul felt a warmth settle over him, a quiet hope that had become rare. "It's more than something," he said softly, looking around at the faces of the villagers. "It's what's left of humanity."

They spent the day in the village, each of them taking in the simple routines of the people around them. Mara led them through the gardens, explaining how they had learned to grow crops in the poor soil, their methods of trial and error, and old gardening wisdom. Lars showed Saul and Jace how they'd reinforced their shelters, using scavenged materials and even parts of old vehicles to make the houses more resilient to storms.

Hannah found herself chatting with a young woman named Lily, who was gathering herbs in a small patch near the fire. Lily showed her how to identify wild plants, sharing tips on finding food in unlikely places. Hannah listened eagerly, her mind absorbing every detail.

As the afternoon wore on, they gathered by the fire again. Saul and Hannah sat close as they listened to the villagers talk about their lives, their laughter filling the quiet valley with a sound that felt foreign but welcome.

Mara settled down beside them. "You said you're heading for the coast?" she asked.

Saul nodded. "It's just an idea, really," he admitted. "Somewhere isolated, maybe even an island. I don't know if it's possible, but the mainland…it just feels too dangerous. We're hoping we can find somewhere safer, somewhere we can build a life."

"I think I understand," Mara said softly. "Sometimes, to survive, we need to imagine a place like that—a place untouched, where we can start over. It's a powerful thing, that kind of hope."

Hannah glanced at Saul as she reached for his hand. "It's more than hope. It's what's keeping us going."

Mara nodded. "You know, we've often talked about finding somewhere new, somewhere even more secure than here. But this valley has become our home. It's not much, and it's certainly not an island, but it's enough."

"I can see why you'd stay," Jace said. "Places like this…they feel like miracles these days."

Mara smiled. "It's no miracle. Just a few people who decided to fight for each other, even when it seemed impossible. Sometimes, that's all it takes."

As the fire died down, Mara stood and reached into a small pack she carried with her. She pulled out a bundle of dried herbs, a few carefully wrapped packets of seeds, and a cloth bag filled with dried berries and roots. "Take these," she said. "They'll help you on your way."

Finn reached out and took the offer. "Thank you, Mara. For everything."

Mara placed a hand on his shoulder. "Just keep going, all of you. This world can be harsh, but there's still good in it. You've got each other, and you have a vision. Hold on to that."

As they made their way out of the village, the night air cooled around them, and they felt the weight of Mara's words settle over them. The stars stretched above them, and Saul glanced at Hannah, his hand finding hers in the darkness.

"We'll find it," he said. "That place we're searching for. Somewhere we can finally rest, finally feel safe."

Hannah leaned into him. "I believe it," she replied. "And after today…I feel like we're closer than ever."

Chapter 41

The sun was setting behind a distant line of hills when they first spotted her. Standing by a cluster of twisted trees, her figure silhouetted against the fading light, she stood alone in the open field. Her face was shadowed, her posture calm, and as they approached, she held her ground, watching with a steady gaze.

"Hello there," Saul called out.

The woman inclined her head, a faint smile flickering across her face. "Hello. Didn't expect to see anyone out here."

As they got closer, Saul noted her appearance—a little older than Hannah, perhaps in her early forties, with dark hair pulled into a rough braid and a face lined by sun and wind. Her clothes were well-worn but practical, patched in layers fit for the road.

"I'm Nora," she said with a small nod. "Been traveling alone for a while. Just me and my knowledge of plants." She patted a small leather satchel at her side as if it were a trusted companion.

"I'm Saul," he replied. "This is Hannah, Finn, and Jace. We're heading toward the coast."

Nora's expression softened. "The coast…it's ambitious. It's been a long time since I saw the ocean. You think there's something better out there?"

Hannah glanced at Saul. "We think it's worth a shot. Better than staying out here, exposed."

Nora nodded slowly as though weighing her own thoughts. "Can't disagree. And it's not bad company you've got here." She looked at each of them in turn. "Mind if I walk with you for a while?"

Saul exchanged a glance with Hannah and Jace before nodding. "You're welcome to join us. But we take precautions. Everyone pulls their weight, and no one goes off alone without telling someone. Agreed?"

"Agreed," Nora replied. "I've survived this long by being careful. Trust me, I'll follow the rules."

They moved forward, Saul and Nora walking side by side as she pointed out plants, identifying leaves and roots that could serve as medicines or add nutrients to a meal. Her easy humor and steady knowledge fit into the rhythm of their group—her presence was a welcome comfort after so many days of travel.

As night settled, they made camp near a sheltered grove, setting up a small fire to ward off the chill. Nora pulled a few dried herbs from her satchel, showing Finn how to crush them into tea. She explained that this would help with energy and stamina.

"Try this," she said, passing him a steaming cup. "Not exactly gourmet, but it'll do."

Finn took the cup with a cautious smile, sipping it slowly. "Thanks, Nora. It's actually not bad."

Nora chuckled. "A little know-how goes a long way. You'd be surprised at what you can find in the wild."

They sat around the fire that night, sharing stories, their laughter mingling with the crackle of the flames. Nora listened intently as they spoke, her face softening as she absorbed their hopes, their dreams, the vision of the coast they held close. There was something soothing about her presence, a quiet confidence that drew them in and made them feel safe.

Hannah leaned into Saul, her hand resting lightly on his arm as she watched Nora with a thoughtful smile. "It feels nice," she whispered. "Having someone who knows so much about the world around us. Almost like things used to be."

"It does," Saul nodded. "But let's keep our guard up. Just in case."

The fire died down, and one by one, they drifted off to sleep, the quiet of the night settling over them like a blanket. Nora volunteered to take the first watch, reassuring them she'd keep an eye out for any threats.

But when dawn broke, it wasn't Nora's face that greeted them. The campsite was empty, and as Saul sat up, the cold realization struck him—a quick glance around revealed their bags hastily rummaged through, the food stores, and a few other supplies missing.

"Where's Nora?" Finn asked groggily, rubbing his eyes.

Saul's face was grim, his eyes scanning the camp. "Gone. And so is a good bit of our supplies."

Hannah stared—her face paling as the reality sank in. "She took them?"

Jace shook his head. "Looks like it. Damn it...I should've known."

They searched the area, hoping she hadn't taken as much as it seemed. But with each bag they checked, the truth became painfully clear: she'd taken nearly half their food, a few blankets, and even some of the tools Saul kept in his pack.

Finn's face was filled with anger. "We trusted her. She seemed like she was one of us."

"Sometimes that's exactly the kind of person you have to be careful of," Saul said. "She knew how to earn our trust. And we let her."

"We can't let this get to us," Hannah said. "Yes, she betrayed us, but we're still here. We'll find a way to make it work."

Jace shook his head in frustration. "You're right, but damn it…she knew we were struggling. She knew what it would cost us. And she still took it."

"I don't get it," Finn said. "Why would she do that? We helped her. We shared what little we had. Why?"

Saul knelt beside him. "Some people…they only know how to look out for themselves. They've been alone so long that they can't see past their own survival. And it hurts. But that doesn't mean we give up on trusting others. It just means we have to be careful. Smarter."

Finn nodded slowly, though doubt shadowed his face. "It's hard, Saul. Every time we meet someone, it feels like we're risking everything. I don't know if I can keep doing that."

Saul's expression softened. "I know, Finn. And maybe that's what this journey is teaching us. But we don't survive this alone. And if we close ourselves off, then what are we really fighting for?"

Hannah knelt beside them. "Nora's gone, and she took more than just supplies. But we still have each other. And I don't know about you, but that's what I'm holding on to."

"We'll get through this," Saul said as he looked at Hannah.

"Together," she said.

Chapter 42

The days dragged on as they continued their journey. They'd made camp in a small grove off the main trail, surrounded by tall, gnarled trees. The fire was only embers now—the flames carefully smothered to avoid drawing attention. Exhausted from the day's travel, they'd settled down early, feeling the weight of the road in their bones.

Finn was the first to drift off. Jace sat by the fire, head bowed, lost in thought, while Saul and Hannah kept close, whispering softly as they reviewed their plans for the days ahead. The quiet was soothing, lulling them into a rare sense of peace, and for a moment, it felt as though they were the only ones left in the world.

Then Saul heard it—a faint rustling, barely audible, coming from beyond the edge of the camp. He froze, his body tense as he strained his ears, listening intently. It was quiet again, just the whisper of the wind in the trees, but he was certain he'd heard something. He exchanged a glance with Hannah, who had gone still beside him, her eyes sharp.

"You hear that?" he whispered.

Hannah nodded. "Something's out there."

Jace looked up, alert. "What do you think it is?"

Saul shook his head, his gaze sweeping over the darkened landscape. "I don't know. Could be animals…but we should be cautious."

They moved carefully, staying low as they scanned the area, their eyes adjusting to the shadows. The rustling sound came again, closer this time, followed by the snap of a twig. Saul's stomach tightened as he tried to gauge the distance and direction. This wasn't the sound of animals. This was deliberate, calculated movement—someone was out there, watching.

He gestured for the others to get down, signaling for silence as they crouched, their breaths held, listening intently. The sounds grew louder, subtle footsteps moving through the underbrush, closing in around them like a tightening net. A faint whisper carried on the breeze, too quiet to make out the words but enough to send a chill down their spines.

"Raiders," Jace said, his eyes wide.

Saul nodded. "We can't let them know we're here. Get low, stay hidden. Hide the supplies, make it look like we've already left."

They moved quickly as they stashed their packs behind the thick roots of a nearby tree, covering them with leaves and dirt to conceal them from view. Finn stirred, his face filled with confusion as he woke, but Hannah placed a hand on his shoulder, "Stay down," she whispered.

Saul motioned for them to spread out, each finding a spot to take cover, their bodies pressed against the cold ground, hidden among the shadows. The darkness was thick around them, but the faint glimmer of moonlight through the trees cast just enough illumination for them to see the figures moving through the underbrush—four, maybe five men, their shapes blending with the shadows, moving with a predatory caution.

One of the raiders stepped forward. He was tall, his face obscured by a scarf wrapped tightly around his mouth and nose, his eyes dark and searching. He held a knife in one hand, the blade glinting in the moonlight as he scanned the camp, his gaze sweeping over the fire pit and the scattered signs of their presence.

"They've been here," the man muttered.

Another figure stepped forward. "Then where are they?"

The leader narrowed his eyes, his gaze sharp as he surveyed the area. "They're close. I can feel it. Spread out. Find them."

The raiders fanned out as they began to search the area. Saul's heart pounded as he lay perfectly still, his breathing shallow. He caught Hannah's eye from across the camp, her hand resting lightly on the handle of her knife.

The minutes dragged on, each second feeling like an eternity as the raiders moved through the camp, their footsteps crunching softly over the leaves, their voices low murmurs that carried on the breeze. One of them stopped just a few feet from where Finn was hiding, his head turning slowly as he scanned the area, his hand resting on the hilt of his knife. Finn's face was pale, his body pressed tightly against the ground.

Saul's mind raced, his thoughts flashing through a hundred different possibilities, each one more dangerous than the last. If they were found, it would be over in seconds. They were outnumbered, out-armed, and they didn't have the element of surprise. The only chance they had was to remain hidden, to wait it out and hope the raiders would give up.

But the raiders were thorough as they searched every inch of the camp. One of them paused by the tree where they had stashed their supplies, his hand brushing against the leaves that concealed their packs. Saul's heart stopped, his body going rigid as he watched, his mind screaming at him to stay hidden.

The raider's hand lingered for a moment, his gaze sharp as he studied the ground, but then he moved on, his attention shifting to another part of the camp. Saul let out a slow, silent breath, his relief tempered by the knowledge that they weren't out of danger yet.

Finally, after what felt like an eternity, the leader of the raiders stepped forward. "They're not here," he muttered. "They must have left before we got here. Move out. We'll pick up their trail in the morning."

When the last of the raiders had disappeared into the darkness, Saul let out a slow, shaky breath, pushing himself up and glancing around to check on the others. Hannah was already on her feet, moving toward him. "They're gone," she whispered. "For now."

Finn sat up slowly, his hands shaking as he took a deep breath. "I thought they were going to find me. I've never felt anything like that…just lying there, waiting."

"We're safe, Finn," Jace said. "They didn't find us. That's what matters."

But despite Jace's words, the fear lingered as they gathered their supplies. The silence felt heavy, each of them acutely aware of how close they had come to disaster.

As they sat around the fire, Jace's voice broke the silence. "I don't know if I can keep doing this. Every day, it feels like we're just one mistake away from the end."

Saul looked at him. "I know it's hard, Jace. But we can't give up now."

Hannah nodded. "We have to keep believing…keep moving forward."

Jace let out a heavy sigh. "I want to believe that. But sometimes it feels like we're fighting a losing battle."

"We're fighting for something worth holding on to," Saul said. "A place where we can finally stop running. A place where we can be safe."

Finn looked up. "Saul's right. We're all we have. And if we don't keep going, then what was all of this for?"

Jace shook his head. "I don't know, Finn," he said. "But hopefully, it's not for nothing."

Chapter 43

The sky was deep and endless, filled with stars that shimmered in the quiet night. The group had settled around a small fire, its warmth a gentle reprieve from the cool night air, each of them exhausted but content in the calm of the open field. It had been days since they'd had a night like this—no looming trees, no oppressive shadows. Just the stars above and the vast, open world stretching out around them.

Saul glanced at Hannah, catching her eye as they both sat near the fire. She gazed at him as if sharing a silent conversation. After a while, Saul shifted, clearing his throat. "I think we're running low on firewood," he said, glancing at the others. "Hannah, why don't you give me a hand? It'll only take a minute."

Hannah nodded, a smile tugging at her lips. "Sure," she replied, pushing herself to her feet. "I think I saw some branches nearby."

Jace and Finn barely noticed—each lost in their own thoughts, and so Saul and Hannah slipped away from the camp, their figures vanishing into the night. They walked a short distance, moving quietly through the field until the glow of the fire was just a faint, distant flicker. The night stretched around them, open and vast, filled with the sounds of crickets and the occasional rustle of wind through the grass.

When they were far enough from camp, Saul stopped, turning to face her. "Been a while since we've had a moment to ourselves," he said.

Hannah stepped closer, her eyes searching his, her face softening as she took in the familiar lines of his expression. "Feels like forever," she whispered, reaching up, her fingers brushing lightly against his cheek. "But here we are."

He wrapped an arm around her, pulling her close, and they stood there in the darkness, the world falling away as they held each other. His hand slipped into hers, their fingers intertwining as he pressed his forehead gently against hers, his gaze warm and filled with a depth of feeling that words couldn't capture.

He leaned down, his lips brushing softly against hers, a gentle spark that seemed to carry all the words they hadn't yet said. The night wrapped around them like a quiet witness, embracing the bond that had grown stronger with every hardship and every step of their journey. They kissed again, slow and lingering, the weight of the world slipping away as they clung to each other, their breaths mingling in the cool night air.

Hannah reached up, her fingers tracing along the line of his jaw, feeling the familiar roughness that had become a part of their shared life. He held her close, his arms a steady comfort as if he could shield her from all that lay beyond them. In that moment, there was nothing else—just the quiet, the night, and each other.

When they finally pulled back, she looked up, her eyes filled with a tenderness that softened the shadows around them. "When we get to that island..." she whispered, "we'll have more nights like this. No more looking over our shoulders, no more fear. Just us."

Saul nodded, his hand cupping her face as he brushed his thumb across her cheek, feeling the warmth of her skin beneath his touch. "That's what I want more than anything," he said. "To build a life with you. A real one. A place where we can breathe, where we can just be."

They stayed there, wrapped in each other's arms, letting the silence speak for them. The stars above stretched like a canopy, filling the night with a soft light that seemed to blanket them in a rare peace. It felt like a gift, a moment untouched by the world's chaos, just the two of them beneath the endless sky.

Hannah leaned her head against his chest, listening to the steady rhythm of his heartbeat, a grounding presence that reminded her of the life they had fought to protect. She could feel the strength in his embrace, the promise it held. The future felt closer, more real, something within reach rather than a distant dream.

After a long while, Saul pressed a soft kiss to the top of her head, his lips lingering as though he could pour all his hopes into that one touch. "We'll make it there," he whispered.

Hannah smiled. "I'll hold you to that," she said softly.

The night seemed to stretch around them, each heartbeat, each breath, tying them more deeply to one another, creating a moment that felt infinite. At last, with a reluctant sigh, Saul pulled back slightly, brushing a strand of hair from her face. "We should probably get back before they think something's up," he said.

Hannah laughed, her fingers still intertwined with his. "Let them wonder," she replied, holding his gaze for one last lingering moment before they stood up.

They gathered a few pieces of wood to keep up appearances and then made their way back to the camp. As they returned, the others barely looked up, too engrossed in their own thoughts to notice. They settled back in by the fire.

Finn turned to Jace. "Do you think we'll all make it there? To the coast, I mean?"

Jace nodded slowly, his face creased with thought as he looked over at Finn. "I think we have a real shot, kid. And it's not just the coast we're going for—it's what it represents. That island…it's hope. A chance to finally put down roots."

Finn looked at Saul and Hannah. "They give me hope," he admitted. "Watching them…it makes me feel like there's still something worth fighting for. Like maybe there's a place for all of us."

The fire crackled softly as they settled into a comfortable silence, the night wrapping around them like a protective cloak. For a while, they shared stories, each voice weaving a thread into the fabric of their small, makeshift family, their laughter and warmth filling the quiet.

Hannah looked around at each of them, her gaze lingering on Finn and Jace, and then finally Saul. "We've all come so far," she said quietly. "Every step, every choice… it's led us here. And I think, no matter what, this journey has been worth it."

Jace nodded, his face solemn. "There's no question. I can feel it in my bones—reaching that island is worth everything."

Chapter 44

They'd been on the road for days, traveling through the forested hills that seemed to grow wilder with each passing mile. Saul led the way, his gaze sharp as he scanned the path ahead, while Jace and Finn kept close behind, alert to any sound that might signal trouble.

"Think we're the only ones out here?" Jace asked.

"Feels like it," Finn replied. "But we've thought that before."

Hannah suddenly raised her hand, signaling them to stop. "Look," she said, nodding toward the stream just off the path.

A lone figure crouched by the water, her back turned to them as she filled a tin cup. The woman looked lean and strong, her hair tied back with a frayed cloth, and her clothes were worn but sturdy. She moved quietly, with the ease of someone used to being alone.

"Another traveler?" Jace whispered, barely audible.

"Looks like it," Saul replied. "Let's not startle her. We'll approach slowly."

They stepped out from the shadows, keeping their hands

visible to show they meant no harm. The woman tensed at the sound of their footsteps, her hand moving to the knife strapped to her thigh as she turned to face them, her eyes sharp.

"Easy," Saul said, stopping a few feet away. "We're just passing through. Don't want any trouble."

She studied them. "Passing through?" she repeated. "Not many people pass through here anymore."

"We're the rare exception," Saul replied with a nod. "Heading to the coast. We've got a…goal, you could say."

She tilted her head, a faint glimmer of interest sparking in her eyes. "A goal?"

Hannah stepped forward. "We're trying to reach an island—a place we can start fresh. It's kept us moving."

The woman's eyes flicked over each of them, seeming to weigh their words. "An island…" she said. After a moment, her hand lowered from her knife. "I've been out here a long time. A place like that sounds worth the journey."

Jace stepped forward, extending his hand. "I'm Jace. This is Saul, Hannah, and Finn," he said. "If you're interested, maybe you could join us?"

She hesitated, glancing at the horizon before looking back at them. Finally, she took his hand briefly. "I'm Mira," she said. "And…yes, I think I'd like that. Been too long since I had real company."

Saul nodded. "Alright, let's go. We've got some ground to cover. You can tell us your story along the way."

They walked on, and Mira fell into step beside Saul, her eyes focused on the trail. She pointed toward a patch of green near a fallen tree. "See that plant there? Good for stomach trouble. Keep a few leaves on hand just in case."

Hannah moved closer, studying the broad, deep-green leaves. "How'd you learn that?"

Mira shrugged. "Trial and error. You learn fast when you're alone." She picked a leaf and handed it to Hannah, showing her how to roll it between her fingers to release the scent.

Finn lingered at the back. Mira caught his eye and offered a slight nod before standing up. "Guess I haven't convinced you yet, huh?"

Finn shifted, crossing his arms. "It's not personal. Just hard to trust people on the road."

She nodded in understanding. "That's smart. I'd be cautious, too." She looked between him and Saul. "But if I wanted trouble, I'd have picked a different target."

Saul chuckled, glancing back at Finn. "We've had our share of run-ins. But I don't get the sense you're here to make things difficult."

"Nope," she replied simply. "Had enough of that. I'm just looking for…" She paused, considering her words. "Something close to what you're looking for. If you let me tag along, I'll pull my weight."

Jace grinned. "If you're crazy enough to follow us to some far-off island, that's good enough for me."

Finn softened a bit but stayed quiet. They moved onward, Mira taking point and pointing out little details—tiny, often invisible signs she'd learned to read over her years alone.

"Step light here," she warned as they passed through a muddy patch. "Ground's soft; it'll pull you down if you're not careful."

Saul followed her lead, testing the ground with each step. "You really know this land."

"Spent a lot of years with just me and the wilderness," she replied. "The land teaches you to survive if you listen."

Hannah studied Mira's confident movements. "What's the hardest thing about being out here?"

Mira's expression grew distant for a moment. "The silence. It can start to feel heavy, like it's closing in. But you get used to it. Sometimes, it means you're safe. Sometimes…it means something's watching you."

Her words sent a chill through the group, each of them

glancing around the trees. Saul nodded. "We've been there, in a way. That kind of silence sticks with you."

"Out here," Mira said, "the quiet forces you to confront yourself. Every day, you figure out a little more about what you're made of."

As they climbed a steep incline, Finn slipped, his foot catching on a root. Mira grabbed his arm. "Careful. This part's tricky," she said, offering him a quick smile.

Finn pulled back, mumbling, "Thanks," before looking away.

Mira just nodded. "It's only common sense to help each other."

Hannah moved closer to Finn as they walked. "She's not Nora," she whispered. "I get why you're wary, but Mira seems different."

Finn's face softened, though he still kept his guard up. "Maybe. But we barely know her. I just don't want us to get hurt again."

"I know," Hannah said. "But trust is a choice, Finn. Sometimes, we have to take chances."

They trudged on, the incline testing their endurance. When they finally reached the top, Mira stopped, crouching down as she scanned the ground. "Looks like someone was here recently," she said.

Saul knelt beside her, eyeing the faint footprints she pointed out. "Can't be more than a day old."

"More like a few hours," she corrected, glancing up at him. "They were heading south."

Hannah's face tensed. "You think they're close?"

Mira shook her head. "Not unless they've doubled back. But we should keep quiet, just in case."

Jace squinted, scanning the ground but seeing nothing. "How do you know all this?"

Mira pointed to a broken twig, still fresh. "Tiny signs. A broken twig…disturbed soil. You learn to read them if you live long enough."

The group shared a glance, each of them slightly more cautious as they continued. "Thanks for the heads-up," Saul said.

By dusk, they had found a sheltered spot for camp. Mira helped gather firewood and arrange the tents. After they'd eaten, they sat around the fire, each of them absorbed in their own thoughts. Mira leaned back, gazing up at the sky.

Hannah watched her, curiosity finally getting the better of her. "How long have you been alone out here?" she asked.

Mira's gaze didn't waver from the sky. "Since I was seventeen," she said. "I was fifteen when that disease broke out. My parents died because they were starving themselves to feed me. I didn't know they were doing that 'til it was too late. I tried to stick with others at first. That didn't last long. I've been on my own ever since."

Hannah's expression softened. "I'm so sorry, Mira."

Mira shrugged. "It was a long time ago…like what? Sixteen years since they died. I survived because I had to, not because I wanted to."

Jace shook his head. "No friends, no one at all?"

She gave a small, sad smile. "After a while, you stop trying to find people. They don't stick around, and it's easier that way. Less to lose."

Hannah reached over, touching her arm. "You've found us now. It doesn't have to be that way anymore."

For a moment, Mira looked down at Hannah's hand, then met her gaze. "Maybe it doesn't," she said. "Feels strange…good, though."

* * *

The next day, as they made their way through a particularly dense stretch of forest, Mira took the lead. "Stay close," she said over her shoulder. "This part's tricky. Step where I step, and don't make too much noise."

Saul followed her carefully. "It's like you're reading the forest."

"In a way, I am," Mira replied. "Every sound, every shift—it tells you something."

Finn watched her, reluctantly impressed. "How'd you learn to do this?"

Mira glanced back. "Had a few close calls. You learn soon enough."

They reached a river cutting through the forest, and Mira stopped, testing the water. "Freshwater here. Safe to drink."

Jace let out a relieved sigh. "Thank god."

As they refilled their canteens, Finn approached Mira. "I'll admit it…you're better than I thought."

She raised an eyebrow, smirking. "Didn't think I could handle myself?"

"Guess I've just learned not to trust too easily," Finn replied.

Mira met his gaze. "Fair enough. But trust goes both ways. I'm putting my faith in you all too."

Finn hesitated, then nodded. "I'll try to remember that."

They moved carefully along the riverbank, and by nightfall, they'd found a new spot for camp. Sitting around the fire, Mira looked around at each of them. "Funny," she said softly. "I didn't think I'd ever find good people again."

Saul looked up. "We're glad you found us, Mira. You seem to belong here with us."

Jace raised his cup in a mock toast. "To our guide, who knows more than the rest of us combined!"

They laughed, and for a moment, the burdens of the road felt lighter. Even Finn smiled faintly, nodding at Mira.

"Guess you're stuck with me," Mira said.

As their laughter faded, the warmth lingered. The fire crackled softly as they settled down and drifted off, wrapped in their blankets as the fire burned low.

Chapter 45

The industrial site loomed ahead. Rusted metal beams jutted from crumbling buildings, their outlines jagged against the gray sky. Empty windows stared like hollow eyes, and vines crept over the concrete walls, slowly reclaiming the abandoned structures. It was the kind of place that had once pulsed with life and noise but now stood silent, left to decay.

As they walked through the narrow paths between the buildings, their footsteps echoed faintly, swallowed by the oppressive stillness. Finn shivered, glancing around. "I don't like this," he said. "Feels like something's watching."

Hannah nodded, her eyes scanning the surroundings. "It's eerie," she said. "But we need to rest, even if it's just for a short while. We've been pushing hard these last few days."

Mira looked around. "Places like this…they feel heavy. Like they're holding memories."

Saul nodded, gesturing toward a partially intact awning. "We'll rest here," he said. "Everyone stay alert. Keep your weapons close, and don't wander off. We move out as soon as we've regained some energy."

They set down their packs and huddled together, trying to ignore the chill that seemed to seep from the walls. The place felt unnatural as if memories of those who had once worked there lingered like ghosts in the air. They took quiet sips from their water and nibbled at small portions of their dwindling food stores. The silence was thick, making every creak of metal and every whisper of wind feel amplified, feeding their unease.

Just as they were beginning to relax, a faint shuffle echoed through the empty corridors. Everyone froze, turning toward the sound. Saul stood up slowly, his hand on his knife, his gaze fixed on a shadowed figure emerging around the corner of a crumbling wall.

The man who appeared was thin, his clothes tattered, and his hair unkempt. His face was pale and gaunt, his eyes hollow, filled with a haunted, almost manic intensity. He stopped when he saw them, his gaze sweeping over their weapons, their packs, and the small circle they'd formed.

"Travelers," he muttered. "Didn't think I'd see any of you in these parts. Thought they'd all gone. Thought I was the last."

Hannah stepped forward cautiously. "Are you alone?" she asked. "Do you need help?"

The man let out a harsh laugh. His eyes drifted over the site as if searching for something lost. "Help," he said. "No one can help. Not out here. Been alone too long. No one cares."

Mira stepped in. "We care," she said. "We're trying to survive, like you. Maybe we can help each other."

The man's gaze shifted to Mira, but he shook his head slowly. "They all say that. But in the end, people only care about themselves."

Saul exchanged a glance with Hannah, his hand still hovering near his knife. "We're just passing through," he said. "We don't want any trouble. We're just trying to find a place where we can start over."

The man's eyes narrowed. "A better place?" he repeated. "That's just a dream, a lie they tell themselves so they don't lose hope. No one escapes."

The words hung heavy in the air, darkening the silence. The man's face twisted as if he were wrestling with memories too painful to bear. "I tried to trust people once," he continued, his voice cracking. "Thought we'd make it, thought we'd find something better. But they turned on me and left me with nothing. People don't care. They only care about themselves. The rest of us are just shadows."

"Maybe he's right," Finn said. "Maybe we're just chasing a dream. Maybe there's nothing better out there."

Hannah shook her head. "No, Finn. We're not like that. We have each other, and that's more than he had. We're not just shadows."

Mira stepped closer to Finn. "He let his pain consume him, Finn. We can't let that happen to us."

The man laughed, his voice bitter. "That's what they all say. They think they're different, that they're better. But when it comes down to it…when survival is on the line…they show their true colors. I watched it happen. Friends, family—they all turned. In the end, it's every person for themselves."

Saul's face hardened. "We're not like that," he said. "We've come this far together, and we'll keep going. We don't abandon each other."

The man's gaze softened briefly before fading back into cold emptiness. "Believe that if you want," he muttered. "But I've seen too much, lost too much. There's nothing left."

He staggered back, his eyes distant, as if retreating into memories only he could see. His shoulders slumped, his body seeming to collapse inward, and he turned away, disappearing into the shadows as silently as he'd come, leaving them alone once more. The group sat in stunned silence, his words echoing in their minds.

Finn looked down, his hands clenched into fists. "Maybe he's right," he whispered. "Maybe this is all just hopeless."

Jace placed a hand on Finn's shoulder. "He's been through hell, Finn. But that doesn't mean he's right about us."

"We have each other," Mira said. "As long as we have that, there's hope."

"That man lost his faith," Hannah said. "He let the darkness consume him."

Saul nodded. "I don't know what happened to him, but it's not our fate. We're heading to the coast, and we're not turning back."

Finn looked around at each of them, his expression softening. "Okay, then. I guess we'll just keep going."

They gathered their things and moved forward. As the ruins faded behind them, they held tightly to their dream, their faith rekindled, their hope renewed. They would reach the coast, find the island, and prove that even in the darkest places, there was still light, still something worth fighting for.

Chapter 46

The days had grown harsher, each one taking a heavier toll. They moved through rolling hills and forested paths, where birds flitted overhead and patches of wildflowers dotted the landscape. Despite the abundance around them, finding food remained a challenge. Edible plants were sparse, and small animals darted away at the slightest sound, leaving them to ration what little food they had left.

As they walked, Finn stumbled slightly, his face pale. "I don't think I can keep going like this," he said. "We need something, anything."

Saul looked back at him, noticing the exhaustion etched into each of their faces. Jace's eyes were rimmed with fatigue, and even Hannah's usually bright gaze seemed dulled by worry. He knew they were all struggling—hunger clawing at their insides. They found a sheltered spot in a small clearing surrounded by trees and settled down to rest.

Jace finally broke the quiet. "We can't keep going like this," he said, looking at each of them. "If we don't find food soon, we're not going to make it to the coast."

Hannah nodded, worry in her eyes. "We've tried everything, but the animals here are fast, and we don't have much to trap them with. We need to think of something."

Finn looked up. "What are we supposed to do?" he asked. "Are we just supposed to keep starving?"

"There are other people out here," Jace said. "People like us, trying to survive. If we came across someone with food, someone who's better off than we are…we could take what we need."

Saul clenched his jaw. He knew what Jace was implying and understood the desperation that drove him to say it, but it felt like a line that, once crossed, could never be undone. "We're not those kinds of people, Jace," he said firmly. "We don't take from others just because they might have more. That's not who we are."

"We are just trying to survive," Jace replied. "If it's a choice between us and someone else, maybe it's time to do what's necessary."

Saul shook his head. "There's another way. We keep moving, we find food, we adapt. But we don't turn on others just to make our lives a little easier. That's not the kind of people we've been, and I'm not letting us become that now."

"I don't want to lose who we are either," Hannah said quietly.

Jace's face twisted with frustration. "Survival doesn't care about principles, Saul," he muttered. "Sometimes you have to be ruthless."

Saul met Jace's gaze. "Maybe you do, but we're better than that," he said. "I won't let us become the kind of people who prey on others. Not now, not ever."

Silence fell over the group as Saul's words sank in. Finn looked at the ground, nodding slowly. "He's right," he said. "If we lose who we are, what's the point?"

Jace's expression softened. "I just don't want us to starve."

"We won't," Saul said. "We'll find a way."

Mira, who had been watching the tree line, pointed ahead. "I saw rabbit trails a few yards back by those bushes."

"Well, that's a start," Saul said. "Why don't you go set some snares, and we'll call it a day and set up camp."

"Sound's like a plan," Mira said. "Be back soon."

They watched as Mira slipped into the forest, then they moved to a nearby clearing to set up camp. Moments later, she returned, dusting off her hands.

"The traps are set," she said. "We'll check them in a few hours. If luck's on our side, we'll have dinner tonight."

Finn glanced at Saul. "What Jace mentioned earlier…about taking from others. Do you think it'll ever come to that?"

Saul looked away. "I don't know, Finn. I really hope not."

Hannah reached over, resting a hand on Saul's arm. "I don't want us to lose who we are," she said. "Not to this."

"Neither do I," Saul replied, taking her hand gently.

As dusk settled over the clearing, Mira stood, glancing toward the traps. "I'll go check the snares," she said, nodding to Saul. "Care to join me?"

He stood up, following her through the trees. When they reached the first snare, she smiled, gesturing to the ground where a small, gray rabbit lay caught in the trap. "One down," she said.

Saul watched as Mira crouched down, resetting the snare. He shook his head. "You make it look easy," he said. "I had a rifle back when all this started, but we ran out of ammo a long time ago. We were staying at a cabin, no longer moving, so scavenging for more ammo stopped. I used what I had left on a couple of deer and small game. Hannah and I had to learn how to trap, but…well, let's just say we weren't naturals."

Mira looked up. "Trapping isn't easy to learn. Guessing you still made it work, though."

"Barely," Saul replied, chuckling. "We survived, but it was rough. It's clear you know what you're doing."

She shrugged as she finished resetting the snare. "It's just been me for a long time, so I didn't have much of a choice. If I wanted to eat, I had to figure it out." She stood, brushing dirt from her hands. "But you've done more than just survive. Trust me, not everyone makes it as far as you have."

Saul nodded. "I guess we got by on luck as much as anything else," he said. "But I'm glad you're here to keep that luck going."

She smiled, tilting her head toward the next snare. "Let's see if we can get you a better meal than luck alone."

By the time they returned to camp, they had two rabbits, their small bodies a welcome sight after days of near-starvation. Jace let out a relieved laugh, and his face filled with gratitude as he looked at Mira. "You really know what you're doing."

Mira shrugged. "It's just something I've picked up over the years."

They set up a small fire, the smell of cooking meat filling the air as the rabbits roasted over the flames. The warmth and the scent brought a sense of comfort that had been missing for days. They sat close to the fire as they ate slowly, savoring each bite. The meal was simple, the meat barely seasoned, but to them, it was a feast. The tension from earlier melted away, replaced by a sense of unity.

When they had eaten their fill, Finn leaned back with a satisfied smile on his face. "It's amazing how different things look when you're not starving."

Hannah laughed softly. "Guess we're lucky Mira came along," she said. "I don't know what we'd do without her."

Mira glanced down, a hint of humility in her expression. "We all bring something to the group. It's not just me."

Saul nodded, "This… it's what keeps us going."

The fire burned low as the forest around them fell silent. One by one, they settled in and drifted into sleep.

Chapter 47

Saul moved cautiously at the front of the group; each footfall placed carefully on the narrow, winding trail. The forest felt strange tonight—like it was watching them. He could tell the others felt it, too; their movements were tense, hands hovering near weapons, each of them looking for a danger they couldn't yet see.

Jace, who was bringing up the rear, paused, his fingers tapping lightly on the handle of his club. "This place feels wrong," he muttered. He glanced over his shoulder, then around the shadowed forest.

"I don't like it," Mira agreed, her gaze scanning the tree line. "It's too quiet like something's waiting for us."

Saul was about to respond when a sudden rustling to their left caught his attention. In an instant, the silence shattered. Branches cracked, bushes rustled, and six figures emerged from the shadows.

"Raiders," Saul said under his breath, feeling his muscles tense. He gripped his knife, adjusting his stance.

The tallest raider, a man with a thick scar running across his cheek, stepped forward, a sneer on his lips. "Looks like we caught ourselves some prize travelers," he said. "Hand over your supplies, and maybe you get to walk out of here."

Saul's gaze hardened as he met the raider's eyes. "We're not giving you anything," he said. "If you want a fight, you'll get one."

The raider laughed, tightening his grip on his club. "So be it," he snarled, signaling his men forward.

The raiders lunged, and chaos erupted. Saul reacted quickly, sidestepping a blow aimed at his head. He slashed low, his knife sinking deep in the raider's thigh. The man howled, stumbling back, clutching his leg as Saul stepped back, resetting his stance.

Beside him, Hannah ducked under a raider's swing. She jabbed her elbow into his ribs. As he staggered, she followed up with a swift kick to his knee, causing him to collapse.

A third raider lunged at Finn, who raised his club, blocking the blow. He was visibly shaking, but he held his ground, his eyes fierce. He managed to deflect another strike as he kept his stance, refusing to back down.

Mira was darting in and out of the fray. She sidestepped a swing, retaliating with a sharp jab to his side. When he staggered, she took advantage, striking his knee with a hard kick that sent him down. She didn't wait, shifting immediately to face her next opponent.

Then, a sharp cry cut through the chaos—Saul turned just in time to see Jace falter, clutching his side. One of the raiders had landed a deep strike, and blood seeped through Jace's fingers, staining his shirt.

"No!" Mira's voice rang out, raw with emotion. She broke away from her fight, rushing to Jace's side. She caught him just as he began to sink to the ground, her hands pressing over his wound in a desperate attempt to stop the bleeding. Blood seeped between her fingers, and her face was pale as she looked down at him."

"Jace, stay with me," Mira said. "You're going to be fine.

We'll get you through this."

A raider saw her distraction and closed in. Finn moved without hesitation, stepping between Mira and the raider. He swung his weapon as he held off the strike.

"Stay away from them!" Finn shouted. He forced the raider back, his grip tightening on his club.

Saul watched as the raiders hesitated—frustrated by their resistance. Taking advantage of the pause, he lunged forward, tackling the closest raider and pinning him to the ground. He landed a solid punch to the man's jaw, followed by another to his gut, leaving him winded. Rolling away, Saul jumped back to his feet, knife in hand.

The raiders regrouped, and with a few muttered curses, they began to retreat, slipping back into the shadows, their figures quickly lost among the trees.

The clearing fell silent once more, but the air was thick with tension. Saul surveyed his friends, his heart pounding as he took in their battered faces. Then his gaze fell to Jace, slumped in Mira's arms, his face ashen and slick with sweat.

Saul knelt beside him. Blood soaked Jace's shirt, the edges of the wound jagged and raw. "Jace," he said, urgency in his voice. "We'll patch you up. You're going to be okay."

Jace gave a faint, tired smile, his voice barely a whisper. "Don't lie to me, Saul. I've...I've seen wounds like this before. It's bad."

Hannah knelt on his other side, her hand resting on his shoulder. "You're strong, Jace," she said, her voice trembling. "You'll pull through this."

But Jace's gaze held a quiet resignation. "Even if I do...I won't be able to keep up," he said. "You know that."

Mira's face crumpled, her eyes welling with tears as she held him close. "You can't just leave us," she whispered. "We need you."

Jace's hand reached up, his touch light on her arm. "You're

strong, Mira," he said, his gaze soft and filled with warmth. "Stronger than you know. You'll get them to that island. That's what matters now."

"There has to be a way," Finn said. "We can carry you, help you. We'll figure it out."

Jace shook his head slightly, looking at each of them, his gaze lingering on Finn. "Listen to me," he said. "This island…you can't let anything stop you—not even me."

Saul clenched his jaw, feeling the weight of Jace's words settle over him. "Jace," he began. "We can't just…leave you."

Jace's fingers tightened around Saul's arm. "Saul," he said, "I'm done for here. I'm not going to make it. All of you need to move on and stay strong."

Hannah reached out, taking Jace's hand in hers, tears glistening in her eyes. "We'll make it there," she whispered. "We'll make it for you."

Jace nodded. "That's all I ask. Get there…find the peace we've all been looking for."

They stayed with him a little while longer, each of them sharing quiet, final words. But when the time came to go, each step felt like a burden, a part of themselves being left behind. They continued to walk as the sun dipped lower. They would carry his memory forward, a tribute to the friend who had helped them this far and to the hope he had given them, even in his final moments.

Chapter 48

The village emerged slowly from the afternoon haze, its quiet, worn structures nestled between rolling hills and bordered by lines of overgrown hedges. From a distance, it looked almost untouched by the world's collapse—like a place frozen in time, sheltered from the storms that had swept across so much of the land. The village wasn't much, just a handful of houses with faded paint and sagging roofs, but there was something welcoming in the way they leaned together, clustered as if in quiet solidarity.

As they approached, Saul felt a pang of both caution and yearning, the need to protect his group mingling with a deep, quiet ache for something familiar, something kind. It had been so long since any of them had seen kindness from a stranger.

"Think anyone's home?" Finn asked.

"There's smoke," Saul replied, pointing to the thin, gray curl rising from the chimney of a house. "Someone's definitely here."

They moved forward slowly, stepping over the cracked cobblestone path that led to the center of the village. Doors opened, and people began to appear, eyes peeking out from behind worn curtains and open doorways, watching them with guarded curiosity. Then, from the house with the smoking chimney, a man and woman stepped out, their faces lined with age and sun but softened with a gentleness that felt foreign after so many weeks on the road.

The man raised his hand in greeting. "Good afternoon, travelers," he called, his voice warm and deep. "You're just passing through?"

Saul exchanged a glance with Hannah. "Yes," he replied, taking a small step forward. "We've been traveling for…well, longer than I'd like to count. We're hoping to find a place to rest for the night if it's no trouble."

The woman, her eyes bright despite the weariness etched into her face, nodded. "You look like you've had a long journey," she said. "We don't have much, but you're welcome to stay with us. A meal, a bed—we're happy to share."

It was so rare, so unexpected, that for a moment, none of them could respond. Hannah's face softened, a faint, grateful smile tugging at the corner of her mouth as she met Saul's gaze. "We'd be grateful," she said.

The couple introduced themselves as Earl and Elara, leading them into their small home at the edge of the village. The house was modest, the walls lined with worn quilts and old, handmade decorations, shelves filled with jars of preserved food and trinkets that hinted at lives lived with quiet purpose. The smell of something savory filled the air, the warmth of the fire adding to the coziness of the room. It felt like a sanctuary, a momentary refuge from the cold, unrelenting world beyond.

Elara gestured for them to sit at the long wooden table, her hands steady as she ladled steaming bowls of stew, thick with vegetables and chunks of tender meat. The aroma was almost intoxicating, and Saul watched as Finn and Mira settled at the table.

Saul and Hannah sat together, their hands brushing under the table. Saul glanced at her, his gaze lingering, noting the faint lines of exhaustion that creased her face, the way her eyes softened in the firelight.

"Feels strange, doesn't it?" he whispered, leaning in so only she could hear. "To be somewhere with other people who are so kind."

Hannah's eyes met his, and she nodded, her gaze filled with a depth of feeling that words couldn't quite capture. "I almost forgot what it feels like," she replied.

After the meal, Earl showed them to a small room in the back of the house. It was simple, with a bed covered in a worn but clean quilt, a small table beside it, and a window that looked out over the fields, where the last of the daylight was fading into twilight.

"We don't get many travelers these days," Earl said. "Especially since we're nestled away out here in the middle of nowhere. But you're welcome here. It's nice to see new faces. I hope you can rest."

As he left, Saul and Hannah stood in the quiet of the room, absorbing the stillness and the privacy. The walls were thin, and the sounds of the household murmured faintly around them—Elara humming softly in the kitchen, Finn and Mira talking in low voices in the next room. It was an unexpected intimacy, this little slice of quiet, and Saul felt a surge of gratitude, a longing that he hadn't let himself feel in so long. Hannah set her pack down and turned to him, her hand reaching up to rest against his cheek.

"It's strange," she said. "Having a room…just for us."

Saul's hand covered hers, pressing it gently to his face as he closed his eyes. "Feels like we're borrowing a memory from the cabin," he whispered.

She smiled. "Maybe it's not just a memory," she said quietly. "Maybe it's a promise. A reminder that we can have this again someday."

He opened his eyes, meeting her gaze, and in that moment, the world outside faded. It was just the two of them standing together in this small, quiet room, sharing a moment that felt both ordinary and monumental. He wrapped his arms around her, pulling her close, his lips brushing softly against hers. They stood together, letting the warmth of their embrace banish the cold, letting themselves believe, if only for a moment, that they were safe.

The world beyond the walls of this room ceased to matter. The fears, the losses, the betrayals—all of it faded in the face of this connection, this quiet sanctuary they had found in each other. When they finally pulled back, they lay together, side by side, wrapped in each other's arms, their bodies fitting together as though they had been carved for this very moment. Saul held her close, his fingers tracing gentle patterns on her back, his breath warm against her hair.

As they drifted into sleep, he could feel the quiet intimacy of her presence, grounding him in a way he hadn't felt in so long. Here, in this room, he felt a peace he hadn't thought possible, a sense of belonging that reminded him why he fought, why he endured.

* * *

Morning came, and they woke to the smell of bread baking over the fireplace. They dressed quietly, reluctant to leave the comfort of the bed. Elara and Earl welcomed them to the table where Mira and Finn were already waiting. They ate in silence, the atmosphere warm with an ease and familiarity that made them feel, just for a moment, as though they were part of something whole and real.

As they prepared to leave, Saul tried to offer Earl a few of their remaining supplies in gratitude, but the older man shook his head with a gentle smile.

"We don't need payment," he said. "Just remember there's still good in this world. That's payment enough."

Hannah's eyes glistened with tears as she looked at Elara, her voice filled with quiet gratitude. "You've given us more than a meal. You've given us more hope."

Elara's smile was soft, and her gaze was kind. "Then take that hope with you," she said. "And when you reach your destination, remember us. We'll be here, holding on to the same faith that kindness is still worth offering."

"Thank you for everything," Mira said with a smile.

Elara nodded. "You are very welcome, my dear."

After saying their goodbyes, they set off, their footsteps leading them back to the open road. As the village disappeared behind them, Saul reached for Hannah's hand. They still had miles to cover before reaching the coast, but the thought of finding small communities like this along the way sparked a quiet hope in him. If places like this could survive, maybe humanity still had a chance to rebuild—to find its way back to something close to normal.

Chapter 49

The landscape had become rougher as they moved deeper into the foothills, the ground uneven and littered with rocks, each step a calculated risk. The air was dry, filled with the scent of earth and pine, and the trail was narrow, winding around steep inclines and sudden drops. They were already exhausted and their bodies sore from days of relentless travel, but the terrain forced them to push on.

Mira was in the middle of the line, just behind Finn, her eyes scanning the ground, trying to avoid the loose rocks that littered the path. But the trail was unforgiving. Just as they rounded a sharp turn, Mira's foot caught on a jagged stone, her ankle twisting painfully as she stumbled, a sharp cry escaping her lips before she fell to the ground.

The group froze, turning to see Mira crumpled on the rocky path. Saul was at her side in an instant as he helped her sit up. "What happened?" he asked.

She winced, pressing a hand to her ankle. "I must have

stepped wrong," she muttered, her face pale as she shifted her leg. "Feels like it's twisted or something. It hurts to move."

Hannah knelt beside her as she examined Mira's ankle, which was already beginning to swell. "It's definitely sprained," she said. "We need to get you off your feet, at least for a few days."

Mira looked up, worry etched on her face. "But we can't stop now," she said. "We're low on food, and we need to keep moving."

Saul looked between them and nodded. "I'll go set some snares," he said, giving Mira a reassuring smile. "You showed me how to do it right, remember? I'll bring back enough to keep us going while you rest up."

Mira nodded. "Well, at least one of us can still trap," she said.

"Don't worry," Saul said. "If I don't get anything, I'll just blame your training."

Mira laughed. "Hey, I trained you well," she said. "Now go get those rabbits."

Saul headed out to set some snares, returning shortly after with a handful of berries he'd found along the way. "Mira, can you check these?" he asked, holding them out.

Mira examined the berries, nodding. "They're safe. Finn, go ahead and gather more if you're up for it. These will be a good addition."

Finn nodded, grateful for something to focus on. As the rest of the group worked to set up camp, they found a small clearing tucked between two large boulders that offered protection from the wind. Hannah and Saul helped Mira settle on a blanket, her ankle propped up on a makeshift pillow of folded clothes, while the others gathered firewood from what the forest had to offer.

After a couple of hours, Saul went to check the snares. When he returned, he carried a rabbit and two squirrels, which he held up with a quiet smile of accomplishment. "Looks like we'll have a decent meal tonight," he said.

They quickly skinned and prepared the game, cooking it over the fire. The aroma of roasting meat mixed with the earthy scent of the berries Finn had foraged. As they ate, the fire crackled softly. The warmth seemed to settle over them, momentarily easing the weariness from days of walking and tending to each other's needs. They all knew how lucky they were to have found food tonight, and even Mira managed a faint smile despite the pain in her ankle.

When they had finished, the group began to drift off to their makeshift beds. Saul and Hannah lingered by the fire as the others settled in. They both felt the responsibility that had grown heavier with each mile they traveled, a weight they shared but rarely spoke of. They walked a short distance from the camp, just far enough to talk freely without disturbing the others.

Saul leaned against a tree, arms crossed, as he looked out into the forest. "Feels like every step forward comes at a cost," he said. "Every choice we make…it's like we're gambling with something we can't afford to lose."

Hannah nodded as she glanced back toward the camp. "I feel it, too. It's like they're not just following us. They're depending on us to hold everything together, even when we're barely holding on ourselves."

Saul sighed, rubbing his temples. "Sometimes I wonder if I'll make the wrong call…if one mistake will be the thing that costs us everything. It's hard not to think about."

Hannah met his gaze. "We're doing everything we can, Saul. You're doing everything you can. They trust you, and so do I. For now, that's enough."

Her words settled over him, a quiet reassurance that eased the tension he hadn't realized he was carrying. They stood together in silence for a few moments, listening to the night sounds. After a while, they walked back to the camp. They settled down beside each other, the stillness of the night gradually easing them into sleep.

* * *

Over the next few days, they took turns keeping an eye on Mira's injury, carefully rationing their supplies, and catching small game when they could. Each meal, though modest, became a small victory, a necessary effort to keep up their strength. They moved slowly, supporting Mira as she hobbled along, helping her through rough patches in the terrain. As they were preparing to break camp, Saul noticed the swelling in Mira's ankle had gone down, and her steps more confident though still cautious. With a nod of approval, he gathered everyone together.

"We've made it through a tough few days," Saul said, meeting each person's gaze. "We're still here, still moving forward."

Hannah nodded, reaching for his hand and giving it a steady squeeze. "Let's go get that island now."

Saul turned toward the trail, setting off with a determined stride as the others fell into place behind him. With every mile, the weight of responsibility settled on him, but he knew he'd do everything to bring them all safely to the coast. Moving forward as one, they pressed on, each step drawing them closer to what lay ahead.

Chapter 50

The climb had felt endless, each step laden with exhaustion and silent aches. They had been pushing through dense foliage and uneven ground for days, with the promise of the coast as their only fuel. Now, as they crested the final ridge, the landscape opened before them like a revelation, filling them with a raw, collective relief.

Ahead lay a vast expanse of mist-draped coastline, where the endless blue of the sea met the rugged shore. The sight was almost too much to take in as if it were both dream and reality blurred together. Saul halted, and for once, the hard lines of his face softened. This vision of the ocean—felt like the beginning of everything he had imagined in his quietest, most vulnerable moments—a place that might hold answers or perhaps simply a place to breathe. Hannah stepped up beside him, her hand slipping onto his shoulder. Together, they stood in silence as they took in the scene before them.

"Look at that," Finn said. "It's…beautiful."

Saul nodded. "We've come a long way," he said quietly.

"Do you think it's as close as it looks?" Finn asked.

"Closer than it's ever been," Mira replied.

They lingered in the moment, each one processing what it meant in their own way. Saul finally turned, scanning the ridge for a suitable spot to set up camp for the night. "Let's find a clearing," he said, glancing at the others. "We'll need a plan for tomorrow."

Once their camp was set up, they shared a meal. The rations were sparse, but no one complained. As the light began to fade, they gathered to discuss the details of their next steps.

"The coast could be full of surprises," Saul said. "If anyone's left, if there are settlements or groups nearby…we need to be cautious. We can't assume the coastline's safe just because it looks untouched. Things have a way of hiding just beneath the surface."

Hannah nodded. "We'll need to stay off the main paths until we're sure it's clear. Maybe split up once we're closer so we don't all risk exposure at once. We can't afford to lose anyone."

"What about supplies?" Finn asked. "We've been careful, but we're running low. If there are people, maybe they'll have something to trade."

"Or something to take," Mira added. "Not everyone's going to be friendly. We've seen that before."

After a long pause, Saul nodded. "We'll scout carefully. Tomorrow, we split into two groups and survey from different angles. No one takes unnecessary risks. If we sense trouble, we retreat. This far along, we're not gambling with anyone's life."

A murmur of agreement passed through the group, and the tension eased just enough for a hint of relief to settle over them. As they prepared for sleep, the atmosphere around them softened, the weight of their caution momentarily lifting. Saul felt the ocean air settle into his bones, refreshing something deep inside that he hadn't acknowledged in a long time.

"When we reach the island," he said, breaking the quiet, "when we finally get there…it'll be a place where we can stop running. A place we can make ours. We'll be more than just survivors.".

"I wonder what it'll be like," Finn said. "A place to live, I mean…really live."

Hannah glanced at him. "It will be our own paradise," she said. "We'll make it work, one way or another. We're not going back. This is it."

Saul nodded. "We've got each other, and that counts for something. Maybe more than we realize."

"Still," Finn said, rubbing the back of his neck, "what if we run into others at the coast, and they're…less than welcoming?"

Hannah let out a soft laugh. "Like we'd just pack up and leave after all of this?"

Mira smirked. "If we can handle each other, I'm pretty sure we can handle anyone else. We're practically experts at survival now."

Saul raised an eyebrow. "I don't think anyone's giving us badges for that."

Finn chuckled. "Maybe we'll make our own badges when we get there. 'Expert Survivors' or something. Give each other titles."

Mira shook her head. "Finn, if we give you a title, it would be 'Chief Worrier.' You're always the one talking about what could go wrong."

Finn sighed. "Someone has to think about those things! I mean, if we're not careful, we could—"

"—fall off a cliff or get attacked by wild animals!" Hannah interrupted. "That's why we're still here, right? Because of our 'Chief Worrier' keeping us on our toes."

Finn rolled his eyes. "You're welcome, by the way. I'll take that title as long as it means we keep making it to the next day."

Hannah looked over at Saul. "So, what's your title, then?" Saul thought for a moment, a rare smile creeping onto his face.

"I think I'll just stick with 'Saul.' Titles sound like a lot of responsibility."

"Too late," Finn said, grinning. "You're already responsible.

We follow you, don't we?"

Saul nodded. "Yeah, I guess so." He paused, looking around at each of them. "But we've all made choices that kept us here, kept us alive. It wasn't just me."

Hannah reached out, her hand resting on his arm. "You're right, but you're the one who's kept us moving forward. We might not say it often, but we wouldn't be here without you."

Saul absorbed her words, letting them sink in. He wasn't used to gratitude, but tonight, it felt like something he needed to hear.

"So," Mira said after a while. "what's the first thing everyone wants to do when we get to the island?"

Hannah closed her eyes, leaning back with a sigh. "Sleep. For days. And without keeping one eye open."

Finn grinned. "I think I'll go for a swim. Haven't been in water that wasn't freezing in…I don't even remember how long."

Mira laughed. "You'd swim the second we get there?"

"Why not?" Finn replied. "After all this, I think we deserve a little celebration."

"What about you, Saul?" Mira asked. "First thing you'd do?"

Saul paused, taking his time. "I think I'd just stand there. Really look around, take it in. We've spent so long just fighting to get to tomorrow. I don't want to forget what it feels like to reach something real, something we chose."

Hannah leaned forward. "And after that?"

Saul chuckled softly. "After that…maybe a swim doesn't sound so bad."

They all laughed, the sound of it surprising in the stillness of the night. It was rare for them to share a moment like this and even rarer to let themselves imagine what the future might actually hold. They sat by the fire, talking into the night, sharing stories and memories that hadn't surfaced in months, letting themselves finally imagine what life could be beyond survival. The ocean's steady rhythm accompanied them, a quiet reassurance in the dark, as if it, too, knew they had come a long way. And under the stars, they allowed themselves to believe—just a little—in the future that waited beyond the dawn.

Chapter 51

They rose with the first light, gathering their packs in silence. Saul cast a glance back at the trail they'd left behind, a landscape now miles and days away. Ahead lay the coast, its promise pulling them forward.

As they began the descent, Saul's voice cut through the silence. "Let's stay sharp. We're close, but we don't know what's down there. We just keep to our plan. Mira, lead the way. Keep your eyes open."

Mira moved to the front, her steps quiet as she navigated the uneven trail with ease. They had fallen into a rhythm over the weeks. Finn lagged a step or two behind, his pack nearly overwhelming his lean frame, but his determination pushed him onward.

They descended slowly, each step calculated, each sound drawing their attention. Around midday, with the coast faintly visible between breaks in the rocks, they rounded a bend and stopped short. Saul's hand shot out, motioning for everyone to halt.

Below them, perhaps fifty feet away, sat a lone figure—a woman perched on a rock, scanning the horizon with a quiet intensity. Her hair was streaked with gray, and she wore a faded jacket that had seen better days. She hadn't seen them yet, her back turned to their vantage point.

"Someone's there," Finn said.

Hannah's hand tightened on Saul's arm, her eyes locked on the woman. "What do we do?"

"Stay quiet," Saul replied. "Finn, stay back. Mira, don't take your eyes off her. Any sign she's not alone, and we're gone. We can't take any chances."

They crouched, watching the woman in silence, trying to assess the situation from afar. After a moment, she shifted as if sensing them. She looked up, her gaze snapping to their position, her eyes meeting Saul's with a guarded calm.

Finn muttered under his breath, "Guess we're not hiding now."

Saul took a steady breath, signaling for the others to hold back. He stepped forward, careful but open, his hand hovering near his side. "Are you lost?"

The woman's eyes swept over them, one by one. There was a quiet tension in her stance, like someone used to being on guard. "No," she replied calmly. "Just…alone."

"What's your name?" Saul asked

"Lyla." She met his gaze directly, then briefly glanced toward Hannah, seeming to take in every person in the group. "You're not from around here."

Saul gave a slight nod. "Just passing through. We're headed to the coast."

Lyla smiled. "You really think you'll make it?"

"We'll worry about that," Hannah said.

Lyla raised her hands in a gesture of peace. "Fair enough."

A quiet tension settled over them as Saul studied her face, gauging her intentions. "Are you really alone?"

"As alone as one can be," she answered. "Haven't seen anyone out here in months. Most who come through don't stay long. The coast doesn't have much to offer."

"Why are you still here, then?" Finn asked.

Lyla glanced at him, then back at Saul. "I don't have much left to lose. Nothing better calling me back. But I know the coast… well enough to survive here." She paused, letting her words settle. "Maybe I could help you."

Hannah crossed her arms, watching Lyla carefully. "And why should we trust you? For all we know, you could be hiding others out here."

"If I were hiding something, I wouldn't be standing here talking to you, would I?" Lyla said. "Besides, I don't need your trust. I'm just offering what I have."

Saul raised a hand, quieting the group. He looked at Lyla thoughtfully. "We've come a long way to get here and met some good people and…some who weren't so good. So, yeah, we're a bit cautious right now. If you're coming with us, stay where we can see you. No wandering, no surprises."

Lyla nodded, her face relaxing slightly. "I wouldn't expect anything less." She took a step back, giving them space. "Besides, the coast isn't as safe as it looks. I can help you avoid trouble, but you'd be smart to keep your guard up."

Hannah gave Saul a slight nod, and he turned to the group. "All right. Lyla, you walk with us. But remember—no tricks. If there's anyone else out here, we need to know."

"Understood," she replied, moving into step beside them as they resumed their descent.

As dusk approached, they reached a plateau where the rocks broke into a small clearing. Lyla stopped, motioning toward a group of boulders up ahead.

"Good place to camp," she suggested. "Not visible from below, and the ground's stable. It's safe…for now."

Mira crossed her arms. "Convenient."

Lyla didn't flinch. "Just offering my two cents. You can take it or leave it."

Saul considered her for a moment, then nodded. "We'll camp here." He dropped his pack and gestured to the others to do the same. "But keep watch."

They settled in slowly, each one taking on a watchful stance. Saul kept his eyes on Lyla, who sat cross-legged on a rock, her gaze steady on the coastline beyond. Once the camp was set, they ate a sparse meal in silence, each person listening for any sound beyond the clearing.

Finally, Lyla broke the quiet. "Where are you headed, really?"

Saul looked at her, then at Hannah, who gave him a small nod. "We're looking for a way across to an island off the coast."

Lyla's face shifted, a flicker of interest passing over her eyes. "An island? You think there's something better out there?"

"That's the idea," Hannah replied. "A place to live without looking over our shoulders. Somewhere safer."

Lyla smiled. "Sounds almost too good to be true."

"It's a chance," Saul replied. "And it's better than what's here."

She gave a slow nod, her eyes thoughtful. "I've been on my own for years. Got a little shack nestled not too far from here. Nothing fancy…just a small room and a cot."

Hannah studied her face. "You sound like someone who's given up on finding something better."

"Not given up," Lyla replied quietly. "Just learned to get by with less. It's what you do to survive."

Finn spoke up. "Do you really think it's possible, then? Reaching an island?"

Lyla met his gaze. "Depends. It'll take everything you have… maybe more. But if you're all still here, still pushing on…that's a strength not everyone has."

Saul glanced at the others, sensing that Lyla's hard-earned wisdom might just be the edge they needed. But for tonight, her guarded companionship was enough. As they lay down under the darkening sky, each of them drifted into sleep with the same thought—a fragile hope, a sense that despite everything, they were one step closer to the life they had imagined.

Chapter 52

As dawn broke, a quiet excitement hummed in the air. The faint sound of waves drifted up from below, mingling with the scent of salt and earth, urging them forward. They had been close to the coast for days, catching glimpses of the ocean through the trees and over hills. But today, they knew, was different. Today, they would reach it.

Saul adjusted his pack and glanced at the others. Finn was wide awake, eyes bright with anticipation, and Hannah looked quietly resolved. Mira, as always, wore her steady, focused expression, though Saul could see the slight lift in her gaze as she scanned the path ahead.

"Let's keep moving," he said. "The beach is close."

Lyla nodded in agreement. "The coast is not always friendly. I've seen traps set up by folks guarding old territory—fishing lines rigged to nets, shards of glass hidden in the sand. Don't let the view fool you."

Mira gave her a skeptical glance. "Convenient how you know

so much about the coast, isn't it?"

Lyla shrugged, seemingly unfazed by Mira's suspicion. "I'm still here, aren't I?"

As they descended, the landscape began to change. The dense brush gave way to patches of sand and low shrubs, and the smell of salt grew stronger.

"Not much grows out here," Lyla said, crouching by a patch of green near a rocky outcrop. "But you learn to make do. This one here," she pointed to a small cluster of leaves with pale purple flowers, "won't fill you up, but it'll take the edge off hunger if you chew on it."

Finn bent down and picked a leaf, eyeing it before placing it in his mouth. He made a face as he chewed. "Tastes like dirt."

"Better than starving," Lyla replied.

They moved carefully around a dense cluster of thorny undergrowth, each one navigating the path to avoid injury. Saul took the lead here, hacking through the vines and thick brush with his knife, clearing a way for the others to follow.

"Let me," Finn offered, stepping forward.

"Go ahead," Saul said, stepping back.

Finn hacked at the vines, sweat dripping down his brow as he cleared a narrow path. Mira and Lyla followed closely, keeping an eye on the surroundings. Finn glanced over his shoulder at Saul, a small smile of satisfaction on his face as he cleared the final vine.

"Not bad," Saul said, clapping him on the shoulder as he passed.

A few steps beyond the thicket, they stumbled upon an abandoned campsite. The sight gave everyone pause. A small ring of rocks marked an old fire pit, long extinguished, with charred bits of wood scattered around. Nearby lay the remains of a rusted fishing hook and a tattered tarp, half-buried in the sand. It was clear someone had been here, though how long ago was hard to tell.

Hannah crouched beside the fire pit, sifting through the ashes with a stick. "Doesn't look fresh. Could have been here for years."

"Or months," Mira countered, scanning the area. "Could be someone who still uses it."

Lyla shook her head. "There would be signs if that was the case. Footprints, maybe. Fresh tracks."

Saul studied the site, a faint unease prickling the back of his neck. "We don't take any chances. Don't touch anything, and stay close."

They moved past the abandoned camp, leaving it undisturbed. As the afternoon wore on, the dense thicket finally gave way to an open expanse. Before them lay a wide, sweeping beach, the sand pale and untouched, stretching toward the horizon. The ocean stretched out beyond, its waves rolling gently against the shore, calm and unbroken.

Saul stopped, his breath catching slightly as he took it in. The beach felt both familiar and surreal as if he were stepping into a memory he had never lived. Hannah stood beside him, her eyes bright with wonder.

"Look at it," Finn whispered. "It's…it's real. We're really here."

Saul placed a hand on Finn's shoulder, feeling his energy like a spark. "We made it this far, and that's something. But we still need to be careful."

Lyla nodded, her gaze distant as she looked over the beach. "Could be empty…could be full of threats. We don't know who or what might come through."

Saul surveyed the area, his mind running through the possibilities. "We'll camp near the rocks," he said, nodding toward a cluster of large boulders at the edge of the beach.

They set up camp as dusk began to fall. They gathered by the fire, each one gazing out toward the ocean, the vast expanse that promised so much. Lyla sat a little apart from the group, her eyes distant as if the sight of the beach had stirred memories she kept tightly guarded.

Hannah broke the silence. "So, what's the plan, Saul?"

Saul looked at her, then at the others. "We find a way across. Tomorrow, we start looking for anything that can float."

"Float?" Finn asked, eyebrows raised. "You mean like a boat?"

"Or pieces of one," Saul replied. "Or anything we can make into one."

Lyla nodded thoughtfully. "Fiberglass, wood…if it's big enough and it floats, it can get you across."

Finn grinned. "So, we're going to make a boat?"

"Something like that," Saul said. "Or fix one up if we find one worthy. But first, we find what's here. We don't get ahead of ourselves."

As the fire crackled, they each sat quietly, the vastness of the journey ahead settling over them. The island felt close now, close enough to touch.

Chapter 53

The morning sun rose over the beach, casting a soft, golden light across the sand. The rhythmic sound of the waves against the shore was a strange lullaby, both calming and unsettling. Saul took in the sight of the coast stretching ahead, its serene beauty contrasting sharply with the urgency they all felt.

"Today, we spread out along the shore," Saul announced to the group gathered around him. "Keep an eye out for any boats big enough to carry us all. Anything that looks seaworthy." He gave each of them a steady look. "And stay close. No wandering off."

Hannah nodded, glancing around to catch the eyes of those in the group. "Let's stay within sight of each other. We've made it too far to risk getting separated now."

"Do you think we'll actually find a boat?" Finn asked.

"I think we'll find something," Saul replied. He turned to Lyla, who stood scanning the shoreline. "You know this place. Any advice on where to look?"

Lyla shaded her eyes with her hand, squinting into the

distance. "If we're lucky, we might find something washed up around the bends in the shoreline. Small harbors and inlets tend to catch what the tide drags in. If there's a boat, that's where it'll be."

With Lyla's guidance, they moved in pairs along the beach, scanning for any sign of wreckage or vessels pushed ashore by the elements. Saul's group took the lead, moving across damp sand, eyes sharp for anything unusual among the driftwood, seaweed, and shells.

They were rounding a bend when Finn's voice rang out. "Saul! Over here!"

Saul followed Finn's pointing finger, and his heart gave a small leap. Just beyond a cluster of rocks and tucked into a shallow inlet was a large yacht, its hull tilted at an angle, partially buried in the sand. The white fiberglass was weathered and dulled, but the boat itself looked mostly intact, as though it had simply waited out the years, sheltered by the cove.

Saul quickened his pace, and as he drew closer, he could see that the yacht was substantial—large enough to hold them all, with a cabin spacious enough to protect them from the elements. The hull, though scuffed and worn, was solid.

"This could work," he said. "It's almost too big, but it could work."

Hannah, Mira, and Lyla joined them, each assessing the boat. Mira circled the hull, running her hand along the sides. "It's got its scars, but it's in surprisingly good shape. We might have actually caught a break."

Finn's gaze turned to Saul, hopeful. "Do you think we can get it moving?"

Saul shook his head. "Not with the engine. After all these years, we won't have any fuel."

Lyla climbed onto the deck and surveyed the yacht, her eyes tracing the remaining rigging and mast. "It's a sailing yacht, after all. We've got the framework here; we just need to patch up the sail. If we find some tarp or fabric sturdy enough, it could work."

Saul nodded, his eyes sweeping over the boat, assessing its potential. "Then we gather supplies. If we're going to make this seaworthy, we need ropes, tarp, and anything we can use to reinforce the hull."

They split into smaller teams, each one setting off in different directions along the coast. Saul, Hannah, and Mira went north along the beach, searching for any remnants of past life—campsites, huts, or any signs of people who might have left something useful behind.

It wasn't long before they stumbled across an old fishing hut, half-buried in sand and tangled in vines. Saul approached cautiously, motioning for the others to hang back as he pushed the creaking door open. Inside, the air was thick with the scent of damp wood and decay. The hut was sparse, with only a few crates and a sagging wooden table.

Saul pried open one of the crates, uncovering coils of frayed rope and a large, faded tarp that looked battered but intact enough to hold up under the wind. He lifted the tarp, inspecting the material.

"Hannah, Mira," he called.

Hannah ran her fingers over the tarp, nodding. "It's a bit worn, but this could work for patching the sail."

Mira tested the rope's strength with a tug. "This will help reinforce things on the boat. If we're careful with it, it should last."

They loaded the tarp and ropes, gathering up what they could carry before heading back to the yacht. When they arrived, Finn and Lyla were already there, unloading their own small stash of supplies: a few more pieces of tarp, some metal scraps that could be used for patching, and a set of rusty but functional tools left behind at an abandoned campsite.

Lyla laid everything out. "Not much, but it's a start."

Finn, however, was grinning. "With what we've got, we can make this work, can't we?"

Saul nodded. "It'll take effort, but yes. Every bit we've got will help.”

The group spent the day working steadily under Lyla’s guidance, focused on patching the sail and reinforcing the yacht.

“See this spot?” Lyla said, pointing to a particularly worn section of the sail. “We’ll layer the tarp over it like this.” She laid the tarp down and pressed it firmly, making sure it covered the weakened area. “Make sure to stitch it tight around the edges.”

Finn nodded, following her lead. “Got it,” he said, threading his needle with concentration. “These patches are really going to hold, right?”

“As long as you double them up in the thinnest places,” Lyla replied, patting his shoulder. “And don’t rush it—one solid patch is better than two flimsy ones.”

Mira leaned closer, inspecting her own patch. “Like this?” she asked, showing Lyla her work.

“Perfect,” Lyla affirmed, smiling. “Just keep it steady. That’ll hold even if we hit rough winds.”

Meanwhile, Saul and Hannah worked on the deck, securing loose areas with ropes and patching up small gaps with scraps of metal they’d salvaged.

“Think we’ve got enough rope?” Hannah asked, tying off a section near the hull’s edge.

“Barely,” Saul replied, giving the knot a firm tug to test it. “But we’ll make do. Every bit of this boat’s going to count.”

Hannah nodded, glancing up at the patched sail. “They’re doing a good job up there. Looks stronger already.”

Saul followed her gaze, watching as Finn and Mira added the final patches under Lyla’s direction. “Solid and reliable—that’s all we need it to be,” he said, a note of quiet pride in his voice.

That evening, they gathered around the yacht. Saul looked around at the group, feeling a renewed sense of hope. “One step at a time,” he said. “Tomorrow, we’ll keep at it. We still have a lot of patchwork to do.”

They sat together in the fading light, the sound of waves

creating a rare sense of calm. As darkness descended, each of them found a place to rest for the night, knowing the hard work still ahead. For tonight, they had a boat—weathered, patched, and imperfect, but it was theirs—a fragile vessel carrying not just the weight of supplies but the faint promise of freedom.

Chapter 54

The next few days went by in a blur. The group worked from dawn to dusk, reinforcing the yacht, gathering provisions, and making their final preparations for the journey. The boat was patched and ready, but they needed every bit of food, water, and supplies they could gather to sustain them on the open water. Beneath the weariness etched on each face was a shared sense of purpose. Tomorrow, they'd leave the mainland behind, taking their first steps toward a new life.

"Today's about gathering what we can to survive the crossing," Saul said, scanning the group's faces. "We'll set some snares in the woods and bring back water from the stream. Stick together and stay alert. Let's not take any risks."

They nodded in quiet agreement, splitting into smaller teams. Finn and Hannah moved inland toward the woods, setting snares and checking for signs of small game, while Saul, Mira, and Lyla made their way to a nearby stream, each carrying a container to fill with fresh water.

By midday, the group had begun to trickle back to the beach with their supplies. Finn and Hannah returned with a few rabbits caught in the snares, which they dressed and prepared for a fire that evening. The water containers were filled and stowed away on the boat, ready for the journey. It wasn't much, but it was enough to get them through the first days.

As they were sorting through the supplies near the boat, the sound of footsteps caught their attention. Saul looked up, signaling to the others to stay alert. Three figures approached from down the shore—a woman in the lead, with two men just behind her.

Saul stepped forward, keeping his expression neutral, his hands in plain sight. "Hello," he called out. "Something we can help you with?"

The woman's gaze was direct as she studied him. "We've been watching you work on that boat these past few days," she replied. "Curiosity got the better of us. Thought we'd see what was going on."

"I'm Saul," he said simply, nodding toward the yacht. "We're preparing to leave."

The woman's interest sharpened. "You're leaving the mainland?"

"It's a risk," Saul admitted. "But staying here isn't much safer."

"I'm Talia," she said. "This is Leo, and that's Callum. We've been scraping by out here, same as you, I'd guess. Care to have a few more?"

Talia's calm, direct approach put Saul on guard. He could feel the tension ripple through his own group, and he knew they all shared the same wary curiosity.

"You've been watching us," he said. "But we don't know anything about you. If we let you join, it would have to be under a few ground rules."

Talia didn't flinch. "Fair enough. We're not looking to take anything from you. Just curious about what you were planning."

Hannah stepped up beside Saul. "It's a hard journey. And if we bring more along, we all need to be able to pull our weight. No hiding, no holding back."

Leo, standing beside Talia, nodded. "We've got supplies of our own," he said. "We're just looking for a chance to get away from here."

Callum, quiet until now, spoke up. "We've been on this coast long enough to know there's nothing left for us here." He looked toward the boat with a hint of longing. "If you're heading to someplace safer, we're willing to do our part."

Saul exchanged a glance with the others. They needed all the hands they could get, but there was no room for uncertainty or half-hearted commitment. "If we let you join, it's because we're trusting each other. Out there, there's no room for second-guessing."

Talia nodded, her gaze steady. "Understood. And we're willing to help with the last of the preparations."

With a silent agreement, the group fell back into their routine, with Talia, Leo, and Callum joining the efforts. They helped prepare the fire, adding what little they had to the evening's provisions. Leo, careful and methodical, worked with Finn to clean the snares and set new ones nearby, adding to their food stores for the journey. Talia worked alongside Mira, inspecting the ropes and water containers on the boat, ensuring everything was secured.

By dusk, they gathered around the fire, sharing a modest meal of roasted rabbit and boiled stream water. The newcomers blended in quietly, joining the subdued conversations as stories were exchanged in low voices. Talia shared brief accounts of her group's survival on the coast while Leo and Callum filled in small details —how they'd scavenged for supplies, tracked game, and kept their small camp secure. It was clear they were skilled, resourceful, and familiar with the harsh realities of life here.

After a lull in the conversation, Finn broke the silence, looking across the fire at Talia. "So…do you think there's really something out there?" he asked.

Talia looked into the flames, her expression thoughtful. "I don't know for sure," she admitted quietly, "but if there's even a chance, I think it's worth taking. There's nothing left here for any of us."

Callum nodded in agreement, his gaze shifting toward the boat. "We've scoured this coast, searched every lead. It's time to move on."

Saul listened, feeling the weight of the decision they'd all made. He looked around at his group—newcomers and friends alike—seeing the same exhaustion and determination in each face.

"Tomorrow," Saul said finally, "we leave this place behind. Whatever's out there, we'll take it on together. No turning back."

Leo raised his water bottle in a toast. "To new beginnings."

When the fire dimmed, Saul looked around the circle, feeling a rare swell of gratitude for the people surrounding him. "Get some rest," he said quietly.

The group nodded, each finding a spot around the dimming fire, settling into the cool sand as night enveloped the beach. The gentle murmur of waves blended with the crackling of the last embers, creating a soothing backdrop that lulled them, one by one, toward sleep.

Saul lay back, pulling Hannah close as they gazed up at the stars. The vastness of the night sky stretched above them. For a while, neither spoke, content to let the silence fill the space between them.

Then Hannah shifted slightly, her voice soft. "It's strange, isn't it?" she whispered. "To see everyone together like this. To have more than just us here."

Saul nodded, brushing a strand of hair from her face. "We started with just us and an idea," he said. "Now…it's more than an idea. It's real. They're all here because they believe in it, too."

She rested her head against his shoulder, smiling faintly. "Maybe that island isn't so far off after all."

Chapter 55

Saul and Hannah moved through the group, rallying everyone for the final preparations. The air buzzed with a mix of anticipation and anxiety; they were on the edge of a new beginning, but the weight of the unknown lay heavy over them.

"All right, everyone!" Saul called. "Let's do one last check on supplies and remember your roles. Today, we make this happen." He turned to Hannah, whose expression reflected his own determination tempered by caution.

Hannah gave a brisk nod. "And stay focused," she reminded the group, her gaze scanning their faces. "We've been over the safety protocols—work together, and we'll make it."

They moved into action, each person taking on their task. Saul supervised as they began digging a narrow trench from the shoreline to the boat. Their plan was simple: dig the trench while the tide was low, then wait for the incoming water to fill it, creating a channel deep enough to buoy the boat.

"Keep it steady!" Saul urged as they dug, heaving sand to the side with shovels and makeshift tools. Finn worked beside him, his energy unwavering despite the effort. Mira and Lyla gathered supplies by the boat, securing their packs with determined faces. Nearby, Talia and Leo reinforced the boat's rigging while Callum studied the map and looked at the compass they had found while scavenging.

As the trench neared completion, they watched the horizon, waiting for the tide to rise. The minutes stretched into an hour as the ocean inched closer, and finally, water began trickling down the channel. Slowly but surely, it filled, creeping up toward the yacht.

"We're getting there," Hannah said.

The water rose higher, filling the trench and reaching the hull. Bit by bit, the boat began to lift, rocking slightly as the incoming tide worked its way under the hull. Saul directed everyone to stand by, ready to secure the yacht as it floated free of the sand.

"Hold steady!" he called. They gripped the boat's sides, guiding it as it swayed gently, the tide giving them just enough lift to maneuver it. Just as they were about to make final adjustments, a shout broke through the rhythmic sound of waves.

"Wait! Don't leave yet!"

Saul turned, squinting at the figures approaching along the shore. A surge of adrenaline hit him as he recognized the man leading the group—Colm, a member of Elara and Earl's community. Behind Colm were nine others, their faces tense and weary but determined.

"Colm!" Saul shouted, motioning them closer. "Help us get this secured!"

The group surged forward, and Saul quickly directed Colm to a large piece of driftwood nearby. "Tie the boat off to that driftwood—it's anchored deep enough to hold!" he called, his voice urgent as the rising tide lifted the yacht higher. Colm and his group moved swiftly, securing the ropes around the driftwood as others steadied the boat.

After the boat was stabilized, Saul turned to Colm. "What's

going on, Colm?" Saul asked. "What are you doing here?"

Colm's expression was strained. "Saul," he said. "We need your help. Raiders invaded our community. They took everything."

Hannah stepped forward, her eyes wide with concern. "What about Elara and Earl?" she asked, her voice trembling slightly.

Colm shook his head. "They didn't make it...along with others. They were killed. We managed to escape, but..." His voice faltered as he took a deep breath. "We're all that's left."

The words hung in the air like a thick fog, and Saul felt a knot tighten in his chest. He looked at the survivors behind Colm, each face marked by fear.

"Tell me what happened," Saul urged.

Colm's face darkened as he recalled the events that had unfolded. "It was early morning. We were still sleeping when the first cries went up. At first, we thought it was just another wild animal, maybe a boar or something. But then we heard them—shouting, shouting like demons. Raiders."

His hands clenched into fists at his sides. "They stormed in without warning. I grabbed Elara and Earl and told them to gather the others, but it was chaos. People were trying to flee, but they were already inside."

Colm's voice broke, and for a moment, he looked lost in the memory. He took a deep breath, forcing himself to continue. "They started setting fires. I thought we were going to die there, trapped between the flames and their blades. I managed to grab a few of us, but the others...they were taken or killed. I saw Earl try to fight back, but they overwhelmed him."

Saul could see the pain etched on Colm's face, the burden of survivor's guilt weighing heavily on his shoulders. "I'm so sorry," he said. "You did what you could."

Colm took a deep breath, regaining some composure. "We fled into the woods, but they pursued us for a while. We had to hide among the trees, waiting for the sun to rise and the chaos to settle. When it was finally quiet, we moved. I thought we'd lost everyone, but we found each other—just a few of us who managed to escape."

Hannah looked at Saul, and in that moment, they both understood the gravity of their situation. This was not just a journey toward survival; it was a fight to reclaim their lives.

"Join us," Saul said. "We're setting sail. We'll leave this place once and for all."

Colm glanced back at his group, then nodded, relief washing over his features. "Thank you. We don't have anywhere else to go."

With their group now larger, Saul realized the logistics of their departure had changed dramatically. "We need to gather more supplies before we can leave," he said. "Instead of eight, we now have eighteen. Let's make the most of the day. A small group can go out to set snares to get more game for the trip. The rest of us will focus on getting more tools and supplies. Whatever we left behind before, get them now."

The group sprang into action, urgency replacing the initial excitement. Hannah paired with Talia and Leo to search the nearby bushes for anything they could forage, while Saul led Finn, Mira, and Callum back toward their previous campsite, hoping to scavenge what they could from the remnants of their last days on land.

As they moved, Saul felt the weight of leadership pressing on him. The reality of Colm's news was a stark reminder of how fragile their existence had become. The people who had once been part of their lives, their homes now reduced to memories, were gone. They were all that remained—a band of survivors bound together by shared struggle.

In the distance, the sun dipped lower as they gathered supplies. Saul kept his focus as the pressure continued to build within him. They set up camp on the beach, working together to prepare a simple meal, their conversations punctuated by the crackling of the fire and the distant roar of the ocean.

As they ate, Saul listened as Colm recounted the beauty of

their community before the raid, how laughter once filled the air, and how children played in the streets without a care.

"Earl always said that as long as we had each other, we could rebuild anything," Colm said. "But it's hard to believe that now. All that's left is ashes."

Hannah placed a comforting hand on Colm's back. "We're all here together now. We can build something new, but it will take time."

Colm nodded, but the pain in his eyes remained. "I wish Earl were here to see this. He always had a plan, a way of bringing people together."

"Tomorrow, we set sail," Saul said. "It will be a long journey, and we need to be ready. We're not just surviving anymore; we're moving toward a new life."

Hannah nodded. "Tomorrow, we take the first step toward a new beginning."

Chapter 56

As dawn broke, Saul moved swiftly through the group, performing a final check on the supplies and equipment. They couldn't afford any delays—the tide was coming in, and the time to leave was now.

"Finn, double-check those ropes," he instructed.

"Aye, Captain!" Finn joked, grinning as he set to work.

"Mira and Lyla," Saul continued. "Make sure all provisions are secured. We can't afford to lose anything overboard once we're moving."

The sun climbed higher as the tide inched closer, slowly filling the trench they had dug the day before. The water crept up, and the group remained focused, each person preparing for what was to come. Colm approached Saul by the edge of the trench, watching as the yacht rocked gently, the rising tide lifting it bit by bit.

"I still can't believe this is happening," Colm said. "After everything, we're really about to leave."

"It feels surreal," Saul agreed.

Finally, with the water high enough to support the boat, they felt the full weight of it lift as it floated freely, anchored only by the ropes tied to the driftwood. Saul gathered everyone one last time.

"This is it," he said. "Once we're moving, stay close and keep communication open. If something feels wrong, speak up immediately."

Each person took their position, waiting for the final signal. Saul moved to the helm, gripping the wheel as Hannah stood beside him, her gaze focused on the horizon.

"Are you ready?" he asked.

"More than ever," she replied.

When the tide had fully lifted the yacht, Saul gave the signal. "Release the ropes!"

Colm and his team untied the driftwood anchor, and the yacht drifted free, rocking gently on the open water. With everyone on board, the boat settled, and a collective sigh of relief mingled with anticipation.

As they edged away from the shore, the cries of seagulls echoed overhead. Soon, the familiar shoreline faded, and the vastness of the ocean stretched out before them. As they moved further from the shore, Saul could feel his heart race. The realization that they were finally embarking on this new journey was thrilling, but the unknown loomed large in his mind.

"Look at that!" Finn shouted, pointing at a pod of dolphins leaping joyfully alongside their boat.

Laughter bubbled up among the group. The sight of the playful creatures was a reminder that life continued even out here.

Hannah smiled. "They seem to be welcoming us," she said, her eyes sparkling. "Maybe they know we're starting a new adventure."

"Let's hope they bring us luck," Talia chimed in, her voice bright as she leaned over the edge to look. "I could use some good fortune right about now."

As they navigated through the calm waters, the initial excitement began to settle into a rhythmic routine. The morning wore down, and each person found their place aboard the vessel.

The sky darkened ominously, and Lyla squinted, noticing the shift in the weather.

"Everyone, keep an eye on the horizon," she called out. "We might be in for a change."

A tense silence fell over the group as they exchanged worried glances. The water, once calm, began to churn slightly. Hannah moved closer to Saul. "What do you think is coming?" she asked quietly.

"Hard to say," Saul replied, scanning the clouds. "We need to stay vigilant. The sea can change in an instant."

Just as he spoke, a gust of wind whipped across the deck, sending a shiver through Saul. The temperature dropped, and the once playful dolphins vanished into the depths, leaving an eerie stillness in their wake. Saul's heart raced as the boat began to sway, the gentle rocking morphing into something more forceful.

"Everyone, brace yourselves!" he shouted, his voice cutting through the rising wind. "Secure everything! We need to be ready for whatever comes next!"

As if in response to his warning, the sky opened up, and rain began to pour down in heavy sheets. The sound of water crashing against the boat was deafening.

The group sprang into action, shouting commands and securing loose items as chaos erupted.

"Saul, I can't see!" Finn yelled, his voice strained with panic.

"Stay close to me!" Saul shouted back, fighting against the wind as he kept the boat steady. "Hannah, help Finn with the ropes! Colm, keep an eye on the horizon! Everyone else, get below deck!"

Saul gripped the steering wheel tightly, his knuckles white as he fought to maintain control. "We need to head into the waves!" he shouted above the roar of the storm. "If we let them hit us broadside, we'll tip over!"

Hannah moved beside him. "I'm with you," she shouted. Together, they adjusted the boat's course, aiming to cut through the waves rather than against them.

The rain fell in torrents, but they pressed on. Just when it felt as though the storm might swallow them whole, the winds began to die down, and the rain eased to a steady drizzle. The waves calmed slightly, but the ocean remained choppy. Saul exhaled, realizing how tightly he had been holding his breath.

"Is everyone alright?" he called out, his voice hoarse but steady.

"I think so!" Hannah replied, shaking water from her hair as she glanced at the others. "We just need to catch our breath."

They took a moment to regroup, standing on the deck and surveying their surroundings. The once-stormy ocean was now a mix of rolling waves and calm patches as if the sea itself was breathing a sigh of relief. Saul couldn't help but feel a sense of triumph wash over him.

"We made it through," he said, looking around at his companions. "That was one hell of a test, but we did it."

The group erupted into relieved laughter, the tension of the storm lifting like fog in the afternoon sun. Even Finn, his face pale from the fear of the storm, managed a shaky grin. "Can we get a little more excitement next time?" he joked.

As they continued to navigate the now calm waters, Saul felt a renewed sense of purpose. The storm had tested them, but they had emerged stronger, more united. They had faced a challenge together, but they were still far from their destination. As the sun dipped lower in the sky, Saul steered the boat into a more stable course. The night was approaching, and he knew they needed to make decisions about where to anchor for the evening.

"Let's keep moving until we find a safe place to rest for the night," he called out. "We can't let our guard down just yet."

As the sun finally set, the sky darkened around them, and the stars began to emerge, twinkling like beacons of hope in the vast expanse of the night. As night enveloped them, they sailed into the unknown. The journey was just beginning, and Saul felt a spark of hope ignite in his chest. They were still alive and surviving what this world had to offer.

Chapter 57

As the days passed at sea, the tumultuous waves began to settle into small pockets of calm, allowing the weary group a chance to catch their breath. The mornings greeted them with gentle sunlight spilling across the deck, illuminating the faces of those who had weathered the storm together. Each sunrise felt like a new beginning, a moment to regroup and refocus.

Saul stood at the helm, surveying the horizon. The water was a tranquil blue, dotted with patches of sunlight that danced upon the surface. He could hardly believe they had made it through the worst of it.

"Hey, Saul!" Finn called. He was leaning over the side of the boat, watching the wake trail behind them. "Look! The fish are jumping!"

Saul chuckled, turning to join him. "They're probably happy to see calmer waters, too," he replied.

As Saul glanced around, he noticed Elise—one of the survivors from Colm's group—joining Finn's side. She watched the lively movement of the fish, her expression softening. "They seem to be enjoying themselves," she remarked, a warm smile spreading across her face as she took in the scene.

"They're lucky they can swim," Finn replied. "I wish I could swim like that."

"You'll get your chance once we find land," Elise encouraged. The two had grown closer during their time at sea, finding comfort in each other amidst the uncertainty. Finn often sought her out, and Elise, with her gentle demeanor, offered him reassurance as they faced the vast unknown together.

They spent the rest of the day in their routines, falling into a rhythm that felt strangely normal. Each person had a task, and each task had its own quiet importance. The steady flow of their day was a welcome change, a reprieve from the chaos they had faced just days earlier. The endless horizon no longer seemed like a barrier but rather a path guiding them forward.

As the sun dipped low on the horizon, Saul gathered everyone around the deck. The soft glow of twilight and a cool breeze brushed across their faces, carrying with it the faint scent of saltwater.

"I think it's time we share some stories," he suggested. "We've all come from different places, and it might help us to get to know each other better."

Hannah nodded in agreement. "It can be therapeutic. We're in this together, after all."

The group settled into a loose circle, their faces illuminated by the last light of the setting sun. Finn, always eager, spoke up first. "I'll go first," he said, glancing at Elise beside him. "I grew up in a small town by the river. My dad taught me how to fish there." He paused. "I remember the first time I caught a fish. It was bigger than my arm!"

"What kind of fish?" Colm asked.

"Uh, I think it was a bass!" Finn replied, laughing. "But it got away before I could even get it to the shore."

"I grew up in a place surrounded by mountains," Mira chimed in. "I loved hiking up the trails, finding hidden waterfalls. It felt like my own little world, away from everything." Her eyes glistened as she spoke.

"I miss the mountains," Colm admitted. "I was a ranger once, you know. I spent years patrolling the forests, ensuring people respected the land."

"Really?" Talia asked. "I didn't know that about you, Colm."

He shrugged, his expression shifting. "I've been many things. But out here…" he gestured toward the endless sea, "it feels like I'm just floating, without purpose."

Saul sensed the vulnerability in Colm's tone. "You have a purpose," he said gently. "We all do. We're navigating toward a new life together."

As the stories continued to flow, a newfound bond began to form among them. Colm shared tales of his family and his home, a place filled with laughter and love, while Hannah spoke of her childhood dreams of adventure and exploration.

Elise, who had been quiet, finally spoke up. "I didn't have a normal childhood," she began. "We moved around a lot after…" She hesitated, but Finn encouraged her with a nod.

Elise took a deep breath, continuing, "After my parents divorced, my mom and I lived in a different place almost every year. I was always the new kid, trying to fit in." She smiled wistfully. "But I found comfort in books. They took me to places I'd never seen."

"That's wonderful," Mira said. "Stories can take us anywhere, even when we're stuck."

"I'd love to hear some of those stories," Finn said with a grin.

"That sounds like a great idea," Hannah agreed as she looked at Elise. "We can create our own stories, too, as we go."

As night fell, the stars began to twinkle overhead, casting a comforting light against the vast expanse of the sea. They settled down for the night, each person lost in their thoughts, feeling the gentle sway of the boat beneath them. Saul lay awake beside Hannah, feeling the weight of responsibility settle over him like the darkness. Even as they grew closer as a group, he couldn't shake the feeling that danger still lurked somewhere on the horizon.

"What are you thinking about?" Hannah whispered.

"I'm worried about what lies ahead," he admitted. "We're navigating an unpredictable world, and I don't want to let anyone down."

"You won't," she assured him, her hand resting gently on his. "You've brought us this far."

He searched her face, finding comfort in her steady gaze. "We have to stay strong. For them."

Hannah nodded. "And we will."

They lay there in silence, feeling the presence of the others around them. Though they had all forged bonds that would last a lifetime, each member of the crew was acutely aware of the precariousness of their situation.

As Saul finally drifted into sleep, he clung to the hope that they would make it to the land they dreamed of, a place where they could rebuild, find peace, and, most importantly, build a life with Hannah worth living.

Chapter 58

The last few days had offered them a rare peace, but tonight felt different—a charged tension hung in the air, wrapping around the crew like a heavy, invisible shroud. Each person sensed it, moving quietly as they worked to ready the boat.

"Everyone!" Saul called out. "We have a storm on the way. I need everyone to secure supplies and hunker down. Move quickly!"

The urgency in his voice snapped the crew into action. Finn and Elise exchanged worried glances before scrambling to gather loose items on the deck. Mira rushed to the cabin, her hands moving swiftly as she ensured everything was stored properly. Colm moved with purpose, his earlier vulnerability replaced by stoic determination. Nearby, Talia and Leo worked side by side, tension tightening their expressions as they checked the ropes around supplies.

"Saul, how bad do you think it's going to be?" Colm asked.

"I don't know, but we need to be ready for anything," Saul replied. "Let's secure everything and brace ourselves."

The wind began to howl, and the ocean churned beneath them, transforming from a gentle swell into an angry beast. Saul felt the boat sway as the first drops of rain began to fall, punctuating the tense atmosphere.

"Get to your stations!" he shouted. "Everyone, hold on tight! We're going to face this head-on!"

Hannah joined him at the helm. "What can I do?" she asked.

"Help Finn and Elise secure the supplies below deck," Saul instructed. "We need to make sure nothing gets lost in the storm."

As Hannah rushed off and Saul focused on the horizon. He gripped the wheel, bracing himself against the fierce gusts that threatened to throw them off course. The boat began to pitch and roll violently.

"Hold steady!" he shouted to Colm, who was adjusting the sails. "We need to keep our course!"

But even as he spoke, the first wave crashed over the side of the boat, drenching them in icy water. The crew scrambled to regain their footing.

"Stay close!" Colm shouted. "We can't afford to lose anyone in this!"

Rain fell in sheets, blinding them as the waves crashed against the boat. The sound of thunder rolled across the sky, echoing the turmoil within Saul's chest.

"Everyone, brace yourselves!" Saul shouted, his voice nearly drowned out by the chaos. "We need to work together!"

The boat pitched violently as a massive wave crashed over the deck, sending Finn sprawling to the ground.

"Finn!" Hannah screamed, rushing to his side as the crew struggled to maintain their footing.

"Get the ropes!" Colm shouted to Callum. But before Callum could respond, another wave hit, slamming him hard against the deck railing with a sickening thud. He collapsed to the floor, clutching his side in pain.

"Callum!" Saul shouted. Talia and Leo were already at his side, their faces pale as they saw the agony in Callum's expression.

"We've got him," Talia shouted. "We need to get him inside!"

"Saul!" Leo shouted. "Help us carry him to the cabin!"

With Talia and Leo's help, Saul managed to lift Callum, struggling against the force of the waves. The boat lurched again, nearly sending them all sprawling as they made their way to the cabin.

"Hold on, Callum!" Talia urged. "We're almost there."

Once inside, they carefully set Callum down, and Saul slammed the door shut against the raging storm. He glanced at Callum's pale face, noting the way he clutched his side, his breaths coming in shallow gasps.

"Are you okay?" Hannah asked, kneeling beside him.

Callum grimaced, attempting to move but wincing as he gasped in pain. "Something…hurts bad," he managed, his voice strained. "Feels like I got crushed."

"Stay still!" Saul commanded. "We need to assess the damage."

Hannah looked over Callum's injuries, noticing the deep bruising forming along his side. Talia knelt beside him, her eyes wide with worry as she gently pressed near the bruised area. Callum winced and gasped.

"We need to keep him as comfortable as possible," Talia said.

Saul nodded, quickly gathering supplies to stabilize him. Leo offered his jacket to prop Callum up while Talia held his hand.

"It'll be okay, Callum," Talia reassured him softly. "Just hold on. We're here."

Outside, the storm continued to rage, the furious sounds of thunder mixing with the crashing waves that battered the boat.

"Hang in there, Callum," Hannah said gently. "We're getting through this."

The hours dragged on, exhaustion setting in as the storm

battered them without mercy. Mira and Lyla took positions near the door, watching the storm through a small porthole.

"It's still rough out there," Mira said, her voice tight with worry.

"The boat can take it," Saul replied. "We just need to hold on."

After what felt like an eternity, the winds began to ease, diminishing to a quiet whisper. The rain slowed, and the waves calmed to a gentle swell. Saul exhaled, glancing at Callum, who lay exhausted but visibly weakened, his breathing shallow.

"Are you alright?" Saul asked, kneeling beside him.

Callum shook his head faintly, wincing as he tried to speak. "Just...hurts," he said. "Hard to...breathe."

Saul looked at Hannah, his concern deepening. "We need to keep him warm and monitor his breathing. If it gets worse..."

"I know," Hannah replied. She wrapped a blanket around Callum, and Talia stayed by his side, her hand on his shoulder.

As the storm finally subsided, the group emerged from the cabin, stepping onto the deck to assess the damage. The boat was battered but afloat.

Saul looked around at his crew. "We made it through," he said. "But we need to take care of Callum. We can't move until we assess the injury properly."

Colm joined Saul. "I'll keep watch," he said.

As they took stock of their supplies, Saul couldn't shake the feeling of dread that lingered in the back of his mind. The storm had tested them in ways they hadn't anticipated, and while they had survived, Callum's injury added a new layer of difficulty to their journey.

Chapter 59

The days following the storm were marked by a somber calm, the sea's relentless waves now gentler, though Callum's condition grew worse with each passing hour. The crew felt the weight of his suffering, knowing full well how limited their resources were. Yet, each of them clung to hope.

Hannah had taken it upon herself to check on him regularly—her medical training rekindled out of necessity. Kneeling by Callum's side, she pressed her fingers gently along his ribs and side, feeling for any signs of deeper injury. His breathing grew more labored, his face drained of color. After a long silence, she looked up, her eyes filled with worry.

"I think it might be internal bleeding," she said softly.

"Internal bleeding?" Lyla asked. "How can you tell?"

"Hannah worked at a hospital before all this," Saul said. "She knows what she's talking about."

Hannah's hands moved with steady care as she continued her examination.

Callum managed a faint smile, his eyes half-closed. "Not exactly…the place I pictured…for getting hospital care," he said with a faint smile.

Hannah returned the smile, though sadness lingered in her eyes. "Just hold on, Callum. We're here with you, and we'll do everything we can."

Despite their best efforts, Callum's pain seemed only to intensify. They had little to ease his suffering, their supplies reduced to makeshift bandages and meager comforts. The crew felt their helplessness more acutely with each passing hour. Every look exchanged between them held an unspoken fear as they realized how limited their abilities truly were.

Finn, who had grown close to Callum over the journey, shifted uncomfortably beside Saul, his face pale with worry.

"Do you think he'll be alright?" Finn asked.

Saul rested a hand on Finn's shoulder. "We're doing everything we can for him, Finn. We have to keep hoping."

But as night fell, Callum's breathing grew more shallow, his face losing even the faintest hints of color. Saul knelt beside him in the cabin, watching helplessly as Callum fought against the pain, his breaths coming in strained gasps. The quiet of the room made the sound of each labored inhale all the more haunting.

"Hannah," Saul whispered, "is there anything else we can do?"

Hannah shook her head. "If it's what I think it is, he would need surgery…and we don't have the equipment or even a fraction of what we'd need."

Talia and Leo stayed by Callum's side, neither willing to leave him, even as his strength faded. Talia held his hand gently, her voice a soft murmur as she tried to comfort him, though her own tears shone in the dim light. Leo sat beside him, his face lined with exhaustion and quiet grief.

"You're not alone, Callum," Talia said, her voice trembling as she spoke. "We're all here with you. We won't leave you."

Leo nodded. "Just hold on a little longer. We'll see this

through together."

The night wore on, each moment stretching into the next as Callum's breathing grew increasingly labored, each gasp fainter and more strained than the last. Dawn was breaking when his eyes fluttered open, his face pale. Talia leaned close, her hand gripping his tightly as tears filled her eyes.

"Callum, stay with us," she whispered. "Please, don't go."

Callum's eyes focused briefly on her. "I...I wanted to see the island," he whispered. "I wanted...to see you all make it."

Talia's voice cracked as she replied, her words a plea. "We'll make it there, Callum. We'll make it there, I promise."

But with a final, shuddering sigh, Callum's eyes drifted closed, his body sinking into a stillness that left the room heavy with silence. Talia let out a soft gasp, her hand flying to her mouth as the reality sank in. Leo bowed his head, whispering a quiet goodbye as he gently placed a hand on Callum's shoulder.

The silence that followed was profound. Saul felt the world around him slow, every sound fading away as the weight of what had happened settled over him. Callum was gone.

"No..." Finn's voice broke the silence. He moved forward, reaching out to Callum as if, by some miracle, he could bring him back. "Please, wake up, Callum! You can't..."

Hannah wrapped her arms around Finn, who buried his face against her. "I'm so sorry, Finn," she whispered. "He's at peace now."

The crew gathered around, and quiet tears fell as they stood together. They had come so far together, only to lose one of their own, and the pain of that truth settled over them like a shroud. As the first rays of sunlight began to pierce the horizon, Saul felt a new resolve harden within him. He stood, calling the crew to gather on the deck.

"We need to give him a proper farewell," he said. "He deserves that."

"What do you have in mind?" Lyla asked.

Saul took a deep breath. "We'll commit him to the sea. It's what he would have wanted."

The crew nodded, a shared understanding passing between them as they gathered items to remember him by. Finn placed a flower he'd saved by Callum's side, a simple token that meant more than words could express. Talia brought a small carving that Callum had once admired, setting it beside him as her own quiet tribute.

They gathered at the edge of the boat, Callum's body wrapped in a simple blanket. Saul took a deep breath, looking over the crew, feeling the weight of his responsibility.

"Today, we honor Callum," Saul began, his voice thick with emotion. "He was a friend, a brother, and a brave soul who gave everything he had. His spirit will stay with us as we continue this journey, and though he's no longer with us, he'll live on in our memories."

As they lowered Callum's body into the sea, watching as the water gently embraced him, Saul continued. "Together, we'll remember him," he said. "We'll carry his memory forward and finish this journey in his honor."

The crew stood in silence, watching as the sea claimed their friend. They held each other close, bound by the shared sorrow and determination to carry on. They set sail once more, the ocean shimmering beneath the morning light. They were no longer just survivors; they were a family united in grief and resilience. And as the horizon stretched out before them, they felt Callum's spirit with them, a guiding presence as they continued toward their uncertain future.

Chapter 60

After what felt like endless days adrift on the vast ocean, the survivors were beginning to lose hope. Each day bled into the next, marked only by the ceaseless rhythm of the waves and the monotonous tasks they repeated—fishing, rationing, watching the endless blue expanse stretch on and on. The silence among them grew heavier as days passed, weighted with fatigue and a gnawing doubt that whispered this journey might never end.

Saul took his place at the helm as usual, his eyes sweeping over the still, dark water. The soft light began to ripple across the surface, casting fragile streaks of pink and gold. His gaze drifted as he scanned the horizon, almost out of habit—but then he froze. Something stirred in the distance, a shape faintly breaking the surface. Saul leaned forward, his heart pounding, squinting to make out the movement, hoping against hope it wasn't a mirage.

"Hannah!" he called. "Come here, quick!"

Hannah, who had been resting nearby, jumped up, alarmed by the tone of his voice. She hurried to his side, her eyes wide as she searched his face. "What is it? Do you see something?"

"Look." Saul pointed toward the horizon. "Birds. Flying low."

Hannah's breath caught as she followed his gaze. "Birds… Saul, do you think—are we near land?"

He nodded. "It's possible. Birds like that usually stick close to shore. This could be it, Hannah."

Nearby, Finn overheard and ran over, his face lighting up with excitement. "Did you say land?" he asked. "Are we really close?"

Saul gave a cautious nod, his gaze still locked on the birds. "We don't know for sure yet, Finn. But it's a good sign. Let's stay calm and keep a lookout."

Finn, unable to contain his excitement, bounded over to Elise, who was scanning the horizon with wide eyes. "Did you hear?" he asked. "We might actually be near land!"

Elise's face softened with relief, a tear slipping down her cheek. She wiped it quickly, her voice catching as she said, "After all this time…"

Colm joined Saul at the helm, shading his eyes against the early morning light. He squinted into the distance. "If we are near land, we'll need to approach carefully," he said. "The last thing we want is to run aground after all this."

Saul nodded. "You're right. We'll take it slow." He steadied his breathing, forcing himself to stay calm. They weren't there yet. He couldn't let himself get carried away.

The next few hours slipped by, and as they continued to sail toward the horizon, other signs began to appear—patches of vegetation drifting by, small branches floating in the water, fragments of a world beyond the ocean.

"Look!" Lyla called, her voice trembling with excitement as she pointed toward a patch of sky. "There are more birds!"

Overhead, a dozen seabirds flitted back and forth, their wings bright against the sky. Saul felt his breath catch, the reality of it sinking in. They were close. After everything, after every storm and hardship—they were finally close.

Hannah moved quickly, securing their provisions. The others followed suit, checking ropes, securing gear, and readying themselves for whatever lay ahead.

"I never thought we'd see land again," Elise said.

Finn nodded. "Neither did I," he admitted. "But here we are."

Eventually, the dark outline of trees came into view. Saul felt his heart leap as the land became clearer—a narrow stretch of beach fringed with thick foliage, its sand glowing under the sunlight.

"Land ho!" Finn's voice rang out. "We made it!"

A cheer rose from the group, their voices mingling with the sound of the waves. After everything they had endured, they were here. They had found land.

"Alright, everyone," Saul called. "Let's prepare to anchor. We're going in slow."

The boat rocked gently as they approached the shore, the soft bump against the sand grounding them in the reality of their accomplishment. Saul took a deep breath, his gaze sweeping over the beach and the dense trees beyond. They had made it.

Without hesitation, Finn jumped over the side of the boat, his feet sinking into the warm sand. He looked back, grinning wildly. "We're here! We really made it!"

One by one, the others followed, stepping onto the shore with joy. They looked around, taking in the sights—the lush greenery, the soft stretch of beach, and the chorus of birds calling from the treetops. After so long on the water, the sensation of solid ground felt surreal, almost too good to be true.

"We should look around," Saul suggested, his voice low as he gestured toward the trees. "Make sure we're alone."

"Do you think there could be other people?" Lyla asked, her gaze sweeping the treeline.

"I don't know," Hannah replied, scanning the area. "But we need to be careful. We don't know what's out here."

They moved toward the edge of the forest, the shadows of the tall trees stretching across the sand. The air was thick with the scent of leaves and soil. Saul's senses were heightened, every sound and movement sharpening as they entered the underbrush.

As they ventured deeper into the forest, something unexpected caught Saul's eye—a faint, narrow line cutting through the undergrowth, barely distinguishable from the wilderness around it. He paused, his gaze tracing the outline of what seemed like an old, overgrown road, almost hidden beneath tangled vines and moss.

"Is that... a road?" Finn asked, stepping closer.

The group gathered around, each of them struck by the sight of the faded, time-worn trail. With a sense of purpose and awe, they began to follow the road, pushing aside branches and wading through tall grasses as they moved cautiously along its barely visible outline.

The path led them to a small village nestled within the trees— a cluster of old stone houses, half-buried under ivy and creeping moss. The walls, though weathered, stood firm, marking the remnants of a past life that had once thrived here. Silence fell over the group as they took in the sight, the air heavy with the echoes of forgotten voices.

Elise knelt beside one of the houses, her fingers brushing the rough stone. "People lived here," she whispered, her voice filled with wonder. "An island community...left behind."

Hannah looked around, her eyes wide with sadness. "I wonder what happened to the people here," Hannah said softly.

Saul looked at her, a sad smile touching his face. "Maybe they left when everything started. When the disease broke out, maybe they thought the mainland would be better."

Hannah nodded, her gaze lingering on the crumbling structures. "It's strange, thinking they may have left this place looking for something we're trying to escape."

Finn ran his hand over a stone wall. "It's like we've come full circle. A place left behind, found again."

Colm nodded. "Maybe we're meant to be here. To make

something of what they left."

As the day wore on, the group continued exploring, each step renewing their sense of purpose. They had finally found a place where they could lay down roots, a sanctuary untouched by the chaos they had escaped.

As the sun began its descent, Saul reached for Hannah's hand, holding it tightly. He gazed out over the landscape, then looked down at her, a soft smile on his face. "We made it," he whispered.

Hannah met his gaze, her eyes shining with joy. "Yes," she replied. "And together, we'll make it ours."

Saul leaned in, pressing his forehead to hers, savoring the closeness. Then, with tenderness, he kissed her.

"This," he whispered as he pulled back, "this is our home."

Epilogue

Three years had passed since the day they first set foot on the island; each one etched with memories of growth, challenge, and quiet, simple triumphs. The group had transformed that unknown shore into a place of shelter and sustenance, crafting lives that, though modest, were fulfilling in ways none of them could have imagined. From the early morning routines to the quiet evenings by the fire, every day felt like a testament to the resilience that had carried them here.

Saul stood by the edge of the forest, watching as the morning sun poured through the canopy. The air was filled with the hum of insects and the occasional call of seabirds swooping overhead. The island had come alive in their care, and they, in turn, had found life again within it.

A few yards away, Finn, Elise, and Colm worked by the main garden, their voices carrying in soft laughter as they harvested the rows of vegetables they'd cultivated together. Finn, now stronger and more sure of himself than the young man who had joined them so many years ago, was a picture of satisfaction. He looked over at Saul and greeted him with a wide smile on his face.

"Saul!" he called, "We're adding another row today. Seems like our yield keeps getting better every season!"

Elise nudged him, a playful grin lighting her face. "That's because you fuss over these plants more than anything else on the island, Finn."

Saul grinned back, moving toward them. "That's what happens when you've got a natural touch. This island likes you, Finn. I'd bet it knows you were the one who first spotted it all those years ago."

Finn chuckled, glancing at Elise. "Maybe so. I think it's starting to trust us."

Elise laughed softly, brushing a stray leaf from Finn's shoulder. "Well, it definitely trusts you more than anyone, Finn. I'd say you're practically part of this place now."

As Saul joined them, they took stock of the garden—a bounty of tubers, greens, and other vegetables they'd gradually introduced into the island's soil. It had taken trial and error, patience, and hours of work, but the land had finally begun to give back to them, allowing them to live without the threat of hunger hanging constantly over their heads. In the first year, fishing had been their main source of food, and it remained essential, but each new row of vegetables planted was a step toward full sustainability.

Hannah approached Saul, a soft smile tugging at her lips as she caught his gaze. The morning light filtered through the trees, casting a gentle glow over the clearing. She had grown into her role here on the island with grace, a quiet strength that reflected her commitment to the life they had built together.

"Good morning," she greeted him, slipping her hand into his.

Saul squeezed her hand gently. "Morning," he replied. "Feels like everything's settling into place, doesn't it?"

Hannah nodded, her gaze following his. "We've come a long way, haven't we?"

Just then, Lyla appeared, her arms full of herbs she'd gathered from the wild plants they'd nurtured along the northern edge of the island. With her knowledge of plants and natural remedies, she had become the group's healer, a role she carried with skill and care. She smiled as she joined them, her presence calming.

"Thought I'd bring some fresh herbs for breakfast," Lyla said, offering a few sprigs of mint to Finn, who took them with a grateful nod.

Colm inhaled deeply, the fresh scent filling the air. "Lyla, I don't know how we'd manage without your touch around here. You make it feel like… like this island really is home."

Lyla chuckled, brushing off the compliment with a modest shrug. "I just listen to what the island offers," she said.

As they turned back toward the main settlement, a sudden rustling in the underbrush caught their attention. From between the bushes emerged a small, skittish animal, one they'd only recently started to notice on the island. It was sleek and reddish-brown, with large eyes and ears that flicked alertly at the sound of their movements—a species they'd guessed might be some kind of mongoose or civet, likely surviving on insects and small reptiles.

Hannah raised a hand, gesturing to the others to stay still. "There it is again," she whispered. "I've seen a few of them around lately, usually in the mornings."

"Do you think it's dangerous?" Finn asked, glancing at Elise, who held his hand a bit tighter.

Hannah shook her head. "No, they're timid. They stay away from us, mostly. I think they've started coming closer because they're curious."

Saul watched the creature as it sniffed around the garden's edge, its eyes darting nervously before it disappeared back into the brush.

"It's strange, isn't it?" he said, "seeing life here that we hadn't noticed before. It's almost like the island is starting to trust us too."

Hannah smiled, nodding. "That's how it feels. Maybe it's just that we're learning to see better, to be more a part of the island than we were."

They continued walking, reaching the central clearing where the stone houses stood, each structure carefully restored and strengthened over the years. The stone walls, weathered but sturdy, gave the settlement a timeless feel as if it had always been a part of the island. Ivy crept up some of the walls, and small gardens flourished beside each house, filled with herbs, wildflowers, and vegetables.

Nearby, Mira and Talia were tending to the smokehouse they'd constructed a year ago, a way to preserve fish and other food they gathered. Mira waved them over, her face flushed from the smoke and heat.

"Catch of the day's in here!" she called, her grin wide. "Finn, Colm—you're going to love what we pulled in."

Saul peeked into the smokehouse, his eyes adjusting to the dim interior as he took in the rows of fish hanging from hooks, drying and curing in the slow, steady warmth. The fish had become a staple of their diet—the island's waters providing an abundance of life that had sustained them in their earliest days. Today's haul was particularly good—a mix of mackerel and snapper, the silver scales glinting in the soft light.

Finn clapped Colm on the back. "Looks like we're in for a feast tonight," he said, his tone lighthearted. "The garden, the fish…We're practically self-sufficient now."

Colm grinned, nodding in agreement. "Who would have thought? We've come a long way from rationing scraps and hoping the nets would be full."

Saul and Hannah moved toward the small workshop they had built on the edge of the settlement, a space where they kept tools, stored firewood, and crafted what they needed. Hannah pulled out a carved wooden box and opened it to reveal a collection of seeds carefully wrapped in cloth.

"I've been meaning to try these," she said, her eyes bright with anticipation. "They're from a wild melon we found further inland. With a little care, maybe we can get them to grow here near the settlement."

Saul took a seed, rolling it between his fingers. "You think it'll work?"

Hannah nodded. "It's worth a shot. If it grows, we'll have more fresh fruit. If it doesn't…well, we'll learn something. That's how it's been all along, hasn't it?"

He smiled. "That's right. We try, we adapt, and we keep going."

They planted the seeds together, carefully pressing them into the soil, covering them with earth. Saul watched as Hannah worked. In moments like these, he felt as though he were glimpsing a different side of her—a woman who had learned to draw strength from the land, who understood that every seed held a story of resilience and hope.

As the sun began to set, the community gathered in the central clearing. Finn and Elise helped bring out the smoked fish, laying it out on a wooden table they had crafted themselves, while Talia and Leo prepared a simple stew from the vegetables harvested earlier in the day.

They ate together, their voices mingling in laughter, and shared memories. The fire crackled softly, and as they ate, their conversations turned to the days that had brought them here. As dusk settled, Saul looked around at the faces of his friends. Finally, his gaze rested on Hannah, who sat beside him, her eyes reflecting the firelight as she smiled.

Hannah leaned in close. "This is the life we dreamed of, isn't it?"

Saul nodded, his heart full as he took her hand in his. "It is. And we made it."

And although it was the whispers of hope that brought them all to the island, they were already living whispers of life.

Part Three

Whispers of Life

Prologue

Saul walked along the shoreline, as he did almost every morning over the last five years, feeling the familiar crunch of sand beneath his feet and the gentle warmth of the morning sun on his face. The waves rolled lazily in, their edges capped with white foam, spilling onto the shore before retreating. Not far off, two small children ran barefoot along the edge of the woods, their laughter ringing through the quiet morning. Saul watched them, his heart warmed by the sight. These were the first children born on the island, now three and four years old. They had never known the world beyond this place, their lives shaped by the rhythms of the island and the community they built.

Hannah walked beside him, her hand wrapped loosely around his. She, too, watched the children, her expression softened by a quiet contentment. She gave his hand a gentle squeeze, a silent acknowledgment of the life they had built here. Saul looked over at her, catching the glint of the sun in her hair, and marveled, as he often did, at the strength that lay beneath her calm demeanor.

"Did you ever think we'd come this far?" she asked.

Saul took a moment to respond, letting the question settle over him. The years on the island had been filled with struggle but also resilience. They had come here as fractured people, survivors clinging to fragments of themselves. Now, watching the community thrive felt like a small miracle.

"I hoped we would," he replied. "But I never thought it would feel like this. Like…home."

Hannah nodded. "It does feel like home," she said. Her eyes drifted to a group of people tending to the gardens. Every day, these fields provided the food they ate, the result of years of trial, labor, and faith. "Everyone has a role, a purpose. I think that's what makes it feel different than before."

"Before," Saul echoed, almost tasting the weight of the word. For them, "before" meant a world that no longer existed, a world where the ground didn't need to be tilled by hand, where supermarkets lined with endless shelves provided everything they needed. Now, their lives revolved around the soil, the sea, and each other.

As they continued their walk, a familiar figure emerged, waving to them from the gardens. It was Finn, his face alight with his usual energy. In these past years, Finn had become more than a friend to both of them. He was an integral part of the community, a voice that brought laughter, curiosity, and hope.

"Morning!" he called, wiping dirt from his hands as he joined them. "What's the plan for today, boss?" His eyes twinkled as he gave Saul a playful nudge.

Finn may have been younger than Saul by several years, but the lines of worry on his face revealed a history of hardships, ones they all carried in their own ways.

Saul chuckled, shaking his head. "Plan? Don't know if we've ever truly had one."

Hannah smiled, leaning into the conversation. "And yet, somehow, here we are."

Finn looked out at the waves. "Do you think there's anyone else out there? Beyond the horizon?"

Saul's gaze followed Finn's, his own thoughts pulled beyond the tranquil scene before them. "I don't know," he said quietly. "Sometimes, I wonder if we're the only ones left after all these years."

"Sometimes, I think about it too," Hannah said softly, looking between them. "The people we met before coming here; what happened to them? Where did they end up?"

Finn let out a sigh. "It's strange, isn't it? We finally found peace, but there's still this...restlessness. Like a piece of us is still missing."

"We've built something beautiful here," Saul said. "But maybe we need to know, for certain, if this is all there is."

Finn nodded. "It's comforting, knowing I'm not the only one wondering." He paused. "But hey, if we did go out there...who knows what we might find?"

Saul's heart tightened at the thought. It was a temptation he had buried time and again, convinced that contentment lay in preserving the life they had built. Yet, watching Finn's eagerness and the glint of curiosity in Hannah's eyes, he felt the weight of his own wonder grow heavier.

"Maybe one day," Saul said, as though testing the words. "But for now, let's focus on what we have here."

Hannah took his hand again. "One day," she echoed.

As the sun continued to rise, they returned to the heart of their community, where work awaited them. People were scattered across the fields and by the shoreline, busy with the tasks that kept their world spinning. The scene was one of harmony—a delicate, hard-won balance that relied on everyone's hands, their dedication, their hope.

Later that day, Saul found himself helping the young boy repair his fishing net. The boy, only four years old, had been the first child born on the island, a living symbol of the future they were building. As Saul knelt beside him, threading the twine through the net's broken seams, he felt a strange, almost fatherly pride.

"Think it will hold, Saul?" Noah asked, his eyes wide.

"Stronger than ever," Saul replied with a reassuring smile. "Just like us."

But even as he said it, his thoughts strayed once more to the open sea. Was this life they'd built truly all there was? Or was there a chance—a faint, fragile hope—that somewhere out there, other people were doing the same, building small worlds out of the ruins?

That night, after the sun had dipped below the water, Saul sat outside his weathered stone house, the waves a steady, rhythmic pulse in the background. Hannah joined him, resting her head on his shoulder. For a moment, they sat in silence, wrapped in the quiet of the island night.

"Do you think we'll ever know?" she asked.

Saul didn't answer immediately. Instead, he closed his eyes, letting the sound of the waves wash over him.

"Maybe," he said finally. "Maybe one day."

Chapter 61

The dawn was soft and pale, spilling light over the waves and casting a silvery glow across the shore. Finn's gaze drifted along the horizon as he went about his morning routine, stretching the stiffness from his limbs and watching the ocean's gentle rhythm. His mind wandered, lost in thought, when something unusual caught his eye—a faint shape in the distance, bobbing up and down with the current. He squinted, leaning forward, his pulse quickening as he realized what it was—a boat.

"Saul! Hannah!" Finn's shout echoed across the quiet shoreline. He broke into a run, his bare feet pounding the sand, and soon enough, Saul and Hannah joined him.

"There's a boat!" Finn gasped as he reached them. "It's coming this way!"

Saul's eyes sharpened, following Finn's pointed finger out to the horizon, where the small, weathered vessel was drawing closer. Hannah's hand found Saul's, squeezing tightly.

"What do you think?" Hannah asked, glancing between them.

"It could be anyone," Saul said. "Or anything."

The three of them stood in silence as the boat drifted closer. By now, others had begun to gather. As the boat neared the shore,

Saul held up his hand, signaling for everyone to stay back. He stepped forward, Hannah and Finn close behind him, as the boat finally scraped against the sand. Two figures sat within it—faces gaunt, shoulders slumped, and eyes wide with the haunted look of people who had seen too much.

Saul met their gaze. "Welcome," he said, his voice carrying over the murmurs. "Can we help you?"

The two strangers exchanged glances, hesitating as if weighing their words. Finally, one of them—a man with sun-weathered skin and deep-set eyes—nodded slowly.

"Thank you," he rasped, his voice cracked from salt and exhaustion. "We…we weren't sure anyone else was out here."

Saul stepped forward. "How long have you been out there?"

The man swallowed. "We were running. Raiders cornered us at the beach. We knew they wouldn't let us go, so we took a risk." He gestured to the raft. "We'd hidden it a while back…figured if we ever needed to escape fast, it would be our best shot."

The woman beside him, a wiry figure with sharp, tired eyes, nodded. "We cut the ties and drifted out with the current. We hadn't planned to go this far, but…we didn't have a choice. The current was too strong. By the time things settled down, we lost our direction."

As a few of the community members moved forward to offer water and dried fish, the strangers drank greedily. The man sighed deeply, his shoulders relaxing as he set down his cup.

"My name is Caleb," he said, glancing between Saul, Hannah, and Finn. "And this is Sadie. We thought it would be a quick escape, but the sea had other plans. Days passed, and we weren't sure we'd make it. And then…we found this place."

Sadie nodded, her voice soft as she scanned the crowd. "We didn't expect…anyone. Just water, maybe an empty island, but not…this. It's like a miracle."

Finn exchanged a look with Saul. "What's it like out there?" he asked. "On the mainland?"

Caleb sighed. "It's…a patchwork," he said slowly. "There are small enclaves—people trying to rebuild, to hold on to some kind of order. Some groups have created communities, trying to cultivate food and keep the peace. But there are others…" He paused, swallowing hard. "There are others who have given up on anything but survival."

Saul's jaw tightened. "Given up?"

Sadie nodded. "They've turned savage," she said. "More than ever before. We've seen groups who live by violence, taking what they want, driven only by fear and hunger. It's…a harsh place."

The crowd murmured, whispers of shock and sympathy rippling through them. Finn leaned forward. "But there are still people trying to rebuild, right? To live together?"

Caleb managed a small nod. "Yes. There are some. We've met groups trying to restore old knowledge, even attempting to rebuild some sort of society." His face softened. "They haven't given up on the world, even if it feels like the world has given up on them."

After a moment, Saul turned back to Caleb and Sadie. "You're welcome to stay here," he said. "We have food and shelter…stay as long as you need."

Caleb inclined his head. "Thank you," he said. "It's been…a long time since we felt safe."

As Caleb and Sadie were led away to rest, Saul, Hannah, and Finn stepped aside.

"What do you think?" Finn asked. "Should we…try to find others? See if we can help?"

"I don't know," Saul admitted. "We've found peace here. Safety. Going out there…we could lose everything we've built."

"But what if we could make a difference?" Finn pressed. "If there are others out there, trying to survive, trying to rebuild… maybe we could be a part of that."

Hannah placed a hand on Finn's shoulder, her expression torn. "It's a risk," she said softly. "But it's also…an opportunity. If people are out there, people like us, we could find them. Bring them together."

Saul glanced between them. "I can't deny that the thought is tempting," he said finally. "But we need to think carefully. If we decide to leave…there's no guarantee we'll make it back. Or that what we find will be worth it."

Finn's shoulders squared. "But we can't stay hidden here forever," he replied. "If these savage people are as bad as Caleb and Sadie say they are, who's to say they won't eventually find us here?"

Saul gave Finn a nod. "As much as I hate to admit it, you have a point."

Hannah's hand slipped into Saul's. "Whatever we choose," she said, "we'll choose it together."

Saul took a deep breath, letting the tension melt from his shoulders as he met her gaze. "We'll figure it out together," he agreed.

The three of them stood there as the morning sun climbed higher, casting light across the island and illuminating the path that stretched out before them—a path they had never thought they might take but one that now seemed inevitable. The stories Caleb and Sadie had shared stirred something in each of them, a quiet yearning to understand what lay beyond their fragile sanctuary.

Chapter 62

The following morning, quiet anticipation settled over the community as people gathered around Caleb and Sadie. The newcomers' weary faces spoke of struggles that went beyond words, etched deep into the lines around their eyes. For a long time, their stories were wrapped in silence—delicate, unbroken—until Sadie finally began to speak.

"We've seen pockets of hope out there," she said, looking around at the gathered faces. "Places where people are trying to restore some sense of life, of normalcy. But it's…fragile."

Caleb nodded. "Some groups are trying to keep a semblance of the old ways, rebuilding in small communities. There's one settlement working on restoring old farming practices and another that's managed to set up a basic form of trade. They're barely hanging on, but they're there." He paused. "Yet, the land is hard, and trust is harder."

The community listened. They had spent years forging a life on this island, isolated yet protected. The thought of other survivors enduring far harsher conditions sparked both hope and fear.

"We came from a place known as Haven's End," Caleb went on. "They call it that because it's where hope is supposed to start again. They've set up an irrigation system, and they're trying to cultivate crops. They even have rudimentary schooling for the children—anything to preserve a sense of the world that was."

"But the world outside Haven's End is…different," Sadie said. "There are groups who have abandoned anything resembling order. They survive by taking, by tearing down. They look at people like you, like us, and they see…opportunity." Her eyes dropped to the ground. "If they knew about this place…"

Finn glanced at Saul. "But it sounds like there's still hope out there," he said. "Communities like Haven's End…they're still trying. Isn't that what we're doing too?"

Saul nodded, his gaze thoughtful as he looked over the people gathered around them. "We have safety here," he said. "We've built something real. And the world out there…" He hesitated. "It could undo everything."

"But maybe it doesn't have to," Finn replied. "Maybe we could help their communities grow bigger and stronger."

* * *

Later that evening, Saul called for a meeting, gathering everyone around the central fire. He looked over the familiar faces, many of whom he had come to see as family. His voice, when he spoke, was calm but carried an undertone of gravity.

"Caleb and Sadie have shown us that we're not alone," he began, his gaze moving over the crowd. "But they've also shown us that the world out there is…a little worse than it was before. It's harsh. It's dangerous. And we don't know what would happen if we ventured beyond this island."

A murmur of agreement rippled through the group, though

uncertainty lingered in the air. Some of the older members exchanged concerned glances, while others looked toward Caleb and Sadie with a faint glimmer of hope.

Finn spoke up. "But if there are people out there—people trying to rebuild, trying to survive—we could find them. We could bring them together. Isn't that what we've been doing here, in our own way?"

Hannah nodded. "We've built something worth protecting," she said. "But maybe…we're meant to share it. To reach out and help others do the same. If we don't, we may not be safe here forever."

Elise stepped forward. "So you really want to leave, Finn?" she asked quietly.

Finn turned to her, his face softening. "Elise, it's…it's not that I want to go," he replied. "But if there's even a chance we can help people, maybe we should try. They're out there, like we used to be, just trying to survive."

Elise hesitated, glancing between him and the others. "I get that, Finn. I do. But it's dangerous out there. We've heard the stories," she said, her voice wavering slightly. "What if something happens to you?"

He reached out, placing a reassuring hand on her shoulder. "I'll be careful," he promised. "I wouldn't do this if I didn't believe it was important. But I'll come back. I promise."

She gave a small nod. "Just…don't take unnecessary risks. And if things feel wrong, promise you'll come back. Don't try to be a hero out there."

Finn managed a small smile, squeezing her hand. "No heroics. I promise."

An older woman, Helen, spoke up, her voice frail but strong. "The world outside…we left it for a reason. This island became our refuge. We have peace here. Are we willing to risk it?"

There were murmurs of agreement, but a few younger faces looked hopeful, inspired by the idea of connecting with others.

Caleb glanced around the crowd. "The mainland has its dangers," he said slowly. "But it also has its beauty. There are people who still believe in each other. Who still fight for something better."

Hannah met Saul's gaze, her eyes searching his. She saw in him the same fear, the same caution, but also a glint of something deeper—a spark that had been quietly growing since Caleb and Sadie's arrival.

"I think we should go," she said softly. "Not all of us. Just a small group."

Saul hesitated. But as he looked at Finn, at Hannah, and then out at the people he had come to care for, he felt the pull of something he couldn't quite name: a quiet yearning, a whisper of possibility that he couldn't ignore.

After a long pause, he nodded. "We'll go," he said. "A few of us. We'll see what's out there. And if there's a chance to help…to make a difference…we'll take it."

As the meeting came to an end, people drifted away in pairs and small groups. Saul, Hannah, and Finn lingered by the fire as they shared a quiet moment.

"I think we can do some good out there," Finn said. "You and Hannah found me. You found the others. And you brought us all together. Now we can go back and bring others together, too."

Saul gave him a small, measured smile. "I don't know what we'll find out there. But we won't know unless we try."

The three of them stood in silence, and in that moment, they were bound together by something more than survival—by a shared belief in the possibility of something greater, something worth risking everything they had built. They would go beyond the island, into the unknown, to seek whatever remnants of humanity were left in the world.

Chapter 63

Saul stood at the edge of the village, taking in the scene, knowing it might be the last time he saw these faces. Behind him stood the old sailing yacht, weathered and sturdy—a symbol of the journey that had brought them here. When they had first arrived, they'd dug a long trench to pull the boat inland, believing they might never need it again. Now, the same task lay before them in reverse: they had to dig the yacht free and return it to the sea it had once carried them across.

Saul glanced over at Hannah, who was clutching a small bundle. In it lay various items the community had pressed into their hands—tokens, charms, small symbols of protection. Each item spoke of their shared lives, a life that felt distant and yet heartbreakingly close.

"These aren't just gifts, you know," she said. "They're pieces of everyone here. Like they're coming with us, in a way."

Saul nodded, his gaze sweeping over the crowd that had gathered. Their faces were solemn, too, some glistening with quiet tears, others marked by expressions of pride. He could see the love in their eyes. Just ahead stood Helen, her back straight despite her years. Finn appeared beside them, his face unusually quiet.

"I didn't think it'd feel like this," he said. "Thought leaving would be easier, like I could just close a door on it all. But now…" He trailed off.

Saul placed a hand on his shoulder. "Home has a way of settling in you, Finn. When you leave it, you feel every piece you've grown attached to."

They moved toward the yacht, where the community had lined up to help push it toward the water. The trench they'd spent days digging stretched out before them. Caleb and Colm stood nearby, ropes in hand, waiting to help with the final push. Caleb would guide them on the mainland, though Saul knew it would cost him dearly to leave Sadie behind.

"You're sure about this?" Sadie's voice cut through the quiet.

Caleb turned to her, reaching out to take her hand. "Sadie," he began, "this is something I have to do. Out there, there are people who need help, who need to find their way. I can't leave them to struggle alone."

Sadie's gaze dropped, her hand squeezing his as if anchoring herself to him for just a moment longer. "I want to come too," she whispered. "I want to be there with you."

Caleb's grip tightened. "I need to know you're safe," he said. "This island…it's safe. And they need you here, Sadie. I need you here. Promise me you'll look after everyone?"

After a long pause, she nodded. "I'll stay," she whispered, stepping into his arms for a final embrace. Caleb held her close, whispering words too soft for the others to hear, before releasing her and turning back to the yacht.

Elise approached Finn and reached out to touch his arm. "Finn," she began. "I know why you're going. I do. But…I need you to promise me something."

Finn looked at her, the usual spark in his eyes softened by the weight of leaving her behind. "Anything, Elise," he said, his hand finding hers and giving it a gentle squeeze.

She took a shaky breath. "Promise me you'll be careful. And come back," she whispered. "No matter what you find out there… just come back to me."

A small, reassuring smile spread across Finn's face as he held her gaze. "I promise, Elise," he replied. "I'll come back. You have my word."

She wrapped her arms around him, holding on tightly for a moment. Then, with a soft smile, she stepped back. Finn gave her hand one last squeeze before moving to join Saul and Colm.

"Let's get this boat moving," Colm said, rolling up his sleeves. "No use in talking about what's ahead until we're back on the water."

Together, they worked with the others to guide the yacht along the narrow, water-filled trench. The community lined up along the trench, each member ready to lend a hand, gripping the ropes and guiding the boat carefully along its path. Inch by inch, the yacht floated forward, rocking slightly as it drifted along the shallow channel. With one final push, it reached open water, its hull dipping into the waves as the ocean welcomed it back.

Helen stepped forward, holding a small cloth bundle, and pressed it into Saul's hands. Her voice, strong yet trembling, carried a quiet power. "You're doing something important," she said. "We don't know what's out there, but whatever you find… bring it back. Bring us a piece of hope."

Saul swallowed. Hope was a fragile thing, and yet it was the foundation of everything they'd built on this island. He looked her in the eye. "We'll come back," he promised. "With whatever we find."

With that, he and the others climbed onto the yacht, the boat swaying beneath them as they adjusted to its familiar, gentle motion. Finn clambered up, leaning against the mast, his face alight with excitement. Hannah, ever the steady anchor, placed a hand on his shoulder, giving him a soft smile.

"We've done this before, Finn," she said. "We made it here. We'll make it back."

Caleb and Colm took their positions at the bow, and as they adjusted the sails, Caleb nodded toward the small raft tied up at the makeshift dock. "If we're careful, we can anchor the yacht far enough from shore and use that to get to land," he suggested. "No sense bringing the yacht close in. Safer that way."

Saul nodded. "Good thinking. We'll use it to get in and out. We don't know what we'll find along the coast, so let's keep the yacht as our lifeline."

With everything in place, the yacht glided smoothly into the waves, its sails unfurling to catch the morning breeze. The crowd onshore watched in silence, hands raised in farewell. There were no cheers, no loud calls—just a shared, quiet understanding that this moment was both an end and a beginning.

They stood on the deck, watching the island shrink behind them. For a long time, no one spoke, each absorbed in the sight of the only home they'd known for years, receding slowly into the distance.

Finn broke the silence first. "It feels weird, doesn't it?" He glanced at the others. "Almost like we're leaving a piece of ourselves behind."

Saul nodded, gripping the helm. "That's because we are, Finn. But we're also carrying a part of them with us."

They sailed through the morning, the island a shrinking silhouette behind them until it became little more than a dark line on the horizon. As noon approached, the air grew warmer, the waves rolling gently beneath them. Saul paused to take a sip of water, passing the canteen to Hannah, who accepted it with a grateful nod.

Hours slipped by, the sun climbing high above, casting a bright glare over the water. The sea stretched endlessly around them, its surface glinting like shattered glass. The quiet rhythm of the yacht's movement became almost hypnotic, each wave a steady beat marking the passage of time.

Hannah looked back toward where the island had once been visible. "It's strange how a place can hold so much of you, even when it's out of sight."

Saul glanced at her. "Home isn't just a place, is it? It's people and memories. All the things we shared."

Finn, overhearing, looked back with a grin. "Well, wherever we end up, I'm glad it's with you all. Couldn't imagine doing this alone."

As evening approached, the sky began to change, the light softening to hues of amber and rose. They took turns at the helm, their movements slower now, the exhaustion of the day settling into their muscles. Saul's hands ached, but he welcomed the sensation—it was a reminder of his purpose.

Finally, as the sun dipped below the horizon, casting the world into shades of twilight, they allowed the yacht to anchor. The vastness of the sea surrounded them, an endless expanse of water and stars, and in that moment, they were completely alone—cut off from the life they had known, bound only by the shared dream that had driven them forward.

The five of them sat in silence, letting the calm of the night wash over them, the gentle lapping of the waves a steady, rhythmic lullaby. The island was gone from sight, swallowed by distance and darkness. Each of them felt the quiet, unyielding pull of purpose. They were leaving behind the safety of their world, but in doing so, they were embracing something greater—a hope that somewhere out there, humanity still held fragments of light—fragments worth reuniting.

Chapter 64

The stars hung low in the sky, their reflections dancing across the dark water as the yacht rocked gently beneath them. Two days had passed since they'd left the island behind, each hour blending into the next as the ocean stretched endlessly around them. The day's exhaustion had settled into a quiet contentment among the group, each of them lost in their own thoughts as they drifted closer to the mainland.

Colm stood at the helm, his hands steady on the wheel as he navigated the yacht through the gentle swells. Caleb leaned against the railing nearby, his eyes fixed on the distant horizon. Finn leaned back against the mast, watching Caleb with curiosity.

"You know," he started, "you've mentioned bits and pieces about the mainland. But I'd like to hear more. What was it like? The community you came from?"

Caleb glanced over. "It wasn't much to look at, really," he began. "Haven's End…funny name, isn't it? More of a village than anything, but to us, it was home."

Hannah, seated on the deck beside Saul, leaned forward. "What was it like?" she asked. "Did you have structure? People working together?"

Caleb nodded slowly. "Yeah, it took a while to figure things out. But we had farmers, hunters, and people who knew how to build and fix things. It wasn't easy. Every day was a new struggle, but we had one rule that kept us going: help each other, no matter what. It was the only way we survived."

Saul raised an eyebrow. "That sounds almost civilized. I didn't expect that."

Caleb chuckled. "It wasn't always civilized, trust me. People don't always get along when they're starving or scared. But we tried. We built a sort of council and made decisions together. It wasn't perfect, but it gave people something to hold onto. That's why it was so painful when we lost some of them."

The air grew heavier as Caleb's eyes darkened, his gaze shifting to the endless sea as he spoke again. "There was a community near ours, about a day's walk. They called themselves Gray Pines."

Finn tilted his head, intrigued. "Gray Pines?"

Caleb nodded. "They had built a kind of fortified camp. They kept mostly to themselves. I think, at first, they just wanted to survive, like everyone else. But over time, they changed."

Colm, who had been listening quietly, looked over with a frown. "Changed how?"

Caleb took a deep breath, glancing out over the water before he spoke. "When the raiders came for them, they fought back fiercely and managed to defend their community. But it left them…different. Paranoid. They saw threats everywhere. And they began taking what they wanted from other nearby groups—food, tools, anything they thought they'd need."

"Did they turn on Haven's End, too?" Hannah asked.

Caleb shook his head. "No, thankfully. They left us alone out of respect, or maybe they just didn't see us as a threat. We had a history of trading with them before things turned, so maybe that bought us some time. But Gray Pines started to act like a storm passing through. They'd sweep through other settlements nearby, taking whatever supplies they felt they needed."

A heavy silence settled over the group. The thought of one community turning on others—neighbors they might once have trusted—was sobering.

After a moment, Finn spoke up. "And Haven's End…they're still out there? They managed to hold on?"

Caleb's face softened slightly. "Yes. We're still holding on. It's a quieter life now, more guarded than it used to be. But Haven's End has learned to be careful and stay under the radar. We've managed by being self-sufficient, growing what we can, and trading only with groups we know are safe. We try to avoid Gray Pines and keep our distance. So far, it's worked."

He paused, glancing at each of them, his face serious. "What happened to Gray Pines is sad. They turned hard and closed themselves off to anything but survival, but…they're not the worst out there. Not by a long stretch."

Hannah leaned in. "You mean there are groups even harsher than raiders?"

Caleb nodded slowly. "Much worse. Some places don't just take supplies. They take people. They live off fear and control everything through violence. Raiders might raid and move on, but these groups…settle in and make everything and everyone theirs. You can feel it even before you see it. Those places—they give off a kind of silence like the land itself is afraid to breathe."

"It's hard to imagine anything more dangerous than raiders," Finn said.

Caleb's gaze grew distant. "In a way, I think raiders are easier. They take what they need and move on. These other groups…they take everything from you—and they don't leave."

Saul shook his head. "It's still a relief to know some people can make it without losing their humanity. That there are still places like Haven's End."

Caleb managed a small smile, though it didn't quite reach his eyes. "It's not the place it once was, but it's survived. And honestly, that's something I hold on to. Knowing there are still pockets of people, like all of you, like the folks at Haven's End, who want to keep going. People who haven't let the world's darkness consume them."

Hannah looked out over the sea, her face reflective. "We all need that hope, don't we? That somewhere, people are trying to make things right."

"Yeah," Caleb replied quietly. "It's what keeps us moving forward, isn't it? The belief that we're not alone in trying to rebuild something better."

"You know," Colm said, "it's easy to think of the mainland as some dark, hopeless place. But I wonder if it's possible to fix it somehow. You know, bring people together and bring back humanity once and for all."

Caleb's expression softened. "I'd like to believe that too. There were whispers. Stories of people forming alliances and small groups trying to bring back a sense of normalcy. I never found them, but…well, that's why I'm here with you all, isn't it?"

Finn grinned. "Maybe we'll find them, or maybe they'll find us. Either way, it feels like we're doing something that matters."

Saul adjusted the sail, his gaze fixed on the horizon. "We're all carrying pieces of those we lost," he said quietly. "And maybe, when we find those people out there, we'll find something worth building together. A future."

Hannah placed her hand over Saul's, offering a warm, reassuring smile. "And if we can bring even a little bit of hope to others…well, that's enough reason for me."

The group sat in silence, letting Caleb's stories settle like a quiet weight around them. The yacht glided steadily through the water, the stars bright above, casting a gentle light over their faces. They stayed up late into the night, sharing quiet stories, laughter, and the weight of old memories. The vastness of the ocean surrounded them, but it no longer felt isolating—it felt like a new beginning, one they would face together, no matter what lay ahead.

Chapter 65

The first glimmer of land appeared just as the sun was beginning to rise, a dark line on the horizon that slowly grew and sharpened as they drew closer. Saul was seated at the bow as the coastline took shape. After days spent in the vast expanse of the ocean, they were finally reaching the mainland. Beside him, Hannah's fingers traced the edge of her satchel absently, her eyes wide with wonder. Finn, Caleb, and Colm sat quietly, each absorbed in his own thoughts.

Colm broke the silence. "We're getting close now. Let's find that sandbar and drop anchor before we get any nearer."

Saul nodded, keeping his gaze on the coastline, and adjusted their course slightly to steer toward the sandy patch Caleb had mentioned. As they neared the shallow stretch, the water took on a different hue, lightening as it reflected the sandy bed below. Here, they would anchor the yacht far enough from shore to keep it hidden from view but close enough to take the raft the rest of the way.

"Let's drop anchor," Saul called out. "This is where we'll leave the yacht."

Finn and Caleb moved to secure the anchor, watching as it sank into the clear water below. The boat stilled, gently rocking with the waves, and they began to lower the raft into the water.

"Everyone ready?" Saul asked.

Caleb gave him a nod. "We're ready, Saul."

Hannah reached for Saul's hand briefly before stepping into the raft. They piled into the raft, arranging their packs and supplies, and pushed off from the yacht. The raft bobbed as they paddled toward shore, the silence broken only by the rhythmic sound of their paddles cutting through the water. Caleb kept his gaze fixed on the shore, his expression calm but focused.

"Land looks…different than I remember," he said softly, mostly to himself. "Harder somehow."

As they neared the shore, they could see the skeletal remains of a town rising against the dawn, buildings choked with vines, and windows shattered. Nature had reclaimed much of it, pushing through the asphalt streets and filling the gaps in broken walls. Saul felt a pang of sadness.

When the raft scraped against the shore, Finn jumped out first, pulling it onto the gravelly sand. Saul, Hannah, Caleb, and Colm followed, each casting a cautious glance at the silent town ahead.

"Let's go slow," Saul said, his voice low. "We don't know what—or who—might be out here."

They moved cautiously; footsteps muffled on the overgrown grass creeping up through cracks in the road. The town was eerily quiet; abandoned cars lined the streets, and rusted signs hung at odd angles. Broken windows peered out like hollow eyes, and the faint breeze carried the scent of salt and decay.

Hannah paused beside a rusted metal railing, running her hand over its surface. "It feels haunted," she whispered. "Like walking through someone else's memory."

Caleb's face darkened. "It was like this when Sadie and I left.

Quiet, empty. But there's life out here, too."

Saul absorbed the scene in silence, the reality of it hitting him harder than he'd anticipated. It was one thing to imagine the world beyond their island; standing here was another entirely. They continued, alert to every shadow, every rustle until they reached a small clearing at the edge of town.

There, they found a makeshift camp—a few scattered belongings, a blanket, and a tin cup half-buried in the dirt. The remnants looked recent, as though someone had abandoned them quickly.

Finn knelt beside the items, frowning as he examined them. "Someone's been here. Not long ago."

Colm touched the stones in a small fire pit, his fingers feeling the faint warmth. "Hours, maybe. Whoever it was, they left fast."

Hannah scanned their surroundings, her body tense. "You think they're still nearby?"

"Could be," Saul replied, straightening up. "If they left in a hurry, they might not want to be found. But let's keep an eye out. "

As the group sat around the remnants of their campsite, Caleb looked to the others. "Haven's End isn't far from here," he said softly. "We can make it there by nightfall if we set out now."

Without hesitation, they gathered their belongings before following Caleb into the woods. The path grew narrower, winding through thick undergrowth until a soft glow appeared through the trees. Caleb held up a hand, motioning for them to pause.

"There it is," he whispered. "Haven's End."

As they approached, the lights sharpened, casting warm glows over a low wooden fence that enclosed the settlement. Two guards straightened as they caught sight of the group, their weapons raised cautiously.

"Caleb?" one guard called. "What happened to you? And… where's Sadie?"

Caleb raised his hands in a gesture of peace, stepping forward. "It's a long story," he said. "Sadie and I were forced off the mainland. Raiders drove us out to sea, and we barely managed to escape." He motioned to Saul, Hannah, Finn, and Colm. "These are the ones who found us. They're allies. They saved Sadie, and now they're here to help."

The guards exchanged uncertain glances before nodding. "Alright. The council will want to hear this."

As they moved through the settlement, people gathered around, whispering and casting questioning looks at Caleb and his new companions. Finally, they reached the large council hall at the heart of Haven's End, where a small group of leaders awaited them, expressions ranging from relief to suspicion. The woman seated at the center, a figure of authority with sharp eyes, leaned forward as she took in the unfamiliar faces.

"Caleb," she said. "We feared the worst. You were gone, and no one knew what happened. Where's Sadie?"

Caleb's expression was somber. "Sadie's safe, I promise. When the raiders chased us off, we drifted until we found a community on an island—a group that's survived quietly, away from the dangers here."

He glanced at Saul and the others. "These people are from that place. They're here to learn, to help us, to find ways we can rebuild together."

The council members exchanged wary glances, still unsure, though the leader's gaze softened slightly as she listened.

"Very well," she said finally. "Caleb's word means much here. You'll be given a place to rest for the night, and tomorrow, we'll talk more."

They followed the woman through the quiet paths of Haven's End until they reached a modest shelter. Inside, she gestured to two small adjoining rooms, each barely big enough for a bed and a place to set down their packs.

"By the way," she said. "I'm Amara. Get some rest. We'll talk tomorrow." With a nod, she turned and walked away.

Caleb turned to Saul, lingering at the door. "I'll see you off here. Tomorrow, we'll talk with the council and go over everything. They'll want to know where I've been and…what happened."

"Thanks, Caleb. We appreciate you bringing us here." Saul replied. They'd be getting into more than just introductions tomorrow.

Finn and Colm gave brief nods before retreating into one of the rooms, exchanging a few quiet words as the door clicked shut behind them. Saul and Hannah stepped into the other, the silence enveloping them as they finally let their bags slip to the floor.

For a moment, neither of them spoke. Saul watched Hannah as she crossed the small room, her fingertips grazing the worn wood of the single nightstand, taking in the unfamiliar surroundings.

As the door clicked shut behind them, Saul set his pack down, stretching his shoulders with a relieved sigh. Hannah glanced around the small, quiet room, her eyes softening.

She turned to him, a teasing smile on her lips. "You know, it feels like we haven't had a moment alone together since we left the island."

Saul's mouth curved into a grin as he stepped closer, reaching for her hand. "Believe me, I noticed," he said, his fingers gently tracing over hers.

Hannah let out a soft laugh, leaning into him. "Feels strange, doesn't it?" she whispered. "All these walls again, a real bed…" Her voice trailed off as her gaze met his.

"Almost too good to be true," Saul replied, pulling her closer. He brushed a stray strand of hair from her face, his hand lingering as he looked at her. "But I'll take it."

Their lips met in a slow, lingering kiss, savoring the warmth and familiarity they'd craved through all the days of their travel. In that small, private moment, the tension of the journey faded away, replaced by a comforting sense of belonging. They held each other close, finding solace in each other's touch.

Hannah leaned her head against his chest, letting out a long, contented sigh. "Think we'll actually get some rest tonight?"

"Let's hope so," he replied. "Feels like it's been too long since we've both had a real night's sleep."

With a final kiss, they slipped into bed. As the silence of Haven's End wrapped around them, they let themselves relax fully for the first time in days. Within minutes, both had drifted into a deep, restful sleep, holding on to the hope of what lay ahead.

Chapter 66

T he morning sun filtered through the narrow windows of Haven's End's council hall, casting muted beams across the worn wooden floor as Saul, Hannah, Finn, and Colm entered, their faces set with a quiet determination. Caleb walked beside them, leading the way to the council that had gathered in a semicircle, each member seated in a sturdy but faded chair. At the center sat Amara, her sharp gaze taking in every detail of the newcomers.

Caleb nodded to Amara. "Thank you all for meeting with us. I know you were concerned when Sadie and I disappeared, but I want you to hear these people out. They're here with good intentions."

Amara leaned forward, hands folded. "We've heard a little from you, Caleb. But we need to know more. What brings you here from this island community you spoke of?"

Saul glanced at his companions before speaking. "We've been on that island for years, keeping to ourselves, building a life away from the chaos. We managed to survive, even thrive in some ways. But over time, we realized isolation has its own dangers."

"And why risk that safety now?" Amara asked. "What has changed?"

Hannah took a breath before adding, "Because we know there are others like us—groups who want to live peacefully, to rebuild. But on our own, we're all vulnerable. We've seen the power of our community in working together, and we think there's a chance to expand that. To create something stronger, something that can withstand…those who don't share that vision."

Another council member, an older man, leaned forward. "And what exactly is this vision of yours?"

"To connect communities," Finn interjected. "We don't want to control or lead anyone. We just want to give people a chance to be part of something bigger. If we work together, we can share knowledge, resources, even protection. We're stronger united than on our own."

There was a murmur among the council members. The older council member leaned back, eyeing the group critically. "So, you're saying we risk our own security to help others? How do we know we aren't just inviting trouble to our doorstep?"

"Because that risk is already there," Colm replied. "Every isolated community is just one raid, one disaster away from losing everything. But if we're united, if we know who our allies are, we have a chance to stand strong together."

Amara's gaze flickered between them, absorbing their words, but her expression remained unreadable. She turned to Caleb. "You've seen what it's like out there, Caleb. Do you truly believe that these people can make a difference?"

Caleb nodded slowly. "I do. They came all this way to help us and offer what they can. I know these people. They have the same values we do. And they've built a community that's survived. We have to try, Amara, because what we're doing alone might not be enough. You saw what happened to Gray Pines."

Amara's expression softened slightly. "And what do you expect from us?"

Hannah stepped forward, meeting Amara's gaze directly. "Nothing. We aren't here to ask for supplies or even your support. We came to start a conversation. To see if there's a way we can all be part of something that lasts, something we can rely on. We just want the chance to talk to other communities and hear their thoughts."

The older man nodded thoughtfully. "This…alliance. You're asking people to put a lot of trust in strangers."

"That's true," Saul acknowledged. "But we're willing to earn that trust, to show you that this is more than just talk."

Finn leaned forward. "We're here because we believe it's possible. I know it might sound far-fetched, but there's something worth fighting for here."

The room fell into silence as the council members exchanged glances. Amara's gaze softened as she looked at Caleb, who gave her a small nod of encouragement.

Finally, she spoke. "You're asking for something ambitious, something that could change everything. But if we're to do this, it has to be done carefully. We'll need time to talk to our people here and make sure they're on board."

"We understand," Saul replied. "We know trust takes time. But we're willing to stay and help, to show you that this is possible."

Amara glanced at the other council members, who gave small nods of agreement. Then she turned back to the group. "Very well. Caleb, you'll go with them. You know the areas nearby and can introduce them to communities who might be open to this idea. But be cautious. Not everyone wants peace, and not everyone will listen."

Caleb gave her a respectful nod. "Understood, Amara. I'll make sure we approach with care."

As the council meeting concluded, Amara's eyes softened as she addressed Saul and the others. "I hope your optimism isn't misplaced. We'll talk more when you return. Get some rest tonight —you'll need it."

After expressing their gratitude to the council, they stepped out of the hall and into the heart of Haven's End, where life hummed with quiet resilience. They spent the afternoon weaving through the settlement, meeting members of the community—faces worn but kind, hands weathered from years of hard work. Children darted between makeshift homes, their laughter a hopeful counterpoint to the adults' cautious nods. Conversations were brief yet warm, each exchange giving Saul, Hannah, Finn, and Colm a deeper sense of the people they might soon call allies.

As the day waned, they returned to the cozy shelter Haven's End provided. The air had cooled, bringing with it the scent of damp earth and faint smoke from cooking fires. A calm, restful night settled over them, the world beyond momentarily forgotten as the settlement grew quiet under the stars.

Once inside, Finn glanced at the others, his face alight with excitement. "Did you hear that? They're really letting us try this."

"It's a good start," Saul replied, giving Finn an encouraging nod. "But we'll need to be careful. This isn't going to be easy."

Colm sighed. "We'll need to be prepared for anything. Some communities might see this as a threat."

Hannah placed a reassuring hand on Colm's shoulder. "We'll face whatever comes our way. We knew this wouldn't be easy."

Caleb stood by the door, listening quietly before speaking. "We'll leave early tomorrow. I'll take you to the closest community, and we can start there."

As night fully enveloped Haven's End, the soft glow of moonlight filtered through the small window in Saul and Hannah's room. They lay close together, whispering softly—the day's events settling in their minds.

Hannah traced small circles on his chest, her head nestled against his shoulder. "I still can't believe we're actually doing this," she said. "All those nights on the island, imagining what it would be like. Now we're really here."

"Neither can I," he replied softly. "But we've come too far to turn back now."

Hannah lifted her head, her gaze lingering on his face. Her hand drifted up to his cheek. He caught her fingers, pressing a gentle kiss to her palm, his eyes never leaving hers. His hand moved from her back to cradle her face, drawing her closer. Their breaths mingled, slow and warm, as his lips met hers in a kiss that was both familiar and charged with new meaning—a promise of closeness amid the uncertainty of their journey.

They lingered like that, wrapped in the quiet intensity of each other's presence, letting the world beyond their room fade away. And as the night deepened, they sank deeper into each other's embrace, savoring this rare, quiet moment together. Eventually, they settled into a peaceful silence, holding each other close and drifting off to sleep.

Chapter 67

The sun was just cresting over the hills, casting a warm, golden glow over the path as Saul, Hannah, Finn, and Colm followed Caleb into new territory. They'd only been on the road since dawn, but already they could see the outline of the village below.

"There's a good chance they'll listen," Caleb said, breaking the morning quiet as they crested a ridge. He pointed to the cluster of buildings below. "Stone Hill has been on its own for a long time, but Abel—their leader—has been open to new ideas before. Just…let's be patient. Trust isn't easy for people out here."

Finn nodded, adjusting his pack as he peered at the village below. "We're not here to rush them, just to show them that we're offering something real. I just hope they're ready to hear it."

As they made their way down the hill, villagers began to notice them, some pausing in their work to glance up with wary expressions. Whispers spread, and soon, a small crowd had formed in the village's main square. Caleb led the way, greeting a few familiar faces as they entered. At the center of the gathering, an older man with silver hair stepped forward.

"Caleb," the man greeted, his voice carrying a note of recognition. "It's been a while. Who are your friends?"

"Good to see you, Abel," Caleb replied. "These are friends from Haven's End. They've come to talk about something that might help protect everything you've built here."

Abel listened as Caleb introduced each member of the group. When he finished, Saul stepped forward, meeting the man's gaze with calm assurance.

"We appreciate you meeting with us, Abel. We're here because we believe that we can be stronger together. As you are aware, there are dangerous groups forming, and none of us are safe on our own. But together, we can create a future where we don't have to live in fear."

A few murmurs rippled through the crowd, but Abel's expression remained skeptical. He crossed his arms, his gaze sharp as he looked Saul over. "And what does this alliance mean for us? Are you asking us to leave our land, our homes?"

"Not to leave, exactly," Hannah said, stepping forward with a reassuring smile. "To bring what you've built and join us in a place where we can all stand together. At Haven's End, you'd still have your independence, but you wouldn't be facing threats alone."

Abel's gaze softened slightly, but the wariness didn't fade. "It sounds good in words. But we've had people make promises before, and they never last."

Colm nodded. "I understand the hesitation. But we're not here to take anything from you. We're here because we believe in something real—a community where people look out for each other. It's your choice to join us, but it's one that could make all of us stronger."

The villagers around them seemed to relax slightly, exchanging cautious glances and murmurs. Just as Abel opened his mouth to reply, a sudden shout rang out from the edge of the village.

"Raiders!" someone cried, their voice sharp and panicked.

The tension in the air snapped as people scrambled, pushing children toward the safety of their homes. Caleb gripped Abel's arm. "Get everyone inside. We'll help hold them off."

Abel hesitated, but he nodded quickly, shouting orders for his people to take shelter. As Saul, Hannah, Finn, and Colm positioned themselves at the edge of the village, a handful of villagers joined them, gripping whatever tools they could find—spades, wooden poles, and rusted metal bars. They looked nervous, but determination blazed in their eyes.

The raiders emerged from the tree line, rough-looking men with scavenged weapons who moved with the swagger of those accustomed to taking what they wanted. Their leader, a wiry man with a scar running down his cheek, paused as he noticed the defenders waiting for them, a mocking smile spreading across his face.

"Well, look at this," he sneered. "Got ourselves some heroes."

"Turn around," Saul called out. "You're not welcome here."

The leader chuckled, glancing back at his men. "Hear that? They think they can tell us what to do."

Finn took a step forward. "Last warning. Leave now, or you'll regret it."

The leader's smile faded, replaced by a scowl. He signaled to his men, and without another word, they charged.

The clash was swift and brutal. Saul moved with controlled precision, blocking blows and driving the raiders back. Hannah darted in and out of their reach, her movements agile as she struck with quick, sharp hits that sent her attackers reeling. Finn fought with fierce determination while Colm held steady beside him, pushing back anyone who came close.

Beside them, the villagers swung their makeshift weapons with raw strength, forcing the raiders to fight for every inch. Together, Saul's group and the villagers held their line, forming a barrier that the raiders hadn't anticipated. Their initial confidence wavered, and as they found themselves met with unexpected resistance, the raiders began to falter.

Seeing his men struggle, the leader cursed and shouted for retreat. The raiders pulled back, scattering into the trees, the leader casting a venomous glare over his shoulder before disappearing into the shadows.

As the dust settled, Saul's group and the villagers caught their breath, relief spreading through the square as people emerged cautiously from their hiding places. Abel approached them, his face filled with gratitude.

"I…I've never seen people fight like that," Able said. "You defended us without asking for anything."

Saul nodded, wiping a smear of dirt from his face. "This is what we want to offer. Protection, support, and a place where you don't have to face threats like that alone."

Abel looked around at his people, his eyes filled with a new understanding. He took a deep breath before meeting Saul's gaze. "We'll come. I see now that we need more than just walls and weapons to stay safe."

The other villagers murmured in agreement, nodding as they looked at Saul's group with newfound respect.

"We'll need a little time to gather our things," Abel said. "But we'll go to Haven's End."

Saul smiled, feeling a surge of relief. "We'll give you instructions on the safest route and prepare for your arrival. You won't regret this."

Over the next few hours, Saul's group worked with the villagers, helping them make preparations and teaching them basic defensive techniques for the journey. They shared maps and discussed travel routes, taking time to answer the villagers' questions and reassure them. As evening approached, Abel gathered the villagers together, addressing them with a tone of determination.

"This isn't an easy choice," he said, his gaze sweeping over his people. "But today, we saw something—a chance to build a safer life. We're not just surviving anymore. We're joining something bigger."

Before they left, Finn sat with a group of younger men and women, speaking quietly but earnestly. "It's different when you're part of something bigger. You don't just have allies—you have people who care about you, who want to see you succeed."

One of the young men asked, "How do you know they won't betray us? That happened to people here before. I don't know if I can trust like that."

Finn met his gaze. "Trust isn't built overnight. But in the coalition, we protect each other because we choose to. We build trust by showing up every single day. You'll see—it's different when you're part of a community that believes in you."

As the villagers set off toward Haven's End, Abel paused, turning to Saul. "Thank you," he said quietly. "For giving us something to believe in again."

Saul clasped his hand, meeting his gaze. "This is only the beginning. Together, we're going to build something that lasts."

They watched as the villagers began their journey, disappearing into the distance, carrying with them the promise of a new future. As the last of the group faded from sight, Saul turned to the others, a sense of accomplishment settling over him.

"One step closer," he said softly, his voice filled with hope. "They're not alone anymore."

Chapter 68

The late afternoon sun cast long shadows as they approached the next town, each of them moving carefully, alert to every sound and movement. The place was deathly quiet, the silence only broken by the occasional creak of an old, battered door swinging in the breeze. Dust swirled in the light, and broken shards of glass and rusted metal lay scattered across the ground.

"This place..." Finn murmured. "It feels like we're walking through someone's nightmare."

Caleb nodded, his expression grave as he scanned the buildings. "It's been stripped clean. But not just that—it's been marked. Look."

He pointed to a series of strange symbols scrawled on a nearby wall, crude markings in ash and what looked disturbingly like dried blood. They were simple, almost childlike in their execution, but there was something unsettling about them—an intentional chaos, a message meant to disturb.

Hannah's face darkened as she traced a finger over the closest marking. "This isn't a typical raid. Whoever did this wanted to leave a reminder, to make sure anyone who saw it wouldn't forget."

Saul nodded. "Fear as a weapon. They're using this place as a warning, making sure no one feels safe."

They continued cautiously through the town, moving in a tight formation. The buildings around them showed clear signs of recent violence—doors splintered, windows smashed, and the remnants of personal belongings scattered and trampled. Toys, torn clothing, and the occasional pot or pan lay abandoned.

As they approached the town square, a flicker of movement caught Saul's eye. He signaled for the others to stop, narrowing his eyes as he focused on the faint outline of a figure hiding in the shadows near a toppled cart.

"Over there," Saul whispered, gesturing toward the figure. "Someone's watching us."

Hannah and Finn exchanged a tense glance, and Caleb moved forward slowly, hands raised in a gesture of peace. "We're not here to hurt you," he called out gently. "We're just passing through."

The figure shifted, emerging slowly from behind the cart. It was a man, his eyes wide and haunted. His clothes were torn and stained, and he clutched a rusted metal pipe with both hands.

"Who…who are you?" he rasped, his voice trembling with fear. "What do you want?"

Saul approached cautiously. "We're travelers from Haven's End," he said. "What happened here?"

The man's grip on the pipe loosened slightly, and his shoulders sagged as he lowered his weapon. He glanced around as if afraid someone might be listening, then swallowed hard.

"They…they came in the night," he whispered. "Didn't take anything. Didn't hurt anyone, not directly. Just…left those markings. Told us they'd be back to finish what they started."

Finn frowned. "Why would they do that? Why terrorize you

without taking anything?"

The man's eyes darted nervously around as if the walls themselves were watching. "It's not about what they want to take. It's about what they want to leave behind. Fear, distrust. They don't need to steal from us. They want us to break down, to scatter, so that when they come back, there's no resistance."

Saul's gaze hardened. "Who are they? Did they say what they were after?"

The man shook his head. "They didn't give a name…just left those symbols. They called themselves 'scouts'—part of something bigger. Said they were just the beginning."

Caleb's eyes darkened. "They're the forward force for the savage group. They move in first, create chaos and fear, and by the time the rest of them arrive, the community's already falling apart."

Hannah's face tightened as she looked at the man. "How many others were with you? Did anyone else make it?"

The man's face twisted with grief. "I don't know. I've been hiding here, watching, trying to stay out of sight. Most people fled when they saw the markings. I haven't seen anyone else in days."

A heavy silence fell over the group as they absorbed his words. The thought of people—families, friends—forced to flee from their homes, leaving everything behind to escape a threat they couldn't face alone, filled them with a renewed sense of urgency.

"We can help you," Saul said gently. "Come with us to Haven's End. We have a community of people who work together and protect each other. You don't have to stay here alone."

The man hesitated, his expression conflicted. "But…but what if they follow? What if they bring that kind of horror to your place?"

"We'll be ready," Caleb replied firmly. "We're gathering strength, creating a network so that when they come, they face more than just a scattering of scared people. They face a unified front."

The man's shoulders sagged, and he took a shuddering breath, nodding slowly. "I…I'll come. I can't stay here any longer. It's like they're still watching me."

Hannah placed a hand on his shoulder. "You're not alone anymore. We'll help you get to safety."

As they led the man back through the town, the unsettling silence seemed to deepen, pressing in on them like a tangible weight. The buildings loomed like silent sentinels, bearing witness to the violence and fear that had taken place within their walls.

They passed more of the strange symbols scrawled on doors, windows, and even the ground. Each one seemed to radiate a sense of menace, a reminder of the terror that had driven the residents away.

"This is more than just a warning," Finn said. "This is psychological warfare. They're trying to break people down before they even step foot in these places."

Caleb nodded. "This is why we need the coalition. Alone, every one of these communities is vulnerable. But if we bring them together, give them a place to stand, we can break this cycle of fear."

Saul turned to the survivor. "Do you know of any other communities nearby? People who might still be holding out?"

The man nodded slowly. "There's a group a few miles south of here. They're small, but they've managed to stay under the radar. If the scouts haven't found them yet, they might still be there."

"Then we'll go to them next," Saul decided, glancing at the others. "If they're isolated, they need to know what's coming. They need to understand that staying alone isn't an option anymore."

The man's eyes flickered. "You really think we can stop them? That there's a chance to fight back?"

"There is," Saul replied, his voice steady. "But only if we stand together."

They spent a few more minutes gathering what they could from the town—a few supplies left behind in the ruins, bits of food and water—and then prepared to move on.

"I'm Rian, by the way," the man finally said.

As they walked, Rian shared more details about the scouts he'd encountered. "They're methodical," he said quietly. "They don't rush in. They watch, wait, and when they strike, they do it in a way that leaves people too scared to resist."

Hannah's face darkened as she listened. "They're trying to destroy communities from the inside out without ever lifting a weapon."

"That's why this has to work," Saul said. "We have to give people something stronger than fear to hold onto. A place where they know they're not alone."

They traveled through the night, the air growing colder as the stars appeared overhead. The quiet was both comforting and unsettling. By dawn, they reached the outskirts of Haven's End, the familiar sight of the settlement filling them with a sense of relief. Rian looked around, his eyes widening as he took in the buildings and the people moving purposefully around the perimeter.

"This is more than I expected," he said.

Saul placed a hand on his shoulder. "And with every new person who joins, it grows stronger. This is what we're fighting for."

Rian nodded. "Then I'll stay. I'll help however I can.

As they settled Rian in, Saul turned to see Abel and his villagers already mingling with the others at Haven's End. A wave of relief and satisfaction swept over them, and Saul broke into a smile as he made his way over.

"You made it," he said warmly, clasping Abel's hand.

Abel nodded. "We're here, just like you promised we'd be welcome."

Caleb appeared beside them, his usual calm demeanor softened by a smile. "Good to see familiar faces. Haven's End will be all the stronger with you here."

Just then, Amara approached, her sharp gaze assessing the

newcomers. "It's good to see our numbers growing," she said. "You'll find what you need here."

Abel inclined his head respectfully. "We're grateful, Amara. We know what it means to be part of this."

When the stars began to appear overhead, Saul and his team finally took a moment to rest. They settled in around a small fire, the familiar crackling of flames bringing a welcome calm. Hannah leaned against Saul, her eyes heavy but content, while Finn stretched out nearby, his usual wariness softened by exhaustion.

Colm sat quietly, watching the flames with a contemplative expression, his shoulders relaxing in the warmth of the fire. Caleb and Amara joined them, sharing a few last words about the day and the progress they'd made. There was a shared understanding between them all—a feeling that, despite the challenges still ahead, they were building something real.

Chapter 69

Dawn had barely broken over Haven's End, casting a soft glow over the settlement as Saul and the others gathered around a small campfire, sharing a quick breakfast. The air was filled with the quiet bustle of new arrivals from Abel's village, a comforting reminder that their coalition was beginning to take shape.

Caleb approached as he joined them by the fire. "There's a small settlement nearby," he began, glancing toward the forested hills to the east. "It's called Hollow Creek. They're a tight-knit, deeply religious community, very guarded. I know a few of them from before, but they don't usually take kindly to outsiders."

Hannah listened intently, glancing over at Saul, Finn, and Colm. "What do you think our chances are?"

"They're cautious by nature," Caleb said, "but things have been harder for them lately. I think they might be open to hearing us out if we approach them with respect. They know me, so at the very least, we won't be strangers."

Saul nodded, adjusting his pack. "Then we give it our best shot. Every community that joins us is a step closer to safety for everyone."

Without further delay, they set off, making their way through thick woods and along winding trails as the morning sun rose higher. When they finally broke through the trees, Hollow Creek came into view. It was a modest settlement, a dozen or so buildings clustered together and enclosed by a low stone wall. Smoke drifted from a few chimneys, curling into the morning air.

As they approached, villagers gathered near the entrance, their expressions cautious and curious. A tall woman stepped forward, her gaze sharp and assessing. She recognized Caleb and nodded, though her expression held a hint of wariness.

"Caleb," she greeted him. "It's been a long time. You know Hollow Creek isn't open to visitors.

"Good to see you, Liora," Caleb replied. "We're coming to discuss something that may benefit both of our communities. This is Saul, Hannah, Finn, and Colm."

Liora's gaze shifted over the others, her face softening slightly but still holding an edge of skepticism. "We don't take lightly to outside influence, Caleb. Hollow Creek has managed on its own for years."

Saul stepped forward, his tone respectful but steady. "We understand, Liora. We're not here to change what's working for you. But there are threats growing outside—raiders and hostile groups targeting communities like yours. We're helping bring settlements together in a coalition, a way for everyone to look out for each other. We wanted to offer that choice to Hollow Creek."

A murmur ran through the crowd, a few villagers exchanging uncertain glances. A broad-shouldered man stepped forward. "So you're offering us safety?" he challenged. "We've managed just fine on our own. What can you offer that we don't already have?"

Before Saul could respond, Hannah stepped in, her voice calm but persuasive. "It's not about taking away your independence.

We're offering a partnership. Having allies means that when times get tough, you have people to turn to. It could be the difference between facing these dangers alone and knowing someone has your back."

The man's expression didn't soften, but a few younger villagers exchanged thoughtful looks. A young woman near the back spoke up. "Maybe we should at least listen. Things have been harder lately, and it wouldn't hurt to consider options."

The man turned to her sharply, his face hardening. "We don't need strangers to protect us, Tess. Hollow Creek has always relied on itself. Why should we risk everything by depending on outsiders?"

Finn took a step forward, speaking directly to the man. "You're right to value what you've built. Trust is essential. But sometimes, facing things alone isn't the strongest choice—it's just the hardest. Wouldn't it be better to know you have people to rely on, especially in a crisis?"

The man crossed his arms. "And what happens when you change your mind? How do we know you won't just leave us when things get rough?"

"We're not here to control anyone," Colm said. "This coalition is about mutual support. Each community comes together to help each other. It's about making sure that no one has to face these times alone."

Liora shook her head. "We've relied on each other here for years, on our unity and our beliefs. If we give that up, what will we become?"

Hannah met her gaze. "We're not asking you to give up anything. There's strength in community. It's not just about surviving but about creating a future where you don't have to live in constant fear. A coalition doesn't take away who you are—it strengthens it."

The crowd fell silent as her words settled. Saul could see the mix of hope and doubt in the villagers' expressions. He took a step forward. "No one's forcing anything on you. We're here because we believe that working together makes us all stronger. But the choice is yours."

The tall man's expression remained set, but he seemed to waver slightly as he looked at his neighbors, some of whom seemed open to the idea.

Liora looked between him and Saul, clearly wrestling with the division within her community. "We'll think about what you've said. But Hollow Creek has survived by relying on itself, and we're not quick to change that. Caleb, out of respect for you, I'll allow you and your friends to stay the night—but come morning, you'll need to be on your way."

Caleb inclined his head. "Thank you, Liora. We respect your decision, and we'll leave at first light."

As the villagers dispersed, Tess lingered a moment, casting a curious glance at Saul and the others. She stepped closer, her voice lowered to avoid being overheard. "Not all of us want to stay cut off," she said quietly, glancing back over her shoulder. "Some of us believe there's more to life than just survival."

Saul nodded, offering her a reassuring smile. "If you or anyone else decides to join, Haven's End is open to you."

Tess gave him a small, grateful nod before returning to her neighbors. Liora returned, gesturing for Saul and the others to follow her.

"There is a place for you down the path," she said curtly. "It's simple, but it'll do for the night."

The shelter, a patched-up structure at the far end of the square, looked as though it had been pieced together from salvaged materials over the years. The roof was held together with old metal sheets, and the walls showed signs of various repairs, with mismatched boards and nails reinforcing weak spots. Inside, the furnishings were sparse—two cots, a worn table, a few blankets, and an oil lamp that cast a dim glow over the room's scuffed walls.

"Thank you, Liora," Saul said, nodding respectfully. "We

appreciate the hospitality."

Liora gave a curt nod, her gaze lingering on Caleb. "It's because of Caleb that I'm extending this courtesy. Tomorrow morning, you'll be on your way."

With that, she left, closing the door softly behind her. The room fell quiet, and each of them took in their surroundings, the weight of the day's conversation settling over them.

Finn leaned against the wall, crossing his arms. "Well, that could've gone worse. At least some of them were willing to listen."

Colm nodded. "It's a start. People like Tess seem ready for change, even if they're hesitant. But it'll take time for the others to see the same."

Hannah sat at the table, resting her chin on her hand as she considered the conversation. "Tess isn't alone in wanting something more. I think others are beginning to see that staying isolated might not be enough anymore. They just need to come around to it in their own time."

Caleb nodded, glancing around the dimly lit room. "Hollow Creek has relied on itself for so long that it's become a part of who they are. But it won't last long. The world outside their walls is changing, and they need to change with it if they want to survive."

Saul looked around the room. "We've done what we came here to do. Now it's up to them. Even if they're not ready to join us, at least they know they have options."

Hannah looked over at Saul. "Sometimes, planting that idea is the best we can do. They'll remember it when the time comes."

Finn yawned. "Well, I'm ready to turn in." He looked at the two cots in the room, then at Saul and Hannah. "Looks like you two can fit on one of the cots." He turned to Caleb and Colm. "Rock, paper, scissors, anyone?"

Colm laughed. "You're on!"

They battled it out for a few rounds before an excited shout broke the silence. "Got it!"

"Lucky you, Caleb," Finn laughed.

Colm threw his arms up. "Well, I guess it's you and me on the floor tonight, Finn. Toss me a blanket."

They all shared one last laugh before settling in for the night. They drifted into sleep with the hope that one day, Hollow Creek might come to see that a united future, even in a broken world, was still possible.

Chapter 70

The early light filtered into the shelter through thin cracks in the patched walls, casting streaks across the floor as they stirred from their sleep. Outside, the morning air was filled with the quiet sounds of Hollow Creek beginning its day. As they gathered their belongings and prepared to leave, Saul decided one last attempt to reach Hollow Creek was worth making.

When they stepped outside, they found Liora waiting for them. The morning light cast a cool glow over her face, hardening the lines etched by years of self-reliance and unyielding strength.

"Liora," Saul began gently, "we want you to know that the coalition's offer is still there."

For a moment, Liora's expression softened, a flicker of hesitation crossing her face before she quickly composed herself. "Hollow Creek doesn't rely on outsiders," she replied firmly. "We've survived by keeping to ourselves, Saul. And we'll continue to do so."

Caleb stepped forward. "Thank you for letting us stay, Liora.

We understand this isn't an easy decision."

Liora gave him a nod. Without further words, Saul and his group turned and left, heading down the narrow forest path toward their next destination. The air was cool and silent as they walked toward the next community.

An hour later, they arrived at the edge of a lively settlement, one far more vibrant than any they'd encountered in recent days. This place was bustling with movement and warmth, with people tending fields, carrying baskets of produce, and setting up market stalls displaying fresh vegetables, herbs, and handmade tools. The air was filled with the sounds of laughter and chatter.

As they entered, a few villagers noticed Caleb and greeted him with warmth and familiarity, quickly guiding them toward the village center. Saul observed the neat rows of crops, the repaired shelters, and the sound of children playing near the well. This was a place that, despite the hardships of the world, had managed to preserve a sense of hope.

"This place is different," Finn said, taking in the scene with quiet awe. "It's like they managed to keep some of the old world alive here."

Hannah nodded, her eyes bright with optimism. "If any community is open to the idea of a coalition, I'd say it's this one."

Soon, they were brought to the village's leader, a man named Damon. After introductions were exchanged, Damon led them to a large, sturdy table in the community's common hall—a simple but well-kept space where villagers often gathered for meetings and discussions.

Damon listened attentively as Saul and Hannah shared the vision of the coalition, his gaze thoughtful. Hannah leaned forward, speaking passionately about how working together could enhance everyone's security and prosperity.

"We're not just talking about defending against threats," she explained. "The coalition would mean each community has the support of others—through resources, knowledge, and mutual protection. By coming together, we create a foundation that protects everyone."

Damon watched her closely. "We at Oakridge have always placed value on self-sufficiency here. Tell me, though, how does the coalition protect that independence?"

Saul leaned in, his voice steady. "The coalition isn't about control; it's about support. You keep your voice, your customs, your way of life. The alliance exists so that we can help each other when it's needed. It's entirely your choice to join, and every community has an equal voice."

"What about land?" Damon asked. "We're farmers here."

Caleb nodded and spoke up. "There is plenty of land just outside of Haven's End. It may need some work to get it started, but it's there."

Damon nodded slowly, absorbing their words. Around them, other village leaders exchanged glances, and some of the younger villagers leaned in, clearly intrigued.

Outside, Finn and Colm had wandered among the people, mingling with curious villagers. Finn listened as they shared stories about their planting cycles, asking thoughtful questions and exchanging techniques he'd picked up in other communities. Colm, meanwhile, discussed ways to fortify tools with a local blacksmith, trading insights that quickly built mutual respect.

As these conversations unfolded, a sudden commotion arose near the edge of the settlement. A figure was running toward them, stumbling over the uneven ground, his face flushed and breath coming in gasps. Saul, Hannah, and the others turned to see a young man from Hollow Creek, clearly exhausted from his journey.

The young man staggered to a stop before Saul, clutching his side as he tried to catch his breath. "Hollow Creek…we were attacked," he managed, his voice rough. "They came out of nowhere—raiders. They took nearly everything. But everyone's alive. Tess and some others left for Haven's End."

A murmur of shock and concern swept through the villagers nearby, and Damon's expression darkened as he absorbed the young man's news.

"This is what we're up against, then?" Damon asked quietly. "It sounds like this coalition might be the only way forward."

"If we stand together," Hannah said, "we have a better chance against these threats. No community should have to face them alone."

Damon looked to the other community leaders. "We can't wait for danger to reach our doorstep. We'll join the coalition. If this alliance can protect our people, then it's the right choice."

"I'll stay here," Finn said. "I'll help them get back to Haven's End."

Saul nodded. "Hannah and I will go back to Hollow Creek with Caleb and Colm. We need to help them any way we can."

Saul thanked Damon and the others, moved by their willingness to act. The farming community quickly organized preparations to head for Haven's End. Leaving them to prepare, Saul, Hannah, Caleb, and Colm set off with the messenger from Hollow Creek.

* * *

Evening was settling over the valley by the time they reached Hollow Creek. Signs of the raid were evident—barrels overturned, bags slashed open, and scattered belongings littering the ground. Villagers moved quietly in small clusters, their faces reflecting fear.

Liora stood by the entrance, arms crossed tightly, her expression hard as she watched Saul's group approach. Her gaze sharpened, and she stepped forward, a flash of anger lighting her eyes.

"You led them here," she accused. "Those raiders were never a problem until you arrived. Now look at what's happened."

Saul took a breath, meeting her gaze calmly. "Liora, we didn't bring anyone here. These raiders are growing in number and targeting isolated communities. This attack was going to happen, whether we were here or not."

Liora's lips pressed into a thin line. "You talk of unity and protection, but all your words brought us was destruction."

Hannah stepped forward. "Liora, this attack wasn't because of us. The world beyond these walls is changing. Raiders are becoming bolder, and they'll keep coming as long as we stay divided."

Liora looked back at her people, many of whom had gathered to listen. Her face softened momentarily before hardening again. "If anyone wants to leave, I won't stop them. But Hollow Creek will remain as it is. I won't abandon our ways."

Several villagers exchanged glances before a few stepped forward, moving quietly to join Saul's group. An older man among them spoke, his voice filled with gentle conviction.

"Liora, we've done this alone for years. But maybe it's time to consider something more. Tess saw a future beyond this place. Maybe we should, too."

A visible division formed within Hollow Creek. Those who chose to stay with Liora did so with solemn expressions, while the others, hope and fear mingling in their eyes, gathered their few belongings to join Saul's group. Saul looked at Liora one last time.

"Liora, we'll leave that door open for you and anyone else here who wants a chance at something different. The coalition will always be there."

Liora's face remained set, her gaze hard and distant as she turned back toward the quiet, dismantled remains of her village.

Hannah placed a gentle hand on Saul's shoulder, nodding toward the new additions to their group, each carrying what little they had. "They're choosing a future they can believe in. That's something."

As they led the departing villagers down the winding path, the air was thick with both the sadness of leaving and the hope of the unknown. A young girl clung to her mother's hand, looking up at Saul with wide, uncertain eyes. He offered her a reassuring smile.

"It's not easy to leave what we know," he said gently, "but it's the first step toward something new—a life where we don't have to face the world alone."

Chapter 71

The warmth of the afternoon sun seeped through the walls of Haven's End's main meeting hall. Amara sat at the head of the broad table, her gaze sharp as she studied each face around her. Each person here knew the risks they had taken to come together, but there was a glint of hope, too, a fragile yet determined vision of a future they were beginning to build.

"Thank you all for joining," Amara began. "We're here because of what we're creating together. It's not lost on any of us that each of you has taken a risk in joining this coalition. Today, we're here to talk about that future—how we're going to build it, sustain it, and most importantly, defend it."

Damon leaned forward, resting his arms on the table. "We've got land out there—good land. The soil just outside Haven's End is solid, and with a bit of work, we can start planting. With enough hands, we could be harvesting by next season." He looked around at the group, his eyes settling on Saul. "If you're looking to make Haven's End self-sufficient, farming is our foundation."

Abel, sitting across from Damon, nodded in agreement. "Farming's key, no doubt. But, well, we're coming here without much to give. We don't have expertise like Damon's people or tools to offer. But if you need strong hands, people who'll pull their weight, my people are more than willing."

Saul nodded with a look of appreciation. "You've got more to offer than you might think, Abel. Every skill and every willing hand counts. The willingness to help is what will make this place strong."

Abel offered a humble smile, glancing at Damon. "I've seen what Damon's people can do. Their skills with the land are something to behold."

Damon nodded in acknowledgment, his eyes glinting with pride. "We've had to adapt to the land. I have a few people who can teach others how to farm and keep the soil healthy. And if we're serious about sustaining Haven's End long-term, irrigation is essential. There's a small creek nearby we could divert if we build channels and trenches. It's labor-intensive, but it'll pay off."

Hannah nodded thoughtfully, tapping her fingers on the map. "Self-sufficiency will give people a reason to stay. Once they see that we can produce food, Haven's End won't just be a safe place —it'll be a place worth building."

Caleb leaned back, arms crossed, as he considered Damon's words. "Farming and irrigation are key, but security is our backbone. We can't risk all this work falling apart because of a single attack. Abel, your people know the land around here. Would you be willing to help organize some regular patrols?"

Abel's gaze turned serious. "We don't have many fighters, but we do know the terrain. If you need people to watch the borders and set up signals, we can manage that."

Colm nodded, looking around the table. "I've noticed there are people with potential here, people who can learn to defend themselves. We can train those who are willing. It doesn't have to be much—just enough to prepare them for whatever comes our way."

Amara leaned forward, glancing at Saul and the others. "So, we're starting with irrigation, farming, and defense patrols. That's a solid foundation. We need everyone to feel that they're part of something vital. If we're going to build this coalition, they have to know they're contributing to it—and benefiting from it."

Damon turned to Amara. "Let's say we're able to get the crops going and build this foundation. What happens when the community grows? Do we stay here or look for more land?"

Amara looked at Saul. "This is where we need a plan that can scale. We can't risk expanding too quickly, but we also can't hold everyone in one place if we're expecting the coalition to grow."

Saul glanced at the others. "The core of Haven's End will stay here. But once we're established, we can set up small outposts— places nearby where people can settle and still be close enough to come back for resources and help. This way, we're keeping a strong, central location while allowing people the space to contribute and grow."

A silence fell over the group as they all considered the scale of what they were attempting to create. Abel broke the quiet, his voice low and steady. "We're all putting something on the line here, but the risks go deeper than just survival. There are dangerous people out there—people who want to see places like Haven's End destroyed."

Saul nodded solemnly. "That's something we need to talk about. We've dealt with smaller groups before—bands of raiders, isolated threats. But there's a larger group out there, which is more organized. We don't know much about them yet, but they've been sending scouts, watching and waiting."

Damon's expression hardened. "So they're not just opportunistic scavengers—they're watching us. Planning, even."

Saul nodded. "Exactly. These scouts aren't random. They're disciplined and cautious. They know what they're doing. If they see what we're building here, they might see us as a threat."

Amara looked around the table. "And they would be right. What we're building here challenges the order they're trying to impose."

"If this coalition is going to last," Caleb said, "we need to stay a step ahead. We should be collecting information—anything we can find out about who they are, where they're coming from, and what they're after."

Finn, who had been quietly listening, leaned forward. "We need to show everyone here what we're up against. If people understand the danger, they'll want to help protect this place, too. We can't just build defenses—we need everyone to be ready to stand together."

Hannah nodded, glancing at Finn with a smile. "You're right. People need to understand what's at stake. This isn't just about protecting ourselves—it's about preserving a way of life that others are trying to take from us."

Colm glanced around the room. "Our goal is more than just survival. We're offering these people a future—one they can believe in. We need to make them understand that while this is a haven, it's not a hiding place. We're ready to defend what we're building."

Damon raised his hand. "What about weapons? We're farmers. We have a few tools that could be used if necessary, but nothing to stand up to a group of trained fighters. If this threat comes, we need to be prepared."

Saul nodded. "We've discussed this. We're working with what we have, but it's clear we'll need more. Caleb and I can work on finding sources—places that might still have supplies."

"We may not have weapons, but we're used to adapting," Abel said. "If there's anything we can do to reinforce the perimeter, I'll organize people to start working on it. Defensive barriers, lookout points—anything that can buy us time if an attack comes."

Caleb nodded. "We can set up a network of lookouts in the nearby woods, places where we can stay hidden but still see far enough to spot any approaching threats. With regular shifts, we'd be able to cover the area."

Hannah glanced at Amara. "With regular shifts and a communication system, we could respond quickly to any threat. Smoke signals, flares—whatever we have."

Amara nodded. "That's a start. If we combine Damon's resources with Abel's experience and the training Colm, Finn, and Caleb can provide, we'll be able to establish a perimeter strong enough to hold them back."

The leaders exchanged glances, the weight of the discussion settling over them. Saul looked around the table. "This is a good start, but we need more people—more communities. The greater our numbers, the stronger our defenses and resources."

Caleb nodded. "There are more out there. With a little convincing, they could become part of what we're building."

Amara gave a nod. "Then we have our next goal. We'll secure what we've started here, and you'll leave tomorrow to find others willing to join us. The more allies we have, the safer we'll be."

The leaders looked at one another, each one nodding in agreement. One by one, each leader rose, a shared sense of purpose filling the room as the meeting adjourned. As the camp settled for the night, Saul and Hannah found a quiet spot just beyond the gathering. Finn joined them, sitting nearby while the stars began to emerge, filling the darkening sky. The faint sound of laughter and murmured conversations drifted from the camp, the sounds of a growing community beginning to take root.

Hannah wrapped her arms around her knees, gazing out over the quiet landscape. "Today felt real," she said softly. "Like we're not just trying to survive, but actually building something."

Saul nodded. "I know what you mean. There was a time when I didn't believe it was possible—any of this." He glanced over at her. "But here we are. People are coming together. They're believing in this place, in us."

Finn looked between the two of them with a hopeful smile. "I didn't think we'd actually find this, you know? A place where people actually care about the future. It's…different."

Hannah looked at Finn. "Do you think we're ready for everything that might come? For the threats? The challenges? It feels like we're balancing on the edge of something huge."

Saul reached out, taking her hand in his. "Maybe we are. But we have each other. And we have people here—people who believe in this as much as we do. As long as we have that, we'll face whatever comes."

Hannah rested her head on Saul's shoulder. "Then that's enough for now."

Above them, the stars watched over Haven's End, a place that was no longer just a refuge but a promise of something greater, a promise they would both protect with everything they had.

Chapter 72

Thick clouds hung low in the sky as the group approached the next settlement, their path winding through dense woods. Caleb led the way, though his face was drawn with thought, his steps slower than usual. Saul walked close behind him while Hannah stayed at his side. Behind them, Finn kept pace, occasionally glancing toward Colm, who brought up the rear. Each of them felt the chill in the air, a dampness that seemed to cling to their clothes and deepen the weight of Caleb's words.

"This next settlement…it's different," Caleb began, glancing at the others. "Edgewood's strength has always been its people, but there's a deep divide here. Disagreements over who should make decisions, who has access to resources, who even speaks for the community. Tensions have grown, and mistrust has festered. They're still holding on, but barely."

Hannah looked at Caleb with concern. "And they're willing to listen to us in the middle of all this?"

"They know me," Caleb continued, "and I know a few of the

key people here. I helped them through a rough patch some years back, but things were different then. Edgewood has always been proud and self-sufficient, and they see any outside influence as a threat. We'll need to approach carefully, tread lightly."

Finn let out a low whistle. "So, they're already on the edge. And we're supposed to convince them to join a coalition?"

Caleb's gaze softened as he met Finn's eyes. "Sometimes, people just need someone they trust to help them find their way. It won't be easy, but maybe we can remind them of what they once had together. And the danger they're in if they stay isolated."

The group grew silent as they emerged from the dense forest and caught their first glimpse of Edgewood. Nestled in a shallow valley, the settlement was modest, with a dozen or so wooden buildings clustered together, all showing signs of wear. A group of people was gathered in the central square, casting wary glances toward them as they entered the village. An older man stepped forward, his posture tense but familiar as he recognized Caleb.

"Caleb, you're back."

"Yes, Lucas, it's good to see you," Caleb replied. He glanced at the others. "These are friends of mine, people I trust. We're here to talk about a coalition that's already helping other communities. And there's something important Edgewood needs to hear."

A woman stepped up beside Lucas. She had strong, clear eyes and an air of calm authority. Caleb nodded at her. "Anna, good to see you again."

Anna gave him a slight nod, but her gaze remained steady on Saul and his group. "We've heard stories about groups trying to pull others together, Caleb. Promises that sound good until things fall apart."

Lucas crossed his arms. "We've been doing just fine on our own, Caleb."

Caleb's tone grew more serious. "Until when? I've seen what happens to communities that think they can go it alone, Lucas. Hollow Creek was raided, and their supplies were nearly wiped out by raiders. They barely made it through, and only because a few chose to join us."

The murmurs in the crowd grew louder, faces turning from Caleb to one another, concern and fear sparking in their eyes.

Hannah stepped forward. "We understand your concerns, and we're not here to impose anything on you. We're here because we believe that all of us can stand stronger together. Stone Hill and Oakridge have already joined Haven's End. Caleb thought you might be open to hearing how it's already helping others."

The villagers around them murmured softly, exchanging looks. Caleb met Lucas's gaze. "Things haven't been easy here. You've dealt with more than your share of hardship, but things have changed. Other communities have already joined us. They're standing together, sharing resources, and protecting each other. Hollow Creek is learning this firsthand."

Anna's eyes flickered with interest. "So you're saying others are already doing this? And they're getting along just fine?"

Caleb nodded. "Yes, they are. And it hasn't always been smooth, but they're seeing the benefit of working as one. It's not about giving up who you are. It's about finding a way to support each other in a world that's getting harder by the day."

Lucas looked at Anna. "Support doesn't come for free, Caleb. There's always a cost."

"That's why we're here to listen," Saul said, "not to tell you what to do. We want to understand what matters to you and what Edgewood needs. The coalition isn't about forcing you into anything. It's about knowing that when times are hard, there are others who will stand with you."

A young man near the edge of the crowd shook his head. "Stand with us? We can barely stand with each other right now. Look around. We've got people arguing over every decision, every piece of food, every bit of wood we find. How are we supposed to 'stand together' with people we don't even know?"

Finn stepped forward. "Maybe that's exactly why a coalition

would help. Sometimes, it takes new connections to remind us that we're not alone, even if things feel divided. We've seen other communities go through something similar, and they're coming together now."

Lucas gave a derisive snort. "Easy to say when you're not here day after day, seeing people fight over scraps."

Anna's expression softened slightly as she looked at Finn. "It's true that things have become difficult here, but we've worked so hard to make this place ours. Sharing what little we have."

"I know what it's like to feel you're barely holding on to what you have," Colm said. "But imagine what it would mean if you didn't have to defend your food alone or ration every piece of wood. Imagine knowing someone out there has your back."

Lucas's face softened slightly, though he still looked unsure. "This all sounds good, but words are easy. We've seen others make promises, and those promises haven't fed anyone."

Anna looked at Lucas. "Maybe it's time we think about things differently, Lucas. We can't keep running ourselves into the ground, fighting each other over what little we have. We're doing more harm to ourselves than good."

Caleb put a hand on Lucas's shoulder. "There's risk in everything, Lucas. And I know Edgewood has faced more than its share. But I've seen what happens when people stop fighting each other and start helping each other."

After several tense moments of silence, Lucas looked around at his people. Finally, he nodded. "All right. I'm willing to give it a chance."

Anna's face softened. "We won't lose anything, Lucas. We're gaining allies."

As the crowd began to disperse, Anna turned to Caleb. "We'll talk more in the morning. You're welcome to stay the night—there's an empty shelter near the western edge of the village."

"Thank you, Anna," Caleb said, nodding.

Finn gave her a smile. "We appreciate it. And thanks for

listening."

They made their way to the shelter as dusk settled over Edgewood. The village was finally quiet as people retreated indoors. The small building was worn, but it was warm and dry, with thick blankets folded neatly by the door.

Saul sat down beside Hannah on one of the blankets, glancing at her with a faint, tired smile. She leaned into him, resting her head on his shoulder as they let the day's events settle.

"This feels like a step in the right direction," he said.

Hannah nodded. "It's more than that. It's hope. For them and for us."

He and Hannah stretched out together on the blanket, her hand resting on his as they drifted into a comforting silence. They shared a final, soft glance before they closed their eyes, her head nestled against his chest. The warmth of new alliances and the familiar comfort of old bonds carried them into a restful sleep.

Chapter 73

Saul jolted awake to the sound of shouts and pounding feet, the thin walls around him rattling as if struck by a powerful storm. It took only a second to clear the fog of sleep, his instincts sharpening as he heard the unmistakable clash of chaos unfolding outside. He turned to Hannah, sleeping beside him, and shook her shoulder.

"Hannah," he whispered urgently. Her eyes blinked open, confusion flickering across her face before another crash outside filled the room, loud and close, shattering the remnants of sleep.

"What's happening?" she murmured, already reaching for her boots.

"Raiders," he replied. "Get the others."

Within moments, everyone was scrambling into action. The sounds outside told them all they needed to know. Saul held Hannah's gaze for a moment before he motioned toward the door. "Ready?"

She nodded. "Let's go."

They pushed the door open and stepped out into the fray. The village square was unrecognizable. Raiders were everywhere and tearing through Edgewood. They moved like a wave, smashing windows, splintering doors, and dragging people out of their homes like animals. People screamed and stumbled out of their beds, families clutching one another in terror as they were rounded up and herded into the open.

Saul clenched his fists. He turned to his group. "Hannah, you're with me. Finn, Colm, Caleb got everyone inside somewhere secure."

Caleb nodded sharply. "Come on," he said, motioning to Finn and Colm, who immediately sprinted off toward a group of villagers clustered by a crumbling fence.

"Inside!" Finn shouted as he waved to a family huddling behind an overturned cart. "Come on, quickly!"

Colm guided a mother and her young children toward the safety of a nearby building. "Stay close," he said. "We'll get you inside. Go, go!"

Saul and Hannah sprang into action, their movements sharp and instinctive as they moved to protect the villagers who hadn't yet found cover. A raider rushed at Saul, swinging a heavy club. Saul sidestepped, catching the raider's wrist mid-swing. With a quick twist, he jerked the arm back, forcing it past its breaking point with a sickening snap. The raider cried out, his face contorted with pain as he crumpled to the ground. Saul didn't hesitate—he seized the fallen club, his eyes scanning the chaos for the next threat.

Just a few feet away, Hannah faced off with a second raider. He swung at her, but she was faster, slipping to the side and planting a precise, bone-jarring kick to his knee. The man's leg buckled, sending him to the ground with a guttural shout of pain. Before he could recover, Hannah pulled her knife and drove it into his chest. Her gaze hardened as she watched him slump to the ground.

Around them, the chaos thickened. Smoke rose in heavy, acrid clouds as the raiders set anything they could alight—wooden carts, fences, and even bundles of hay that quickly turned into blazing infernos. Flames leaped toward the rooftops, casting an eerie, flickering glow over the square. Villagers screamed as they were herded from their homes, their terrified voices drowned out by the raiders' twisted laughter that mingled with the crackling of the fires consuming the heart of Edgewood.

"Over here!" Finn's voice carried across the square as he waved to another group of villagers hiding by the well. He beckoned them urgently, his face drawn and tense. "Move, now! Go!"

Saul turned, the firelight casting a hellish glow across the square, and caught sight of a figure standing apart from the chaos, watching the destruction unfold with a calm, almost amused detachment. He was tall, with a cruel confidence in the way he carried himself. His stance was relaxed, his arms folded as if he were simply watching a show rather than orchestrating terror.

The man's cold gaze locked onto Saul, and without hesitation, Saul shouted, "Hey! You!"

The figure didn't flinch, his face breaking into a slow, chilling smile. He raised a hand, gesturing to his raiders. As if choreographed, they ceased their rampage, standing down and beginning to gather the stolen goods they had piled up. The fires still crackled as the raiders fell silent, their eyes flicking toward the man.

The leader took a few steps forward, closing the distance between him and Saul, his smile widening as he did. "Name's Aldrick," he said, his voice smooth, almost mocking.

Saul glared at him, his fists clenched. Hannah was at his side, her gaze unwavering as she stared down the man who had turned Edgewood into a nightmare. Finn, Colm, and Caleb joined them.

Aldrick's gaze flicked over each of them before he continued, "A little birdie told me there's a coalition brewing among the communities. Very noble of you all…trying to play hero. How's that going for you?"

"What do you want from these people?" Saul shouted. "They've done nothing to you."

Aldrick laughed. "Nothing? They exist. They occupy land, hoard resources, live free." He shook his head, amusement glinting in his eyes. "See, you're all under this quaint impression that the world is a place for the meek to rebuild. But it's not. It's for the strong to rule, to take whatever they please. That's what the Revenants believe, and that's why we always win."

Hannah stepped forward. "You're nothing but a piece of shit," she spat. "People are coming together because they want a future —a real future, where there's more than just fear and violence. The world was destroyed once, and we're not going to let it happen again."

Aldrick's smile faded, replaced by a look of cold contempt. "You think your pretty words mean anything? That the world is a place where everyone holds hands and lives happily ever after?" He sneered, his voice dripping with disdain. "This world is for the strong, not for those who hide behind dreams of peace. Your coalition will crumble. It's nothing more than a fool's paradise."

"We're not backing down," Saul said.

Aldrick's eyes narrowed. "You truly don't understand, do you? The Revenants aren't just a band of raiders. We're an empire. We're everywhere. And we don't play by your rules. You think you're safe behind your little alliances? You think you can stand against us?"

A tense silence fell over the square as Aldrick's words sank in, his gaze lingering on Saul. "I'll give you one warning: give up this coalition, or watch it burn. Because we are bigger than you could ever imagine, and you are nothing but ants in our path."

He turned as if to leave, his men already starting to retreat with their stolen supplies. Saul's voice cut through the silence, firm and unyielding. "We will not back down!"

Aldrick stopped mid-step. He turned and pulled a gun from his side. The metallic glint caught the faint glow of the firelight as he raised it and fired.

The crack of the gunshot shattered the night. Saul barely had time to register the flash before he heard a gasp.

Colm staggered, his face contorted with shock as he looked down at the red stain blossoming across his chest. His mouth opened as if to speak, but no words came. His eyes, wide with disbelief, found Saul's before his legs gave out.

"Colm!" Hannah cried, reaching out, but it was too late. Colm crumpled to the ground.

A stunned silence settled over the square. The faint crackle of flames, the quiet sobs of villagers watching from the shadows—everything else seemed to fade as Saul stared at his friend lying motionless before him. His mind raced, trying to process the reality of what had just happened.

Aldrick's gaze lingered on Saul for a brief moment before he turned and walked away, his men following close behind, their laughter echoing through the silence.

Chapter 74

A low murmur filled the council hall as the leaders took their seats around the long, battered table, its surface scarred from years of use. Amara sat at the head, her posture rigid, though her face bore the heavy strain of recent events. One by one, the others joined, each carrying the weight of what they had seen and lost. Saul took his place beside her as Hannah and Finn settled in next to him. Across from them, Caleb sat with a brooding expression, his usual ease replaced by a wary intensity.

At the far end, Lucas and Anna from Edgewood shifted uneasily, still visibly shaken by the destruction that had driven them here. From Stone Hill, Abel sat with his arms crossed, his face creased with a frown as he absorbed the grim atmosphere. Beside him, Damon from Oakridge looked tense, his fingers tapping an anxious rhythm on the tabletop.

Amara let her gaze sweep over the group, taking in each face before she finally spoke. "Last night, Edgewood was ravaged. Homes were destroyed, supplies stolen, and lives shattered. Many of you spent the night traveling here to Haven's End. We're up against something far bigger than one raid. We need to talk about what we're really facing and what we're prepared to do."

Saul leaned forward. "They call themselves the Revenants. They're not just raiders—they're organized and ruthless, and they're looking to conquer. This isn't about supplies or fear; it's about control."

Finn looked at Saul. "How did they know about the coalition?" he asked. "Aldrick said they were tipped off."

"I think I can answer that," Caleb said. "There's only one way they know. I would bet anything it was Liora."

"From Hollow Creek?" Hannah asked. "Why would Liora do that?"

"I don't know," Caleb said. "But you saw how Liora acted when we offered her to join the coalition. You also saw how angry she was after Hollow Creek was raided. She blames us for that. She lost half of her people to Haven's End.

Lucas shook his head. "If they're after us, taking down communities one by one, it's only a matter of time before they come for Haven's End."

Abel nodded grimly. "We need more patrols. More eyes on the borders, day and night. If they come here, we can't be caught off guard."

Saul looked at him and nodded. "Agreed, but patrols alone won't hold them off. Haven's End isn't fortified to withstand an organized attack. They have weapons; they have an army. We need something stronger than just eyes on the perimeter."

Damon leaned forward. "What I don't understand is how they're armed at all. It's been years since the world went dark, and guns and ammo don't exactly grow on trees. Where are they getting them?"

Silence followed his question. Caleb's gaze flicked to Amara. After a moment, he cleared his throat. "There's…a place that might explain it. A place we don't talk about much. But if we're going to stand a chance against the Revenants, it's time we talked about Ironwood."

Amara stiffened. She raised a hand. "No."

Caleb's jaw tightened. "Amara, we can't bury our heads in the sand. Ironwood—"

"I said no," she repeated. "We are not discussing Ironwood."

Saul looked between them, confusion and curiosity flickering in his eyes. "What's Ironwood?"

Amara's gaze turned icy, her lips pressed into a thin line. "It's nothing worth wasting time over," she said.

Caleb's frustration broke through. "With all due respect, Amara, this isn't the time to protect old grudges. Ironwood might be the only thing that stands between us and annihilation."

Hannah leaned in. "Caleb, what is Ironwood?"

Amara's shoulders sagged slightly as if weighed down by a history she hadn't intended to revisit. She hesitated, her gaze drifting over the group. Finally, she took a deep breath, resignation. "Ironwood is…a place we barely speak of anymore. It is the most isolated and skilled community we know. They've mastered weapons—guns, ammunition, even traps. They're not reliant on the old world's relics. Their guns work, and they know how to make more."

The silence that followed was thick. Abel shifted uneasily. "And you think they'd be willing to help us? They closed themselves off years ago."

"What happened?" Hannah pressed.

Caleb rubbed a hand over his face. "Years back, Ironwood was known for its weapons and for…strict rules. They only traded with those they trusted. Most of us didn't meet their standards, so they were left alone. But Sadie and I wanted to try our luck one day. Sadie's brother came with us."

His voice faltered as he recalled the memory. "We didn't make it to their gates. The second we were in their line of sight, Sadie's brother was shot. No warning. No second chance. Just gone."

The weight of his words settled over the group like a shroud. Saul's voice cut through the silence. "What happened that made them react like that?"

Caleb's expression twisted with anger. "A few days before we tried to visit, raiders posed as travelers, gaining access to Ironwood under the pretense of trading seeds for weapons. They went at the end of the day, hoping Ironwood would let them stay the night for rest, which they did. During the night, they killed guards and stole weapons. Ironwood was humiliated and weakened. Since then, they have stopped trusting anyone. They shoot on sight."

Amara sighed. "You see why it's out of the question. Ironwood doesn't want anything to do with us. They don't want anyone near them."

"But they have the power to help us," Saul insisted. "If we don't reach out, the Revenants may overpower them someday. Imagine the Revenants with Ironwood's firepower. It would be the end of everything we've worked for."

Anna's voice was wary. "If Ironwood is so unforgiving, why would they listen?"

"We don't know if they'll listen," Hanna said. "But if we don't try, the Revenants will keep coming, and we'll be defenseless. Haven's End is growing—our farms are strong, and the community is rebuilding. Maybe if Ironwood sees that, they'll understand we're asking for an alliance, not weapons."

"And if Ironwood doesn't care?" Abel asked.

Damon leaned back, crossing his arms. "What if they see us as no different from the last people who tried to take from them? Why would they risk helping us?"

Caleb's gaze hardened as he looked at Amara. "Because Ironwood knows what it's like to be attacked, to have everything you've built taken away. If they're the people I remember, there's a chance they'll listen. We can't give up on that."

Amara's eyes narrowed. For the first time, a flicker of hesitation crossed her face. "And if they turn on you? If they kill you before you even reach the gates?"

Saul didn't flinch. "Then we'll know we did everything we could. But I won't sit back and let the Revenants tear through every community while we do nothing."

Hannah nodded. "If we're going to protect Haven's End and every other community out there, we have to take this risk. It's the only chance we have."

Finn, who had been listening intently, finally spoke. "Amara… I get why you're reluctant, but what's the alternative: just waiting until the Revenants come for us, too? Ironwood might not welcome us, but they're survivors, just like us. Maybe they'll understand what's at stake."

The room fell silent as Amara's gaze moved over each of them, torn between duty and fear. She closed her eyes, exhaling a long breath before meeting Saul's gaze. "You know what you're asking, don't you?" she said softly.

Saul nodded. "We know. And we're ready to face it."

A silence stretched, filled with the weight of their decision. Finally, Amara's shoulders dropped. "If you're willing to risk your lives, I won't stop you. But understand this—Ironwood isn't the ally they once were. You're risking everything, facing people who might see you as enemies."

Saul nodded solemnly. "We understand. But we can't let fear hold us back. The Revenants are only getting stronger, and if we don't act now, there'll be nothing left to fight for."

The meeting ended with a heavy silence. As Saul, Hannah, and Finn left the hall, a silent understanding passed between them. They had chosen their path, and there was no turning back.

Chapter 75

The morning was veiled in a pale mist, the forest around them cloaked in shadows as Saul, Hannah, Caleb, and Finn began their trek to Ironwood. The forest was quiet, an unsettling kind of silence that amplified the soft rustle of leaves and the occasional snap of a branch underfoot. The journey to Ironwood was not one to be taken lightly—every step forward felt like crossing into dangerous, unknown territory.

Caleb took the lead, his steps sure and deliberate, guiding them through the dense underbrush and narrow paths that wound through the trees. Behind him, Saul walked in tense silence, his mind racing with the possibilities of what awaited them in Ironwood. Beside him, Hannah moved with quiet determination, her gaze steady, occasionally drifting to Saul as if gauging his thoughts. Finn followed at the back, his usual energy subdued, replaced by a wary tension that matched the seriousness of their mission.

The path grew steeper as they climbed, the landscape shifting from dense woods to rocky hillsides littered with remnants of the world before—the twisted skeletons of old vehicles, rusted metal fragments, and broken glass glinting in the faint sunlight filtering through the clouds. As they continued, the landscape around them began to change. They passed through the remnants of abandoned campsites, fire pits filled with ashes long cold, tents shredded by time and neglect. The air grew heavier, each step feeling like a descent into the past—a place littered with memories of lives lost or left behind.

Caleb pointed out subtle signs of Ironwood's presence. "See these markings?" He gestured to faint notches carved into the bark of a tree. "Ironwood scouts. They keep track of anyone moving through here, and they're watching us right now, even if we don't see them."

Hannah's gaze followed Caleb's gesture. "Do you think they will actually see us as a threat?"

"Maybe," he replied. "But they won't act until we get closer. Ironwood doesn't waste bullets."

Finn let out a low whistle. "Efficient. Sounds like they've got it all figured out."

Caleb's expression turned serious. "They do. They have a way of making their own ammunition, cobbling together materials from whatever they can salvage. It's rough, not like what we had before everything collapsed, but it's effective. That's what sets them apart from the rest—most communities lost that ability years ago."

Their conversation was cut short as Caleb halted abruptly, signaling for them to be quiet. They'd entered a clearing, open and exposed, with no place to hide. He motioned for them to move slowly. As they crossed, a sound broke the quiet—a faint rustling, followed by the unmistakable glint of metal hidden among the trees on the opposite side. Caleb's eyes narrowed, his posture tensing.

"Revenant scouts," he whispered.

The group moved instinctively, lowering themselves into the

undergrowth. Saul felt his pulse quicken as he caught sight of two figures moving through the trees. The scouts were careful, their weapons glinting in the sparse sunlight as they scanned the area.

Hannah shot a questioning look at Saul, who nodded, indicating they'd need to handle this without drawing attention. They couldn't risk a gunfight—not this close to Ironwood's territory.

As the scouts drew nearer, Saul signaled to Hannah and Finn. They split off, positioning themselves strategically to surround the scouts without being detected. Hannah moved like a shadow, her footfalls barely audible as she closed in. Saul watched Finn take position, noting the young man's steady hands and focused gaze.

The tension was electric as they waited, holding their breaths, each of them poised to strike. One of the scouts paused, glancing around, suspicion evident in his posture. But it was too late—Hannah was on him, disarming him with a swift, silent maneuver that left the man crumpled on the ground. Simultaneously, Finn sprang forward, his movements precise as he dispatched the second scout with a quick, efficient blow.

They regrouped, the tension slowly ebbing as they caught their breaths. Finn wiped his brow. "That was easier than I thought it would be."

"Not bad," Saul said quietly.

Finn managed a faint smile. "Guess I'm learning a thing or two."

They continued onward, the encounter with the scouts leaving them more alert, and their senses heightened as they approached Ironwood's territory. The shadows grew longer as they walked, night beginning to descend, casting an eerie stillness over the landscape.

Caleb led them to a secluded spot near a cluster of trees, gesturing for them to settle in for the night. "We'll camp here," he said. "No need to approach Ironwood in the dark."

They gathered around a small, carefully concealed fire, the

warmth a brief comfort in the cool evening air. Caleb sat back, his gaze distant as he spoke. "Ironwood doesn't see alliances as strength. To them, reliance on others is a weakness—a vulnerability."

Saul's expression hardened. "We can't afford to fail. If they don't help us, the Revenants will tear through every settlement they come across. Ironwood may think they're safe, but they're just as vulnerable as the rest of us."

Hannah placed a reassuring hand on his arm. "We'll make them see that, Saul. But we have to go in knowing that this isn't just about convincing them. We're asking them to change everything they believe about survival."

Finn spoke up. "What if they do agree? Would they come to Haven's End? Or would we have to wait until the Revenants come knocking?"

Caleb's gaze flickered with uncertainty. "Ironwood won't leave their territory easily. But if they see value in a coalition, maybe they'd consider moving closer. But I'll tell you right now, that is a long shot."

Around them, the night settled in, the quiet punctuated only by the crackling of the fire and the distant hoot of an owl. As they prepared to sleep, Saul found himself staring into the flames, his mind turning over the possibilities, the risks, and the hope that Ironwood's help might finally tip the scales in their favor.

Chapter 76

The thick, towering trees thinned as they neared Ironwood's borders, the dense forest giving way to open terrain marked by jagged ridges and an eerie stillness. Caleb raised a hand, signaling the group to halt just beyond the last line of trees. Ahead, a faint path twisted toward Ironwood's domain, its edges littered with remnants of old traps and subtle markers that hinted at hidden sentries.

"From here on," Caleb whispered, glancing over his shoulder, "we're officially in Ironwood's sights. They're known to shoot first, ask questions later, so every step we take has to be intentional."

Saul's gaze settled on the barely visible border, a line drawn between the safety of the forest and the unknown dangers beyond. He tightened his grip on his pack, feeling the weight of the risk they were taking.

As the structure came into view, Finn squinted as he studied the imposing walls rising in the distance. "Looks like a prison," he muttered under his breath.

Caleb nodded, a faint smirk crossing his face. "That's because it is," he replied quietly. "Ironwood's founders made their home inside an old penitentiary. Those walls were built to keep people in —or out, depending on your view."

The revelation settled over them, and the stark reality of Ironwood's fortress-like structure became clear. The high, weathered walls loomed ahead, fortified to withstand anything. The prison walls explained the fortress's reputation—no one entered or exited without permission, and escape would be nearly impossible.

Saul's eyes traced the line of the reinforced barriers, piecing together what this meant for them. Ironwood's strength didn't just come from its people but from the prison's very bones—a place designed to resist intrusion, now repurposed to keep strangers at bay.

"They're not going to let us just stroll in," Finn said.

"No, they won't," Caleb replied. "This close to their gates, they'll be watching. Any sudden move, any hint of threat, and they won't hesitate."

The group stood in silence, absorbing the reality of what lay ahead. Ironwood's impenetrable walls felt more daunting now, a physical manifestation of the community's hardened, isolationist mindset.

"Let me go ahead," Hannah said.

Saul's reaction was immediate, his hand reaching out to grasp her arm, a flash of protective resistance in his eyes. "Hannah, no. We don't know how they'll react."

"Exactly," she replied. "They see an entire group of us, and it looks like an invasion. If one of us goes alone, it might seem less threatening. And they're less likely to see me as a danger. They can't be savage enough to shoot a lone woman."

A cold knot formed in Saul's stomach. The idea of letting her approach Ironwood's gates alone, unarmed and vulnerable, felt like a gamble he wasn't willing to take. He shook his head, his fingers digging into her sleeve. "We don't know that, Hannah. We don't know how they'll react to anyone. Going in alone is a risk."

"It's a risk either way," she countered. "We didn't come all this way to cower in the woods. If Ironwood is going to help us, we need to show them that we're serious and that we're willing to trust them first. They know that kind of strength, Saul."

The intensity of her gaze, the unbreakable resolve in her stance—it was something Saul had seen before in her, something he'd come to admire even as it terrified him. He held her gaze for a long moment, his heart pounding, before he released her arm.

"All right," he said. "But if they show any sign of—"

"I know," she interrupted. "I'll be careful."

Hannah took a breath, then stepped forward, leaving the cover of the trees. Her shoulders were squared, her hands raised high above her head, and her fingers spread to show that she held no weapons. Each step she took echoed in Saul's mind, his pulse pounding as he watched her figure grow smaller, isolated against the vast stretch of Ironwood's land.

She had barely gone a dozen yards when a crack filled the air, a sharp, echoing gunshot that shattered the silence. Saul's heart leaped as he watched a plume of dirt kick up by her feet. She stopped, but only for a moment, before continuing her walk, her hands still raised.

Another warning shot rang out, followed by another, each one landing inches from her. Saul's breath caught in his throat, his fists clenched so tight he could feel his nails biting into his palms. Every instinct told him to run forward, to grab her and pull her back to safety, but he forced himself to stay still, trusting her strength.

The shots stopped, replaced by a heavy, oppressive silence. Hannah's steady gait never faltered as she neared the massive, imposing gates of Ironwood. Moments ticked by with agonizing slowness, each second stretching into eternity as the three men watched, breathless, from their hiding place.

Then, with a low creak that seemed to shiver through the earth itself, the gates of Ironwood opened. A shadowed figure emerged, signaling for her to approach, and within seconds, Hannah disappeared behind the towering gates, swallowed by the unknown.

Saul exhaled, his breath a shuddering release. But the relief was short-lived, giving way to an aching anxiety as the gates closed again, sealing her inside. He exchanged a look with Caleb and Finn, the tension between them thick and tangible.

They waited, the minutes dragged on, each one heavier than the last. Saul's mind raced, conjuring up scenarios—was she safe? Had they accepted her presence? Or was she already facing interrogation, locked behind walls that would refuse to let her go?

Finally, after what felt like an eternity, the gates creaked open once more, and several armed guards stepped out, their faces obscured by shadows and makeshift armor. They raised their weapons as they signaled for the group to come forward.

Saul glanced at Caleb and Finn, both of whom looked equally tense, but they knew what they had to do. With measured steps, they left the cover of the trees, approaching the gate slowly, hands lifted in a mirror of Hannah's gesture. The guards watched them with cold, appraising eyes, their expressions unreadable behind their rough, makeshift masks.

As soon as they reached the gates, the guards moved in, brusquely patting them down—checking them for hidden weapons before motioning them forward. Saul kept his expression neutral, trying to project a calm he didn't feel as they stepped inside Ironwood's fortified walls.

Once past the gate, they were each grabbed by separate guards and pulled in different directions, a jarring, disorienting division that left Saul struggling against the urge to resist. But he knew any resistance would only worsen their situation. He allowed himself to be led, his gaze darting around as he took in the surroundings.

As he was shoved into a narrow corridor, he caught sight of

Hannah in a cell, separated by thick, iron bars. Their eyes met, and she gave him a reassuring nod though her face was marked with worry. She mouthed something to him—*We'll get through this*—before the guards closed the door, locking them both away from each other.

Saul's cell was cramped and dimly lit through a small barred window. He leaned back against the wall, his mind racing, straining to come up with a plan, some way to communicate with Hannah, Caleb, and Finn. Ironwood's distrust of outsiders was more severe than he had anticipated.

Hours passed, marked only by the muffled sounds of Ironwood's operations outside—the clang of metal, the steady, rhythmic beat of hammers. Through the narrow slit of the window, he could see guards moving in disciplined patrols, their weapons at the ready. It was clear that Ironwood had honed itself into a well-oiled machine of defense and survival, a society that thrived in isolation and guarded its autonomy fiercely.

He heard a shuffling movement nearby and realized Caleb was in the cell next to his, separated by only a few feet of thick stone wall. Caleb's voice drifted over. "Well, this isn't exactly how I pictured our big diplomatic mission."

Saul managed a grim smile. "They're not taking any chances with us. Can't say I blame them."

Caleb's sigh was laced with frustration. "I just hope they're willing to listen before they decide we're not worth the trouble."

Finn's voice came from another cell down the line. "And if they don't? If they just leave us here to rot?"

Saul closed his eyes briefly, grappling with his own fears. "We're not giving up that easily. Ironwood needs to understand that the Revenants aren't just another band of raiders. Eventually, they'll come for Ironwood too. People have broken out of prisons before. They can break in, too."

Silence fell, the weight of their predicament pressing down on them all. Saul leaned back, his mind racing, wondering how they could break through Ironwood's walls—both physical and ideological. Across the room, he caught sight of a guard watching them through the bars. Saul met his eyes, a silent challenge in his own. He wasn't here to surrender, nor was he here to be dismissed. Whatever Ironwood's leaders thought, whatever doubts they held —Saul and his group had come with a purpose, and they would find a way to make that purpose heard.

Chapter 77

S aul paced the small confines of his cell, his mind running over every possible argument, every way to make Ironwood see that their alliance was not a weakness but a chance at survival. Finally, the clang of iron doors jolted him from his thoughts. Guards moved down the hall, their faces shadowed under heavy helmets, stopping before each of their cells.

One by one, Saul, Hannah, Caleb, and Finn were led out, shackles clicking around their wrists. The metallic rattle echoed through the hall as they were herded toward a dimly lit chamber, the air thick with an unfamiliar, acrid scent of metal and smoke.

The chamber was stark and unadorned, its rough stone walls casting shadows that seemed to narrow in on the figures at the far end. A tall, formidable man stood before them. His gaze was sharp, surveying each of them with a cold intensity.

"I am Cyrus," he said. "Leader of Ironwood."

Beside him, another man inclined his head slightly, his gaze equally intense but with a watchful calm that contrasted with

Cyrus's direct, unwavering scrutiny. "And I am Rowen," he added, his voice quieter. "Second-in-command here."

Cyrus took a step closer, his gaze narrowing as it settled on Saul, then moved slowly to take in each of their faces. "Outsiders do not make it to Ironwood without purpose," he said. "So tell me —what brings you here?"

Hannah spoke first. "We're here because Ironwood is part of this world, too. There is a group out there. They call themselves the Revenants. They are growing, and they are a threat to all of us. We're here to offer a coalition. Other communities have already joined."

Cyrus's lips twisted into a faint, mocking smile. "The Revenants…I've heard of them. Ironwood has stood alone all these years. We don't need alliances to survive." He folded his arms. "You come here, pleading for aid, but alliances have brought nothing but betrayal and blood. Your coalition will be no different."

Saul leaned forward, his hands clasped on the table. "Your isolation might protect you now, but the Revenants are different. They're not just raiders looking for supplies. They're organized, and they're expanding their reach. If they continue unchecked, they'll come for Ironwood, too."

Cyrus's expression barely shifted. He glanced at Rowen, who gave a subtle nod before turning his attention back to the group. "Ironwood has no need to fear raiders," Cyrus replied. "We have more than enough defenses to handle any threat."

"And how long do you think that will last?" Caleb spoke up. "The Revenants have numbers. They have resources. And they're not just interested in picking at scraps. They're looking to dominate, to wipe out anything they can't control."

Cyrus leaned back, crossing his arms over his chest. "You ask us to join your coalition, to expose ourselves to the very dangers we've spent years avoiding."

"Not to expose yourselves," Hannah replied softly, meeting Cyrus's gaze, "but to protect yourselves—and others. Your skills, your defenses—they could save countless lives. Ironwood would still remain Ironwood but stronger with the coalition's support. And in return, we stand together against the Revenants."

Cyrus's lips thinned, his eyes flicking between Hannah and Saul. Finally, he shook his head. "Alliances bring weakness. They are a liability. Ironwood has survived because we do not let outsiders compromise our strength."

He pushed back from the table, nodding to the guards stationed near the door. "Take them back to their cells. I have no more interest in this conversation."

The guards moved forward, seizing Saul and the others by their arms. Saul caught Rowen's gaze just as they were pulled to their feet, and he saw something there—a flash of understanding, or perhaps doubt, lurking behind Rowen's stoic expression.

As they were marched back through the dim corridors, Caleb's frustration simmered over. "This is pointless. Ironwood's too rigid and closed-minded to see that this coalition is their best chance. We're wasting time."

Back in the cold confines of their cells, the reality of their situation settled heavily over them. Saul leaned against the damp wall of his cell, every muscle in his body tense with frustration. His mind raced through the events that had led them here—every step, every conversation, every desperate plea to make Ironwood see reason. They were so close, yet now they were imprisoned, trapped within these walls like criminals. Across from him, he could just make out Caleb's silhouette in the faint light, pacing back and forth.

Then, there was a sound—faint but distinct, the echo of footsteps approaching in the corridor. Saul straightened, his eyes narrowing as the footsteps grew louder, more deliberate. The torchlight flickered as a figure emerged at the edge of his cell door.

"Rowen," Saul breathed. He glanced around, catching the curious, tense looks of Caleb and the others. "What are you doing here?"

Rowen raised a finger to his lips, gesturing for silence. He moved to each cell in turn, ensuring that all of them were listening before he spoke. "I'm taking a risk by being here," he said. "But I needed to speak with you without Cyrus knowing."

Saul's pulse quickened. Rowen was clearly uneasy, his eyes darting toward the corridor every few seconds as though expecting someone to interrupt them at any moment.

"I may not agree with every decision Cyrus makes," Rowan continued, "but Ironwood is still my home. It's just..." He paused, taking a steadying breath. "Things weren't always this way. We used to help people before raiders tricked us and stole weapons. I've also seen the Revenants out there. I've seen what they do, how they break people down, destroy communities."

Saul leaned forward. "So you've seen what the Revenants are capable of," he said. "You know that standing alone won't protect you forever."

Rowen's gaze was steady. "Ironwood's survival has always come from its isolation," he said. "But isolation can't protect us from everything. The Revenants are growing stronger. Cyrus thinks we're untouchable, but I'm not so sure anymore."

Finn stepped forward. "Then help us, Rowen. Ironwood doesn't have to face them alone. You're sitting on the one thing that could turn the tide—your weapons, your ammunition. If you join us, we could stand against them together."

Rowen shook his head. "It's not that simple. Cyrus has been Ironwood's leader since the beginning. He believes in strength through self-reliance, that trusting outsiders is a weakness."

Hannah's eyes fixed on Rowen. "You know what's at stake here, Rowen. This isn't just about Ironwood anymore. It's about all of us, about preserving what's left of humanity. If the coalition falls, Ironwood will eventually fall, too. No one survives alone forever."

Rowen looked away, his expression darkening. After a long silence, Rowen nodded. "You're right," he said. "Ironwood can't afford to stand alone. Not anymore.”

“Then help us,” Hannah urged. “We need you, Rowen. The coalition needs Ironwood.”

Rowen hesitated, glancing back down the corridor before leaning in closer to the bars. “I’ll talk to Cyrus,” he said. “I’ll arrange for you to have another meeting with him. If we’re going to make him see reason, it has to be now before he shuts down completely.”

“Thank you, Rowen,” Caleb said. “This means everything to us.”

But Rowen’s face remained grim. “Don’t thank me yet,” he said. “Cyrus won’t be easy to convince. He’s not a man who changes his mind lightly.”

The group watched as Rowen left, his footsteps echoing down the corridor until the darkness swallowed him once more.

“This is it,” Hannah said. “This is our last chance.”

Chapter 78

The dawn arrived cold and gray, casting a pale light through the narrow, barred windows of the Ironwood holding cells. They waited in tense anticipation, the hours passing in silence as they prepared for what felt like their last chance. The heavy iron door clanked open, and Rowen appeared, his expression as serious as the shadows that hung across the room.

"Cyrus has agreed to see you," Rowen announced.

The group exchanged glances. Saul straightened. "Then let's make sure he understands what's at stake."

With a nod, Rowen led them through the narrow corridors, the echo of their footsteps swallowed up by the thick stone walls. Finally, they reached a vast hall, its walls lined with maps, some worn and torn, others meticulously annotated with markers of surrounding territories. At the far end of a long table sat Cyrus, his gaze sharp as if daring them to present anything that could shift his convictions.

Cyrus's eyes narrowed as he looked them over. "You've

already spoken once," he began. "So understand, this is the last time I'll hear your arguments. I didn't bring Ironwood this far to see it compromised by false hope and empty promises."

Saul took a breath, stepping forward. "Cyrus, we're not here to ask for something without giving back. We're here to show you that Ironwood's strength doesn't have to be isolated strength. We're not asking you to give up what you've built. We're asking you to see that Ironwood could be part of something greater."

Cyrus's jaw tightened, and he glanced at Rowen. "Isolation is what's kept Ironwood alive."

Rowen stepped forward. "Cyrus, with all due respect, we're reaching a breaking point. The Revenants' numbers are growing, and their influence is spreading faster than ever. I've seen it myself. And if they come for Ironwood, it won't matter how strong our walls are if they outnumber us."

For the first time, a flicker of doubt crossed Cyrus's face, but it was quickly masked by his usual composure. "And what makes you think the coalition will be any different?"

Caleb's voice cut through the tension. "Because the coalition is more than just a pact of convenience. We're bringing communities together, each with different strengths—farming, resource management—to form something resilient. Haven's End, Edgewood, and others—we've managed to create a system that can support itself. But we need what Ironwood can bring to the table. We need to protect that system."

Cyrus's gaze turned to Caleb. "And what exactly does Ironwood gain from this arrangement?"

Hannah didn't hesitate. "You gain a future not just for Ironwood but for something beyond it. Right now, you're surviving—but imagine building something more. A world where communities thrive and grow together, where humanity isn't just scraping by, but rebuilding."

Finn took over. "I saw the children in Ironwood, Cyrus. You know as well as we do that they deserve more than just survival.

They deserve the chance to see a world rebuilt, a world where people can live without constant fear, where there's hope. You have the power to make that a reality, not just for Ironwood, but for everyone."

Hannah nodded. "There's a whole world out there, Cyrus. You know that the Revenants are not the only savage group out there. If communities like us don't come together and fight against them, all of humanity will be lost forever. There's no coming back from that."

"Cyrus, this isn't about opening Ironwood to weakness," Rowen said. "It's about strengthening it with allies who have as much to lose as we do. Ironwood's technology and weapon-making abilities are unmatched. But even we can't last forever on our own."

"We're not asking you to take unnecessary risks," Caleb added. "We're asking you to consider that maybe, just maybe, there's a way to be strong and secure without being isolated. A way to pass on not just survival tactics, but a life worth living for generations to come."

The silence stretched, pressing down on each of them, until finally, Cyrus looked directly at Saul. "And you're certain," he said slowly, "that this coalition is strong enough to withstand the Revenants? That it's worth putting Ironwood at risk?"

Saul nodded. "I am. Because we've come this far, and we haven't fallen. Because every person in that coalition knows what's at stake. We're not going to give up, not now, and not ever. The Revenants won't stop until there's nothing left. Together, we can stop them. But only together."

Cyrus leaned back in his chair. The room fell silent again, the air thick with anticipation as they awaited his decision.

Finally, he spoke. "Ironwood will join this coalition," he said. "But I retain command of Ironwood's forces, and I will not compromise our methods or defenses. If your coalition falters, Ironwood will cut ties immediately."

Saul inclined his head in agreement, relief flooding through him. "We wouldn't expect anything less."

Without another word, Cyrus stood and exited, his footsteps echoing down the corridor, leaving them with Rowen. The weight of the moment settled on them, the gravity of the alliance that had just been formed.

As they filed out of the hall, Rowen walked alongside them. "You did it," he said quietly. "You actually did it."

Saul gave him a grim smile. "We did it together, Rowen. Ironwood will be an invaluable ally. But this is just the beginning. Now, we need to make sure that this alliance lasts."

Rowen nodded, his face thoughtful as he glanced back toward the direction Cyrus had gone. "He's a hard man, Cyrus. But I think he understands now. And as long as we keep showing him that this coalition is strong, he'll keep Ironwood committed."

As they exited the hall and the morning sun met their faces, Saul felt a surge of hope. They had Ironwood's support and a chance to fight back against the Revenants with renewed strength and purpose. They had forged an alliance from the ashes of distrust and isolation.

Chapter 79

As they neared Haven's End, Caleb picked up his pace, the familiar landscape around them sparking a glimmer of relief. Finn's shoulders relaxed slightly, and even Saul allowed himself a faint smile. They had made it back without any trouble.

The gates to Haven's End loomed ahead, and as they approached, guards opened them, recognition and relief evident in their faces. Word of their arrival spread quickly, and soon, they were surrounded by familiar faces, coalition members who had been waiting anxiously for their return. Amara and the other leaders gathered, their eyes scanning the group, taking in the exhaustion and determination etched into their faces.

"You're back," Amara said. "What news do you bring?"

Saul took a deep breath, stepping forward to address the gathered leaders. "We've secured Ironwood's support," he announced. "They've agreed to a provisional alliance. Cyrus is cautious, but they've committed to standing with us—for now."

A murmur rippled through the crowd. Amara's eyes narrowed

slightly, assessing. "And what are the terms?"

Hannah stepped in. "Ironwood will remain autonomous, but they'll lend us their strength and their weapons. They understand the threat the Revenants pose—not just to us, but to their own survival. We're united by a common purpose."

"If the Revenants come," Caleb said, "we'll be prepared."

Amara's gaze softened as she absorbed the weight of their words. The other leaders exchanged glances. Abel crossed his arms, studying them with his usual critical eye.

"Ironwood's people have been known to be ruthless in the past," he said. "What assurance do we have that they won't turn on us the moment things get difficult?"

Saul met Abel's gaze. "There are no guarantees, Abel. But Ironwood has just as much to lose if the Revenants take control. Cyrus understands this, even if he's reluctant to admit it."

Abel's expression softened. "And do they see themselves becoming part of what we're building here? Or are they just in this for their own gain?"

"It's more than just a transaction for them," Hannah said. "They're starting to see the world beyond their walls—how much they've missed, how much humanity has lost because of this endless survival mentality. They have skills, weapons, and the means to protect themselves, but they don't have what we've managed to rebuild here. That's what we're offering them. It's not just a coalition; it's a future."

"If Ironwood truly sees that," Amara said, "then maybe they can help us rebuild. But we'll need to tread carefully. Trust isn't something that can be forced, especially after so much has been lost."

Saul nodded. "We're prepared for that. But Ironwood's people are cautious, not indifferent. They want to survive, and they're willing to stand with us if it means securing that survival."

"We'll proceed, then," Amara said. "We'll prepare Haven's End, strengthen our defenses, and integrate Ironwood's people into our community. If they're willing to trust us, we'll offer them the same. This is our best chance at survival—and at rebuilding."

The crowd began to disperse, each person heading off with a sense of purpose. As they walked away from the gathered crowd, Saul glanced at Hannah, a quiet smile breaking through his usual stern expression. "We did it," he said. "For once, it feels like we're actually building something, not just fighting to survive."

Hannah returned his smile. "We've still got a long way to go. But we're not alone anymore. That makes all the difference."

Caleb clapped Saul on the shoulder, "Now comes the hard part —convincing a bunch of stubborn people to live together in peace."

Finn chuckled, his expression lightening. "If we can survive Ironwood, we can survive anything."

* * *

A dawn breeze stirred the leaves as the first light poured into Haven's End. The heavy, wooden doors groaned as they opened, and Amara entered. She took her seat at the head of the worn table, her gaze sweeping over the familiar faces gathering around her. Saul, Hannah, Caleb, and Finn sat nearby, each carrying an intensity born from days of brutal journeying, countless sleepless nights, and a purpose that now defined them. Damon and Abel, too, joined the council—their roles crucial in the coordination and defense of their community.

A weighty silence settled over the room as if each leader carried the burden of every man, woman, and child in Haven's End. This was more than a meeting; it was a reckoning. Amara's gaze lingered on each face before she spoke, her voice cutting through the silence.

"We're on borrowed time. The Revenants are no longer just a shadow. They're here, and if we don't prepare now, there won't be a Haven's End left to defend."

Just then, the council doors opened with a low creak, and all eyes turned as Rowen entered, accompanied by a select few Ironwood fighters. They were clad in armor crafted from reclaimed metal, plates fitted precisely to their bodies, scratched and weathered but undeniably sturdy. These were not just weapons but symbols of Ironwood's grit and commitment.

Rowen nodded to Amara, his calm gaze sweeping the council. "Ironwood stands ready. We're here to fight with you. We've brought armor, ammunition, and the best we have to offer. We won't turn away."

"If Ironwood's committed," Damon said, "we need more than supplies. We need to know you'll hold the line when the Revenants hit us hard. We're not looking for allies who'll retreat when things get rough."

Rowen met his gaze. "This isn't a fight we intend to turn our backs on. We've fought on our own for years, but we're here now because we believe this fight is ours, too."

Amara leaned forward. "If Ironwood's here to stay, then we have a chance. But we can't just rely on promises. We need plans —solid ones." Her gaze shifted to Caleb. "You know their tactics. What are we up against?"

"The Revenants don't fight fair," he began. "They'll use every weakness they can find. They hit fast and disappear, using chaos to break apart organized defenses. They'll come at us from all sides, testing our patience and looking for a crack. We'll need patrols, round-the-clock watches, and fighters ready to defend the walls."

Hannah nodded. "And it won't just be at the borders. We need people stationed within the walls. If even one of them gets through, the damage they could do would be catastrophic."

Rowen stepped closer to the table, gesturing to his men. "Ironwood has weapons that can help. We've brought gear that's been forged to withstand this kind of combat."

The Ironwood fighters laid out an assortment of weapons: makeshift rifles, long blades crafted from salvaged metal, and a few grenades, rudimentary but effective, filled with the powder they'd painstakingly created from reclaimed resources.

Rowen placed his hand on one of the rifles, lifting it slightly for emphasis. "These weapons may look rough, but they've kept Ironwood alive. Every piece has been tested in real combat. We'll train anyone willing to fight with them."

As the coalition members examined the gear, a murmur of admiration rippled through the room. Caleb picked up a rifle and weighed it in his hands. He was clearly impressed by the craftsmanship. Finn, nearby, picked up one of the blades, running his thumb along its edge.

"These will make a difference," he said. "Every weapon, every fighter counts."

Amara's eyes swept over the room. "Ironwood's fighters will stand alongside ours. We need to build trust, not just talk about it. We'll be training together, fighting together, and if we do this right, we'll be defending our homes together."

Rowen nodded in agreement. "Joint training sessions start tonight. Our fighters are prepared to share what we know, and we're here to learn from you as well. Ironwood is with you."

Amara's gaze was firm as she addressed them all. "You've heard your orders. Now let's get them done."

As the crowd dispersed, each person preparing for what lay ahead, Saul and Hannah shared a quiet moment, hands clasped, their eyes meeting in mutual resolve. The day was coming, and they would meet it head-on, side by side, for a future they believed in.

Chapter 80

Over the next few days, Haven's End became a whirlwind of movement and determination. The coalition members threw themselves into preparing for the storm they knew would soon arrive. The air was thick with the steady sounds of hammers, the sharp ring of metal, and voices calling out directions as everyone worked with single-minded focus.

Rowen took charge of fortifying the walls, and his Ironwood fighters assisted as they carefully inspected every weak spot along the perimeter. Ironwood's expertise in defensive structures became a critical asset and even those who had once viewed Rowen and his people with suspicion now turned to them for guidance.

Saul, Hannah, and Finn moved through the camp, organizing work crews and assigning duties. There was no room for uncertainty or hesitation; everyone had to be ready.

"First priority is strengthening the main wall," Rowen instructed. His finger traced the sections that required reinforcement. "If The Revenants break through here, they'll have direct access to the heart of Haven's End. We can't let that happen."

Amara nodded. "I've already assigned crews to the eastern and western flanks. We'll rotate them in shifts to keep everyone fresh."

Saul studied the map, mentally picturing the layout of the defenses. "Good. We also need lookouts posted around the clock on the outer perimeter," he added. "If even a single Revenant scout gets close, we have to know about it."

"We'll need sentries on higher ground, too," Finn suggested, gesturing to the elevated areas surrounding Haven's End. "If we can get some vantage points established, we can spot any approach from miles away."

Rowen considered the suggestion, nodding thoughtfully. "Ironwood's fighters are familiar with elevated watchpoints. We can set up a few lookouts along the ridges outside the walls."

Ironwood's fighters quickly set up sentry stations on the surrounding heights. They constructed makeshift lookout towers from reclaimed wood and metal, securing platforms that would allow sentries to monitor the surrounding area day and night. From these vantage points, the sentries would have a clear view of the distant fields and the tree line, where any movement would be immediately visible. Rowen and his men worked with a quiet efficiency, their years of isolation and defense lending them a certain expertise in matters of security that Haven's End had never before possessed.

Meanwhile, Saul and Finn led teams in reinforcing the main wall. They stripped down old carts, doors, and anything sturdy enough to bolster the perimeter, layering metal and wooden barriers to withstand impacts and even bullets. Each board, each nail, was pounded into place with a sense of finality.

Throughout these intense days of preparation, Finn proved invaluable, moving between tasks with a relentless energy that inspired others. Whether he was helping to haul timber to the wall or organizing shifts for the sentries, his focus was unwavering. He'd found his purpose here, his commitment to the coalition driving him to push himself and those around him.

Hannah caught up with Finn as he was pulling another heavy load of boards toward the western flank. "You've been at this non-stop," she said. "I think even the strongest of us need a break every now and then."

Finn grinned. "Maybe, but I've got too much adrenaline to sit still. Besides, if we're going to hold this place, I want to make sure it's as strong as we can get it."

Hannah smiled, nodding in agreement. "You're not wrong. But just remember, we'll need that energy when the fighting starts."

Finn gave her a quick salute. "Message received. I'll pace myself."

The training sessions were equally intense. Saul, alongside Rowen and Caleb, led drills on combat techniques, working to refine the fighters' skills in close-quarters fighting and defensive maneuvers. Each session began with hand-to-hand training, with Ironwood's fighters demonstrating techniques that made use of minimal weaponry, teaching the coalition members how to turn even a piece of wood into a weapon. They practiced blocking, grappling, and taking down opponents quickly and efficiently.

Saul walked among the fighters as they trained, correcting their stances, offering advice, and pushing them harder. He knew that every movement, every skill honed in these few days, could be the difference between survival and defeat. As he passed Finn, he stopped to observe, a small smile tugging at the corner of his mouth as Finn deftly took down his sparring partner.

"You've come a long way," Saul remarked.

Finn shrugged. "Just doing my part. Besides, I had some good teachers." He glanced at Hannah, who was nearby helping a young woman adjust her grip on a spear.

Meanwhile, Rowen took charge of a specialized group, training them in the use of Ironwood's homemade weapons—guns crafted from scavenged parts, crossbows forged from metal scraps, and improvised explosives that would serve as critical defenses when the time came. He explained the care and discipline required to maintain these weapons, emphasizing that every shot and every strike mattered. He drilled into them the patience and skill needed to reload, to aim, to wait for the opportune moment to strike.

As dusk settled, Amara gathered everyone in the main square. The coalition fighters, Ironwood's soldiers, and the civilians who had pitched in however they could.

"We've done more in two days than most communities manage in months," Amara said. "Look around you. Every one of you has given everything to prepare and fortify this place we call home. We've built walls, set up watch posts, trained together—all so that we can face whatever comes."

She paused, her gaze shifting to Saul, who nodded and stepped forward to address the crowd.

"We've all faced losses and endured hardship," Saul began, his voice steady. "But together, we've become something stronger than any of us could have imagined. Haven's End is more than just a place. It's a symbol of what we're willing to fight for, of the future we want to build."

His eyes traveled over the faces before him, each one marked by determination. "When The Revenants come—and they will come—we'll be ready. And we'll show them what unity and resilience look like."

The murmur of agreement rippled through the crowd, a quiet but resolute signal that they were as ready as they could be. Preparations for the battle loomed over them, yet an uneasy calm settled over the camp as night fell, wrapping the settlement in a silence filled with unspoken fears and unbreakable determination.

Later, as the fires died down and the camp eased into fitful rest, Saul and Hannah walked together along the quiet perimeter, their steps slow, their fingers entwined as they moved. The starlit sky stretched endlessly above them.

"It feels scary, doesn't it?" Hannah said, glancing up at him. "Standing here, knowing what's coming. And yet…"

Saul stopped, turning to her. "It does," he admitted. "But I've never felt more certain about what we're fighting for."

Their eyes met, and for a moment, the future and all its risks seemed to fade, replaced by the quiet understanding that only they could share. Saul brushed a loose strand of hair from her face, his hand lingering as he looked at her.

She smiled at him. "Come on," she said as she took his hand.

As they walked back to their room, the quiet settled around them, yet the weight of the coming battle felt momentarily distant. Once inside, Saul closed the door, turning to find Hannah watching him, her gaze steady but softened with an intimacy reserved only for him. He stepped closer, his hand brushing lightly along her cheek, fingers tracing the line of her jaw. His touch lingered as if they both knew that in this fleeting moment, time belonged to them alone.

Hannah's hands slipped around his waist, pulling him close. "All these years," she whispered. "And here we are."

He smiled, his own hand moving to rest on the small of her back. "Still here. Still together," he whispered.

Their lips met, gently at first, then with a growing urgency that dissolved any remaining space between them. Saul's hands found her waist, drawing her closer as the world outside faded to nothing. Hannah's fingers tangled in his hair, a familiar yet electric touch, and Saul's heart beat steadily, grounding them in the warmth and comfort of each other's arms. They moved slowly, savoring every touch and kiss as if committing every sensation to memory. The tension from days of preparation and planning unwound with every intimate moment, leaving them wrapped together in the safety of their shared love and trust.

As they pulled apart, Saul pressed a lingering kiss to Hannah's forehead, his lips warm and gentle against her skin. She closed her eyes, savoring the quiet intimacy of the moment, letting the world outside fall away. As they drifted into sleep, the heartbeat of the community pulsed softly outside their door—a comforting reminder of what they had fought for and what they'd built.

Chapter 81

The next two days passed in a relentless rhythm of preparation. The walls surrounding Haven's End grew taller and sturdier, fortified with newly raised wooden barricades and towers where vigilant guards kept watch, scanning the horizon for any sign of movement. The atmosphere was charged with urgency as every able hand contributed to reinforcing their defenses.

Throughout the settlement, the echoes of clanging metal and urgent shouts filled the air. Fighters practiced their drills in the open fields, sparring with an intensity that spoke of both determination and the quiet dread simmering beneath the surface. Amara moved among them, offering words of encouragement, while Rowen and his Ironwood soldiers guided the coalition members in new combat techniques. Caleb and Finn organized smaller squads, ensuring everyone knew their roles and responsibilities.

As dusk began to settle, Saul stood atop the wall overlooking the surrounding area. The wind rustled the leaves, a gentle reminder of the calm before the storm. Just as he was about to step away, a cry echoed from one of the lookout posts. "The Revenants! They're coming!"

Saul's heart raced as he turned sharply, sprinting toward the sound. Panic erupted in Haven's End as guards scrambled to their positions, weapons at the ready. "To your posts! Prepare for battle!" he shouted, his voice cutting through the chaos.

Hannah was at his side, her expression fierce. "We can't let them catch us off guard. We need to organize everyone now!"

"Finn! Caleb!" Saul called as he scanned the area, quickly locating the two of them among the chaos. "Get the fighters to the walls! Rowen, gather your people. We need to be ready!"

In a flurry of movement, the coalition rallied, each member taking their designated positions. The atmosphere shifted from the camaraderie of preparation to the raw edge of impending conflict. As Saul took his place among the archers, he felt the weight of their lives resting on his shoulders. The tension was electric, the air thick with anticipation as Finn stood beside him.

"What do we do when they come?" he asked.

"Hold your ground," Saul replied firmly. "We'll wait until they're in range, then we strike. Use the ammo wisely. We can't waste a single shot."

Suddenly, the ground trembled as distant shouts and the sound of heavy footsteps approached. The Revenants were closing in, their presence an ominous shadow against the moonlit sky. Saul glanced at Hannah, who gripped her weapon tightly, her resolve evident. They had fought too hard to let fear dictate their actions now.

"Here they come!" one of the guards shouted from the lookout.

The gates creaked open, revealing a mass of figures emerging from the darkness—The Revenants. Clad in makeshift armor and armed to the teeth, they advanced with a chilling determination that sent a shiver down Saul's spine. Their leader, Aldrick, stood at the forefront, his confident smirk cutting through the chaos as he surveyed Haven's End.

"Prepare yourselves!" Saul commanded, raising his voice above the din. "Fight for your homes! Fight for your families!"

As the first arrows flew, the battle erupted. A hail of projectiles rained down upon the approaching enemy, and the air filled with the sounds of war—the whirring of arrows, the sharp crack of gunfire, and the cries of the wounded. Finn, standing shoulder to shoulder with Saul, released his arrow with deadly precision, striking a Revenant before he could draw his weapon.

"Nice shot!" Caleb shouted, taking cover behind a barricade and returning fire with one of Ironwood's rifles. The sound of gunfire echoed through the night, punctuated by the cries of the attackers as they fell.

Hannah was a whirlwind of movement, darting between fighters, her knife flashing in the dim light as she took down any Revenant who dared to approach the walls. Each thrust and slice felt like a release of pent-up fury.

"Keep pushing!" Saul yelled, his voice hoarse with effort. "Don't let them breach the walls!"

As the battle intensified, the Revenants retaliated with fervor. They surged forward, their numbers overwhelming, but the coalition held firm. Ironwood's fighters, under Rowen's command, coordinated their fire, targeting key members of The Revenants and creating openings for their allies.

As the tide began to shift, the Revenants faltered under the relentless assault. Rowen's voice rang out above the chaos, urging his fighters to press the advantage. "Now! Move forward! Push them back!"

Saul's heart raced as he fought alongside his friends, the adrenaline surging through his veins. They had trained for this moment, and now it was a reality—chaotic and brutal, but they were ready. Finn, who had been hesitant before, now moved with a fierce resolve, his shots finding their mark with unwavering accuracy.

But just as hope began to swell, Saul's heart sank as he spotted Aldrick rallying his men, shouting commands that cut through the chaos. "Fall back! Regroup! We're not finished yet!"

In an instant, the Revenants shifted their strategy, pushing harder against the coalition's defenses. The air crackled with tension as Saul shouted, "Hold the line! We cannot let them break through!"

Hannah fought fiercely beside him, but the relentless assault of the Revenants began to take its toll. The fighters around them were pushed back, and the walls of Haven's End trembled under the pressure.

"Saul!" Finn called out, panic in his voice as he struggled to keep his aim steady. "What do we do? They're coming!"

"Focus, Finn! Keep shooting!" Saul shouted back, but he could feel the tide of battle turning.

Just when it seemed they might be overwhelmed, Rowen's voice cut through the din, commanding and unwavering. "Ironwood! Advance!"

With a fierce battle cry, Rowen and his fighters surged forward, breaking through the ranks of the Revenants and striking with a ferocity that caught the enemy off guard. The sudden shift in momentum invigorated the coalition fighters, who rallied around Rowen's command.

"Push them back!" Rowen commanded, his voice a clarion call amidst the tumult. Ironwood's fighters surged forward, reinforcing the coalition.

As the battle raged on, Saul and Hannah fought together, cutting through the waves of Revenant fighters. The coalition pressed forward, spurred by the sight of their leaders at the forefront. Rowen and his Ironwood fighters launched a decisive counterattack, driving a wedge into the Revenants' ranks and forcing them to fall back in disarray.

Through the haze of smoke and chaos, Saul caught sight of Aldrick. The Revenant leader prowled near the center, barking orders to his dwindling forces, his eyes blazing with fury and desperation. Saul's gaze met Hannah's, and they moved toward him together, cutting a determined path through the crowd.

Aldrick saw them coming and snarled; his blade raised as he charged forward to meet them. Saul blocked his strike, the force of impact reverberating up his arm. Aldrick was strong, his rage giving him a frightening edge, but Saul held his ground, matching him blow for blow. Hannah circled, waiting for an opening.

Aldrick swung again, narrowly missing Saul. But in that instant, Hannah struck, her blade catching him in the side. Aldrick staggered, his eyes wide with fury as he turned toward her, but Saul was ready. With one final thrust, he struck true, his blade finding its mark. Aldrick collapsed, the fight draining from his eyes. His gaze met Saul's in a moment of shock before he slumped to the ground.

The sight of their fallen leader sent a ripple of panic through the remaining Revenants. Rowen seized the moment, shouting for the coalition to press forward. The Revenants faltered, their ranks breaking as fear and defeat swept over them. One by one, they began to retreat, fleeing the battlefield in disarray.

As the dust settled, Saul and Hannah stood side by side, their breaths heavy. Victory was theirs, hard-won and bittersweet. The coalition surveyed the battlefield, the weight of their losses mingling with the hope of a new beginning. They began to mourn those they had lost. Saul stood among them, his heart heavy. They had faced the darkness and emerged stronger, yet the journey was far from over. The coalition would need to continue standing together, united in their purpose, for the road ahead was still fraught with challenges.

"Today, we fought not just for ourselves but for the future we all believe in," Saul began, his voice breaking the somber silence. "We honor those we lost by continuing to fight for what we've built together. This victory is a testament to our strength and our unity.”

As Saul’s words hung in the night air, a ripple of quiet acknowledgment moved through the crowd. Hannah stepped forward, her hand finding Saul’s.

“Together, we’ve proven what we’re capable of,” she said softly. “We will rebuild, honor the fallen, and make sure their sacrifice carries forward into the world we’re shaping.”

One by one, the survivors nodded, their gazes lifting from the scars of battle to the shared hope that tomorrow held. In the darkness, beneath a sky strewn with stars, Haven’s End stood as more than a settlement—it was a beacon of resilience, a promise that together, they would not only survive but thrive.

Epilogue

Ten years had passed since Saul and Hannah had first stepped into Haven's End, a place once marked by fear and uncertainty but now teeming with life and promise. The journey back to the island to bring their remaining friends to the mainland had been one of the first signs of their success, and the small band of survivors they once were had grown into a bustling community.

Saul walked through the heart of the settlement, his steps slower now, his face lined with years of experience, hardship, and triumph. Around him, the village hummed with the quiet sounds of daily life. Paths wove between sturdy buildings, and each plot of land was put to use—gardens blooming with vegetables, children chasing one another in laughter, adults tending to livestock, repairing tools, and sharing stories. It was a village, yes, but it was also home, one they had all created together.

He stopped by a garden patch, watching a group harvesting fresh vegetables. He smiled as they worked in sync, joking easily, their voices carrying on the warm breeze. It was hard to believe how far they had come. Only a decade ago, survival had been their sole focus, but now they had built something that was more than survival—this was a community.

Hannah joined him, slipping her hand into his with a warm, familiar squeeze. She looked out over the settlement, her eyes brimming with pride. "Can you believe it?" she said. "We always dreamed of this, but seeing it now…it's more than I ever thought possible."

Saul nodded, his gaze sweeping over the familiar faces, mingling now with a new generation that had known only this rebuilt world. "It's incredible," he said quietly.

Their quiet moment was interrupted as Finn approached. He was a far cry from the young man he'd once been, the one who had questioned his place in the world and feared each new challenge. Now, he moved with the quiet confidence of someone who belonged here, who had found his purpose and was ready to continue their work.

"Saul, Hannah," he greeted. "I thought you might want to see this." He unfurled a map he'd been carrying, revealing routes and markings that traced the newly formed network of alliances and connections with neighboring communities.

His finger glided over the lines on the map. "We've been working with other groups farther away, helping where we can. And they've been sending back support. We're building something much bigger now. We're really expanding out there."

Saul raised his eyebrows in admiration. "You've done incredible work, Finn. Back then, it was all just an idea. Now, it's a reality."

Finn chuckled. "I couldn't have done it without you both," he said, glancing from Saul to Hannah.

As the evening settled, the entire settlement gathered around the central fire, a tradition that had started in the earliest days of the coalition and continued ever since. Conversations floated on the air—small groups exchanging stories, laughter ringing out as children played nearby, and plans for the future being shared. Saul looked around, his heart swelling with pride. Beside him, Hannah's hand slipped into his once more, her fingers entwining with his as they watched their world glow in the night.

She rested her head on his shoulder, her voice a soft whisper in the quiet. "We did it, Saul. We made it real."

The night sky stretched above them, stars gleaming like tiny beacons of hope, casting their light over the home they had forged against all odds. And as the whispers of life grew louder with each passing day, Saul and Hannah could already hear the whispers of humanity.

About the author:

Adam McKim was born and raised in a small town in Missouri, where he still lives today with his wife and son. He began writing in his early twenties and has authored a growing collection of poems and books. When he's not writing, he enjoys quiet moments with family and the continued pursuit of storytelling.